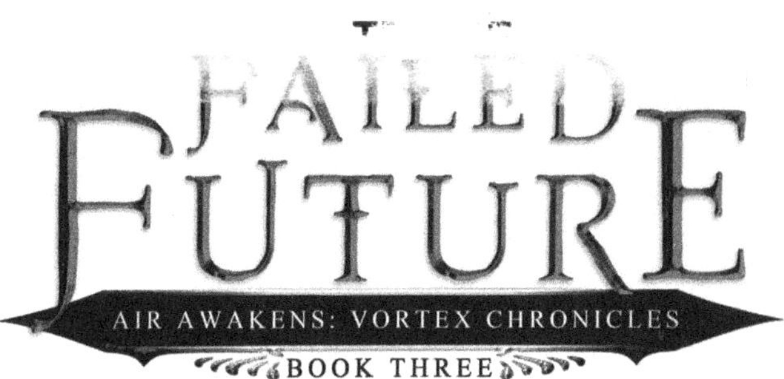
THE
FAILED
FUTURE
AIR AWAKENS: VORTEX CHRONICLES
BOOK THREE

ELISE KOVA

Silver Wing Press

This book is a work of fiction. The names, characters and events in this book are the products of the author's imagination or are used fictitiously. Any similarity to real persons living or dead is coincidental and not intended by the author.

Published by Silver Wing Press

Cover Artwork by Livia Prima
Editing by Rebecca Faith Editorial

eISBN: 978-1-949694-10-9
ISBN (paperback): 978-1-949694-11-6
ISBN (hardcover): 978-1-949694-12-3

Also by Elise Kova

AIR AWAKENS SERIES

Air Awakens

Fire Falling

Earth's End

Water's Wrath

Crystal Crowned

AIR AWAKENS: GOLDEN GUARD TRILOGY

The Crown's Dog

The Prince's Rogue

The Farmer's War

LOOM SAGA

The Alchemists of Loom

The Dragons of Nova

The Rebels of Gold

AGE OF MAGIC: WISH QUARTET

Prince of Gods

Society of Wishes

Circle of Ashes

Birth of Chaos

Age of Magic

http://www.EliseKova.com

for every dream that failed
to make room for the one that came true

CONTENTS

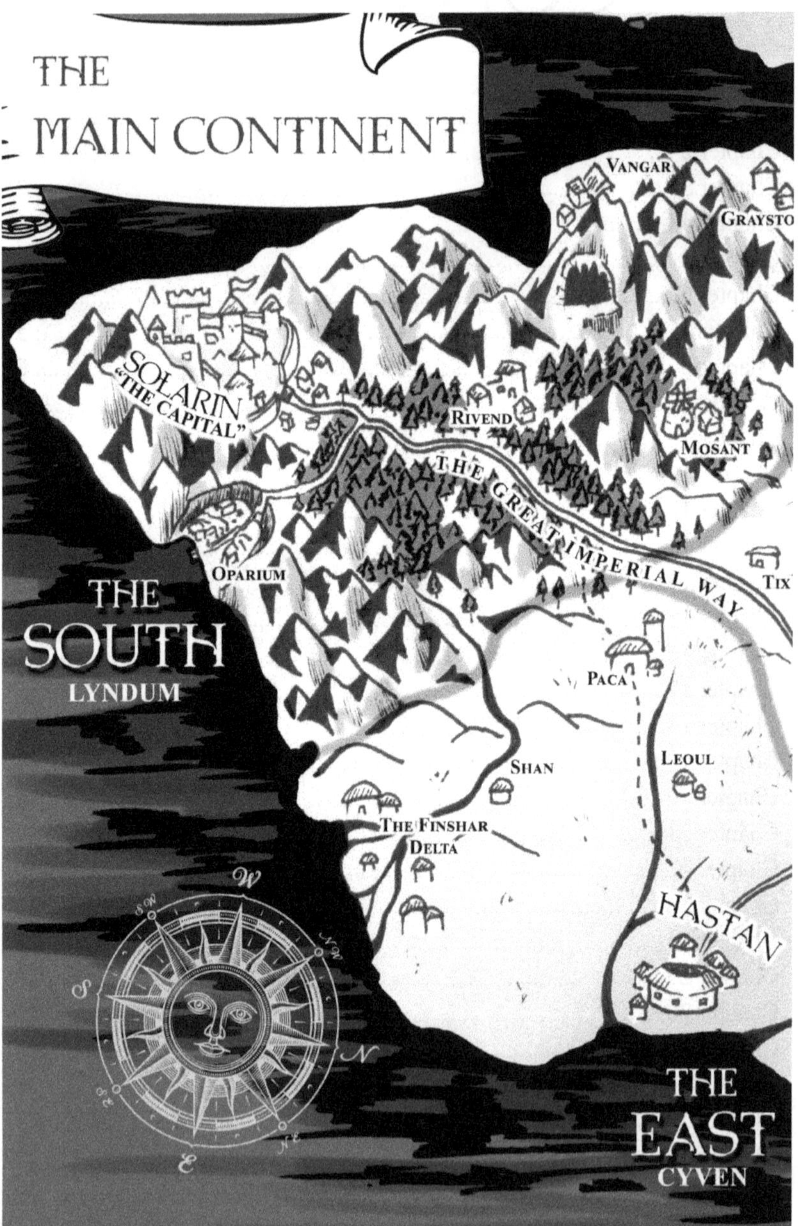

THE MAIN CONTINENT
VANGAR
GRAYSTO
SOLARIN
"THE CAPITAL"
RIVEND
MOSANT
THE GREAT IMPERIAL WAY
OPARIUM
TIX
THE SOUTH
LYNDUM
PACA
SHAN
LEOUL
THE FINSHAR DELTA
HASTAN
W
SW
NW
S
N
SE
NE
E
THE EAST
CYVEN

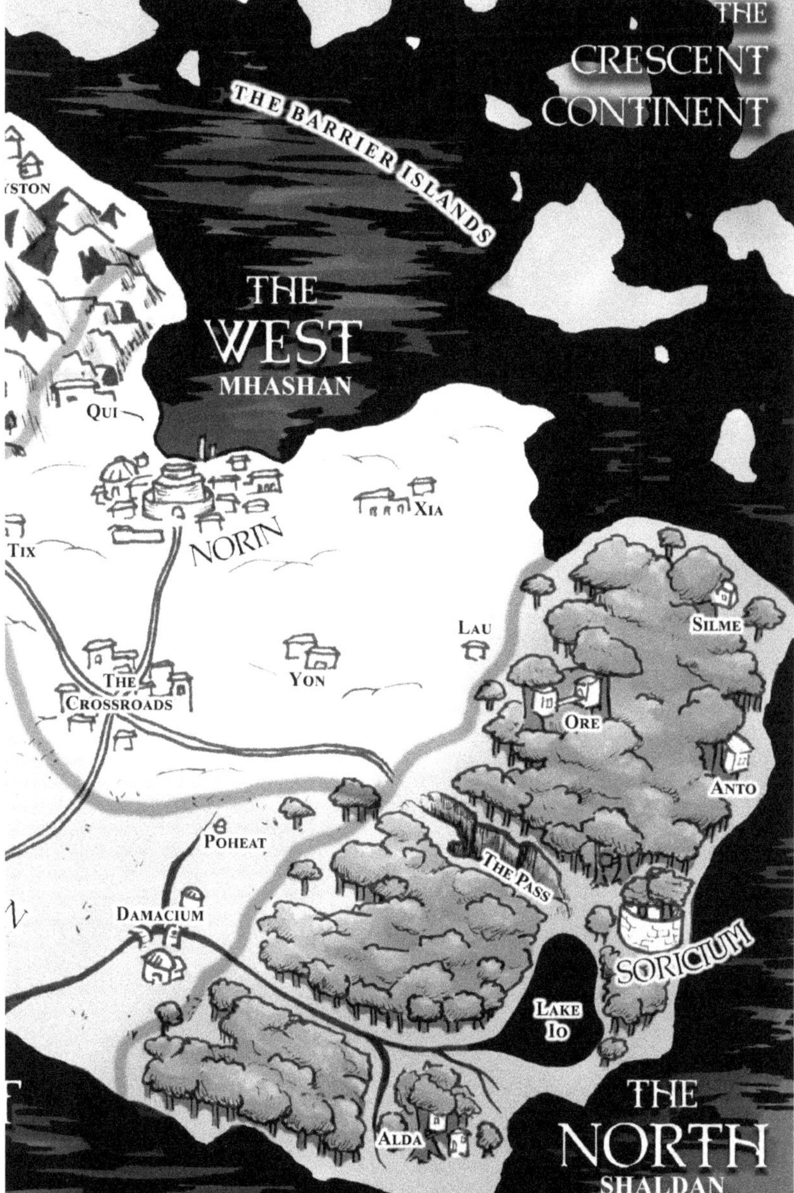

THE CRESCENT CONTINENT
THE BARRIER ISLANDS
THE WEST
MHASHAN
QUI
NORIN
XIA
TIX
LAU
SILME
YON
THE CROSSROADS
ORE
ANTO
POHEAT
THE PASS
DAMACIUM
SORICIUM
LAKE IO
ALDA
THE NORTH
SHALDAN

N
DARK ISLE
DOLARIAN
BEAUTY'S BEND
TEETER ISLE
LITTLE BROTHER BAY
MONLAN
NORIN
GREATER ATOLL
SHATTERED INLET
VARGA
BELLAST
TWILIGHT FOREST
MAROON ATOLL
TORIS
DANT
MALLON
DIAMOND SANDS ISLES
THE SHATTERED ISLES
RISEN
WARICH
MERU
FARTH
ISLE OF FROST
LUTH
HOKOH
CASTAWAY ISLE

1

EVERYTHING WAS A BLUR.

Each memory merged into the next, a hazy mess of color and sound and not-quite-consciousness.

She was on a ship of ice. Frost glittered through the dark memories, illuminating nothing but pain. An ocean of dark water enveloped her—nearly as cold as the vessel itself. She was lost in the vast sea, an invisible fragment among the waves, tossed between each swell, tumbled over reef and stone. There was the feeling of grit, rough against her…

Sand.

Breathing.

Just… breathing. Air sputtering between gasping lips. Heaving as her body expelled the water to make room for every life-giving breath it fought for.

Exhaustion.

More darkness.

Him.

Two hands hoisted her up and liberated her from the soggy grave she had consigned herself to. Arms covered in a delicately embroidered coat that her fingers would know anywhere wrapped around her, sure and warm.

A voice that resonated with her very soul.

Her hair was smoothed away from her face. She was still damp, and felt perhaps this would be her existence from now until forever. Air sucked the moisture from her, setting her body to shivering. Her brow couldn't dry; it was constantly slick with sweat.

Fever raged through her. At least, she thought so. Maybe he told her so.

Cold, hot, cold.

Mumbled words, sparks of light, more darkness.

Time persisted like this. For how long, Vi couldn't quite say. She was alive, but hanging by determined, ragged threads and a body too stubborn to give in.

She screamed herself hoarse as her wounds were ripped back open—something muttered about her clumsy healing needing to be "reset". She gasped as agony ebbed and flowed and her tissue was mended anew. Salves were smeared on her and potions poured down her throat; she had no choice but to drink or drown.

Every time her eyes opened, they stayed that way a little longer. Slow blinking seconds connected in her reforming consciousness.

Wind rattled against the drawn shutters on the sole window of the hovel where he'd stashed her. There was a hearth at her right side, always burning. Too hot, or not warm enough, never right in the middle. But the flames were a familiar and welcome companion. They were the only thing that made sense to her.

At her left was Taavin. He would curl up, leaning with his back against the door, light always surrounding him even when he looked as though he were sleeping.

How was he here? And where exactly was *here* anyway?

If she stretched far enough, she might be able to touch him.

But Vi had neither the strength nor the energy to try.

Sometimes, she would wake to find him fumbling around in a trunk, open like a clam against the wall opposite the fire. She would hear the sound of corks popping before bright herbaceous smells cut through the briny air.

Other times, she opened her eyes and he was hovered over her, lips moving fast and soft. Most of the words she could identify if she thought hard enough—and thinking was very difficult. But a good many she couldn't. So Vi didn't expend too much effort on identifying which was which. She'd forget the next time her eyes opened anyway.

Vi blinked into the twilight.

This time was different than the others.

Her mind was sharper—clearer. She was present in the moment and keenly aware of her own excruciating existence. Her thoughts were still jumbled, but now felt like pieces she could put her fingers on and begin to snap back together.

Vi turned her head toward a soft clinking sound.

"Taavin?" Her lips stretched painfully, and the iron taste of blood swelled where the delicate skin cracked.

"Vi." He turned sharply, nearly spilling what was in the rough-hewn cup cradled in his hands. Their eyes met, and Taavin scrambled over to her in clumsy haste.

He was undeniably Taavin… Yet he looked so different than she remembered. Almost jarringly so. Enough that Vi had to blink, reminding herself that this was, indeed, the same man.

His hair was matted with dirt and grime. Dark circles she'd never seen before shadowed his eyes. The usual vibrancy of his coat was gone, replaced with gray twilight and accented by the dying embers of the fire casting long shadows over them. The only things that had any brilliance to him were his eyes—ever shining—and the small circle of light spinning around his left wrist. The glyph was drawn together so tightly that Vi couldn't identify what it was for.

"How do you feel?"

"Like death, but slightly more animated." Vi shifted onto her side, putting her weight on her left elbow and trying to push herself up. Every joint was stiff and aching. It felt like she hadn't moved in years.

"Don't get up too quickly. 'Animated death' may be an apt description given how I found you and what I've had to do to try to piece you back together properly." But Vi was determined, so Taavin helped her upright, situating her against the wall behind her. Vi knew the space had been narrow, but she hadn't realized that the top of her head was nearly touching one wall and her toes the one opposite while lying down. "Here, drink this—it'll help your body wake up. I've been keeping you in a sort of stasis to let your body focus on healing."

Vi accepted the cup from him, staring down at the muddy mixture within.

"I promise it looks worse than it tastes."

She took a timid sip. It was thick and grassy, but warm on the way down—almost like liquor, but without the strong burn. Vi took another sip, replacing the salt musk of the shack with the bright tang of the drink. This was the earthy note she'd smelled earlier and Vi found it almost pleasant.

"Do you remember everything? Remember me?" Taavin asked almost timidly. "Was your memory affected at all by the trauma?"

"Yes." Vi stared into the cup once more. "I mean, yes I remember everything—and you. No, my memory wasn't affected." The cup rested in her lap, over the rough-hewn blanket that covered her legs. Vi wiggled her toes. They didn't feel like her own… nothing felt like hers. It was as if her soul had been placed into a completely new body. "I think so, at least…"

Her voice faded to nothing. Memories stacked like building blocks around her, closing her in. Vi's fingernails dug into the grooves of the clay cup; the craftsman's mark still present in the indents of fingers fired into permanence. The dull ache in her chest assured Vi that this seemingly new body was, indeed, hers.

Every scar she now wore was like a map, showing how she'd

finally made it to Meru.

"That's good," he breathed a small sigh of relief. "I've been worried I'd not done enough…"

"I'm fine." It was a lie. A lie to save her from having to fight her way out of the deep hole the truth put her into. Vi was many things… but after fleeing her home, abandoning her Empire, fighting for her life, facing off against a pirate queen, and putting a traitor to death… "fine" was none of them.

"How are you here?" Vi flipped the focus on him. Talking about herself was the last thing she wanted to do. "Aren't you trapped in Risen?"

"Clearly not." Taavin sank back off the balls of his feet, drawing his knees up to his chest. Vi watched him and debated passing the mug back. He seemed as if he could use the soothing properties of its contents as much as she could. "I managed to escape."

"How?" Vi looked around the shack. "How did you get here? And how did you know I would be here?"

Questions piled on questions. Nothing was adding up.

"Remember, I told you that you were not the only one who would be on a journey. I vowed to find a way out of my prison." His hand, timidly, rested on hers. "No, I always knew there was a possible escape. I just needed to have the courage to take it."

Vi stared at his hand, willing it to spark light into her chest as it had once before, but she still felt frustratingly little. Every emotion was dulled. Instead, she focused on that conversation they'd had forever ago on Erion's balcony. "You said you were having dreams too… of storms, and death in the water, of me in dark waves."

He gave a small nod.

"Taavin, you dream only of the past," Vi whispered.

"I thought I did." He looked away, lost in his own thoughts. "But the closer you got to me, the stranger my dreams became. Or perhaps it was merely the will of the Goddess that I would find you. Either way, the black sand beaches outside the Twilight

Forest are unmistakable. When I had a brief but particularly violent vision of you on the sand, I knew I had to leave."

A violent vision? She knew he'd spoken of having shakes and going comatose during his visions… Was she nothing but violence to those around her? Was that what she was becoming?

"Then, on my way, I heard word of the pirate Adela sailing along the eastern coasts. I knew you were aboard a vessel. I had these unrelenting visions. It all seemed to compel me to go in a way I simply couldn't ignore; I feared for the worst."

He finally dragged his gaze back to her. Vi stared back, holding his deep and sunken eyes. They seemed all the more harrowed when framed by the gauntness of his face—a sharper edge to his cheeks than she'd ever seen. When was the last time he'd had a good night sleep? Or a full stomach?

"I'm glad you came, whatever the reason." Vi took another sip of the concoction he'd made for her. She didn't know if it was serendipity, the will of the Goddess, or some other magic at play, but she would count her blessings rather than question them.

"Me too. I don't know how long you were out on that beach, but I shudder to think what would have happened if I had been any later."

Vi looked down at his hand, still lingering atop hers. It half-hovered, trembling, as though he was afraid to touch her. Vi finally released the mug and twisted her fingers with his. He shifted closer at the unspoken request.

Both of them stared at the contact for several long seconds. She heard a hitch, and a quiver in his breath. But neither moved. Vi's gaze dragged upward to meet his.

Their shade of green was even more astounding in person. It was the only thing of brilliance in the dark world she now found herself in.

"You're really here," he whispered in wonder, despite the fact that he must have been taking care of her for days now.

"I am. Do I feel different to you in person?"

"Not really," he confessed with a soft laugh. "I can't tell if that makes me happy or sad." His other hand lifted, cupping her cheek. Vi could feel the thin layer of grime on her skin that smeared under the pad of his thumb.

"Why sad?" she dared ask.

"Because you came all this way and endured so much…maybe you summoning me through the watch was just as good."

"It wasn't." Vi placed the cup off to the side, shifting her hands so they covered his. One on her face, one in her lap. "I don't need magic to see you now. Your presence isn't governed by glyphs. Now you can be by my side whenever I need—every moment of the day."

"Only if you permit it."

"I'd permit nothing less." Vi closed her eyes, tipping her head forward to press her forehead against his. Taavin stayed there, giving her comfort without needing to be asked. "Besides…" Her voice trailed off, sandpaper covering her throat, her soul.

"*Besides?*"

Vi shook her head slowly. She needed him to help hold her together. Far from home, he was all she had right now—the only familiar thing in a strange land.

But somehow, needing him felt like weakness. It felt terrifying for a reason Vi couldn't describe.

"Besides," Vi started again, clearing her throat and leaning away, distancing herself from the moment and the sensation of frailty. "My coming wasn't purely social. We have work to do." Vi slowly raised a hand to her watch.

"We do," he said in solemn agreement.

"What do we need to do now?" she asked. There were two reasons she'd struggled and fought and killed to get to Meru, and this was one.

"I don't know yet… May I?" Taavin held a hand right before the watch. Vi ignored his closeness. How soft she knew his lips were.

"Go ahead." Vi rubbed the back of her neck, debating if she should just take it off.

The watch was the last connection she had to the world she'd been born into—to her family. It was perhaps the only thing that could prove she was, in fact, Vi Solaris. Even as her fingertips rolled over the screw-lock that held the chain fast, she couldn't bring herself to undo it.

A different sensation distracted her—the feeling of shorter hair than she was used to. Vi remembered the start of her escape from Adela—smashing a flame bulb and using the remnants of the fire to try to burn off the gag they'd forced on her. Some of the hair had singed away, and now it was shorter at the back of her head than the rest. She fussed with the ends that now extended barely past her shoulders.

The hair the West had so loved… she'd need to cut it. Like everything else, the thought passed through her mind with a dull ache and little other feeling.

Ignorant to her various internal battles, Taavin's fingers closed around the watch.

The moment the metal touched Taavin's skin, magic sparked, exploding out like tiny fireworks from the contact point. Glistening specks sparkled through the air and clung to the barely visible outline of glyphs unknown. Noise filled her mind—so loud and instantaneous that Vi couldn't tell if it was music or voices, singing or screams. Her breathing quickened. She may have even let out a small shout.

The colors and shapes overtook Taavin as well, encompassing them both for what felt like hours but surely must have only been seconds. His eyes flashed brightly right before the room returned to its dim light—though in the wake of such strange magic, it seemed darker than before.

Taavin's breathing was heavy. Vi's heart raced, and she was more alert than she'd felt since she'd woken. They both seemed to be waiting for something else to happen. Yet nothing did.

When Vi could no longer handle the silence, she dared to ask, "What was that?"

"I take it that hasn't happened before?" The intense stare he'd been impaling the watch with was now turned to her. A sensation similar to the first time he'd ever laid eyes on her crawled up her spine and Vi subconsciously leaned slightly away.

"No… What… what was that?"

"I don't—" A knock on the door interrupted him. Taavin looked back to her, his eyes frantic. "My wards broke." The words fell from his mouth, not an answer to her question but several times more horrifying.

"Your wards?" Vi breathed, trying to match how softly he was speaking. Her attention fell with his to his wrist—the glyph that had been there earlier was gone.

"Surrounding this place, keeping us hidden. Now they can sense me, and with that burst of magic—"

"Fallor," Vi finished.

"Fallor?" Taavin looked to her. "Adela's right-hand man?"

"He's after me," Vi answered hastily. "Wait… Who did you think it was?"

"The Swords."

"The what?" As soon as the question left her lips, Vi remembered a brief conversation they'd had in her tent when she'd first begun to demand information from him. "The Swords of Light? The Faithful's militia?"

"They're after me."

The door rattled again, preventing Vi from asking the thousand questions swirling in her mind about the Swords of Light.

"Get ready to run." Taavin grabbed her hand. "*Durroe sallvas tempre dupot. Durroe watt radia dupot.*"

Light spiraled out from him. Vi recognized the chants to deceive ears and eyes. *Radia*, to hide. *Tempre*, to mask? *Dupot*… she'd never heard that word before. Had she? Her mind was in a haze, still sluggish from her injuries and whatever magic was still making her ears ring.

Glyphs surrounded Taavin, condensing onto his left wrist like bracelets. She knew what he was doing, and yet… Vi was struck with awe.

He commanded the magic with a deftness she'd never seen before—not from any sorcerer from any discipline. It put even the poetic nature by which her parents could command the elements to shame. It was more than sorcery, it was art—as breathtaking as a virtuoso musician or master dancer. The magic wasn't just an extension of Taavin.

It *was* Taavin.

The door to the shack was kicked in. Two men stood framed at the threshold, ice crackling around them, reaching inside of the shack. The remnants of the dying fire were snuffled and Vi's eyes worked to adjust to moonlight only.

One man was unknown to her, a nameless and bloodthirsty face. Her focus remained locked on the other: Fallor. The red of his hair and shimmering dots that lined his brow were unmistakable to her now. She'd know them by daylight, moonlight, and nightmare.

His eyes narrowed slightly, sweeping across the shack and past where Vi and Taavin were hidden.

"Search it," Fallor commanded. The nameless man stepped forward into the small space as Fallor remained in the doorway.

Vi bit back a shout of pain as she was tugged into motion. Taavin seized the opportunity, sprinting past Fallor in the doorway. Unfortunately, he misjudged the distance.

Taavin twisted to slip through, but Vi was caught-off balance. She tripped over her own feet; there was still a disconnect between her body's movements and her brain. Taavin pulled at her arm as Vi tried to convince her limbs to move properly.

Barely, just barely, her side brushed against Fallor's giant arm.

The man turned his head, moving on instinct—there could be no other description for how fast he lashed out. She'd touched him, and that meant the magic that had extended from Taavin to her, now extended to Fallor. *He could see them.*

Fallor's arm slammed against her middle, knocking the air from her lungs. It pressed further into Vi's abdomen as he pulled with bone-crushing might.

Vi looked to Taavin, watching his eyes widen slightly as she was ripped from his grasp. He was still moving in the other direction, hand around her wrist. But Fallor was too strong. She felt weightless as she was hoisted into the air. Taavin's fingers slipped from Vi's and she watched as he disappeared, the magic now concealing him from her without their contact.

"Found you," Fallor growled into her ear, a stomach-churning glee making the words all the more terrifying.

"*Juth*—" A LARGE hand clamped around Vi's mouth before she could finish the chant.

"I think not." Fallor turned to his comrade. "There's another, get him."

"Adela only wanted her."

"She'll want this one," Fallor assured him with a confidence that shook Vi to her core.

They knew who Taavin was. That was the only explanation. Otherwise Fallor would've focused only on her.

Vi stared out into the rainy field surrounding the shack, looking for any sign of Taavin. Her stomach and jaw ached from Fallor's unrelenting hold. She hoped Taavin was still running as fast and far as he could get. She'd tangled with the pirates once and survived—she could do it again. She would never forgive herself if he was taken captive, too.

Yet for all she wanted Taavin to look after himself, Vi knew he wouldn't.

She was Yargen's Champion, and if the elfin'ra got their hands on her they would use her blood to summon their dark god Raspian. But even if that weren't the case… This was the man who had dared to escape his captivity, come to her, and nursed her back to health—he wasn't going to leave her behind. Which left Vi with one option before he would do something reckless and expose himself again.

Magic was magic, he'd said once. Every discipline was merely a way to manipulate and channel it. So Fallor could stop her as a Lightspinner by silencing her, but without Adela's terrible shackles, he'd never stop her as a Firebearer.

Closing her eyes, Vi sought out the spark within her. She imagined it springing forth, just as the light did. The only difference was that this power needed no words.

Heat shimmered against the rain, turning it instantly to mist. Fallor must've felt it, but he didn't react fast enough. Tiny sparks ignited in a blink, forming a wall of flame that hovered a few inches off Vi's skin and clothes. It pulsed out from her, forcing Fallor away.

She hit the ground. One hand slid out as Vi sought balance, slipping in the mud. It coated her side and she rolled with it. The taste of earth filled her mouth as she shouted, "*Juth starys hoolo.*"

A glyph formed around the men and the shack as she spoke. Vi squinted at Fallor, rubbing the mud from where it was running in her eyes with her other hand. There was a different shimmer of light surrounding the pirate, but she couldn't make out what it was before the fire she'd unleashed caught the glyph she wrought, erupting in a white-hot blaze.

Screams from the bloodthirsty man who had been investigating the shack filled the air, solo. There wasn't a chorus of cries as she'd expected—but then again, had she ever expected Fallor to go down quietly? Vi stared into the blaze, searching for his outline. The flames burned even brighter, and he was nowhere to be found.

Already ash, she hoped.

The cry of a bird of prey echoed off the cliffside as it rose higher on the updraft created by her flames.

"Vi!" Taavin's voice broke her concentration in tandem with his hand clamping once more around hers. "We have to go."

Vi remained still, staring at the burning hut with the pirate still inside. The screams were quieting. It was a terrible way to go, yet killing the man didn't yield even the slightest bit of remorse or guilt, and that fact made her feel terrible.

All around her was darkness—outside, in the stormy night, and in the hollow of her chest, a chasm opened by betrayal. Dawn would come with the morning—but would light ever breach the inky depths that threatened to drown her?

"Fallor is coming." Taavin yanked at her arm. "We have to go!"

"Fallor? I—"

An eagle's screech interrupted her. The bird she'd seen take to the skies was in full dive, wings tucked. An odd shimmer of light surrounded it. At first, Vi thought the distortion was merely the firelight catching on the rain, but it was more than that. Reality itself rippled, as if nothing more than a reflection in a shimmering pool.

With a magic Vi had never even imagined, the bird was gone and Fallor was there—as if one had disappeared beneath the shifting waves of reality and the other had surfaced. Momentum propelled him through the air as he plunged both of his feet into Taavin's chest, using the other man's body like a springboard. As he pushed away, the same ripple was already beginning to surround him, but Vi didn't watch this time as bird was substituted for man.

Her eyes were on Taavin. Agony singed through her, a silent cry caught in her mouth, left agape in shock.

Taavin wheezed, rolling in the mud, coughing and sputtering.

"Taavin!" Vi fell to her knees, sliding to his side.

"We have to go, on foot… They killed the horse." He barely forced out the words. "More… come."

Vi looked skyward. She searched the darkness and rain for any sign of the eagle, but there was none. With his strange magic, Fallor could be anywhere. In her mind, he was suddenly everywhere.

At any moment they would be attacked. If Fallor's magic could transform him into a bird, she shuddered to think what else it could do. She had to fight back, had to think of a glyph combination that could thwart whatever power he was using. But facing a magic so foreign to her, Vi was armed with little but panic.

"*Durroe sallvas tempre dupot. Durroe watt radia dupot.*" Taavin repeated his earlier words and Vi felt the glyphs slip around them both, cocooning them in his magic. "We have to make it to the trees."

"The trees," Vi repeated, forcing her mind to continue to function. She couldn't freeze up. Not now. Not after all she'd done to get here.

"Over there." He pointed with his free arm as Vi lifted his other and placed it around her shoulders. "We have to get to the Twilight Forest."

Twilight Forest. Her mental atlas flipped through its archives but came up empty. Not because she was panicked, but because she was now in a land she knew almost nothing about, running blindly into the night.

"Let's go." Vi pushed off from the ground.

Taavin was heavier than he looked and Vi hadn't felt so weak in a long time. She ignored the signs of fatigue, pushing her feet into a run over the tall grasses that covered the cliffside.

The flames from the burning shack had been smothered by the torrential rain, and a heavy mist clouded above the quickly cooling remains. Fallor wouldn't give up. And he wouldn't make it easy.

As the thought crossed her mind, a pulse of magic rippled out across the ground, tangling her ankles. Vi felt herself falling, clasping her hand as tightly as possible to Taavin's so as not to break the magicks that were hiding them. But it was Taavin who let go.

The power that had been concealing them shattered under the second pulse of magic that swept over the grassy cliff. Fragments of light swirled in the ripple before blinking unnaturally from existence. It was as if Taavin's power had never been there at all.

"*Loft Dorh Dupot*," Taavin snarled. Vi had never heard such a vicious tone from the man's mouth before and was taken aback by it.

Taavin held out one arm, fist clenched around the center of a spinning circle, as though he was holding an invisible tether. She followed his focused gaze to Fallor. Vi remembered when Taavin had used the same immobilization rune on her.

He'd said it was no easy feat, even if he made it look otherwise.

Which meant Vi had to act fast.

"*Mysst Soto Larrk*!" She sprang into motion, feeling light condense under her palm into the hilt of a sword. She didn't want to risk *juth* interfering with Taavin's magic. She'd take the fight to Fallor.

Vi was nearly to him when Fallor broke free of Taavin's magic with a roar. She shifted her grip on the sword, swinging it with all her might. Fallor dodged, the point of the blade missing his neck by a hair's breadth. She let out a scream of frustration.

"A sword?" Fallor caught her wrist. His fingers looped entirely around and then some, compressing her bones. "Did you learn how to use this from your *friend*?"

Jayme.

Vi's hand released the hilt under Fallor's crushing grip. The magic blade fell to the ground, unraveling into formless strands of light that faded quickly into the night.

"What was the poor wench's name who lived under your boot again?" he sneered.

The narrowing of her eyes was his only warning before magic exploded from her, unfettered. It was light and fire. Both and neither. It was every inch of agony she felt and had not even had a breath to properly address since waking.

Fallor jumped back from the flames. In the same movement, he unsheathed a dagger, nearly the length of a short sword, from his thigh. He reared back, driving it right toward her chest.

"*Mysst Soto Xieh!*" Vi proclaimed, staring up at Fallor, unflinching, as his weapon drove harmlessly into a spinning circle of slight. "Don't you dare mention that traitor's name in my presence."

Fallor stepped back, spun, and launched another attack.

"*Loft Dorh Hoolo*," Vi seethed. She poured every ounce of hate for the man—and Jayme's betrayal—into the words. Fallor was stopped instantly, frozen in time.

Even under the influence of her own word of power from the goddess, Fallor was barely tethered. Rain poured over her shoulders. Mud dripped into her eyes. But Vi ignored the burning sensation, staring at Fallor as she waited for Taavin's words.

Waiting for him to finish the job.

A crack of lightning arced overhead, dancing through the clouds, splitting toward the earth. Her attention wavered as red illuminated the entire bluff.

Red lighting.

Vi found herself flooded by a profound sense of foreboding. The watch at her neck felt hot and whispers tickled the edge of her hearing. She'd seen the phenomenon in the distance on the *Dawn Skipper*. Up close, the lightning was profoundly unnerving. In its wake, Vi felt surrounded by an enemy she couldn't see but could sense lurking, ready to attack.

Unfortunately, it distracted her from the enemy right before her.

"*Mysst Soto Xieh!*" Taavin spoke so hastily the words were barely distinguishable. A shield of light was before her once more, this time shattering under Fallor's blade.

Vi jumped and slid back, putting distance between her and the pirate. "*Mysst Soto Larrk.*"

In her right hand, a bow appeared; in her left, an arrow. Vi brought them together, hands moving with expertise born from years of training. She drew back the bowstring, feeling the aches in her shoulders that accompanied it. Vi ignored every protest her body made—every reminder that she wasn't operating at full health.

She loosed the arrow point blank; it moved only inches to sink into Fallor's shoulder. The arrow exploded into light as Vi reached back to where a quiver would be. Her fingers condensed around something solid—a new arrow where there had previously been none.

Nocking the second, Vi loosed it just as quickly. Fallor stumbled back, raising his hand up to his shoulder, covering the wounds she inflicted. Rain, tinted red by another burst of lightning, merged with the dark blood pouring from the wounds. Vi expected to find anger, rage, or frustration in Fallor's gaze when he trained it upon her.

She hadn't expected the laughter.

"You really think you're a killer?" Her hands were moving to prove him wrong as he spoke. Fallor narrowed his steely eyes. "Do it then," he challenged with a whisper. "Show me you're a killer and not some pampered princess. Kill me, and meet Adela's true rage."

Rainwater shook from her quivering hand. Her fingers cramped in their grip, tighter than death, around the bow. She stared down the arrow, looking at the point right over the soft spot in the center of the man's neck.

Kill him.

It would feel so good to kill him.

She wanted to. But she couldn't. She was trapped between something dark and twisted that kept trying to snarl her in its thorny embrace, and everything she once thought she knew about herself. All the while, he was right there, waiting.

Was he right? Was this why she hadn't shattered his heart as she had Jayme's or Kora's? She had been able to kill them in a moment of blind rage. But would she be able to kill so easily again?

No, she'd chosen this route because it would be more painful. *That was it*, a sinister voice uttered within her. It felt like a person Vi had never met had taken residence in the void of her chest.

"I want to kill you slowly," she whispered. "I will see to it that none of Adela's pirates enjoy a clean death."

Vi let the arrow loose, aimed right for his throat. She wanted to watch the blood drain from his neck in a river. But the arrow only had time to knick his flesh before an unfamiliar voice boomed over the pouring rain. "*Juth mariy.*"

The bow in her hands shattered into harmless light. Vi let out a cry of anguish and readied her magic for her next assault. Enough of letting him off easy. Enough hesitation. She'd end this now.

The familiar grip of Taavin's fingers closed around her. "*Durroe sallvas tempre dupot. Durroe watt radia dupot.*" They were concealed once more.

Fallor didn't look for them. Instead, he turned, squinting in the darkness at the top of the far ridge. There, mounted on white steeds, was a line of men and women illuminated by shining orbs of blue-tinted light cast above their heads.

"Oh, holy Swords," Fallor cursed. There was the tell-tale ripple of power that made her skin crawl and Vi watched as the man slipped between each pulse of magic, disappearing and reappearing as an eagle where a man once stood.

"We have to go." Taavin tugged on her hand. He was going to dislocate her shoulder before the night was up. "Quickly, before—"

"*Juth mariy.*" The man at the head of the group shouted again. Vi could make out little more than his golden armor and dark hair. There was an uncanny similarity between him and the man she'd come all this way to find.

"Father?" Vi said, small and weak.

"Vi, this way!" Taavin pulled on her as his concealment shattered. "We have to make it to the Twilight Forest."

He broke into an all-out sprint, leaving Vi little choice but to follow.

That man atop the steed wasn't her father, no matter how much the armor looked like that of Solaris. She was far from that world of white and gold. Far from her home.

And her father was still the captive of the pirate queen.

An eagle's cry sounded, punctuated by the man shouting, "Archers to the Morphi! Calvary, to them! Loose!"

Vi couldn't hear the bowstrings over the rain and rolling thunder that followed streaks of red lightning. Neither could she hear the hooves of the large horses in pursuit of them. But she could *feel* the beasts.

She pushed her feet harder into the earth as red lightning cracked once more, striking the forest ahead. Every leaping step she took had Vi's free hand pressing into her side, where the flesh felt like it was tearing open anew. She was too freshly healed to be fighting and fleeing.

Taavin slowed. He was wheezing, too, his hand grasping at his shirt above his chest. Vi slowed her pace, looking back to the horses.

"Taavin, we—"

"I know," he hissed. Glancing over his shoulder, he looked back at the horses quickly closing the gap between them. "*Durroe watt radia. Durroe watt ivin.*" He turned forward again, keeping close alongside her, the rings of light he'd summoned condensing around his finger. "Keep running, and don't look back."

Vi heeded his words, running with all she had. Taavin, for his part, managed to keep stride. But every five steps he seemed to stumble, then every three.

"Taavin—" She looked to his face with worry. His eyes were hazy and unfocused. Was he going to make it to the forest? What would happen if the Swords caught them?

"Keep, going," he panted. "We're almost there."

As they ran, nearly at the trees, Taavin's arm swung out, pointing. A tiny glyph still spiraled around his finger. Vi watched as a nearly identical copy of her and Taavin sprinted off at an angle.

An illusion.

The horses continued to charge, shifting course to chase after their fabricated copies. Taavin's illusions vanished into thin air as the mounted men and women overtook them. One of the knights let out a cry of frustration as Vi and Taavin plunged into the welcoming embrace of the tree line, and into the dark unknown that was the Twilight Forest.

THE MOMENT HER FEET hit the mossy, wet earth of the forest, Vi moved faster.

She'd grown up in the jungles of Shaldan, spending her childhood leaping and swinging from branch to branch. The feeling of damp brush and leaves under her feet, the sounds of rain muffled by the leafy canopy—its familiarity was a balm to her panic. She felt more comfortable with trees above and around her than she had in months in the desert and open sea.

There had been a road that led into the forest, but her and Taavin continued to ignore it. Instead, he struck out between the trees. From the corners of her eyes, Vi watched him move. Since entering the forest, her footing had become surer, while his stumbles were happening with greater frequency.

Taavin didn't even so much as glance her way. His face was etched with a fierce determination that unnerved her. Not just because she'd never seen the expression on his features—but because she was afraid of what would happen when that expression vanished. It was the look of a man who was going to run himself until his body gave out. She took a half step closer to him so she'd be there if he fell.

Vi glanced back, looking to where the riders had been. The rainclouds had blotted out the moon, leaving them very little light to see by. She found herself hoping for the cracks of the ominous red lightning to catch a quick glimpse of the knights or Fallor, but there was no such luck and she didn't dare summon a fire.

With every winded breath, the ache in her side ran deeper. Vi pressed a hand into the still-healing wound, wondering how recently Taavin had ripped it open. The pain seemed to spread, shooting straight up into her head.

"Taavin—"

"I know." He slowed his pace, chest heaving with panting breaths. He was faring no better than she. "Looks like I was right…"

"About what?"

"None of them will dare to come into the Twilight Forest," he wheezed, slumping against a tree. Vi was ready, reaching out to support him. But the moment her hand brushed feather-light against his side, he winced and let out a long hiss.

"Your ribs." Vi pulled her hands away, looking at the place Fallor had made contact. "Let me see."

"Let's get out of the rain first. We may be able to find shelter closer to the cliffs—an overhang, perhaps."

They pressed onward, albeit at a slower pace. Vi was soon dragging her feet and Taavin was leaning against every other tree to catch his breath.

"We have to stop. We're not going to make it much longer." She scanned their surrounds for options.

Ahead, the trees gave way for a small stream. Vi looked up and downstream, searching for any sign of Fallor or the Swords. But there was none. In fact, they seemed to be the only life in the forest, the world still other than the whisper of water. Taavin took a step down onto the slick rocks.

"Be careful." Vi quickly leapt to his side. Her arm wrapped tightly around his waist, holding him to her and stabilizing him.

"You're sure-footed."

"I grew up in a jungle, remember?" Vi helped him across to the giant boulders she assumed he was heading toward.

Just as Taavin had suspected—or hoped—the terrain had become rockier the closer they got to the cliffs that met the sea. The banks of the stream became giant boulders that jutted out from the earth. Downstream, Vi could see more rocks than trees.

They made their way toward one particularly large outcropping, a dark gap betraying a space just wide enough for them to squeeze through.

"In here?" Vi asked.

"It's the best I've seen and we should get out of the rain."

"Let me go first and make sure there's enough room." Vi guided him toward one of the two giant boulders on either side of the opening, stepping away from his side only when she was certain he was stable enough to stand on his own.

Squeezing herself into the opening, Vi tip-toed into the dark before allowing a small flame to kindle above her palm. The passage grew so narrow, she was certain she'd have to give up and turn back. But the flame illuminated a more open space ahead, and somehow she managed to twist the curves of her hips in just the right way to pop through with only a small wince.

Sure enough, it was a small cave, formed by four massive rocks leaning against each other. It would barely be large enough for the two of them—but it was dry and certainly well hidden.

It'd do.

"Come on in," Vi called back. "I think there's enough room."

Taavin appeared as he side-stepped between the rocks. Vi reached out, offering a hand and helping him through the rest of the way. He emerged with a sigh of relief, immediately leaning against the rocky wall opposite, hand splayed on his chest where Fallor had used his body as a springboard.

"Sit, and let me see," Vi repeated her earlier demand.

"I'll be fine," he said, as if pain wasn't written on his face in large, block letters.

"Quit being stubborn."

He finally obliged her, sinking down the wall until he was seated. His legs extended until his toes hit the opposite wall, knees bent. Vi crouched at his side, twisting until she found a way to somehow sit comfortably and not be in his lap at the same time.

Her hands paused at the hem of his shirt, the fabric still slick with rain and clinging to every curve of his muscle. Vi raised her eyes slowly to his.

"May I?" she whispered.

"Go ahead." The words were stronger than hers, but far from what she'd call confident. He was as nervous as she was. This was uncharted territory for them both.

She wasn't undressing him. Well, she *was*. But not really. It was for medical reasons.

Her racing thoughts had her heart matching pace as she slowly lifted the shirt, exposing the tan skin beneath. His flesh was bumpy, thanks to the chill of the cave and the exposed damp. Vi continued to ignore the cut curves of his muscles and the line of hair trailing down to and underneath his trousers—an easy task the moment her eyes landed on his ribcage.

"Oh, Taavin…" she breathed.

He winced as her fingers lightly brushed the deep bruising that splotched his skin. "It's that bad?"

"It looks like you had a small mountain crush you." Vi lowered the shirt slowly. "I've used *halleth* before but—"

"Not very well."

Vi narrowed her eyes slightly. She'd been about to say the same thing. But that didn't mean she appreciated him beating her to the punch. As if reading her mind, he wheezed laughter.

"I could tell." Taavin hid a wince between his words. The fight and flight had stolen their focus from their injuries and ailing bodies; it seemed that the pain was settling in on him now, just like she hadn't noticed her aches until they'd slowed their pace in the woods. "The wounds that had been inflicted on you—you tried to heal them with *halleth*—it was clumsily done. The skin was all knotted and scarred in a way that was going to give you trouble long-term. I was forced to rip them back open and set them correctly."

That confirmed her suspicions about why she still ached so badly.

"I was learning on the run," Vi said defensively. "We haven't had a chance to go over *halleth* yet. And Firebearing doesn't cover any kind of healing other than cauterizing wounds."

"You're alive—that means you did more than enough," he said, trying to soothe. "With Fallor on your tail, I assume those wounds were from Adela?"

Vi gave a small nod, lips pursed.

"What happened to you on the way here?" he asked, daring to ask the question that must have been on his mind since he found her on the beach. "I spoke with you on that balcony not more than—"

"Two, three, maybe four weeks ago," Vi murmured. It felt like a lifetime to her as well. Being unconscious for a large chunk of that time certainly didn't help.

"Something has changed since then."

He was right. Something had changed. Jayme's betrayal had awoken a darkness in her that Vi worried she'd never be free of.

"Vi, what is it?" he asked softly, emerald eyes shining in the firelight. Did hers shine as brightly? Or had they dulled with the dust of the long road she'd traveled?

"It's nothing." *Besides being trapped in the dark prison of my thoughts*. "It took a lot to get here. That's all."

He opened his mouth to speak again and Vi knew what he was going to ask. He'd want details. He'd probe for information she wasn't ready to give. Those events were still lost in the depths of the black waters sloshing in the hole in her chest.

"It seems to have been the same for you," Vi countered. His turn to look away. "The Swords of Light, the strong arm of the

Faithful, are after you?"

"Led by Lord Ulvarth, no less."

"Their leader?"

"Yes. Knight of the Sun. Lord of the Faithful. Beloved by Yargen. Sole attendant to the Voice." Taavin enumerated Ulvarth's titles, each more bitter than the last.

"That's a mouthful… Not that I'm one to talk." Taavin gave a small grin at her jest, one he quickly abandoned. "He was there, wasn't he?"

"He was," Taavin said. "At the front." The firelight danced on his skin, casting long shadows. For a man who was filled with the power of light, darkness seemed to love him.

"They want to bring you back to the Archives of Yargen, don't they?"

"As soon as they can. I don't think it's public knowledge that I've escaped yet. If word gets out, Ulvarth stands to lose his rank and title—or the people's faith, at the very least."

She was slowly piecing together the parts of Taavin's life from bits of information he'd dropped like breadcrumbs in a vast forest. A man who was the head of a holy order—who'd ordained the Queen of Meru by his hand. But a puppet for others, a captive to keep under control so that Ulvarth could have power over arguably the strongest organization on Meru.

Her heart ached for him as her blood boiled with rage at the Lord of the Faithful.

"Why does Adela want you? Because you're a Solaris?"

At the mere mention of Adela, Vi's midsection ached. "The elfin'ra have put a bounty out for me," Vi answered simply.

"And Adela will capitalize on anything, even the end of the world." Taavin cursed under his breath.

She'd even capitalize on the lonely heart of a gullible princess, Vi thought bitterly. But she kept her mouth shut.

"Vi, what is it?" Taavin's palm cupped her cheek, summoning Vi's attention back once more from the demons lurking in her heart. “Let me help you,” he said gently.

“You’ve done enough.” It was her turn to take care of him now. And Vi didn’t want to give Jayme another thought or word. Doing so felt like letting the traitor win. “We should plan our next move. You have Lord Ulvarth after you, and I have Fallor—Adela by extension—after me. It’s a lot to deal with.”

“Our next move is to wait.” Taavin shifted, wincing again as his hand fell from her face. Vi caught it, not wanting to let go his warmth just yet. She felt far too cold on the inside to lose his touch.

“We have to keep moving. We’re not safe here.”

“This is the one place we have a chance to be safe,” he insisted.

“Why?” Vi remembered his mention that they wouldn’t “dare” follow them into the forest.

“Because we’re in the Twilight Forest, which is under the protection of the Twilight Kingdom.”

“Twilight Kingdom?” Vi repeated.

“The Twilight Kingdom is inhabited by the morphi, those who command the power of the shift.”

Twilight Kingdom. Morphi. The shift. Her head was spinning, trying to take in all the new information at once. “What’s the power of the shift? Is that another discipline of magic on Meru—like Lightspinning?”

Taavin’s eyes fluttered closed a moment as he took a shallow breath. He looked exhausted and Vi knew she should let him rest. But it was hard to do that when information that might keep them alive hung on his tongue.

“It is. But I admit… I don’t know much. Thc shift is a forbidden topic for the Faithful.”

“What makes it forbidden?”

“You saw the markings on Fallor’s brow?” he asked. She nodded, remembering the glowing dots that he’d covered with grease paint when she’d first met him. “Those are the mark of the morphi. The Faithful teach that they—the morphi—are turning their backs on Yargen by anchoring themselves in the twilight—neither darkness or light. Because of this altered existence, they can *shift* reality—which is an affront to Yargen's goodness."

"That sounds like a more religious than logical reason."

"It likely is." Taavin let out a soft sigh, eyelids drooping. "As I said, I know little of this power. Only the morphi possess it, and they guard the secrets of the shift with their lives."

"Is it because of the shift that Fallor can become an eagle?" Vi asked. "He's shifting the reality of himself—his nature—into that of an eagle?"

"That is my understanding, yes. Physical change is just one of their skills. They can also distort or break Lightspinning magic."

"That's what he did in the field, to break your illusion?"

"Yes."

"So how does this Twilight Kingdom protect us, if Fallor is one of them?" Vi kept her focus on the pressing matter of their survival rather than any questions on magical theory.

"He's a morphi… but the Twilight Kingdom holds no love for him. He's a famous exile from their lands, forbidden from entering their territory."

"And the Faithful won't follow us into the forests because the shift magic is anathema to them?" Dislike of the morphi still seemed an arbitrary and ill-founded prejudice, but if it protected them, she wouldn't complain too much about it.

"More or less."

"Can we seek refuge in the Twilight Kingdom?"

"No, we'll rest here until I can recover." Taavin rested a hand lightly on his ribs. "Which may be some time since we've lost the contents of my trunk."

"Sorry…" Vi muttered. It had gone up in smoke with the rest of the shack.

"It's all right. I didn't have much left anyway after traveling for a good week."

"If we can't seek refuge, can we at least restock in the

Kingdom?" She couldn't blame Taavin for wanting to keep a low profile, given who he was. But surely she could at least go and get what they needed?

"No. The Kingdom is protected by an impenetrable shift. Even if you could get through… you shouldn't."

"But I can—"

"The enemies of our enemies are not our friends in this case. Neither of us should venture to interact with anyone from the Twilight Kingdom." He spoke as though it were a declaration. Vi bristled at the tone but didn't object. He knew far more about Meru and its nuances than she.

"Why would they have a reason to be hostile to us?"

"For the same reason that I will not heal myself with *halleth*… The feeling of hatred is mutual between the Faithful and the morphi. If they sense Lightspinning in their lands, we will be hunted. We conceal ourselves here in body and in magic."

Which meant they weren't really safe at all. Vi turned toward the narrow entrance they'd squeezed through. The rain still pounded outside, perhaps intent on raising the water in the small stream and flooding them out like two rats. In the distance, thunder rolled.

"Raspian is getting stronger…" Taavin mumbled, his eyes finally closing for slumber. "The end of the world is drawing near."

Vi remained silent, allowing Taavin to slip off to sleep.

She didn't bother worrying him with the fact that this was the second time she'd seen red lightning.

4

THE FIRST THING Vi felt was the reassuring warmth of someone next to her.

The soft dripping of the cave filled her ears. Wet *plops* thrummed a rhythm underneath the echoes of the quietly babbling stream that ran by the entrance. The world was far quieter than when she'd gone to sleep.

Vi slowly opened her eyes, her attention drawn immediately to the man at her side. The gray light washed out his features and darkened his hair nearly to black. It clung with grime and sweat around his face, the natural waves of it almost clumping into curls. Slowly, Vi raised a hand, lightly pushing his hair away from his eyes.

Her fingertip brushed the point of his ear, her hand lingering there almost of its own volition.

He truly was different from her. She'd always known it. Yet when she had summoned him with *narro hath*, he'd existed in the framework of her world. Now, she was an occupant of his, and even the princess who belonged nowhere had never felt so out of place.

She'd finally made it to him. Somehow, he felt farther away than ever. They were from different worlds, pulled together by fate. Two people who should have never met and seemed destined for nothing more than heartache.

Vi lifted her hand off his person, though he was still heavy on hers. He was far heavier than Ellene had been when she'd fallen asleep on Vi's shoulder during too-long stories around campfires.

Ellene.

Vi had begrudged her life in Shaldan. Those endless nights of storytelling, the expectations of royalty, her never-ending lessons, the seemingly insufferable captivity. How grateful she would be to have one more night to relax with Ellene and sip cider, safe and protected behind walls meant to keep the world out as much as Vi in. She had never fully appreciated how good she'd had it.

And now it was gone.

The young princess who had sat around those firesides was lost on a beach between the Dark Isle and Meru. She was no longer that innocent, spoiled girl. Vi took a slow inhale of breath. The anger that ebbed and flowed within her had no direction, and would serve nothing. She had work to do; she had to let it go… But she didn't know how.

"Vi…" Taavin murmured, face still pressed against her shoulder. He hadn't even opened his long lashes yet. She shifted slightly, trying to get a better look at his face.

The man was calling for her in his sleep. But her movement seemed to rouse him from the remnants of dreamland.

"Did I disturb you?" she asked softly.

"No." Taavin winced as he rubbed his sides. "I think I disturbed myself." She neglected to mention that she'd been the one to lightly trail her fingers along his face. "It's late."

"Is it?"

"Given how stiff I am, I think so."

"Good to know the stiffness isn't just me." Using the wall for support, Vi pushed herself upward. There wasn't much room to stretch, but she made a good effort of it. "I'm going to wash my face and have a drink."

"While you're out, will you get me a garnet skullcap?"

"You're not coming? Some fresh air would do you well."

"You may be right… But no." Taavin adjusted himself slightly. Vi didn't miss the wince. "I think I shall linger here for a bit more. I'm not quite sure if it's the best idea for me to be moving yet… The skullcap should help relieve the aches and soothe me back to sleep."

"You slept a fair bit." A frown crossed her lips. Could a person sleep too much? Vi suddenly wished she'd paid more attention to Ginger's brief clerical lessons whenever Vi landed herself in trouble. Another thing she'd taken for granted.

"The more I rest, the faster we can be on the road." He gave her what Vi could easily recognize as a brave smile in the face of great pain.

"Taavin, I'm worried—"

"Don't worry about me, Vi. I'm elfin; we're a hearty bunch and heal much faster than humans, even without any kind of clerical assistance." Heal much faster than *her*, he meant. Everything this morning served to remind her of their differences. "Garnet skullcap. Bright white flowers shaped like little bells. Deep crimson leaves—thin and slightly waxy."

Vi quickly repeated the description back to him. "Got it."

"Thank you, Vi."

She gave a nod. "I'll be back soon."

Vi sucked in her stomach and squeezed through the narrow passage and out onto the rocky bed of the stream. Raising a hand to her eyes, Vi shielded them from the bright white light of morning, giving them a chance to adjust.

Motion startled her near instantly. Vi ducked quickly, raising her hand, her spark crackling around her fingers. She jerked her head toward a nearby tree where the projectile had landed.

No, wait, not a projectile… Sitting in the tree was a bird as big as her forearm with a long neck and oil-slick plumage. It almost looked wet with how the light shimmered off its long feathers. Every subtle breeze sent rainbows across its back and breast. From hooked beak to bright blue talons, Vi had never seen anything like it.

The strange looking bird regarded her for a long moment before taking off with an undignified chirp. Vi watched it take flight, the mere sight of a bird sending small shivers down her spine. She wondered if she would ever be able to see a winged creature again without thinking of Fallor.

Vi set off, trying to leave thoughts of the pirate behind her.

In the daylight, the trees were an eerie gray color. Not quite the shade of bleached bone, but brighter than the ashes of a fire pit, and a hue Vi had never seen among the giant sentries of the North. These trees were tall—dizzyingly so. But they were thin from root to canopy. So thin that Vi wondered how they didn't topple over with the slightest of breezes that swayed their canopies.

The forest floor was covered with leaves and little else. There were no smaller shrubs, no fan-like fronds stretching out to block her path. She could see straight through all the trees like bars in a cage until the horizon blurred and it was hard to tell just where anything stopped and started.

That was the real reason she didn't stray far from the stream.

Every tree of the forest looked identical. Sameness and more sameness. It was a forest she felt she could get lost in forever if she wasn't careful.

"Red leaves," she murmured to herself.

She'd been walking for the better part of an hour in search of the skullcap. Vi was about ready to give up when she finally found it. Taavin hadn't specified what part of the plant he needed—and Vi knew all too well that not all parts of a plant were equal, at least not when it came to extracting medicinal properties. So she dug it out, roots to delicate buds.

"I think I have it," Vi announced as she squeezed back into their hiding place.

The skullcap slipped from her fingers, forgotten.

"Taavin!" She knelt at his side. The man's chin was slumped to his chest. His arms hung heavy, palms up. The last person she'd seen in such a state had been dying from the White Death. "Taavin wh—"

"I was merely resting." He lifted his head with a start, giving her a thin smile. "No need to fret."

Vi searched his face. *Lying*. He was lying through his teeth. There was plenty of reason for her to fret.

"You're not okay, are you?" she whispered.

"I will be." Taavin looked toward his feet, seeing the skullcap she'd dropped. "I see you found some."

"I did."

"Good. I'll just need the buds... two for now. Be careful to pinch them off so that you don't get any stem. Here, like this." His hands reached out, covering her fingers lightly. Vi split her attention between what he was showing her and his haggard expression. Even now, even after all that had transpired, a certain grace clung to him and wouldn't let go.

"Here, let me do the next." She focused on the task at hand and tried to replicate his motions.

"Perfect." Taavin took the bud from her fingers, chewing it thoughtfully before swallowing. With that, he leaned back, settling himself once more.

Vi shifted to face him. His feet were at her side, hers at his. Her eyes landed on his hands—folded over his lower stomach and slowly running over a golden bracelet Vi had never seen before. Had they been outstretched, she might have gathered them in her own.

This was the first quiet—and fully conscious—moment they'd had since meeting in person, she realized.

Suddenly, despite all that had transpired, she felt marginally awkward. Her hands couldn't seem to find a good place to rest. How had she been so comfortable around him before? How had she touched him like it was nothing? Vi ended up mirroring his pose.

"How long will it take for you to get better?" she asked.

"With enough rest and any luck, a few days at worst."

"A few days…" she repeated, her mind already turning over the implications of the thought. "I'll need to forage some sustenance for us." He'd said the Twilight Kingdom and Forest were the lands of the morphi, and the last thing Vi wanted to do was slay an animal that was secretly a person. Her thoughts wandered back to the dark bird—it was a good thing she hadn't killed it.

"Do you know what plants are safe to eat?"

"I was going to look for ones I recognized. I realize I'm far from home, but there's likely a few common varieties—Meru and the Dark Isle aren't *that* far apart. Certain mushrooms grow across the whole Dark Isle… I assume they'll be here too. Maybe some fruits or nuts that you can help identify?"

"Brilliant thoughts. Forgive me for forgetting how capable you are." A small, sad smile crossed his mouth. "I sometimes think of our captivity as the same. In reality, you were able to explore far more than me."

The aching and longing in his voice kept Vi from arguing. She hadn't ever really been able to *explore*. Not in the true, untethered sense of the word. But she had been awarded some freedoms. She'd had teachers who wanted her to know how to survive in the wilds if, or when, she needed to. She suspected none of them ever thought she'd have to put theory into practice—but here she found herself, somewhat prepared to face this newest challenge.

Even if she hadn't realized it at the time, she'd had luxuries Taavin had only dreamed of.

"When you're better…" Vi straightened away from the wall, resting a hand on his thigh. "I'll show you every edible plant I can find, and how to harvest them. I'll even show you the ones that I had to taste-test to find out if they're edible or poisonous."

"Don't you go taste-testing possibly poisonous things." His hand covered hers. "I don't want anything happening to you."

"Nothing will."

Taavin gave a dark chuckle. "You say that, when clearly so much has." Vi searched his expression as he effortlessly held her gaze. "You're not the same woman I first met."

"No one stays the same," Vi murmured.

"True… Then, you're not the same woman I stood next to on that balcony." Taavin's fingers worked to lace with hers. Vi's hand remained limp, giving him no encouragement. Yet she couldn't find it in her to pull away either. He was the only comfort she had in this strange world.

"Maybe you never really had a good measure on me to begin with," Vi contested as discomfort worked its way underneath her skin like maggots.

"Truly?" He arched his eyebrows. "You think I don't know you by now? You think I haven't spent my life learning your mannerisms? Memorizing your face?"

"You memorized a woman in a dream. I am not that woman. It was likely my grandmother, remember?"

"Maybe." He shifted slightly, sitting straighter. "Or maybe you're challenging me because you know I'm right."

Vi shifted, caught between wanting to pour out her soul to him, and bolt from the cave to avoid his scrutiny. She'd spent so much time trying to get to him that Vi hadn't really thought about what it would be like when they were together… all the time. When she couldn't dismiss him with a thought or wave of her hand. When his eyes continued to bore into her soul long after she wanted the relief of hiding from things she herself wasn't yet ready to address.

"Vi—"

"I should get to foraging, while there's still plenty of good light." Vi pulled away quickly. Fleeing from her problems would be her choice.

"Wait—" Taavin leaned forward, started to get up, then stopped mid-motion with a wince of pain. His back rested heavily once more on the wall behind him as he grabbed both of his sides.

"Vi, I'm just trying—"

Vi ignored him, pretending she couldn't hear. Once more, she squeezed out into the sunlight, promptly starting upstream.

He was just trying to help. She knew he was. She paused to look back to the rocky entrance of their cave, briefly debating whether or not to return immediately and make amends.

Would it feel good, or terrible, to expose the angry darkness that swirled around in her now? What would he think when he learned of how she'd used *juth calt*?

Vi turned, continuing on, her back to the cave mouth.

At first, she wasn't very active in her foraging. It was more of a walk to try to clear her head. But the more time that passed, the less clear-headed she felt. If anything, things got murkier.

Mirroring her mindset, dusk fell.

"Twilight in the Twilight Forest," Vi muttered. Her feet slowed once more.

The world had certainly taken on an unnatural quality. The ashen trees looked even more devoid of color. Their leaves had become pale—not a fiery red as one might expect with the fading sun. And they cast long shadows on the forest floor, turning it dark gray. It was as though the whole world had been expunged of color and steeped in drab.

The trees in the distance seemed to waver briefly. Vi rubbed her eyes and squinted. Had she only imagined the ruler-straight trunks wobbling?

She stepped away from the rocky stream, scrambling up a large boulder, and started into the trees.

Her first thought was Fallor and his strange magic—*the shift*. Perhaps he had followed them into the forest despite being exiled? Vi balled her hand into a fist, curling the spark under her fingers.

Taavin had said they couldn't use Lightspinning without risking detection. Would her fire be all right? It would have to be, because she wasn't about to fight Fallor bare-handed.

The forest was uncomfortably silent. Nothing but gray sameness as far as the eye could see. She turned, glancing over her shoulder—

The stream was gone.

Her heart raced in earnest now. She couldn't hear the stream over the deafening stillness of the woods. She couldn't see it between the countless trees that seemed to close in on her. Vi spun in place. All she had to do was turn right around and go back the way she came.

It wasn't Fallor, anyway—it couldn't be. Perhaps it was some other morphi. Though Taavin had cautioned her to stay away.

As she spun in place, something caught her eye—another bit of wobbling, this time over the split trunk of a fell tree.

"What is that?" she whispered, slowly drawing near. The leaves crunched under her shuffling footsteps, but Vi could barely hear it. There was a murmuring buzz at the edges of her hearing, the closer she got to the oddity.

It was a tree trunk, split from the inside out. The smell of rot suddenly filled her nose, as though the tree had let out a dying breath. But the aroma was not deep and earthy as one would expect. It was rank and choking, like carrion. She would've long fled were it not for an unnerving fascination with the anomaly—as though she were looking at something she shouldn't.

Tiny sparks of red lightning jumped between each gaping crack in the bark, leaving black spots in their wake. Above it, the air seemed alive, shifting and writhing, distorting the trees beyond. There was a snap, a pop, and Vi could nearly make out lights where there had been none. It was as if the air were tearing open to expose the darkness that existed beyond the veil of her reality. A whole city of darkness, waiting.

Vi squinted and leaned closer in an effort to make out more details before the air shifted again and the city was gone.

She leaned too close.

A tiny bolt of lightning extended upward, striking her fingertip. Though it couldn't have been more than a pin-prick, it felt as though it darted under her skin, crackling across her muscles from finger to shoulder to brow, all the way down to her toes.

She must've let out a scream, but Vi couldn't be certain, because the murmuring in her ears magnified with the cracks of lightning that struggled to break through her flesh. Suddenly it was as if a thousand people were talking over each other at once, all trying to get to her. They said countless names, rapid fire, over a thousand muttered conversations Vi couldn't make out.

She gripped the sides of her face, trying to cover her ears and mute the excruciating, deafening noise. Slowly layering atop them all was a terrible rhythm, a singular repeated word, louder by the moment.

Die, die, die.

There was another bolt of lightning, this time jackknifing right for her heart—too quick for her to move away.

Light burst from the watch at her neck, cutting the impending darkness of the forest, keeping the lightning and auditory assault at bay. Vi stumbled backward, fell, scrambled back to her feet. She panted, breathless. But the only sounds in her ears now were that of her frantically beating heart, and every labored breath as she turned and broke into an all-out run.

"TAAVIN... TAAVIN!" VI pushed herself through the entrance of the cave, not caring for every rough bit of rock that dug into her curves. It barely registered as pain—barely registered at all. "Taavin," she repeated again as she gasped for air. As though his name was the only thing she could manage.

"Vi, what is it?" Through the pain, he forced himself more upright. Distress, but not for his own state, written across his features. "Are you all right? What's happened?"

Vi shook her head. The one voice, that terrible, earth-shattering voice demanding her death still lived in her ears. If she opened her mouth, it may come from her lips. That was how deep it now ran in her.

"It's clearly something." Taavin's voice had gone stern. "Don't shut me out."

She shook her head again, trying to focus on breathing. Trying to dig her nails into the rough wall behind her to keep her focus grounded in the here and now. She needed something stable. But the whole world felt like it could crumble at once.

"Vi—" A small yelp of pain broke through, yanking her back to the present. Taavin was rolled on his side on the ground, his elbow supporting him. Yet even now, he struggled to get back up.

"Don't." She stopped him with a word. "Don't get up again, you'll just hurt yourself." Vi sank down the wall slowly, crouching on the balls of her feet, knees to her chest and arms around her legs.

"Tell me." He reached out with the hand that wasn't supporting him, fumbling until he caught her fingers. "Did you run into a morphi?"

She shook her head no.

"The Swords of Light?"

"No."

"What, then?"

Vi stared at him. Her eyes felt dry, as though they'd been held open too wide for too long. She made an effort to blink them. Somehow, even that hurt. The same sensation she'd had when she'd woken returned: her body was not her own.

"I don't know what it was," she confessed. "There was red lightning around a fallen tree and—"

"Red lightning around a *tree*?" Taavin finally seated himself once more, no longer leaned over on his elbow.

"More like… inside the tree. Maybe it was struck during the storm last night? There was a tree that had fallen, and it looked odd. When I got closer, I could see red lightning jumping between its shattered trunk and it *reeked*. Taavin, it smelled of death."

His expression darkened. "What else happened?"

"How do you know something else happened?" Vi whispered.

"Because you aren't a woman reduced to shaking by a tree that smells of death and has red lightning… however darkly unnatural it may be."

Vi balled her hands into fists, willing her arms to stop

trembling. He was right. She wasn't someone who quaked in fear. She swallowed hard, continuing when her voice was more level.

"The air above seemed... alive. Like it was writhing and ripping. Through it, I saw a city of darkness. Then, a bolt of lightning hit me and... *noise*. Terrible noise." Vi's hands slowly worked their way back up to her ears, as if she still needed to block out the wretched sounds. "Screaming, crying, talking, a thousand people—a whole world of people—all at once."

She couldn't put into words the sensation. She'd known the sound of every voice, as though she'd heard them with her own ears earlier in her life. Yet the words were muffled and unfamiliar.

"Is that all?" He pushed himself forward, sliding along the floor, reaching for her. This time, Vi extended a hand, allowing their fingers to knot together tightly.

This was real, she reminded herself. Taavin was real, and good, and safe, and that... what she had seen in the forest had been... had been...

"It was Raspian," Vi uttered so softly she couldn't be certain she'd spoken at all. "Above it all, I heard him, calling for my death." Taavin's fingers tightened around hers. "He's getting stronger, isn't he?" Taavin gave a small nod. "I saw the land of the elfin'ra, I heard their voices. He's rallying them."

"I'm not sure about that."

"But—"

"I agree... Raspian is getting stronger. He's sinking in his dark clutches wherever he can find purchase, as Yargen's powers weaken. We've seen it in the White Death, we've seen it in his magic streaking through the sky as red lightning. But I don't think the city you saw was of the elfin'ra. I think it was the Twilight Kingdom. I suspect his dark energy is distorting the shift around the city, weakening it. Perhaps, as you describe, tearing it."

"He's rotting the world from the inside out." Vi returned to one of her earlier conclusions.

"But this could be a good thing for us," Taavin mused.

"How so?"

"Because Adela and her like have eluded punishment for years by retreating to her Isle of Frost. The whole of the island is protected by a shift of its own."

"Adela knew the Faithful wouldn't rely on the morphi, not even to get to her." Vi pieced it together aloud, recalling what Taavin had said about the mutual hatred. That made the morphi an easy target for Adela to lure to her cause.

"But if Raspian is breaking down the shift, we may be able to find a way in to the isle. It was something we were going to have to confront, one way or another. This just provides us a simple solution."

Vi dismissed the fact that Taavin was ignoring the obvious, yet again; they could simply seek help from the morphi. Vi likewise filed the idea away, for now. Getting a morphi on their side appealed to her, loathe as she was to bring an unknown element into her plans. She didn't want to leave her father's rescue to the chance of a tear in the shift around the Isle of Frost—she wanted to know for certain she'd be able to get to Adela.

"How is Raspian doing all this without a physical form? Isn't that what the elfin'ra have been after, what they're hunting us to achieve?"

"Yes. For Raspian to reap the destruction he so desires and rebuild the world in his image, he will need to be flesh and blood … But as Yargen's magic continues to fade, Raspian can make bolder plays as he searches for a way to walk among us again."

"What can we do to stop him?"

"Rekindle the flame and restore it to the blazing beacon of life it's always been." Such had been his goal from the start. It had been the one thing he'd sought her out to do all those months ago.

"The watch protected me from one of the bolts of lightning," she said as she clutched the token. "Taavin, I think somehow, it has Yargen's magic."

He hummed in agreement, reaching upward. But rather than going immediately for the watch, his fingertips rested lightly on her cheek. They were almost scalding hot. Vi hadn't realized how clammy she'd become. He searched her face for a long moment before his hand fell, resting atop hers and the watch.

"You may be right. We don't know what it contains, yet, and I desperately want to uncover its secrets."

"How do we do that?"

"I'll need to use Lightspinning to investigate the magic within. Something I am in no position to do."

Taavin pushed himself away and settled back against the wall across from her once more. His eyes fluttered closed a moment and Vi watched the shallow rise and fall of his chest. She didn't know if he meant that he wasn't in a position to do so because of his current state… or because they were in a place he couldn't use Lightspinning.

Likely both.

"Well… you'll just have to get better quickly then." Vi pushed away from her wall, twisting and settling once more next to him. Their sides were flush and she soaked in his warmth.

"I'm trying," he murmured over a bite of skullcap.

"Try harder." Vi nudged him lightly, hoping she'd come off as playful. The emotion was rusty. It felt awkward to her, so she couldn't imagine how it was received.

A smile broke on his lips. "Yes, my Champion."

"Thank you, my Voice."

There was something dangerously endearing to the words. Perhaps their physical proximity added layers of meaning that weren't really there. Or perhaps it was the panic that still popped under her skin like electric shocks, driving her to seek out any feelings of safety and security she could.

"Taavin…" Vi whispered. His breathing had slowed, and she had yet to look back toward him, instead keeping her focus on the dancing shadows her small, flickering flame cast on the wall opposite them. She almost hoped he had fallen asleep.

"Yes, Vi?"

"You told me once, terrible things happen to those you love."

"I did." His voice had grown more lucid, and Vi felt guilty keeping him awake. What was she really trying to ask, anyway?

"Why did you say that?" He sighed softly. "You don't have to tell me."

"I've only ever loved one person, Vi—" She braced herself for the name of some lover she really didn't want to know about, instantly regretting her decision. "—my mother."

"What?" Her eyes were pulled to him in surprise. But Taavin wasn't looking at her. He stared off at the same wall she had been, seeing something entirely different in the shadows.

"Why is it so surprising I loved my mother?"

"I expected you to have a lover… I wasn't thinking of familial love."

He chuckled at that. "How would I find a lover? I was sequestered… The only person who really has unfettered access to me is Ulvarth."

"Right…" She didn't know what else to say. Vi had imagined servants coming in and out, attending him as they had her. Another thing she'd been wrong about. "What happened to your mother?" Vi couldn't imagine a mother condemning their child to such a life willingly. And given all he'd said on the matter, she fully expected the truth to be grim.

"Ulvarth killed her."

She wasn't surprised, not really. After everything Taavin had told her… Her lips pursed into a thin line.

"Ulvarth killed her, to get me." Taavin still wouldn't look at her. His expression was blank, matching the hollow tone of his voice. "There is always a Voice, Vi… When one dies, Yargen chooses another child to serve her for their lifetime. I always suffered from my visions—that was what ultimately drew Ulvarth to me."

"But your mother didn't want to give you up." Vi's mind wandered back to her own mother. Vhalla had made that terrible choice to give Vi up for such an excruciatingly long stretch. But if she hadn't… If the North had attacked during the rise of the Mad

King, her mother and father may not have lived long enough to see Vi into the world.

"No, she said they were wrong. That I was merely a troubled boy, not afflicted by words of the goddess." Taavin raised a hand, running it down the side of his face over the crescent-shaped scar on his cheek. "The struggle wasn't much. What could a boy and a young woman do against Ulvarth and the Swords of Light?"

"You tried to defend her." The scar had an explanation, and a terrible, gut-wrenching one at that.

"I did. They wouldn't kill me… No… Ulvarth needed me alive. But he didn't need me unbroken."

"I'm sorry," she breathed. It wasn't nearly enough. Taavin didn't even address the paltry attempt at consolation.

"She loved me. So she defended me and died for it. If she had agreed to Ulvarth's demands, she would still be alive. Bad things happen to those I love and who love me. So I swore I'd never love again and put someone at risk."

Vi closed her eyes, ignoring the dull ache the words inspired. The halfway status of their relationship, the questions, the time spent wondering what they were… He'd never give them anything more than he already had, she realized. She heard it clearly between his words: *I can't let myself love you.*

Despite all she'd been though, that realization may have hurt the most.

"We should go to sleep," Vi murmured and extinguished the flame.

"We should," he agreed and, within moments, his heavy breathing told her that he had, finally, allowed the world to slip away.

But Vi was still very much grounded in the world. It was a world of men who cut down women to take their children. A world of red lightning.

A world where she had somehow allowed someone into her heart who may not want to be there.

TAAVIN HAD GOTTEN WORSE.

"You should drink something." Vi tapped his cheek gently. His head was limp, chin against his chest. "You haven't drank anything for two days."

His bloodshot eyes cracked open, blinking slowly in the dim light. Sweat beaded on his forehead. Two nights ago, when she'd returned from the red lightning incident in the wood, she'd thought she was cold from fear—that was why he'd seemed so warm to her. But the fever had been ravaging him then. Now, the infection from his broken bones and festering wounds continued to spread.

"Taavin, please, the fever is taking water from you; even if you don't feel you're thirsty, you need to drink."

"Vi…" His lips barely moved as he spoke.

"I'm here, it's me." She held out the wide, flat leaf she'd been cupping in her hand and using as a bowl to ferry water into the cave. "Please, drink."

"I…"

"Please." Vi brought the edge of the leaf to his lips. Taavin didn't have the energy to object further. Most of the water dribbled down his chin and onto his lap, but some got into his mouth. Surely, some had. "Good, that's it."

The knot in his throat bobbed and Taavin's eyes closed. Vi set the leaf to the side. He was fading. She didn't have to be a cleric to know when someone was dying.

"I'm going to find help," Vi whispered. A foolish and dangerous idea had been forming in her head for days now. One that she became less able to shake with each passing morning as he woke worse than the last. "Stay here, and hang on."

Vi emerged from the cave into the familiar haze of the Twilight Forest and struck out upstream as she had all those mornings ago. Part of her was already sick with the notion of what she was about to do. But there was no other choice. Inaction would result in Taavin's death. At least this way he'd have a chance.

How long had she walked that first day? Long enough for her mind to wander… but she hadn't really been paying attention to any actual distances. Vi's eyes scanned the trees to the edge of where the horizon became hazy, looking for a tell-tale wobble in reality itself.

Finding none, Vi stepped off the rocky riverbank and onto the leafy carpet of the forest. She hadn't found the last tear along the water—it had been in the woods itself.

Vi looked back the way she'd come. *No other option*, she repeated to herself. Going back meant Taavin's death. And that was a reality Vi was not about to face.

Tree by tree, Vi ran her fingers along the bark. Her spark tingled beneath her flesh, heating the air between her and the tree. She left singed fingerprints in her wake on every tree she passed. They were signposts for her to use to find her way back, and Vi sincerely hoped she would need to use them—that this foolish notion wouldn't kill her.

The sun was hanging low in the horizon and Vi had lost count of how many trees she'd marked when she finally saw a flash of red light. It was a tiny spark, barely perceptible in the wash of sunset amber. But it was the hope she'd been searching for.

Vi approached the abnormality in the fabric of reality with caution. Another tree had fallen, but this time, rather than landing on the ground, it was propped against its neighboring tree. Tiny bolts of red magic, like ominous fireflies, darted back and forth between the fallen tree and the ground. Scraps of bark were sheered off and hung at an odd angle, dangling in the air—perfectly still, even when breezes swept through the forest enough to rustle the leaves at her feet.

It had been the storm, Vi decided. The bolts of red lightning had struck trees in the forest, creating these abnormalities. She wondered if she went back to the bluffs, would she find red lightning crackling among dead grasses, like footprints of an angry god?

Murmuring returned to the back of her mind, the closer she came to the tree of red lightning. It was a dull, pulsing sensation, but one Vi knew would become sharper if she drew closer.

When she drew closer.

Vi watched the shimmering air in the triangle created by the upright tree, the lightning-struck tree leaning against it, and the ground below. She watched, and waited, keeping her distance. She waited long enough that her feet ached from her toes digging into the ground through the worn-thin soles of her shoes. It wasn't until twilight had fallen on the forest in earnest that Vi caught the first glimpse of the kingdom shimmering beyond—this time more clearly than the last.

Taavin's theory was that Raspian's magic had worn away the shift protecting the Twilight Kingdom—however *that* worked. It was time to put his theory to the test.

Vi gripped the watch around her neck so tightly that she feared she would break it. But that didn't prompt her to unfurl her fingers.

"Yargen, protect me." Vi didn't know if it was a prayer, a demand, or just a wish. She'd take all three, if that's what got her through.

Shifting her feet, Vi launched herself forward like an arrow loosed from the bowstring. Each step was wider than her usual gait, intended to build momentum as quickly as possible. Her body tipped forward, running head-first toward the pulsating air that grew more violent with red magic by the second. She threw her entire weight behind every step. There was no turning back.

There was only one way for her now—into the breach.

Every muscle in her body tensed on impact, ready for the agony she knew was coming. Lightning flared on all sides of her, blinding her, trying to snarl her in its brutal embrace. Vi kept pumping her legs, pushing herself forward, but she didn't know what she was pushing against.

Her eyes had closed instinctively, but now she forced them open. Lightning danced before her vision. It looked as though it was behind her eyes, shooting through her skull—in one ear and out the other. Between every bolt was nothing but pure darkness.

She clutched the watch tighter as the cacophony grew so loud, Vi could barely manage a thought beyond *forward.* She had to keep moving forward. She'd either free herself and be on the other side of this terrible bramble of magic in a world beyond, or she'd push straight through to the Twilight Kingdom as she'd hoped.

A thousand hands worked to keep her back as a thousand voices screamed at her all at once. Vi ignored the feeling of every electric grasp on her body. She ignored the noise as best she could.

Forward.

The word resounded in her chest and Vi realized she'd been saying it aloud the whole time. That was fine. It drowned out Raspian's call for her death. It kept her feet moving. It kept him from claiming her.

Underneath her hand, the watch seared white-hot. It throbbed with every pulse of magic washing over Vi's body. *Forward, and don't let go*. If she let go of the watch, she let go of Yargen. Without Yargen's magic protecting her, Vi knew she would've already been torn apart.

Her long march suddenly had an end. In the distance, beyond the flashes of lightning, there was darkness. Perhaps, it was death waiting for her. Either way, Vi continued relentlessly on and, with a shout, she freed herself of the clutches of Raspian's magic.

Vi took in a gasping breath, only to find the air suddenly thin. Suffocating darkness was around her, so thick that not even air could exist here. She opened her mouth, not getting enough air through her nose alone. But there was no more to be had in this still, blank space.

Still, she forced herself to take a step, and then another.

With every inch, cool light flared underneath her feet until it condensed into a shimmering, solid form. The glowing blue path of magic hardened into stone guided her through the darkness and toward the twilight. Every step brought magic rippling over her like wind, giving her a brief reprieve before the darkness closed in again. But just when her head was throbbing and her eyes felt as though they might explode from her skull, the world slowly rebuilt itself before her eyes.

It was not the world she'd known. The Twilight Forest had vanished before her eyes and was now replaced by a city appearing through shadowy trees that barely had form. With every step closer, there was a brief flash of air, then sound, then light.

Vi emerged from between two dark trees, which seemed now more solid than shadow, and collapsed to her knees. Surrounding her were shards of pale blue stone; they fell off her, like shards of glass, fading to a dull black stone as they hit the ground. She gulped in heaving breaths. Air had never tasted so fresh, or felt so good. Her eyes were blurry, face wet. Vi didn't know if it was from involuntary tears brought on by pain, sweat from the exertion, or immense relief to have made it through.

Likely all three.

Vi rubbed her eyes, sank to her heels, and blinked, taking in the new world before her. It was a city nestled in a valley. Tall ridges extended up on all sides, lined with the same dark trees that were now at Vi's back. It was as if the trees were made of smoke—less solid the farther back one went, turning into wisps of magic that trailed up to form a hazy barrier around the Twilight Kingdom.

A metropolis of wooded magic lit up before her. Large buildings with rope-bridges suspended between them towered overtop wide fauna that served as roofs for bustling markets and businesses below. The construction reminded her somewhat of the North, but with more glass and fitted stone. *There were no Groundbreakers here*, Vi reminded herself.

There were balconies of glass, shining in the moonlight. Some homes had siding that looked like dark metal laid in a pattern that reminded Vi of snake scales. Wood blended into metal set into stone. Nothing seemed right, yet it all connected.

Vi's eyes drifted upward to a moon that had never felt so close. She swallowed hard, her vision of the world's end seared in her memory. Like that vision, this moon, too, was rimmed in a bloody corona, stretching out into the stars scattered on a perpetually dusky sky.

Even here, Raspian had sunk in his claws. Vi wondered how long it would be until the moon in her world looked much the same. And that was when a terrible thought crossed her mind…

What if Taavin's injuries were not fully a result of Fallor's attack? What if the voice was falling prey to Raspian's effects on their world? And if he was—what did that mean for her own susceptibility to the spreading darkness?

Vi gripped her knees, hanging her head. Perhaps that was why, despite Taavin's allegedly superior healing abilities, he was so injured. Vi sniffed, rubbing her nose with the back of her hand. Memories of the White Death—of the clinic in Soricium—drifted through her mind.

No.

She wouldn't let this be his end.

Vi struggled to her feet, using the tree next to her for support. Somewhere in the city beneath her were clerics. She would find one and she would bring him or her back to Taavin by any means necessary.

With one shaky footstep after the next, Vi descended into the Twilight Kingdom.

7

VI MADE SHORT WORK of the walk down the grassy, sloping ridge that ringed the bustling metropolis. Leaning against the back wall of a building right at the edge of the city—Vi took a quick assessment of herself.

Her clothes were ratty and torn. They were sun bleached and salt damaged, hanging like rags on the line that was her too-thin frame. Vi pressed at her stomach and hips. There was less muscle there than she was used to and far less than she'd like.

Rubbing her temples, Vi tried to maintain her focus. It was a difficult task. Her head was still splitting and she could feel the invisible scars of Raspian's infernal lightning on the underside of her skin.

"Think, Vi," she commanded herself. Hearing her voice aloud helped her brain return to task. She glanced around the corner, looking at the group of people lounging on a shared patio area between two buildings.

They didn't seem to notice her, too busy carrying on

laughing, drinking, and playing some kind of game Vi couldn't see and doubted she would recognize. She mostly ignored the conversation—which, fortunately, was carried out in what she knew as the common tongue—and focused on the people's faces. They each looked very much like what she would expect of a human… save for their eyebrows.

Dotted across their brows were faintly glowing spots like those Fallor sported. Every individual seemed to have a slightly different color and pattern. Vi leaned back, running her fingers along her own brow in thought.

There was no way she could create anything convincingly similar without using some kind of Lightspinning. Which meant she'd need to hide rather than masquerade. Perhaps there were humans among them, and Vi's worries were ill founded. But the Twilight Kingdom went to great lengths to protect itself from outsiders, and Vi had yet to see any non-morphi. She wasn't about to take a chance.

It took three side alleyways before Vi found one that wasn't swarming with people. Two men lingered at the opening by the road, their backs to her. Neither so much as looked over their shoulders as Vi slipped in, grabbing a dishcloth off a drying line and quickly tying it around her forehead.

She adjusted it several times, making sure it was secured tightly—tight enough to contribute to her already-throbbing headache. Vi ignored the pain, focusing on running her fingers over her brow and making sure everything from just above her eyes to halfway up her forehead was covered.

It likely looked ridiculous. But given the sorry state of the rest of her, a dishcloth bandanna was the least of her worries. Vi held her breath and kept her strides even as she approached the two men.

Calm—she had to be calm, even when it felt like everything pointed to her being immediately discovered as an interloper.

"Excuse me?" Vi asked. Both men turned, startled to see her. Vi folded her hands, keeping her eyes mostly down in an attempt to be demure and nonthreatening. Just because she was willing to fight tooth and nail for her and Taavin's survival didn't mean she wanted to. If it came down to that, her odds didn't look good.

"Yes?"

"Do you know where I can find the nearest cleric? I don't regularly come this way… and I'm a bit turned around."

"Cleric?" The man repeated, looking to his friend. The other shrugged.

"A healer, I mean?" Vi said tentatively, hoping her difference in word choice wouldn't be what ultimately led to her discovery.

"Oh, why didn't you say so?" The man shook his head, as though she was already burdensome, then looked to his friend. "Who's closest to here?"

"Sarphos has a shop. But he's rarely in it."

"Yeah, he wouldn't be."

"I think after that it's Rem?"

"Rem?"

"Five streets down and over, on seventeenth, the shop with the purple-colored awning."

"*Oh*, her."

"So…" Vi jumped into the conversation. "Purple colored awning on seventeenth," she repeated. "But Sarphos is closer?"

"If you want to try him." The man gave a shrug that showed how likely her success was. "He is in the opposite direction though… Only one street down." He pointed to another intersection diagonally across from where Vi stood. "He's in between here and fourteenth. But he's rarely there."

"Excellent, thank you." Vi gave a small nod and started in the direction the man had pointed. The two men resumed their conversation as if nothing had happened. As if her heart wasn't racing.

She adjusted her makeshift bandanna again and allowed her eyes to wander.

Men and women of all shapes and sizes, skin tones and hair

colors walked around her, ignorant to the stranger in their midst. The only unifying factor among them was the glowing markings dotted above their eyes in place of eyebrows. But that wasn't the most fantastical element of the kingdom.

There was a menagerie surrounding her. Jaguars lounged on balconies, wolves trotted down alleyways, birds of all manner of plumage soared overhead, and towering beasts of scales and feathers that Vi had no name for raced each other down the main streets. Magic pulsed around her, strange and foreign. In a flash those same animals would be replaced by human-looking folk, quickly conducting their business before another pulse of magic brought them back into their animal forms.

Her head was still splitting. Her body still felt ravaged by the toll it took to get here. And Vi knew she should be alarmed with every step—she had more worries than fingers to count them.

But for a brief moment, her chest was tense with delight. Laughter hid behind her smirking lips as she beheld the splendor of the world in perpetual twilight. Every glowing stone and flower, person and dialect, was new.

Turning the corner, Vi scanned the various narrow storefronts. It reminded her somewhat of the market in the Crossroads, with everyone fighting over space. But there were no street sellers here—only quaint doors with signs dangling before them.

Vi looped the street twice before she finally noticed a narrow door crammed between two others. On it was a picture of a garnet skullcap and a mortar and pestle, *Sarphos's Supplies* engraved next to the image. Taking a breath, Vi pushed on the door, pleasantly surprised when it opened effortlessly.

A small bell overhead jingled happily at her entrance. Vi stepped into the crammed space. There were shelves of jars stacked three deep, floor to ceiling, on either side of her. Despite being shut tight, the jars emitted the earthy aromas Vi had associated with clerical salves her entire life. Herbs of all varieties dried from the ceiling, packed between linen bags containing unknown but sweet-smelling items.

At the very back of the store was an empty desk, and behind that a door.

And nothing and no one else.

Vi slowly walked, debating if she should just take something and run while the store was unattended. But she didn't know the first thing about what salve or potion Taavin would need. And worse, she realized she didn't exactly know how she'd get back short of running into that seemingly infinite blackness and hoping she ended up on the other side alive.

A risk that didn't seem wise to take more than once.

"Hello?" Vi called, resting her hands on the counter. Glowing stones hung like pendants on either side, giving the whole room a ghostly light. "Is anyone here?"

"Yes, coming!" a male voice called. Vi heard stomping overhead, then stairs creaking, before a man emerged from the dark doorway behind the counter. "Sorry about that. You caught me right before I was going to step out. How may I be of service?"

He had steel-colored eyes and the dots above them were the same sort of pale blue. His expression was soft, youthful. Kind and yet… painfully sad. Perhaps it was the dim light playing tricks on her, but there was something haunted about this ruddy-haired man.

"Are you Sarphos?"

"I am."

"Excellent, I… I need help." Vi folded her hands on the counter. Were she back in the Solaris Empire, she could always resort to commanding him if she had to. But here, she had no sway, no golden coin bearing the Solaris seal lingering in her back pocket to reassure her even in tough situations that there was always a way out. "Please."

"What seems to be the matter?" His expression grew serious, the dots above his eyes scrunching together.

"My… friend. He's in the Twilight Forest. He's wounded… I think he has broken bones that have become infected."

"Its difficult to diagnose someone from afar… can you bring him here?"

"I don't think I can move him. Can you come to him?"

"I'm afraid I can't—I'm needed at the castle."

Mother above, she would pick the cleric that had some tie to the royal family. Vi briefly debated heading to the other cleric the men mentioned, but she didn't want to waste time. "Please, I… I think he may die."

Sarphos's expression deepened into a frown. He lifted the counter where it was hinged on one side, and slipped through. There was barely enough room for them to stand side by side in the narrow shop.

"Tell me exactly what's wrong, what symptoms he's exhibiting, as much detail as you think would be necessary and then some." Even as he spoke, his eyes were scanning the shelves, hands reaching for jars.

"He had something heavy fall on his chest," Vi answered somewhat vaguely. She didn't think going into the fact that they had been battling with a morphi—even a morphi the kingdom had exiled—would help her cause. "There's a lot of bruising. I think at least one rib is broken. From there… lethargy, fever."

"Infection, likely." Sarphos grabbed three leaves from one jar, filled a small bottle with an inky substance from another, then two dried roots from a third. "Take these to him. He eats the leaves first, and then drinks the potion—but *slowly*. It'll likely make him sick if he goes too quickly. But he does need to get it all down. And then have him chew on the roots for the pain as needed until I can get to him. Come back to me tonight and I'll go out with you."

Vi accepted Sarphos's supplies, realizing two things at the exact same time. The first was that she had no way to pay for this. An Imperial "I owe you" was likely not going to cut it here. The second was that she had no idea how to get back to Taavin.

Sarphos was sidestepping away, already halfway the door.

"I don't know how." Vi hated how weak she sounded, and felt.

She hated being forced to rely on the goodness in this stranger's heart because she had no other option. "I don't know how to get back to him."

"You lost a dying man in the woods?" he asked incredulously.

"No, I don't know how to get back to the woods."

"What?"

"I'm not supposed to be here." Vi pulled the cloth from her forehead.

Sarphos took a step back, and for a brief moment she was afraid he'd bolt for the door. He looked at her like she had begun speaking in tongues—like she was going to attack him at any moment.

"How are you here?" he whispered. "Only morphi are allowed in the Twilight Kingdom." Well, that confirmed one of her suspicions.

"Were it not an emergency, I wouldn't have trespassed on your lands," she assured him, trying to emphasize she meant no harm. If he raised an alarm, Vi doubted she could escape in time. "I just want to get medicine, that's all."

"No." He shook his head, still not taking his eyes off her. Like she was some kind of apparition. "*How* are you here?"

"There was a tear in the… shift, I believe. I fell through." That was technically correct. Still, Vi gripped her watch on instinct, remembering the full details of the ordeal.

"A tear in the shift? The shift doesn't tear."

"It can, and it is," Vi insisted solemnly. "I doubt you'll believe me if I tried to explain why, but—"

"What would a human know of the shift?"

"Frustratingly little." The statement was somewhat snappish. But Vi would practically kill for a decent explanation of the morphi's magic. "But I do know there are nefarious forces at play, and the world is rotting from the inside out."

"I can't say I believe you… But the fact that you're here at all is proof enough something is amiss." Sarphos looked her up and down. "Will you show me this tear you speak of?"

"Only if you help my friend. Come and heal him, and I'll show it to you."

Sarphos chuckled, and a small smile crossed his lips. In a world full of liars and backstabbers, the seemingly genuine kindness caught Vi off-guard. *Don't trust it,* a voice in her mind cautioned. Everyone was out to get something. Everyone had a goal. And she had no idea what this man's were or what he'd do to get them.

"I was going to help you anyway." Sarphos pulled a bag from a cubby near the floor by the door. He took the items from her, and Vi begrudgingly released them. It felt like she was letting go of Taavin's lifeline by relinquishing them back to him. "That's what a healer does, you know… heal people. It's my oath."

"I'll still show you the tear." Vi much preferred a clear this-for-that agreement. The idea of giving someone good faith grated against her new base instincts, re-aligned by Jayme's betrayal.

"And I appreciate that. The morphi need to know of it." Sarphos motioned to the rag. "You may want to wear that again until we're out." Vi nodded, donning the cloth once more. "Right, this way then."

With her stomach clenching with worry to the point of pain, Vi followed him back onto the streets.

THEY ASCENDED THE MAIN street of the Twilight Kingdom. On one end was what Vi assumed to be the palace, given its grand gate, overall opulence, and positioning at the center of the city. On the other end, the road sloped upward over the ridge that surrounded the tree-line to a large archway that was the only break in the ominous black trees.

"Take my hand." Sarphos paused and extended his palm to her. "I'll need to guide you through the shift. Don't let go, or you could find yourself trapped in the in-between."

Vi still didn't fully understand the shift, but she did as instructed. She didn't need in-depth knowledge to know she wanted to get through as quickly as possible. Given her last experience, Vi didn't want to spend any extra time in the space that was neither here nor there.

"And keep quiet as we pass. It looks like Ruie is on duty today. At least it's not Arwin…"

She nodded, not even daring to speak now as they continued

their approach.

A woman lounged at the side of the archway, arms folded, looking board. She had bright golden hair that reminded Vi achingly of Romulin's, though hers was cut shorter. Billowing fabrics tucked into simple boiled leather armor covered her lanky, lithe form.

"Sarphos… didn't Arwin want to see you today?" she said dully, by way of greeting. "She's back at the palace."

"I realized I was low on a few supplies I'll likely need for her."

"Need a few things or…" Ruie pushed off from the stone column of the archway. "Are you ditching my sister to take someone special out for a late-night *stroll*?" She grinned wildly. "I don't think Arwin will take too kindly to playing second-fiddle."

"Wh-what? Stroll? You mean—no. Me?" Sarphos blubbered. Vi couldn't tell if he was embarrassed, or worried about what this Arwin may think. Either way, she committed the name to memory.

"Someone special perhaps?" Ruie took a few steps forward. "What's your name?"

Vi opened her mouth to answer, but Sarphos spoke too fast.

"She's no one. J-Just an apprentice of mine."

"I didn't think you took apprentices. You sure it isn't something more?"

"I don't mind if you say something." Vi gave a grin and a wink to Sarphos, trying to mirror Ellene's voice and facial expressions when teasing Darrus.

"I-I—"

Ruie roared with laughter. "Oh go on, then, don't let me keep you. She's clearly eager."

Vi gave a tug on his hand, taking a step forward. *Let him fall into step*, Vi pleaded mentally. She could almost feel the uncomfortable, nervous energy radiating off the healer who was now scarlet from the crown of his head down to his collar.

Luckily, he didn't actually die of embarrassment, and instead kept moving.

"And good for you Sarphos!" Ruie called after them. "It's good to see you happy after so long!"

Sarphos shot a glare over his shoulder before turning back to Vi. "I thought I said not to speak." He had the audacity to sound bothered.

"It got us through, didn't it?"

"Yeah, but now she's going to tell all her sisters," he muttered. "Oh, never mind." Sarphos sighed. "We're past it anyway. Now, to get through the shift—stay close."

Vi did as she was told, and they continued to walk into the darkness.

She squeezed his hand tightly, not caring if she hurt him. Better that, than allow him to feel her tremble. The last thing Vi wanted to do was go back into this void. But Taavin waited on the other side. At least this time she had a guide.

There was a pulse of magic so faint Vi wasn't sure if she imagined it. Vi took a deep breath and held it, remembering the thin air that came next.

"Not far, now," Sarphos said, low and steady as another pulse thrummed against her, then another, and another, as the world wobbled back into existence from the darkness, like ripples across a pond.

They stepped out between two trees and Vi took a deep breath.

"That was much better than when I did it," she said with relief.

"I'd imagine," Sarphos said. "The shift transforms things from what they are, to what they can be—though that shift is a special one made only by the royal family. We call the transition 'the between'—which is a place you don't want to be stuck in."

"I believe it..." Vi looked behind her, but there were just the same pale trees of the Twilight Forest standing sentry to a quiet night. All traces of the Twilight Kingdom were gone. *The shift transitioned what was to what could be*. She still had many questions about the magic, but they could wait. There were more pressing matters now. "Come on, this way."

Luckily, they'd come out in a location where Vi could hear the stream. She just had to hope they hadn't emerged too far from the cave… and that it was the same stream.

"So what brings a human to the Twilight Forest?" Saphos asked as they walked. "We don't get too many in our borders these days."

"I'm just passing through." Vi had no desire for small talk. This was business. She wasn't about to be his friend. "I would've been gone by now if it weren't for my friend's injuries."

"Where are you going after you pass through here?"

"I have to find my father."

Saphos fell silent. The quiet made the walk seem even longer, fraying the nerves at the ends of Vi's patience. All she had to go by to find Taavin was the stream, so she nearly wept tears of joy when her eyes landed on something familiar. She recognized a boulder—at least she thought she did. She picked up her pace.

"Wait, why are we running?" Sarphos called.

Vi's feet flew over the wet stones, slipping and splashing in the water. Her pant legs were damp up to her knees. But Vi paid it no mind. She was used to running in forests.

What she wasn't used to was this overwhelming, sickening, lightheaded feeling of worry and fear and excitement all wrapped into the shape of a single man.

She came to a stop at the unassuming cave, her chest heaving. "He's in there." She hoped. "Let me go first… there's not much room."

"All right." Sarphos leaned against the large boulders, catching his breath. "Call me when you're ready. I'll just be… you know… recovering from the most exercise I've had in months. Don't mind me."

It was easy to ignore his mutterings due to the racing of her thoughts. What if Taavin was gone? What if she'd somehow gone to the wrong place? *What if he was…*

She didn't finish that last thought.

Vi rested her hand on the rock, took a breath, and pushed through the narrow opening. She emerged into the near darkness, immediately aware of Taavin's form. But he made no sound or movement.

"Taavin?" Vi whispered, summoning a spark for light. "Taavin, please." She crouched down, shaking him lightly. But for the first time, he didn't respond. Her hand flew to his neck, seeking a pulse and breathing a sigh of relief when she found it.

"Sarphos!" Vi shouted, deafeningly loud in the small space. Taavin still didn't wake. "Sarphos, he's not moving!"

Sarphos pushed his way through the opening with a grunt, holding out one of the faintly glowing stones she'd seen illuminating the Twilight Kingdom like a lantern. Vi barely had time to shift herself onto the other side of Taavin to give the healer room. Her hands wrapped around Taavin's, clutching tightly, as if he'd slip away from her for good if she let him go. Her eyes drifted up to the morphi as he finished pulling his bag through.

"This is him?" Sarphos's expression darkened as he stared down at Taavin. His eyes narrowed in a way that Vi could describe as nothing other than pure loathing.

"Yes. You said you would help him," Vi reminded him, the statement coming off more as a curt demand. Then she added, softly, "Please help him." Taavin's pulse was so weak underneath her fingers. It felt as though he could leave the mortal realm any moment.

Sarphos's eyes dragged away from Taavin's prone form, turning to Vi. They stared at each other for several quick breaths—Vi's hastened in panic, Sarphos's in what looked like rage. She braced herself, ready to outright threaten the man's life if that's what it took.

She was ready to burn down the whole world to save Taavin.

"You told me it was your friend… You didn't tell me your friend was the worst, most despicable, wretched creature on this earth: the Voice."

"Wretched?" Vi would've been more angry if she wasn't so confused. "He's not—"

"Was this your plan all along, to lure me here?" Sarphos looked over his shoulder, through the crack in the rocks. "Where is your legion of Swords?"

"I don't want to kill you. I don't wish you ill at all." Vi made every attempt to speak calmly, but Sarphos's rising mix of panic and prejudice was making it difficult.

"Then why would you bring me before the Voice? You're one of them, aren't you? Faithful?"

"He's dying!" Her shrill voice echoed in the small cave. Taavin didn't stir. "Does this look like a man who is trying to kill you? He's fighting for his life."

"Good," Sarphos said darkly. "Let him die. Better for the rest of us."

Sarphos turned, about to squeeze through the opening. Vi stood, and with her rose a wall of flame, filling the narrow opening, licking the healer's face and clothes. Sarphos jumped back, patting a spot on his shirt that caught fire.

"What magic is this?" His eyes darted between the singed spot and her. But Vi ignored the question. Let her powers remain mysterious. There was danger in the unknown.

"You said you were a healer—that it was your *oath* to heal people."

"Oaths can be broken," Saphos seethed.

"I know that too well," she spat back. "Just as I also know that when negotiations break down, force may be necessary. Help him or you will not go back to the Twilight Kingdom alive. Help him or I will find the Lord of the Faithful myself and tell him that the Voice has died because of you."

The last thing Vi ever wanted to do was align herself with Ulvarth. But Sarphos didn't need to know that.

Sarphos continued to stare at her, narrowing his eyes slightly. "If you kill me, King Noct will demand retribution."

"I am not of your land, and I do not fear your king. I am from across the sea—across the Shattered Islands. I am from the Dark Isle, and this man is my only ally here. Do not underestimate what I would do for the people I love."

The glare Vi gave Sarphos hid her shock. She kept her feet on the ground, even if her head was reeling.

People I love… Love… She loved him. Her heart felt like it had just shattered into a thousand pieces only to have them all start beating in unison—a chorus that sang for Taavin alone.

Sarphos spat a curse at her in a language she didn't understand. Vi was unflinching and unremorseful. Sarphos, however, was slowly worn down.

"If I heal him… he will harm my people."

"He won't."

"If you're from the Dark Isle as you say, you have no idea what he's done, or what he'll do."

"I know him far better than you," Vi insisted. "I've known him for nearly a year now. He's not a violent man, regardless of what the Faithful do. They do it without him."

Sarphos grumbled and shook his head, running a hand through his ruddy hair. "You really must be from the Dark Isle if you think the Faithful move in any way the Voice doesn't command."

"Please, Sarphos, as a healer—help him… And I give you my word he won't harm your people."

"*She gives me her word.* What's her word good for?" Sarphos grumbled as he knelt down. Vi let him have his gripes; she'd clearly won. His eyes trailed over Taavin, taking quick stock, before flicking back up to her. "I didn't have you pegged as someone who could be so brutal."

Neither did she a few mere weeks ago. "You have no idea what I'm capable of."

"I suppose I don't," Sarphos muttered, placing his hands on Taavin's chest. Delicately, he lifted Taavin's shirt. Vi looked on warily, making sure he didn't get any smart ideas. But Sarphos was focused, his gaze serious. He had shifted from the morphi loyalist to just a cleric tending to a patient.

Vi held her breath, waiting for his assessment, and praying she'd done enough in time to save the man she'd fallen in love with.

9

VI'S GAZE LINGERED ON Taavin's face. He looked so frail and small—something she never thought she'd say of the man. But wounded and prone, he seemed all too fragile. Her thumb lightly caressed the back of his hand.

"It's not too serious." Sarphos pulled away and began to rummage through his satchel.

"This looks serious."

"It's *becoming* quite serious," he agreed. "But the wound itself is uncomplicated—some broken bones, internal bleeding, and an infection going unchecked brought about by improper hygiene. All of those things have a clear and simple fix. He should be back to his normal, tyrannical self in no time."

Vi pressed her fingertips to her lips, suppressing an involuntary noise of relief. Perhaps Raspian's distortions hadn't gotten on Taavin. She dared to hope.

"Prop him up for me."

Vi did as Sarphos instructed, shifting to slide an arm under

Taavin's back. He was dead weight and nearly impossible to lift, but Vi managed it. Sarphos gingerly tilted his head back, parting Taavin's lips and pouring the inky liquid she'd seen earlier down his throat.

"Will he choke?"

"No, the potion will be absorbed before it even gets to where his lungs split off."

She turned her attention back to Taavin, continuing to hold him. Sarphos continued giving small doses of the medicine, counting quietly to himself. Just when the bottle was almost empty, Taavin's eyes jolted open and he erupted in a fit of coughing.

Vi shifted her arm further around him, patting his back as he wheezed and gasped. Sarphos inched away. She narrowed her eyes at the healer, silently reminding him of her threat if he dared to run. But Sarphos was distracted and soon, too, was Vi.

"Vi?" Taavin whispered.

"Taavin." His name was a breath of relief on her lips.

Vi leaned forward without a thought. Her forehead pressed against his and tightened her arm, their noses nearly touching. Her eyes dipped closed and for three blissful seconds she just listened to him breathe, feeling his frail form against her. Feeling him wonderfully alive.

"You terrified me," she murmured, pulling away.

"That feeling is mutual. I thought you'd gone off on your own and left me." Taavin's hand tried to reach for her face, but only made it to her forearm.

"I wouldn't leave you."

Sarphos cleared his throat, reminding them both of his presence.

Taavin's eyes peeled away from hers. He turned slowly, looking Sarphos up and down. The morphi healer returned the glare inch for inch.

"You did wander far, I see…" Taavin muttered. She could feel the tension rising between Taavin and Sarphos.

"Sarphos is a healer of the Twilight Kingdom. He's the one who's helping you." *Helping*. Not helped. She hoped Sarphos's care would be ongoing until Taavin was back at full strength.

"I see…" Taavin ground out, his jaw tense. Though his face relaxed when he looked back to her. "How did you find a morphi healer?"

"She claims she went through a tear in the shift. Something I have not forgotten she promised to show me," Sarphos interjected.

"A tear? Vi, you didn't—"

"Yes, I did. And I haven't forgotten, I will still show it to you," Vi interrupted and gave Sarphos a look. He'd kept his side of the bargain, she'd keep hers. She turned back to Taavin, putting his protests to rest with a short, "You were weak and getting worse. I had no other choice."

"You have a choice now—don't go with him." Taavin grabbed her arm. "I don't want you leaving my sight… I don't want you going somewhere I can't get to." Taavin's palm finally found her cheek. Vi leaned into it slightly, her eyes dipping closed. He'd been the only one to touch her this way.

"As the crown princess of the Solaris Empire, I must keep my word." Vi gingerly trailed her fingers up his arm. "Just as you must keep the word I gave on your behalf, in exchange for Sarphos's help—that you will not harm any morphi while you're here."

"I will not harm a single morphi, so long as they don't harm you." Taavin's eyes swung to Sarphos.

"We do not harm unjustly." Sarphos seemed to emphasize the word *unjustly* an odd amount—as if to imply Taavin would. His rage toward Taavin was something Vi still didn't fully understand.

"I can protect myself," Vi reminded Taavin.

"I know you can…" Taavin sighed, his eyes shining in the dim light of Sarphos's glowing stone. "Please, be careful."

"I will be."

"We should go," Sarphos needlessly reminded. As if Vi wasn't aware her time was running short. "The king is expecting me."

"I'll come back as soon as I'm able," Vi vowed.

"If anything happens to you I—" His throat closed and he choked on the word. Taavin shook his head, continuing down a different path. "I finally have you in reach and I've barely had a chance to speak to you."

"And we keep getting pulled apart." Vi gave him a small smile. "I know… But the road to my father, to figuring out this—" she touched the watch around her neck "—isn't going to be a short one. We'll have plenty of time. For now, we both need to focus on starting that road at full strength."

"I agree with all that," he reiterated. "But it doesn't mean I want you to go."

Vi searched his eyes. Had their faces always been this close? Or had they been slowly moving together?

Near. Far. Near. Far.

Back and forth they swung, a pendulum that never lost its momentum. The closer she got to him one moment, the further he felt the next. Vi closed her eyes, taking a slow breath through her nose. She leaned forward, resting her forehead lightly against his one final time.

But Vi didn't kiss him, not with an audience. Not now, when he still looked of death and smelled of potion. She'd kiss him when they were next together—when they were both stronger. In her mind, that future joining of mouths and tongues was an unspoken promise—to whom, exactly, she wasn't sure.

"Be careful," she whispered, and quickly stood, giving a nod to Sarphos. The man now wore an entirely new, strange, expression. "I'm ready."

"Very well then. Until I return with stronger, more tailored potions, continue drinking that, and chew on those. And whenever you feel strong enough… do try to take a bath." Sarphos pointed to the various healing accoutrements he'd left before he pushed himself through the crack.

Vi looked down at Taavin once more, already regretting her decision not to kiss him.

"Taavin… I…" Her voice was barely more than a whisper.

"Yes?" Had his breathing hastened? Or was it her imagination?

"I hope you feel stronger soon. I'll be back as soon as I'm able." Vi side-stepped through the craggy opening, reminding herself of the one thing Taavin had made clear: terrible things happened to the people he loved. Thus, he didn't want to love anyone, or have anyone love him.

Under no circumstances could she let him know he'd well and truly stolen her heart.

"Ready?" Sarphos startled her from her thoughts as she emerged from the small cave.

"Yes, this way." Vi started on ahead, walking along the bank of the stream. Just once she considered ignoring her promise to Sarphos about showing him the tear. But Vi knew she had to keep her word. New plans were already forming in her head. "Thank you, Sarphos, for healing him."

"You didn't leave me with much of a choice."

"That makes me no less grateful."

"I suppose, in a way, I should be thanking you." Sarphos ran a hand through his ruddy hair.

"Why?"

"If I hadn't seen it with my own eyes… I would've never thought the monster capable of compassion, let alone affection."

They reached the singed tree that marked the point Vi had diverted from the stream. Sarphos at her side, Vi followed her earlier markers into the dark woods.

"Why do you call him a monster?" She didn't want to make small talk. But when it came to Taavin, she wanted to understand the source of Sarphos's vitriol.

"If you are from the Dark Isle, as you claim—"

"Which I am."

"—then there's no way you could understand. This is not your fight."

Vi sighed, pausing a moment to locate the next singe mark

before moving on. "Maybe not… But Taavin is very important to me, and I'd like to understand the conflict as it relates to him."

"You may not be able to hear the truth, as you have already been taken in by Faithful lies. But if you can, trust me when I say that there's good reason why many in this world would kill me for not letting him die and rot in that cave. Even then, that would be a death far better than he deserves."

Vi wanted to tell him that Taavin had been honest with her about the mutual hatred between the Faithful and the morphi—that she knew it was rooted in fundamental ideological differences in each culture's magic. But the tear had come into view, and the conversation ended.

"What in the…" Sarphos murmured, slowly approaching the felled tree Vi had crossed through earlier.

"Don't get too close." She grabbed his forearm, holding him back. "It's not safe."

"It doesn't look safe." His nose scrunched. "And smells of death. You went through that?"

"Yes. If you watch closely, you can see the Twilight Kingdom, now and then, in the shifting air."

Sarphos stared intently at the air between the trees, but Vi's focus was on the leaning tree itself. It was almost entirely blackened, large splits exposing liquefied innards that glowed with red lightning. The tree looked as though it had been rotting for weeks since she had last been here—not mere hours. She bet that had they arrived a day later, it would've collapsed entirely.

"So it's true," he whispered. Sarphos must've seen the kingdom while Vi was distracted by the progression of the rot. "You can catch glimpses."

"Believe me now?"

"I still don't believe you could've made it through that and survived."

"It wasn't an…*ideal* experience." Vi's hand went to her watch. Without it and whatever power it held, she likely would've died.

"Well, then, I think our business has concluded." Sarphos

adjusted the satchel on his shoulder.

"You won't tell anyone about Taavin?" Vi dared ask. It was too much trust to put in a single man, especially when Sarphos had every reason to betray them. She needed to move Taavin as quickly as possible. But Taavin couldn't be moved yet… Her mind began to whirl around possible solutions.

"So long as he doesn't harm my people."

"Give me your word."

"You have it," Sarphos said with all the sincerity in the world.

Vi wanted to believe him.

She wanted to take him at his word. She wanted to go back to the days when promises meant something. But they didn't any longer. A vow wasn't good enough, not when he had so much to gain by outing them. If she were in his shoes, Vi couldn't be certain she'd honor it.

That meant she had to ensure his silence another way; she had to keep him in her sights.

"Sarphos, wait," she called after him, just as he had taken a few steps.

"What now?"

"You're going to report this tear to your king, aren't you?"

"I am," he responded cautiously.

"Take me with you?" Vi did her best to phrase it as a question and not a desperate plea or command. The only way she could get him to agree was to endear herself to him, truly convince him it was in his best interest, or both.

"Why do you think I would take someone in league with the Voice to King Noct himself?"

"Because I have more knowledge than you on these tears—their cause and how we may be able to stop them." Vi held out her hands. "Because I am unarmed and no threat in the Twilight Kingdom."

"You had that strange fire magic before."

"Firebearing. It's called Firebearing." For a brief second,

Sarphos looked almost intrigued by the notion. "It's a discipline of magic on the Dark Isle and is in no way like the Faithful's Lightspinning."

"It didn't feel like Lightspinning…" He stroked his chin. "You really are from there?"

"I really am."

"But there is nothing on the Dark Isle. It is a barren wasteland."

Vi chuckled. "I thought much the same of Meru." She braved a smile, hoping it came off as casual. Hoping he believed they were finding an easy rapport and she wasn't just looking for a way to keep him in her sights. "Take me to your king, let me tell him of my lands myself."

Sarphos twisted the strap of his bag. Vi wondered if his thoughts mirrored her own—twisting and turning over the various options before him. As she waited, Vi tried to keep her expression light, even though she was already working two mental steps ahead.

Taavin had mentioned a shift like the one around the Twilight Kingdom protecting the Isle of Frost… If she continued building this relationship, perhaps she could ultimately convince Sarphos—or King Noct—to help rescue her father.

"Oh, all right, come on then." Sarphos grabbed her hand. "But don't blame me if Arwin kills you on the spot."

Vi didn't have a chance to inquire further as pulsing magic enveloped them both. She barely had time to hold her breath before the darkness of the between pressed around her.

"TOOK YOU LONG enough," the woman at the archway at the entrance to the Twilight Kindgom droned. "Arwin has already come looking for you."

Vi knew she didn't imagine Sarphos suddenly going pale.

"What did you tell her?" he squeaked out.

"That you were out with your lady friend."

"Why did you say that?" Sarphos groaned, starting down the street.

"Why are you keeping it a secret?" Ruie called after them. "Is it because she dresses poorly?"

"I'd like to see how lovely *she* looks after sailing across continents," Vi mumbled, picking at the fabric of her shirt. They were the same clothes Erion had given her, back when she was pretending to be Yullia.

Should she use another name now? Vi looked up to the castle ahead of them, towering over all the people crowding the street. No… she'd already told Sarphos that she was the crown princess.

And meeting another royal while being honest about who she was may just serve her well.

"When we get to the castle, let me do the talking at first." Sarphos interrupted her thoughts. "Arwin is going to be in rare form, I'm sure. She doesn't take kindly to delays and will be even more irritated when she finds out I've brought a human before the king."

"Who is this Arwin to you? An old flame?"

Sarphos tilted his head back, letting out a bark of laughter. It was rich and warm-sounding, comfortable. Good, she wanted him to be comfortable around her. The more she could endear herself to him, the better.

"No, *no*. Arwin is… Well, she was to be my sister by marriage, once. But that was a lifetime ago." Sarphos kept his eyes forward, focused on the castle, oblivious to Vi studying him.

"So there's history there." Vi didn't press the matter. He clearly didn't want to go into the details.

"To say the least. We'll likely have to get through her to see the King."

"How so?"

"She's one of his core guards and by far the toughest of them all. What she says, goes. But if I can get to King Noct before she gets to us, all the better."

Vi adjusted the bandanna around her forehead. Tough, headstrong, demanding—none of them were personality traits she exactly wanted to work with.

They entered the castle through another free-standing archway. The castle had no outer wall or gates. In fact, there was little to stop the populous from strolling in. In a city protected by a force like the shift, Vi could understand why they didn't feel the need for fortifications.

She wondered if Adela felt much the same. Vi could only dream of catching the pirate flat-footed.

"You finally came." Positioned at the door was another young woman. She had a shade of blonde hair similar to Ruie's, though slightly more ashen. Even so, the family resemblance was unmistakable. "Arwin is waiting for you."

"Tell her I need to speak with the king." Sarphos continued leading them into a large foyer, the girl falling into step alongside them.

"And who are you?" she asked.

"A traveler of sorts." Vi looked up at the ceiling, where a chandelier of glowing stones illuminated the open space with a harsh, bright light.

"Who is she?" the girl asked Sarphos, apparently dissatisfied with Vi's answer.

"She's a traveler."

"From where?"

"Enough questions, Emmie." Sarphos rolled his eyes as they stepped into a hallway in the back of the room. A curtain of small, white flowering vines was strung along the ceiling. These, too, gave off their own magical illumination. Enough to see by, but comfortably dimmer than the entry.

"Why do you only tell Arwin things?" Emmie puffed out her cheeks in frustration.

"I do not only tell Arwin things," Sarphos muttered.

That would be something to keep an eye on—how close Sarphos and Arwin really were. Vi didn't know much about the woman yet. But what she'd gleaned so far assured her that Arwin gaining knowledge of Taavin would be trouble.

"Go find Arwin and tell her I'm with the king." Sarphos shooed Emmie away. The girl gave a huff, but ran off anyway.

Vi paused, looking down the hall where Emmie had disappeared. She saw a different young girl running down in her place, a girl with corkscrew curls and that same streak of childishness. Vi would bet anything Emmie and Ellene were near the same age.

"This way—" Sarphos tapped her shoulder and turned to lead, but stopped abruptly. "I just realized, I don't even know your name."

Vi smiled slyly, proud that she managed to go this long without telling him. "It's Vi."

"Vi… right, this way, please."

They went through two more hallways and three antechambers before entering a rectangular room.

On the far side, an open wall faced a grassy glade where children ran and played; on Vi's right stood a throne crafted from an array of materials, including some Vi would never attempt to piece together; wood and stone were fitted against glass and metal. It was where she would expect to see their King seated.

But the throne was empty.

At Vi's left was a low table and sitting area surrounding it. A plump man sat with his back to the door, watching three children playing with a pair of wolves and a peacock in the field beyond. *This* sagely and content-looking man was not what she'd expected of the Twilight Kingdom's king.

But looks could be deceiving. Vi was a living example of that—with her tattered clothing and grime-coated fingernails, no one would believe her a crown princess. Which meant she'd have to work all the harder to convince these people she was. Vi folded her hands in front of her, rolled her shoulders back, and adjusted her posture.

"My king, forgive my intrusion." Sarphos rounded the sitting area, dropping to a kneel.

"You know you are always welcome in my home, Sarphos." The king spoke with a whispering, weathered voice. "Stand, please."

Sarphos did as he was bid as Vi came to awkwardly stand next to him. "Unfortunately, I have brought ill tidings."

King Noct had golden hair like Ruie and Emmie, that faded into a white beard. But rather than analyzing the familial resemblance between him and the girls, Vi's mind wandered back to her own family. She wondered if she was looking at a much older version of her brother in the man.

"Ill tidings," King Noct repeated. "I do hope this lovely young woman isn't the cause of such things."

"Your highness." It was Vi's turn to kneel. Sarphos may be welcome in this court, but she was an outsider. "I've—"

"Sarphos!" A shout interrupted her. "You got some pair of stones, keeping me waiting." A woman stormed in from a side entrance.

She had bright golden hair, braided back tightly and wound into a large bun at the top of her head. Tiny curls attempted to escape around her face. She was pale, but not unnaturally so like the elfin'ra. Her eyes were muted gray, and landed on Vi with cold, steely calculation. Vi had little doubt that the person currently sizing her up was the infamous Arwin.

"Is *this* the woman you've been hiding from us?"

"I'm not hiding anything!" Sarphos insisted.

"We were just about to find out who this lovely young lady is, and why Sarphos kept you waiting… before you interrupted," the king said slowly, as if fighting back a yawn the entire time.

"If there's a stranger in our midst, shouldn't you be on your throne, father?"

Father?

"I think not being on my throne is far less damaging to my appearance than you questioning me before said stranger," the king answered—though he didn't sound the least bit offended. Vi felt like she was more present to a family gathering than a royal court.

Arwin pursed her lips and gestured for Vi to continue. Vi took a deep breath.

"I've come from an Empire across the sea."

The king stilled. Then, he commanded slowly, "Tell me your name, child."

"I am Vi Solaris, crown princess of the Solaris Empire."

"Solaris?" Arwin looked to Sarphos, who seemed to shrink under the woman's stare. "There is no such Empire."

Vi fought a smile and failed. She remembered being in

Arwin's shoes. The moment the veil was lifted from her eyes was fresh in Vi's memory. She had assumed the rest of the world knew about Solaris—that her people alone had been left in the dark. She had assumed wrong.

"There is, across what you call the Shattered Isles. On the Dark Isle."

"A forgotten and desolate rock?"

"Let her speak, Arwin." King Noct's voice had deepened, his tone becoming far more serious.

"I was born in Solarin, capital of the Solaris Empire, to Emperor Aldrik Solaris and Empress Vhalla Solaris. There, Meru's existence is not common knowledge. Shortly after my birth I was sent to our northernmost territory, Shaldan. I thought my wardship was a purely political arrangement, but it was more than that.

"There was a prophecy about my birth," Vi proceeded delicately. Given the morphi's relationship with the Faithful, Vi didn't know what their reaction would be to Yargen. *Tell the truth, just not the* whole *truth.* Half-lies were child's play compared to the web of fictions she'd had to craft along this journey. "It involves those known as the elfin'ra and Lord Raspian's return to this realm."

"Lord Raspian, elfin'ra? You speak like a Faithful," Arwin said, her voice dropping to a low growl.

"I am not a Faithful," Vi insisted.

"But you are a liar." Arwin stomped over to her. Without so much as a word of warning, she yanked the bandanna from Vi's brow. "Human," Arwin seethed, turning to Sarphos. "You brought a human among us? She could be Faithful."

Sarphos shrank backward. If Arwin pressed, he'd break. And if he broke, there was no guarantee of Taavin's safety.

"I said I'm not Faithful," Vi insisted. "The Faithful don't even exist in Solaris."

"Silence, Arwin." The King sighed tiredly. "Tell me more of the details of this prophecy?"

"My lord, I don't entirely know them all myself…" Vi looked down at her feet for a moment, hoping the body language of respect and deference was the same here as it was at home. "It has been passed to me in pieces, from my mother and from the woman who raised me. All I know for certain is that I have been chosen by Yargen to play a role in preventing the end of our world. I am Yargen's Champion. But what that means exactly… I'm unsure."

"And that is why you have ventured so far?"

"Yes, that… and to find my father."

"Prophecies, the Faithful's goddess, a human in the Twilight Kingdom…" Arwin paced between Sarphos and her father, staring down Vi at every turn. "She spews lies to you, father."

"Have you not seen it, Arwin?" Noct straightened in his seat. In that motion he went from a lounging old man to a king. "The bloody ring that circles our moon? It foretells the end of days."

"Or it's merely a phenomenon we don't yet understand. What's more likely? Ancient prophecies or a natural anomaly to be investigated?"

"Then there are the tears in the shift…" Sarphos said meekly, staring at his toes.

"Tears?" All eyes were on him. Vi watched as he fidgeted with the bag strap over his shoulder.

"Lord Raspian is rotting the world from the inside out," Vi said finally, when Sarphos didn't speak. "On the Dark Isle, people have fallen ill to a deadly plague from which there is no cure; we call it the White Death. There has been red lightning in the sky, now the corona around your moon, and I fear the tears in your shift are his work as well."

"Plague? Did you say plague?" Sarphos's head snapped up.

"Yes."

"What are its symptoms?" He was gravely eager. So much so that Vi had a horrible theory he already knew what she was about to say.

"Stony skin, milky eyes, bulging red veins, madness, and—"

"Sores that break and ooze white," he finished solemnly. Vi nodded in acknowledgement. "It's started to show here too."

"I'm so sorry," Vi said softly. "Our healers couldn't make headway with it. I don't think there's a cure beyond stopping Raspian."

"Don't doubt Sarphos," Arwin said defensively.

"I don't. He's already helped me once."

"The journey looks to have taken a toll on you." The king's voice was almost sad. Vi didn't need sympathy, but she'd gladly take it. "I shall open my home to you, Vi Solaris."

"You can't be serious," Arwin grumbled. Everyone ignored her.

"She is to be my distinguished guest," the king insisted. "See that she is made comfortable until she feels well enough to continue on her journey."

"I am to be saddled with—"

"Enough, Arwin," the king snapped, finally reaching his limit with his daughter's objections. "I have spoken."

"Yes, father." Arwin lowered her head.

"Bathe, rest, eat, and recover tonight, Vi… For in the morning, there is something of grave importance we must discuss."

"Grave importance?" Vi repeated.

"An object was bestowed on my forefathers long, long ago… well before history was recorded in your homeland. And I believe it belongs to you."

"I don't understand." What could he possibly have that belonged to her? Moreover, how would something like that even get to the Twilight Kingdom?

"I never understood either… until this moment. But we shall discuss in the morning, for it is late now and you could use some rest underneath the safety of a friendly roof." Noct gave a yawn, as if for emphasis, and when he finished, he waved them away.

Arwin placed her hand on Vi's shoulder, giving her a small shove toward the door she'd entered from.

"Manners, Arwin." Vi heard a soft snort over her shoulder. "When you have seen her settled… go with Sarphos to inspect these tears, and then return to me. There are things I must share with you regarding the Dark Isle."

Secrets on both sides of the ocean. Vi already knew what King Noct would say, and she didn't envy those revelations. It didn't take a prophecy to see that the hours looming before Arwin were destined to be filled with unpleasantness.

"Very well, father."

"I could help show the tears," Vi offered. Really, the last thing she wanted was for Arwin and Sarphos to be alone in the Twilight Forest. It would be too easy for him to out Taavin and she still had yet to get a firm grasp on their relationship. "Since I know of them."

"Can you find them confidently, Sarphos?" the king asked.

"I can."

"Then you should rest." Noct turned back to her with a small smile. "You look truly exhausted."

She was. But she wasn't too exhausted to try to protect Taavin. "I don't mind assisting."

"It's all right, Vi," Sarphos said. Vi looked to him and the man pointedly locked eyes with her. He gave a small nod that spoke volumes meant to be reassuring, yet it only put her stomach further in knots. "You can trust me to show her the tear."

And nothing else. Vi hoped that's what was left unspoken.

"Now that's settled… Arwin, please see her to the north tower?"

"If I must," Arwin grumbled, before escorting Vi deeper into the palace of the Twilight Kingdom—and farther from the healer who knew her secret.

11

"THERE WILL BE a guard positioned at the entrance to the tower you'll be staying in," Arwin said without so much as glancing at her.

"Am I a prisoner?" Vi looked back to the throne room. Sarphos was still speaking with King Noct. What if they were discussing Taavin? How quickly would King Noct's hospitality turn to hostility? She should be ready to fight her way out of the castle at any moment.

"If it were up to me, you'd already be in irons," Arwin muttered. Then, louder, "No, you're not a prisoner. But that doesn't mean I trust you."

"I'm not here to make trouble."

"That's what all troublemakers say."

"I suppose they do." Vi sighed. No one who was about to stab you in the back gave any warning. There wasn't any kind of armor that protected you from betrayal. The only defense was constant suspicion and vigilance. "I suppose I'll think of this guard as an attendant, rather than a sentry."

"Whatever makes you happy, princess." Arwin said *princess* as though it were a slur.

"Are you not also a princess?"

Arwin let out a massive snort followed by raucous laughter. "I am no princess."

"That's what the daughter of a king is in my land."

"In the Twilight Kingdom, the lineage is passed only through the male bloodline. Daughters become sworn guards of the crown." It was a surprisingly straightforward and informative answer from the woman who had been entirely callous thus far. Even though Vi's questions on the logistics of royal succession abounded, she kept them to herself, not pushing the matter.

Up two floors, Arwin led Vi across a narrow arcade.

On one side was the courtyard she'd seen three stories below from King Noct's throne room. On the other side, the Twilight Kingdom was visible through the archways and stone pillars. Vi admired its ethereal nature as they walked to the tower at the far end of the walkway and up a final flight of winding stairs.

"You'll use this as your room." Arwin stopped at a doorway, the second one up the stairs that spiraled around the tower, and pushed it open.

The soft light of the stars filtered in through a window that couldn't be bothered with glass. Instead, a curtain of white, glowing flowers modestly obscured the view. There was a comfortable looking bed, a side table with a washbasin, and a tall dresser that hopefully had a clean change of clothes. As the king promised, everything she would need to be comfortable for a good night's rest was there.

"One door down is the bathing room for this tower. I do recommend you use it." Arwin scrunched up her nose.

"Yes, I need it." Vi wasn't about to let herself be offended by the obvious.

"While you're in the bath, I'll see to finding you a change of clothes." Arwin walked back down to the first door. "Emmie will be positioned at the start of the bridge. Ask her if you need anything else."

"Thank you." Vi said, stopping before the bathing room as Arwin continued on.

"Don't thank me. I'm just following orders."

"Still, I'm grateful," Vi called after her. Arwin didn't look back.

The bathing room was small but heated to steaming perfection. The nearly scalding water of the tub soaked off grime and eased away her tensions. Her mind wandered to Taavin.

He was alone in that cave while she was enjoying the hospitality of the Twilight Kingdom's royal family. Hopefully, Arwin wasn't currently on her way to meet him. Sarphos was supposed to show her the tears, but could she trust him to do only that?

Despite the heat of the water, Vi's shoulders tightened.

As she wandered back up the stairs to her room, she wondered if there was a way she could sneak Taavin in. If Vi couldn't keep Sarphos in her sights at all times, perhaps she should try to keep Taavin closer. *No*, it'd be impossible, she quickly decided. Gaining the trust of the king and keeping Sarphos close was the best she could do.

When Vi returned to her room, she found the dresser full of lush fabrics in every color from pale grays to vibrant reds, embellished velvets and simple silks. There was everything she could imagine in every size.

She found a pair of voluminous trousers in a dark violet hue that tapered around the ankle. There was room enough for her hips and butt, and they were surprisingly comfortable. After that, Vi donned a thin sleeveless shirt, meant to be worn beneath the coat embroidered with matching silver vines along the hemline.

Vi lifted the jacket from the drawer. Its construction reminded her somewhat of Taavin's intricately embroidered coat—a tight-fitting, tailored torso that split into four panels at the hips. However, where his extended down to his calves, this looked like it wouldn't go past her waist. And where Taavin's coat had a small upright collar, this had a large cowl. Vi ran her fingers over the fabric. It was just as fine as his, from the deep yet colorful dyes to the cut and intricate stitching.

Vi clutched the garment to her chest, imagining what she held was indeed Taavin's. Imagining he was there. She pressed her eyes tightly shut and took a quivering breath.

"I hope I'm doing the right thing," she breathed into the fabric, as though it could somehow carry her words to him. "I want to protect you."

He'd said terrible things happened to the people he loved. But Vi supposed her track record was no better. The only other people she'd loved were plagued, captured by pirates, struggling to keep an empire together, and watching their people die with little hope of a cure.

Maybe they were both cursed.

Vi returned the coat to the drawer and closed it. Her hands pressed on the outside, as if she could trap all her insecurities within. As if she could smother them.

When her emotions had leveled, Vi walked over to the small washbasin. Grooming tools were set out around it, and Vi set to brushing through her hair. The process quickly reminded her of the discovery she'd made earlier: thanks to her escape from Adela, her hair was now at different lengths. Inspecting herself in the small hand mirror, Vi tilted her head left and right, looking at the longer hair on either side. She could braid it up and wait for it to grow out. Or…

A pair of shears caught her eye.

Vi carefully gathered her hair in her hands, suppressing a small shiver at the sound of the blades slicing through. Hair fell to the ground like the remnants of her past life. In just a few moments, it was over, and Vi's free hand played with the freshly sheared edge of her hair—now almost all one length, just past her shoulders.

She couldn't remember the last time it had been this short.

Staring at the pile of hair on the floor, she waited to feel something. Sadness, perhaps? Her hair was part of what had connected her to her grandmother, her father, and to her Western heritage.

And yet… Vi felt very little.

She had far more important things to worry about than hair.

A firm knock on her door jostled Vi from sleep. She'd barely had time to open her eyes before Arwin was barging in.

"Up. I have breakfast," Arwin declared gruffly, standing at the foot of her bed and holding a tray in both of her white-knuckled hands. The silverware on the tray clanked together as a result of her barely contained rage. "I will tolerate no complaints. I am not your servant girl to boss around."

"I wasn't going to complain." Vi yawned and pulled herself upright. Her room was identical to how it had been when she'd gone to sleep—there was no sunrise or sunset in the Twilight Kingdom, no day or night, just the perpetual half-light of its namesake. She looked at the breakfast Arwin held and resisted the easy jab that for not being her "servant girl," she sure looked the part.

"What are you smirking at?" Arwin muttered, setting the tray down heavily at the foot of her bed.

"I'm not smirking. I'm smiling because the food looks good." Vi reached for the sandwich, not inspecting it too closely before taking a large bite. She wasn't dead, and Arwin wasn't throwing chains on her… That must mean Sarphos hadn't told them about Taavin—or at least not told Arwin. Noct was still a wild card, but Vi suspected if he was a smart king, he wouldn't pass up the opportunity to at least capture a valuable enemy like Taavin.

No, Sarphos hadn't told them anything, Vi decided.

"Are you always so trusting?" Arwin's voice cut through the silence and Vi's thoughts like a sharpened axe. "Eating food put in front of you by strangers without so much as a sniff?"

"If you had planned to kill me, you could've done it when I was sleeping, or in the bath, or the first moment you saw me." Vi took another large bite for emphasis. Arwin looked away, staring out the window. When she wasn't glowering at Vi, there was a softness to the woman Vi was unaccustomed to. "Why are you so mistrusting of me? I told you I'm not Faithful and I mean no harm to your people."

The woman tensed. Vi could see the biceps in her folded arms tighten over her hands tucked by the insides of her elbows. She was wearing a sleeveless shirt today and the lines of her bulging muscles were on display. Perhaps another show of power, another subtle threat.

"You truly know nothing, do you?" Arwin said almost delicately. Her steely eyes drifted back to Vi. "You're really from the Dark Isle?"

"I am. And I know a great many things… But I admit there are serious gaps when it comes to knowledge of your land and people." Vi paused, allowing Arwin's continued scrutiny. "But I would like to learn."

"Why?"

Once more, her original question popped into her mind. What had happened that led to the morphi—Arwin—to have such a deep mistrust of all outsiders? Sarphos's words the night before still clung to her thoughts as well: *Why was Taavin a monster?*

Vi wasn't sure she wanted the answers, but she needed to know all the same.

"Why not?" Vi asked simply. "Aren't you curious about the Dark Isle?"

Arwin held her gaze for a long moment. Just when Vi thought she was about to give in, she uttered a simple, "No."

"But—"

"Finish your food. My father is waiting for you."

Vi did as she was told, and quickly donned fresh clothing in much the same fashion as the articles she'd found yesterday. She didn't really need to change—what she'd gone to bed in hadn't gotten dirty. It just felt good that she *could.*

Arwin led Vi down the tower, across the walkway, down another flight of stairs, across a hall, down yet another spiral staircase, and into what Vi would best describe as a council room. The walls were stone, vertical tapestries running from floor to ceiling depicting champions with dotted foreheads standing victorious in battle. Between the tapestries hung weapons, the low light of the glowing stones hung above the center table gleaming off their polished edges.

"I'll get my father." Arwin stepped forward and around the table toward the back of the room. Vi watched as the woman swung her arm in a circle, magic rippling across the wall like waves in a pond. The stones shifted, shimmered, and changed right before her eyes, redesigning themselves in the shape of an archway.

Vi had been watching the whole time, yet, if pressed, she wouldn't be able to tell someone how a solid wall transformed itself into a door. Luckily, Arwin didn't look back before slipping through the new passageway. She didn't see Vi's awe.

With nothing to do other than wait, Vi began to inspect the careful stitching and bright dyes of one of the tapestries. But she didn't get far before Arwin and Noct appeared in the archway.

"Your highness." Vi dropped to a knee.

"Rise, child." He spoke to her, but his focus was not on her. Rather, the king gave far more attention to the small wooden box he was carrying. Noct set it down on the table reverently.

"Are you certain, father?" Arwin asked. For once, she didn't sound indignant. She sounded… concerned. Worried. Ominous.

"I am." Noct turned his gaze to Vi. "My family has protected this with our royal shift for generations. But it is time for the weapon to be among the world of men once more."

He placed his hand down on the box and, in a single blink, it transformed into something entirely different.

Vi's eyes focused on the item wrapped tightly in a deep purple velvet. Time weighed heavy on the fabric, parts threadbare; the gold cord fastening was gray with dust. While Vi couldn't see through the wrapping, it left little to her imagination: a long pole, connected to something flat and curved at one end—a scythe, she'd surmise. Though that only made her more confused.

King Noct rested a hand on the non-bladed end of the weapon, then finally looked up at Vi. "Do you have any idea what this is?"

Her eyes stayed glued to it. The watch was heavy around her neck, hot enough to nearly burn her skin, but Vi hardly noticed. A piece of her had been torn from her body, thrown into a different place and time. The surreal feeling raked up her spine and sank into her skull, impossible to shake, as she stared wide-eyed.

"I don't," Vi said, her voice almost quivering. Though something insisted she did. She knew what it was… but not with her eyes. With something deeper rooted and less explicable.

"The prophecy you mentioned… you said you were chosen by Yargen as her Champion," King Noct began. "It reminded me of a piece of lore passed down in our family, generation to generation, dating back nearly a thousand years. My father told it to me, and his father to him—generations preparing one another should what I believe to be this moment ever come to pass."

Her heart was beating so hard Vi could've sworn she heard the watch chain rattling around her neck.

"This is not of the Twilight Kingdom. We were merely the holders of this relic—protectors or curators, if you will. It came from your Dark Isle." She should feel excited by that fact, shouldn't she? But all Vi felt was sickness rising. The surreal feeling of having one foot in the present and the other somewhere else lingered—her body torn in two. "I was told that long ago, it was used to cultivate the land of the Dark Isle so that it would be fertile for eons to come, giving life to the magickless people who sought refuge there. But its powers could easily be used to end that same life.

"A man, the grandson of Yargen's last Champion, smuggled this off the isle to ensure it never fell into the wrong hands."

"How did it get to the Twilight Kingdom?" Vi murmured. Her

voice felt like it was echoing from a distant place.

"Queen Lumeria has sent spies to the Dark Isle over time. One of those spies was a morphi… back then, tensions weren't as high with the Faithful."

"Why were there spies?" She should be offended by the idea. But Vi had felt very little since the wrapped item had appeared. All she could feel was a deep need to *see it.*

"To ensure those on the isle weren't disturbing forces they shouldn't."

"A lot of good that did," Vi whispered. Raspian had been locked away in the Crystal Caverns, the destruction of which led to the rise of the Mad King Victor. That set in motion a series of events that ultimately led Vi to where she was now.

"So it would seem," Noct agreed solemnly. "But that long-ago descendant of the Champion saw this weapon preserved for the future Champion—perhaps for this very moment."

Noct reached forward and Vi watched as he undid the knots of rope keeping the velvet closed. One of the braided tethers nearly disintegrated beneath his fingers. Vi's heart raced until the fabric was at last thrown back—

All at once, her heart stopped.

There, shining dimly, was one of the four legendary crystal weapons. She knew it was true without needing further proof. She knew it in her marrow.

It glowed with a faint blue light, a microcosm of stars trapped beneath its glassy surface. Vi reached out a hand. She was drawn to it with an undeniable pull. She couldn't turn away if she tried.

Her fingers brushed the top of the blade.

The hazy light that surrounded the weapon slowly drifted over her hand and up her arm, before fading completely into her skin. It swirled within her, like a dust storm over the desert.

The desert.

Images flashed before her eyes, so clear Vi could swear she was standing at the event itself, watching them play out. There was an Eastern man with hazel eyes, working his way through a humble city that was ancient Norin. A shift in the magic, a spark of blue light, and he was now at the docks, speaking with another, passing over the velvet-wrapped parcel. Another shift, and Vi witnessed the man turning away from his precious heirloom.

A chill ran over her as Vi jettisoned back to the present. The sensation of being in two places at once had finally abated. Perhaps because she'd finally seen what she needed to—what the goddess had wanted her to see. Vi lifted her hand away from the weapon, the dim shimmer of magic clinging to her fingers for several seconds before fading.

She turned to King Noct, her voice barely a whisper. "It is a crystal weapon… But what do you want me to do with it?"

King Noct and Arwin were a half-step farther away than she remembered them being. They both stared at her with wary, awe-filled eyes. Vi took a slow breath, not daring to ask what they'd seen when her senses were overtaken by a time long past. She didn't want to know. With one touch to the crystal weapon, something within her had changed, and she wanted no additional proof of the fact.

"I want you to do what you were chosen to do—use it to save our world."

Vi sat on a bench at one end of a large, rectangular training hall.

The floor was wooden, mats lined up on the back wall to her left, mostly forgotten. Archery targets hung on the far wall to the right; weapons of all shapes and sizes lined the wall across from where she stood.

But none of them consumed her attention quite like the weapon in her hands.

Every time Vi shifted her fingers across its surface, magic sparked and crackled within. Power seemed to flow from her to the weapon and back, growing more powerful with every turn. Her breath quickened.

"So, what are you going to do with it?" The question jostled her from her fascination with the magic within the scythe. Vi hadn't even heard the steady *thunk* of arrows sinking into the archery targets come to a stop.

"I… don't know yet."

"You don't know?" The woman huffed, as if disappointed, passing her bow from hand to hand. "Aren't you the Champion?"

"This whole Champion thing doesn't exactly come with a guide book," Vi muttered. There might be someone who could help her… but getting to Taavin wasn't an easy affair at the moment. Vi stood, holding out the weapon with one end on the ground. "Could you teach me how to use it, perhaps?"

Arwin tilted her head to the side, looking Vi and the weapon up and down. "It's a scythe—a *farmer's* scythe, not a war scythe. The blade's all wrong for proper combat. You really want it to be more vertical to get better access to the sharp edge."

"Well, it's all I have, so I'd better learn how to use it," Vi countered.

"Can't you reshape it somehow?"

"*Reshape it?* You think I can reshape something a goddess made?"

"Fair point," Arwin mumbled and crossed the room to a rack of weapons. She tossed her bow from one hand to the next; there was a pulse of magic mid-air, and when Arwin grabbed it again, she wielded a long pole off the wall with an axe on one side. "Even if I'm confident with pole arms… I still have no idea how I'm going to teach you how to use that effectively at all."

"I'd appreciate the effort," Vi said sincerely, meeting Arwin in the center of one of the painted rings on the floor.

"Do you even know the basics of combat?" Arwin asked, slowly twirling the halberd in her hands.

"I've had a bit of training," Vi answered somewhat coyly.

"The fate of the world rests on the shoulders of someone who's had 'a bit of training'?" Vi could feel the vibrations through the floor as Arwin slammed down the butt of her weapon. "We're all doomed."

She should be offended, but Vi couldn't stop laughing. Finally, she managed, "Maybe we are."

"You're really reassuring me now." Arwin's posture went slack, slightly relaxed.

"Let's be honest, you thought we were doomed from the moment you first learned I was Yargen's Champion."

"Can't say I believe all that. Maybe you're an opportunist with a good grasp of history. Maybe you noticed a convenient opportunity to claim you're something you're not, with few to argue against your claims."

"If I'm lying about being Yargen's Champion, I sure went to great lengths for that lie." Vi tried to mimic Arwin's stance, gripping the small handles that extended from the main shaft of her weapon. She barely had time to shift her feet into a wider, sturdier base before Arwin lunged without warning. Vi stepped back, adjusting the distance. She lifted the scythe on instinct, pushing Arwin's blade up and away from striking at her center.

The curve of the axe at the end of the halberd hooked on the main body of Vi's scythe. Arwin gave a firm yank, ripping the weapon from her fingertips. Vi was pulled forward and off balance.

Arwin shifted the halberd back in her hands, allowing the scythe to fall to the floor. She stepped forward, driving her fist into Vi's stomach. Vi doubled over, her muscles contracting around Arwin's hand.

The woman had a fist like a rock.

Wheezing, Vi grabbed her stomach and fell to her knees. When she lifted her head, it was to find the tip of Arwin's halberd at the tip of her nose. Arwin regarded her coolly down the pole arm.

"Was the punch really necessary?" Her stomach was still spasming. *Great Mother above it hurt,* and it reminded Vi that her midsection was still mostly fresh flesh. But she tried desperately to keep her face calm and hide as much of the pain as possible.

"Your enemies won't show you mercy. Especially not with a pathetic showing like that."

A chuckle escaped Vi's lips. "Don't I know it."

Arwin cocked an eyebrow at the bitter remark. She lowered the halberd, replacing it with her hand. Vi stared at the open palm, glancing back to Arwin. She wasn't about to take the bait and be an easy target once again.

"Come on, up with you."

Vi's fingers clasped around Arwin's and she hoisted her up so quickly that Vi's shoulder ached. Vi rolled it backward but said nothing. The woman started for the door.

"Wait." Vi stopped her with a call. Arwin turned, eyebrow arched. "Is that it? Are we done?"

"You actually want to go again?"

"As many times as you're willing." Vi picked up the scythe, adjusting her grip some. It had been too easy to rip from her hands before. Perhaps if she locked her thumbs around the main shaft, it'd provide better support.

"Why? You're fooling yourself if you think that thing will stand up against any trained combatant. At best, you'll have some range over a swordsman. But with the scythe curved as it is, you can't effectively use the slicing edge."

"So you've told me."

"You'll have to use it in more pulling motions, which will be hard to manage at distance."

"Then I'd better practice."

"Do you even have the stamina to swing it more than a few times?"

"Only one way to build my stamina." Vi wasn't backing down and she would make sure Arwin knew it.

"Why not just—"

"Because this may be our only hope," Vi interrupted. "Because all the crystals, and crystal weapons, on the Dark Isle have been destroyed. *This is the only one left*. If it came from the descendant of the last Champion, it may just be the only thing I can use against Raspian. I have no choice. So will you help me learn it or not?"

Arwin stared at her, long and hard, not moving a muscle.

"*Please*." Vi had no choice, no pride. Just holding the scythe filled her with a sense of urgency. The idea of preventing the end of the world was no longer an intangible thing. Vi now held proof of what she'd have to do in her hands, and she couldn't be too arrogant to avoid admitting she was nowhere near ready.

"Very well then," Arwin said finally. "But I'm going to train you as I would any of my sisters. I'm not going easy on you just because you're a guest and princess."

"None of my enemies will go easy on me." The thin line of Vi's mouth turned into a bitter smirk. "Bring on the gut punches."

What followed was a series of beatings the likes of which Vi had never experienced before. She'd always thought Sehra's warriors had stopped going easy on her when she'd come of age. But like most things in her childhood, that too turned out to be a lie.

Arwin didn't miss an opportunity to trip her, smack her sides with the pole of her halberd, knock the scythe from her hands, or rap her knuckles for improper grip. Bruises covered her body and everything ached. She wasn't sure exactly how much time had passed. An hour? Maybe two?

But Vi knew it wasn't nearly long enough. She had just begun to feel comfortable with the weight of the scythe in her hands.

"That's enough," Arwin declared. "You're spent for today."

"For today?" Vi leaned heavily against the scythe for support, panting and wiping sweat from her brow. "Does that mean you'll teach me tomorrow?"

"We'll see. Don't push your luck."

"And here I had you pegged for not passing up the chance to knock me around some more."

"It may be one of the most fun things I've done in some time." Arwin cracked the beginnings of a smile. It wasn't much. But it was more emotion—*positive* emotion—than Vi had seen from her so far. The expression faded as quickly as it came, and Arwin looked between her and the door before starting toward a cabinet in the back of the room instead. "Come here."

Vi obliged her. Toward the back of the room, near the archery targets, was a tall cabinet. All manner of vial and supplies housed within. Vi knew a clerical stash when she saw one. Arwin selected a small jar.

"Drink this now, and then we're taking you to Sarphos for him to give you something stronger. You're still skin and bones and will be far too achy tomorrow to do anything if you don't take steps to ease the pain now."

"So we *are* sparring again tomorrow?" She was excited at the prospect, but the deep ache in her body tempered the fact. Vi leaned the scythe against the wall to take the jar from Arwin and sniff the thick, amber colored liquid inside.

"I said we'll see." Arwin wiped sweat from her face using the bottom of her shirt. "Though, I still suspect there's another, better way for you to use that thing… There must be. I can't imagine a goddess would outfit her warrior with something not designed for fighting."

Vi looked at the scythe as she took a long sip of the liquid. It was cloyingly sweet and as thick as honey—perhaps it was just honey with herbs and salves swirled within. But there was a distinct medicinal aftertaste that was so bitter on the back of her palette that Vi was glad for the sweetness.

"I wish I knew," Vi murmured. She was staring at a crystal weapon. A real, complete, legendary crystal weapon. She could feel its power, even now, thrumming quietly. It whispered secrets to her, inviting her to uncover them. Yet it spoke in a language she couldn't understand. Perhaps Arwin was right and there was some way to change the weapon. There was so much potential waiting to be unlocked, but Vi didn't even know where to start. "Unfortunately, the only people who may be able to help me are the Faithful."

Arwin leaned against the wall, an almost lazy, deadly smile playing at her lips. "Suggest going to the Faithful in my presence again and die."

"Why do you hate them so much?" She'd asked Sarphos. It was time to hear Arwin's answer… and hope it was something more significant than "because they're monsters."

Arwin searched her face as if Vi was hiding the answer to her own question somewhere on it. Finally, "You truly know nothing of the morphi and Meru, do you?"

"I imagine I only know slightly more than you know of the Dark Isle," Vi lied. She would bet she knew vastly more than Arwin knew of the Dark Isle, thanks to Taavin and Sarphos's information. But in the grand scheme of things, that was precious little.

"Fair." Arwin sighed, closing her eyes. When she spoke, it was the first time Vi didn't feel as though she was being spoken down to, or threatened. "The seeds of the hatred were sown about a thousand years ago, not long after the Great War between the entities they call the Goddess Yargen and the God Raspian."

"Entities?" Vi interrupted quickly. "So, you don't think they're actually divine?" Arwin surprised her with a shrug.

"Don't know. I've never seen them. They must be powerful if all the stories are true… But I could be a powerful goddess to a beetle." Her eyes drifted to the scythe. "That weapon, however ill designed it is, combined with the tears and the plague—it all makes a compelling argument for these supposed gods' might. But I don't know if I could confidently say something is divine when I saw it. So how can I trust someone else's claims?"

Vi hadn't considered it that way, and it was almost painful to do so. Some things about her world vision weren't ready to be challenged. Especially not when so much was already cast in doubt. "Well, that being what it is… you were saying? After this great war and the morphi?"

"Yes, well… Yargen and Raspian are said to have battled countless times—starting different eras of light and dark. After their last row, Yargen won dominion over the world—so the Faithful claim—and was seated in Risen for a time. In the aftermath, the elfin'ra were exiled from Meru and locked away on their island as punishment for their support of Raspian. Much like the morphi, their magic was seen as fundamentally twisted. The race of the draconis were eventually cast off as well… though that didn't happen for a couple centuries."

"Did the draconis help Raspian?" Vi had yet to hear of this particular people.

"Some did, some didn't. Find me a whole race of people who's entirely good or entirely evil and I'll eat my boot. But it didn't matter what they *did*. It mattered what people *said*. And people say a lot in the years following world-changing events.

"The core of Yargen's followers, the early Faithful, claim the draconis are descended from Raspian's great dragon, crafted by the god himself. They also say the morphi are tainted by Raspian as well, since our magic is said to derive from twilight—neither here, nor there—the moment when the sun gives up its hold to the darkness where Raspian thrives."

"But the twilight could also be the dawn," Vi contested.

"Thank you!" Arwin threw her hands in the air. "I'm pleased to see you have some sense. Certainly not a Faithful after all."

"So that's why you hate the Faithful? Because they have unfairly labeled your people as allies of Raspian?"

"If only that was the extent of it." A frown lined Arwin's face. "Around twenty, thirty years ago, the Faithful grew bolder and far more wicked. They were always bad, but they didn't have the power they have now. They increased their hold on Meru—on Queen Lumeria herself. They justified their actions by saying the word of Yargen had changed, and the people believed them. They were the first ones to say the end of the world was coming and, as a result, they were more active in cleansing those who would seek to aid Raspian."

"*Cleansing?*" Vi said the word slowly. It had a horrible taste.

"Their words, not mine. They've slaughtered innocent morphi and draconis under false trials in Risen. Really, it was all a display of power. The Lord of the Faithful knows no limits to his cruelty. The draconis don't leave their island just as the morphi can only exist safely here—that's why my father carved out this place for us using the royal family's knowledge of the shift."

"That's horrible," Vi whispered. The potion she held in her hands had been forgotten. No amount of balm could soothe the ache she felt for the people of Meru. "Why does no one stop it?"

"Like I said, their actions supposedly come from the goddess herself. Though I have my suspicions…"

"You don't think they're acting on Yargen's orders?"

"I can't imagine the goddess being quiet for hundreds of years and then suddenly demanding blood. Can you?" Vi shook her head and Arwin continued. "No, it's all the depravity of two power-hungry men."

"Who?" Vi whispered. She didn't want to hear the answer, because she already knew it.

"Who else? Lord Ulvarth wields the sword, but the one who gives him the orders and the power—the real evil—is the Voice of the Faithful."

THE REAL EVIL IS *the Voice of the Faithful.* The words rattled in her ears, drowning out the buzz of magic from the scythe. The conversation took a blessedly lighter turn as they walked back to Vi's room, but the weight of earlier revelations was heavy on her mind and shoulders.

"Leave the blade here, we're going to Sarphos," Arwin commanded. Vi was too tired to argue.

Leaving the scythe without so much as a lock on her door didn't feel like enough. But it had been safe and hidden in the Twilight Kingdom for hundreds of years now, so Vi could only trust it would be safe for a few more days.

Though, knowing her luck, Vi wouldn't exactly be surprised if something happened now that the scythe had been revealed from its hiding place.

Up two floors, Arwin came to a stop before a large, open space. The domed ceiling overhead was framed by metal and otherwise open to the stars in the twilight sky above. Glowing stones hung like pendants over three tables that quite literally *grew* up from the floor—starting as stone, but transforming into branches that wove themselves in the proper shape. In the back of the room was a desk with a familiar red-haired man hunched over it. On either side of his work station were a series of tables, vials, mixing stations, and other workspaces.

Whatever Sarphos was doing must be intense, for his shoulders were pulled to his ears and his hand moved feverishly over the open page before him. Arwin cleared her throat and he nearly jumped from his seat.

"Sarphos."

He looked over his shoulder. "What is it now?"

"Don't look so happy to see me," Arwin leaned her hip against one of the tables.

"Why would I be happy? You're always breaking something," Sarphos muttered. "Or someone, I should say. What did you do to her?"

"She was worse for wear when she came in. Even mild training has her bruising." Arwin motioned between Vi and the table. "Up with you. Let Sarphos give you a once-over."

Vi obliged, pushing herself off the floor to sit on the edge of the table.

"Can I trust you with her?" Arwin asked, already starting for the open door. "I have to get to a meeting with the head of the city guards. *Someone* has been taking up all my time today."

"I'm not sorry," Vi called loftily after the woman.

Arwin just snorted before disappearing, not even giving Sarphos a chance to respond.

"You two seem to be getting along better," Sarphos observed thoughtfully.

"She still doesn't trust me." And that fact could be deadly to Taavin. No matter how much easy banter they exchanged, Vi needed to stay on guard.

"She likely never will."

"Good, the feeling can be mutual then."

Sarphos looked away from his potions, inspecting her in his peripheral vision. His expression made her wonder if she should've kept the thought to herself. But she had little energy to care about whatever verdict he reached about the callous remark.

These people are not your friends, Vi reminded herself. They had their own objectives and histories she didn't understand. They were a means to an end.

"Have the morphi not been kind to you?" Sarphos asked softly, as he placed a hand on her forearm. Vi thought the motion merely reassuring until she felt a pulse of magic reverberate through her body, probing uncomfortably between her muscles.

"Everyone has been kind."

"Yet you do not trust us?" Sarphos removed his hand from her and then pointed at her midsection where Adela had wounded her. "Lie back and let me see that."

Vi did as instructed. "I can't… because once anyone finds out who I am aligned with… the kindness will end."

"Mine hasn't," he murmured, lifting her shirt slightly. Vi looked down at the raised scar on her abdomen. It could've been much worse, given the original wound.

He worked in silence and Vi stared at the glowing stone pendant above her. There was an odd, hollow ache in her—one she didn't think any salve would be able to fix. One that would make tears prick her eyes if she wasn't careful.

"Thank you," Vi said finally.

"It's my oath to heal," Sarphos said simply and lowered her shirt.

"It's not your oath to keep him a secret." Vi didn't have to specify who *he* was. "Perhaps the opposite. So, thank you."

"I still don't know if it was the right decision." He looked her right in the eye. "Make sure you and he prove to me that it was. Prove to me that this prophecy you're involved in, your goals to help all the people of this world, are real. Prove to me… that I didn't just let the murderer of morphi survive for no reason."

Vi gave a small nod, accepting the vial Sarphos held out. She downed it, and the next, feeling steadily stronger. Over the third, she asked, "Take me to him?"

"I had already planned on it."

Vi opened her eyes to the eerie skeletal trees of the Twilight Forest and took a deep breath.

"Are you all right?" Sarphos asked from her side, releasing her hand.

"Yes. It's easier to pass through the shift if I keep my eyes closed and hold my breath. Much less jarring that way."

"Interesting," he murmured. "I've never passed through a shift with a non-morphi before now."

"Glad I could be your experiment." She tried to keep her voice easy. "I see you got us closer this time."

"Now that I know where it is, I can come here directly."

Vi wondered if she should interpret the statement as a thinly veiled threat—that he could lead anyone here in an instant.

"Saves us time." Vi stepped ahead, crossed the stream. Without another word, she side-stepped through the narrow opening of the cave.

"Vi?" Taavin called out. This time, his voice didn't come from the ground, but directly across from her. The glowing stone Sarphos had left the last time illuminated him faintly as he breathed a sigh of relief. "I thought I heard your voice."

"Sarphos is here too." Vi gave him a quick once-over. His eyes were attentive and bright, the luster had returned to his skin and his muscles seemed better defined. Even Taavin's hair looked clean. Whatever Sarphos had given him had truly worked wonders overnight.

Her relief was light and palpable, but only until Sarphos entered, and the atmosphere in the close space suddenly grew heavy.

“Sarphos.” Taavin gave him a wary look.

“Voice,” Sarphos responded just as curtly.

Silence, long and strained, stretched between them. Vi waited, holding her breath. Of course meeting Taavin when he was healthy—healthier—would be different for Sarphos than helping a dying man.

“Shall we just get on with it?” Vi broke the silence, and their staring battle. The less the two interacted, the better. Sarphos was already in too deep to back out now, and he knew it. Taavin still needed his help, and he knew it. At least, she hoped they’d both arrived at the same conclusions.

“Very well.” Sarphos’s tone took on a more detached and clerical nature as he set down the bundle of clothes he’d brought and stepped forward.

For his part, Taavin said nothing, holding out his arms and waiting. Sarphos poked, prodded, and pulsed his magic over Taavin. Vi folded and unfolded her hands before her. Her whole body was tense, every muscle trembling just beneath the surface, though she didn’t entirely know why.

Was it because she was nervous either Taavin or Sarphos would snap, attacking the other? Was it worry that Sarphos would find something terribly wrong? Or was it because of what Arwin had said about Taavin and the Faithful earlier?

“Right, then… the healing so far looks good. There’s still quite a bit of infection so I have a few draughts I’d like to make you.” Sarphos stepped back toward the opening. “Give me a minute or five?”

“Take your time.” Vi caught his eyes, trying to silently stress the words. Sarphos may have picked up on her meaning, giving her the slightest of nods before pushing back toward the entrance.

“You’re certain we can trust him?” Taavin asked.

“Yes.” Vi leaned against the wall behind her by the opening so she could listen for Sarphos’s return. “If he was going to hurt either of us, he would’ve by now. If he was going to out us, he could've—I've tried to keep an eye on him, but I've hardly been with him every waking moment. No one in the Twilight Kingdom knows he's smuggling me out or helping you."

"It's just… the morphi…" Taavin rubbed the back of his neck, staring at where Sarphos departed. "They don't take kindly to Faithful."

"So I hear."

Taavin's arm dropped to his side. "I'd imagine… What exactly have you heard?"

"I've heard that the morphi have been sequestered—forced to hide behind the shift, to fight for their lives to have a mere place on this land." Vi took a step forward. "I've heard how the Faithful will slaughter them just to make a point. I've heard of the brutality of the Lord of the Faithful—that his bloodlust is impossible to sate. I've heard he murders innocents on nothing more than superstitions regarding their magicks." She was standing toe to toe with him, heart racing, struggling to keep her voice and her emotions in check. Yet when she spoke next, her voice had dropped to a whisper. "And I've heard that all of these atrocities come to pass at your command."

Taavin's eyes searched her face as Vi searched his. She held her breath, waiting for a reaction of any kind. But he gave her none.

"Tell me…" She reached up, grabbing Taavin's coat. "Tell me they're lying. Tell me the Faithful of Yargen aren't butchers hiding under the skirts of their goddess, using fear to justify their wicked actions."

Taavin said nothing. He continued to stare with those terribly beautiful green eyes. Vi shook him, anger rising in her once more. She was helpless against its rolling tide.

The darkness threatened to consume her whole. One more betrayal was all it would take, and she may never trust again.

"Tell me it wasn't you." Sparks crackled around her fingers, singeing his once-bright coat. "Tell me it wasn't you who ordered it!"

"I wish I could."

Vi released him. She wasn't sure if she pushed him or he stumbled back. But the net result was the same. Once more, they both stood against opposite walls in too-small space.

"Tell me… the truth." Vi forced out. "No lies, no half-truths." She shook her head and cast a hand through the air, as if she could dispel the shadows he'd spun around her—the mystery that had made him so horribly alluring. "Tell me what you've done. Tell me everything, like I asked of you in the West… and tell me why I shouldn't tell Sarphos to get the whole of the morphi army and kill you as he wanted to from the start."

"Other than the fact that if the morphi killed me, it truly would spell their demise?" Taavin said, painfully deadpan, worrying the bracelet around his wrist.

"Do not deflect!" Vi pointed her finger at him, wishing she could pin him down. His words were slippery things. "What is your role in all of this?"

Tell me you aren't betraying me too, her mind screamed.

Taavin took a deep breath, his eyes fluttering closed. "Everything I've said has been the truth. I was taken from my home as a child by Lord Ulvarth and the Faithful. They murdered my mother and burned everything she'd worked to create to the ground. I was troubled by visions—nightmares of you."

"This is not my fault," Vi growled before he could continue. If he was about to blame his actions on her, he had another thing coming.

"My actions are my own." The man had an uncanny and uncomfortable ability to read her mind. "But you need to understand where I was in life: I was alone, sequestered, *tormented*… And I was a pawn for Ulvarth to consolidate power. The Lord of Swords is nothing without the Voice. He needed someone as a figurehead—someone he could manipulate into saying everything he wanted. Someone who would live in fear of him and never utter a word about the truth of his twisted directives."

"So you told him what he wanted to hear," Vi concluded, all their past conversations falling into logical place.

"He locked me away with the flame at the top of the Archives of Yargen, denied me food and drink. Told me I would receive nothing until I espoused the words of the goddess. At first, I lied, making things up for him." Taavin's words became hurried, almost crazed. "But he would say, 'Taavin, you must have misheard. Listen again.'"

It was Taavin's turn to approach her. With every statement he drew nearer. Arms outstretched, as if begging her for something. But Vi wasn't sure what, or if she had anything to give.

"So I began repeating what he'd say to me—the things I knew, things he all but told me, he wanted. I became his parrot. If I knew he wanted a man condemned, or to march against a city, or to take over a celebration, I would say the words. He would have the Voice's proclamations… and I would eat."

"And with your words, you knowingly condemned innocent people to die." Vi stared up at him, their noses nearly touching.

"If that's what it took to survive."

"How many people saw you say these lies? Was it only Ulvarth? Or did the Swords hear as well? Did the citizens?"

"I did what I had to do to survive. But I took no joy in it. I didn't want to. I knew what I was doing and I loathed myself for it. But I was a captive; I was helpless." Taavin shook his head, running his hands through his hair. When he looked back to her, his eyes were haunted and far more sunken than they'd been just moments ago. This was the shadowed edge of his personality that he'd always kept hidden just below his hopeful, driven exterior. "What would you have done? Curled up and died?"

"I wouldn't have told a power-hungry lunatic to murder innocent people for no reason!" Her voice rose now and Vi shoved him away. Taavin stumbled, reaching out to the cave wall for support. She wouldn't have him looking down at her. "If I had to die to spare them, I would've."

"It's easy for you to say that here, now… but not when hunger is gnawing at you. Not when death is staring you down. You don't know what you'd do then."

"I do know what I'd do. Because I've seen death. I've seen it on my land, in my people, and in visions of the world's end that haunt me even still. I've seen it in the faces that tried to kill me as I risked my life every step to get here." Her voice had gone low. "And I risked it all, not for me, not for you, but for this world. For my family. So don't you *dare* tell me I wouldn't die for a cause greater than myself."

"I never wanted to hurt anyone." He was pleading now. "I didn't—"

"Just because you didn't wield the sword, doesn't mean your hands are clean of blood."

"Had I stopped him then, he would've let me die and found another babe to rip from their home! The Voice is reborn, Vi. Time and again. So even if I had died, it wouldn't have changed anything."

His eyes were ablaze and, for the first time, Vi's mind and mouth fell silent.

"If I hadn't done as Ulvarth asked, if I let myself die, I couldn't have stopped the Swords of Light when I was able. I wouldn't have been able to hear Yargen's words when they came in earnest. I wouldn't have been able to do the best I could from my powerless position for the people of Meru—*all* of them. I wouldn't have been able to help guide you here and begin to make sense of this." Taavin thrust his index finger at the watch and Vi felt it press painfully against her breastbone. "I wouldn't have had the ability to help stop the world's end. He would've let me die, done his will anyway for a few years, claiming he was acting on my last words as the Voice, and then placed another helpless child right back in the position I was in."

Vi looked from the watch to Taavin. Every emotion ravaged her thoughts. There was sorrow for him, frustration, hurt, confusion. He was in more pain than she could imagine—the agony she'd always somehow known was there finally laid bare—

and seeing the hurt unleashed only sparked her own profound sense of suffering.

Above it all, anger thrummed within her. So much that her spark had taken residence in the hole Jayme had left in her chest. Pressing her eyes shut, Vi tried to find sense in the darkness. But there was none to be had, and she was forced to look once more at Taavin.

"I trusted you," she whispered.

"As I did you. I left Risen for you. I told you my story. Forgive me for sparing myself the trauma of sharing the more agonizing details of my captivity."

"How can I believe anything else you'll say? How can I trust you're not keeping something else from me?" Her heart was racing. They were at the point of breaking, she could see it. Yet she couldn't stop herself.

"How can I put my faith in you when you judge me for actions taken when I was in *captivity*?" he seethed back. "I never meant to break your trust, Vi. But know you are dangerously close to breaking mine."

"Maybe that's just what happens to the people we love." Her mind returned to one of the last thoughts she'd had when she'd seen him previously. "Maybe we're meant to hurt and be hurt. Maybe we're just meant to burn."

Vi took a small step away from him. Taavin caught her wrist. Sparks crackled, bright yellow, tangled with a hazy blue glow that Vi knew as the hallmark of his magic—of Yargen's power.

"Fine," he breathed. "If we're meant to burn, then we burn together."

They were both breathing heavily. His exhales were her inhales, until the air between them was thin and she felt dizzy. Vi stared up at his emerald eyes long enough to watch their crystalline depths go hazy. "Taa—"

His hand was in the back of her hair, grabbing, pulling. His free arm wrapped around her, holding her to him. Vi's eyes barely had time to close before his mouth crashed against hers.

Taavin's teeth scraped against her lips and Vi parted them with a soft groan, allowing him entry. The rock wall behind her dug into her back. She managed to squeeze her hands between them. Her fingers fought their way up his chest, to his face, tugging him closer.

Sunlight… Even in the darkness, he smelled of sunlight. He smelled of fields warmed in the afternoon, of the heat on fresh laundry pulled inside on a hot day, of joy and laughter over a cool drink in the balmy hours after dusk.

He shifted his legs and Vi's hips pressed forward slightly, their bodies completely flush. His fingers gripped her hard enough that they might leave bruises. Vi almost hoped they did. She needed proof this moment was real. She wanted something to look at later and remind herself it wasn't just a fleeting daydream.

Taavin finally pulled away a fraction, breathless, their noses rubbing and foreheads nearly touching.

"Perhaps you're right about us burning together, because only you can set me on fire." Vi leaned forward, catching his mouth for several more moments. Taavin kissed her slowly this time, almost sweetly, as if he was savoring every taste. As if they both somehow knew that these desperate, fleeting moments were the best they would have.

"Vi." Her name was husky on his swollen lips. "I've never had much… but this is all I have now. This whole world may need you and not know it, but no one needs you more than I do, I promise you that. I will make mistakes. But I need you to believe in me, trust me." His thumb caressed her cheek as his eyes locked with hers. Gut-wrenching pain filled her with that gaze. He was asking for something she didn't know if she could give any longer. "I need you to accept that this, however perfect it can feel, isn't. I want you to stay with me despite that fact. Stay with me because it is messy, and raw, and something we need but may also be terrified to want."

She pressed her eyes closed. Vi took a quivering breath. *Say yes. Just say yes.* She tried to will the word to her lips.

What would happen if she gave herself to him even more than she already had, and then he betrayed her? Would there be anything left unbroken in her after something like that?

"Taavin," her voice was raspy and thin, barely forced through a thick throat. "What if I can't?"

"Good sense would have me give up on you… But when it comes to you, Vi, I seem to be lacking in good sense."

Vi tightened her arms around his neck and shoulders. "I'm sorry," she whispered.

"As am I," he murmured.

"Sarphos will be back soon and I have so much to tell you. So much we should discuss… but all I want to do is hold you." Vi let out a small, bitter laugh. There was so much to say. She had yet to tell him of the scythe, of Jayme, of Adela. There would never be enough time for all the words unspoken between them.

"Then hold me, and let the world wait."

14

EVENTUALLY, KING NOCT'S HOSPITALITY would run out. Everything had its limits. And before that happened, Vi wanted to be as prepared as possible to start on the road again.

But with so much to do, she wasn't sure where to start.

Vi opened a heavy wooden door to a library, tucked away in a quiet corner of the palace. Cool air rushed to greet her, carrying the scent of stale leather and parchment. The atmosphere was that of opening a time capsule, the room still and coated in a thick layer of dust.

The only evidence that anyone had used this room recently was an open journal sitting out on the table, two empty inkwells and one still full laid out next to it.

The private library of the royal family was small, but tall, and every bookcase that lined its walls was packed. It was more than enough information to keep herself busy yesterday and today… perhaps tomorrow. But Taavin was getting stronger, and so was she. And that meant they needed to continue onward.

Her father was out there, and the longer she dallied, the longer he suffered.

Vi ran her fingertips absentmindedly along the spines of the books, working her way toward the back corner where she'd left off last night. Selecting a narrow, wide book, Vi lifted it off the shelf and brought it over to her table. She flipped through the maps within, landing on the page she'd been working from yesterday.

Settling into her spot at the table, Vi got to work.

"You really have a thing for maps, huh?" Arwin's voice startled her. Vi had filled five pages in the journal and half the inkwell was gone, so she must've been working for at least two hours. "You burned the midnight oil here last night, and were back at it before breakfast."

"I do love maps." Vi looked back down at her transcriptions. She'd been sketching from memory the map Sehra had shown her, the maps she'd grown up with on the Dark Isle. Now, she was making slow work of transcribing the coastlines of Meru—comparing them to what she knew, comparing them to the morphi's records of maps through the ages.

Two pages earlier in the journal, she'd been working on a route to Adela's Isle of Frost.

"Here, breakfast." Arwin held out a sandwich as she sat across the table from her. Vi took a generous bite, ignoring the smear of ink her fingertips left on the bread's hard crust.

"Thanks," Vi mumbled over the food, looking back at her work.

"Why do you like maps so much?"

Slowly, Vi looked up. The question was calm, genuine. There wasn't even a hint of a jab. So Vi answered an honest question honestly.

"I told you, I grew up captive."

"You said you were sent to the northernmost territory of your Empire, for politics and prophecy. Nothing about being captive."

"Well, it effectively made me a captive." Vi glanced up again from her journal, seeing pity in Arwin's eyes. She laughed softly, shaking her head. "It wasn't that bad. I lived a fairly good life..." Her thoughts went to Taavin's imprisonment. Yes, her time in the North could've been *much* worse. "But maps were my window to the world, how I made sense of all the space spreading out around me that I never thought I'd get to see."

"I see," Arwin murmured.

"What about you?" Vi dared to ask. "What are you interested in?"

"Mostly combat."

"Just combat? Nothing else?" Vi knew many soldiers who delighted in honing their skills. But underneath the armor, they were still people. They had passions and hobbies.

"Sometimes I sing." Then, as if suddenly regretting the burst of honesty, Arwin stood quickly. "But speaking of combat, I should get back to training." She nearly bolted for the door, catching herself on its frame and turning back to Vi. "So should you... I'm sure you'll be on your way toward the end of the world soon enough, and you're not going to kill any evil gods with your current scythe skills."

Before Vi could reply, Arwin left.

She spent a few more hours pouring through the maps, working as quickly as possible to get as much information down as she could from the records of the Twilight Kingdom. There was a wealth of information she'd never be able to comb through. As Vi returned the last book to the shelf with a sigh, she scanned the room one more time.

What if, somewhere in here, was information on the scythe? Its history? The history of all the mysterious crystal weapons?

She could spend months looking through every book, searching for information that may well not be there—that likely *wasn't* there. Arwin was right, she didn't have much time, and she had to make the most of what she had. So, clutching the journal to her chest, Vi left the library behind and made for the training room.

"I was wondering how long you'd keep me waiting." Arwin's brow was slick with sweat when Vi entered. A spear in her hand today.

"Thanks for waiting at all." Vi adjusted her grip on the scythe as she crossed over. Magic flowed through her, bright and immeasurably powerful.

"You need me." Arwin shrugged.

"I do." In multiple ways, Vi realized. A plan had been forming in the back of her mind while she had been working on routes to the Isle of Frost.

Taavin had said there was a shift protecting the Isle of Frost, like that surrounding the Twilight Kingdom. Originally, Vi had thought to try to get Sarphos to come with them. But perhaps Vi could convince Arwin to come along to continue her training with the scythe. It was another avenue to pursue and seemed more likely than convincing the soft Sarphos to venture out on a dangerous journey. Vi wasn't about to leave their access to Adela's stronghold to chance.

Vi considered the best next steps as they traded blow for blow in the sparring ring.

"Remember, distance." Arwin knocked the pole of her weapon with Vi's. "You have to manage the distance with that thing." Vi adjusted her feet, and Arwin held up her spear again. "Dodge and slash—catch my hip with the curved part of that weapon and pull."

They repeated the motions again, and again. They did them slowly and at a too-far distance to start, then sped up as Vi became more comfortable. Just when she thought she'd gathered the hang of it, Arwin changed the move.

"All right, put that to the side for now," Arwin finally commanded. Vi's arms were like jelly, limp at her sides the moment she let go of the scythe. "Let's practice a little bit of combat, now that we've run through drills."

All Vi could do was nod. She was winded, legs exhausted,

arms failing. But she wasn't about to back down. Arwin walked over to the weapon rack, grabbing a wooden halberd. With a pulse of her magic, the polearm had turned into a wooden scythe, nearly identical to her weapon. She tossed it over and Vi was shocked she still had the reflexes and strength to catch it.

"Why haven't I been practicing with this the whole time?"

"We weren't moving that fast, or doing anything that dangerous, during the drills. I wanted you to grow accustomed to the actual weight of your weapon. But for sparring… I'm not going to even risk having you knick me with that thing. Who knows what it'd do to me."

Vi looked to the weapon, and agreed. It was likely for the best… She'd always heard crystals led to madness, and monstrous corruptions of mind and body. But the scythe had also been in the hands of the morphi for generations. Perhaps, somehow, they were immune… or perhaps they'd just never handled the weapon enough. Vi wouldn't take chances, in case it was the latter.

"I'll use different weapons each round. Your only objective is to land a killing blow on me."

"Understood," Vi said, and the sparring commenced.

With two weapons, Arwin formed an X to catch her scythe, pushing it off and digging the blunted wooden point of one into the soft part of her throat. When Arwin wielded a single sword, Vi had slightly more luck keeping the woman at distance—until Arwin caught the pole in her hands, yanking the wooden weapon forward and Vi with it. She stumbled and fell, blinking up at the sword in her face.

"I know you have more than that, up with you," Arwin commanded gruffly. They clasped forearms and Arwin pulled her upright. Vi swayed wearily and ignored every stinging pain in her body. "You were good on distance there; you just need to identify openings to attack better. Defense is only useful to create an opening for offense."

"I'll focus on openings, then," Vi said, and they continued on.

Arwin was nimble and skilled—a trained warrior through and

through. No matter how many hours she put in, Vi wasn't about to make up for the difference in their years of experience.

And yet… when an opening presented itself, Vi took it.

Arwin's weight shifted—Vi recognized her preparation for a lunge. She dodged to the side. Swiping the blade low, Vi hooked Arwin's ankle and pulled. The woman was sent off-balance, dancing from foot to foot to try to stay upright.

Vi pushed the blade this time, hitting the fronts of her ankles. Arwin slammed the tip of her wooden sword into the ground, using it for support. She crouched low, about to strike again. But Vi was too fast.

She swung the scythe around, stopping it right at Arwin's neck.

For a brief second, they both panted, staring at each other.

"Well done." Arwin recovered her breath much faster than Vi. "Perhaps you have a fighter in you yet."

Vi eased the scythe away from Arwin, leaning against it for support. "I have a good tutor."

Arwin flashed her a genuine smile, taking the scythe and returning it with her wooden sword to the rack. Vi took the expression as a sign of hope—perhaps she really could convince the woman to go with her on her journey.

"Come along." Arwin started for the exit.

"Where are we going?" Vi grabbed the crystal scythe and followed Arwin out of the training room. They went through the normal doors, into the usual hallway, but then took an unexpected turn down a wing of the palace Vi had never been to before.

"You'll see soon enough." Arwin glanced over her shoulder, making sure Vi was still close behind. "You did well today. You deserve—and need—some recovery."

The potent scents of flowers and woody herbs filled the air on clouds of steam. Arwin led her into a bathing room. There, Vi discovered the source of the aroma—three large tubs, like barrels cut in half, filled to the brim with steaming water.

"Strip." Arwin pointed to a tall table on one half of the room, then to the tubs. "And soak. It does wonders for the body."

Vi hovered as Arwin headed for the tall table on the room's other side. She slowly peeled her sweat-drenched shirt off her skin, revealing a tight leather binding underneath before Vi could look away. Vi would have called it a corset, but it covered the breasts only—not down to the hips. Additionally, it had thick straps that wrapped over the shoulders and—most fascinating of all—it was fashioned to cover the entire breast, accentuating no cleavage, and was tied in the front.

"What?" Arwin caught her staring. "This?" She motioned to a fairly large, crescent-shaped birthmark underneath her collar bone.

"No, not that. Why do you bind your chest like that?" Vi blurted.

"Keeps them out of my way. They'd be way too painful to deal with if they were bouncing about during combat or practice." Arwin paused, mid-loosening of the ties. Her eyes caught Vi's. "What do you do?" she asked cautiously.

Mutual fascination filled the air to the point that Vi felt dizzy with it and couldn't help laughing. And the laughter felt so good that she didn't even bother trying to stop it.

"Look at us," Vi said finally when she was under control. "Fascinated by each other's lives, even when it comes to undergarments." Arwin gave her a small grin. "We have nothing like that where I'm from. Our underclothes are meant to tighten the waist or accentuate the bust."

"We have corsets too," Arwin said.

"I see."

"They're just not practical for my line of work." Arwin started for the laces of her chest leathers and Vi quickly averted her eyes, giving the woman some privacy. "I really don't care how small my waist is."

Vi set the scythe to the side and quickly undressed before crossing to the tub next to Arwin's. She stepped up onto the ledge that surrounded it, dipping her toes into the water—feeling around for the small step she knew must be there. Finding one, she brought the other leg over and sat. What Vi had thought was water turned out to be a bright teal substance that reminded her of the consistency of an egg yolk. Any potential to be unnerved by such a comparison dissolved as a rush tingled up her body to her head, making everything feel light. Every muscle in her body relaxed all at once.

"*Oh my…*" Vi sighed softly, sinking back into the tub, the back of her head resting against the edge.

"Nice, isn't it?" Arwin slung her arms over the side of her tub closest to Vi, chin resting on her forearms.

"I've never felt anything like it. It's as if my whole body has vanished."

"It's one of Sarphos's concoctions, actually. We worked on it together back before…" Arwin's voice trailed off. Vi looked over to see the woman staring off at nothing. Vi didn't question her; whatever memory had drawn her away was hers alone. The last thing she wanted to draw Arwin's attention to was her moment of vulnerability. "It's made from the shift," Arwin continued hastily, as though the pause hadn't happened at all. "Using water and other ingredients, he'll use the shift to merge them together and make something new—shift it into something else."

"He's a skilled healer, and an even better man," Vi murmured, thinking of all he'd done for Taavin and her, despite them being his supposed enemies. That would be another challenge if Vi somehow managed to find a way to convince Arwin to come along with her. How would she get her to ignore Taavin's identity? Perhaps it was better to go after Sarphos; he already knew who he was dealing with.

"He is. And nothing at all like his brother," Arwin continued.

"His brother?" Vi remembered when she'd first inquired about Arwin and Sarphos's relationship—he'd said something about Arwin being engaged to his brother. So the mention now had her more than a little intrigued.

Arwin pushed away from the side of her tub, mirroring Vi's

position with her head lounged back. She stared upward, speaking more toward the ceiling than Vi.

"Sarphos's brother and I were engaged to be married. He was nothing like Sarphos—strong willed, a fighter, reckless, everything a young girl foolishly dreams—or lusts—about. There are times I wonder what would've happened if I knew what I know now, and had been smart enough to fall for the kind and stable Sarphos instead..." Arwin's voice was filled with longing. But Vi didn't know whether it was for Sarphos's brother, or a life that could've been with Sarphos himself.

"What happened to him?" Vi asked gently. "Not Sarphos, obviously, his brother?"

"He's gone now."

"I'm sorry." She straightened, moving the thick waters around with her hands, watching the flowers dance on the surface as she stirred up currents beneath. This could be her opportunity. Vi took a deep breath. She just had to find strength enough to be vulnerable... How was it, out of everything she'd done, that was starting to terrify her the most? "I'm afraid I may lose someone important to me as well."

"Who?"

"My father."

"You said you were here to find him. Why is the King of the Dark Isle on Meru?"

"Emperor—we don't have kings on the Dark Isle anymore," Vi corrected without thinking. Luckily, Arwin didn't seem offended. "My mother is sick with the White Death. So my father embarked on a journey to Meru to find a cure. He didn't know then what the cause was." *Didn't know his journey was hopeless*, Vi thought but couldn't bring herself to say. If only she'd known earlier. If only her father had known. Then he would've been safe and sound back with her mother.

"I take it this journey didn't go well?" Arwin asked solemnly.

"It didn't... He was captured and is being held hostage."

"By the Faithful?"

"No, he never made it to Meru. Adela captured him. Now she has him on her Isle of Frost and… I know he's alive… but every day that passes is another when his life could end. Even when I'm so close to reaching him." Vi turned to Arwin, surprised to see the woman stony-faced and serious. "Before I do anything else, I have to get to the Isle of Frost."

"You're going to the Isle of Frost?" Arwin whispered.

"Yes."

Without warning, Arwin stood. Vi looked away quickly, giving the woman privacy as she left the tub.

Had she said something wrong? Had she offended her somehow? Vi ran through the conversation in her head.

"Get out," Arwin commanded gruffly. Vi turned slowly, but the woman's back was to her as she tightened the bindings on her chest. "We're going to see my father."

"Arwin… I didn't mean to offend—"

"You didn't offend me." Arwin looked over her shoulder with a fire in her eyes. "But you have presented me with a unique opportunity."

15

UNIQUE OPPORTUNITY. VI DIDN'T know yet if she liked those words.

Arwin didn't say anything else as they left the baths, starting up through the palace wordlessly. Vi repeated the conversation in her head verbatim, wondering where she'd gone wrong. Perhaps it was bringing up Adela? Taavin had said that Fallor was a notable outcast of the morphi, and he was in Adela's service…

Vi suppressed a groan. She should've thought of that sooner.

Her mind swirled around the possibilities as they made their way along the spiral staircases of the palace, down to the throne room Vi had been first taken to days before. Just like then, King Noct sat on his large sofa, hands folded over his round belly, watching children play in the courtyard beyond.

"What is it, daughter?" the king asked, slowly drawing his eyes to Arwin. They drifted over Vi as well, pausing. "I see the weapon is becoming a part of you."

Vi shifted her grip on the scythe. It was less cumbersome than she'd originally thought it would be—perhaps because it was surprisingly light. Or because she could feel the power radiating through it underneath her fingers. Either way, carrying it was indeed becoming more instinctive.

"I don't enjoy letting it out of my sight," Vi said quietly. Then added quickly, "I know it's safe here, but—"

"But that is the right decision. You cannot be too cautious… and the weapon must get to know its new champion. Perhaps Arwin can fashion a sling for you to better carry it with." At the mention of his daughter, he turned to Arwin. "Why have you come with such a severe expression?"

"Father, there is something we have overlooked—a detail our guest has neglected to share."

"What is this?" The king looked back to her.

"Well… I had been telling Arwin about my quest to find my father," Vi started, glancing between the two.

"Yes, one of the reasons that you came to Meru."

"It's not that she's finding him—it's *where* her father is," Arwin said gruffly before motioning for Vi to continue.

"He's on the Isle of Frost, your highness," Vi said delicately. "Adela has him."

"The Isle of Frost…" the king repeated softly. His eyes drifted back to Arwin. "I know what you are thinking."

"Father, I must. This is my chance."

"I remain firm in my—"

"Your stance has always been that I cannot go alone," Arwin interrupted, "and that has been enough, because you forbade my sisters from going with me on my mission." Arwin took a step forward. "Well, now I will not be alone. I will have a companion on the journey—a companion who is not your daughter and will be going anyway."

"A companion who also doesn't know this land. Who is not a warrior like yourself and can't protect you."

Were she able to show the king her Lightspinning, he might think differently. But Vi kept her mouth shut.

"I can take care of myself—you know I can. She has the scythe and is improving. At the very least, she can guide the way—I've seen her with her maps, father." Arwin looked to Vi. "You know how to get there, don't you?"

"I do," Vi said with slightly more confidence than she felt.

"If you go, you will die at Adela's hand."

"Your highness," Vi interjected quickly before the conversation could take yet another repetitive turn. "I do not fully understand the depth of all you are discussing… But if Arwin wishes to join me, then I beseech you to let her." Vi glanced at Arwin. The woman had a desperate look to her eyes. Vi didn't know what she was bargaining for just yet—what had given Arwin this fire—but if it resulted in the help she needed, she would handle the rest as it came. "I must save my father."

"You must save this world."

"I know that," Vi nearly snapped back at him. The only thing keeping her voice level was her years of royal training. She had no idea how she was going to save the world—she was still just trying to save the ones she loved. "But I also know this: Arwin is the best teacher I'll be able to find for this weapon." Vi shifted her grip on the scythe. "How will I be ready to fight to save our world if I can't keep training?"

The king was silent.

"I also know that I won't be able to focus on defeating Raspian if I'm worried for my father's life. I want to save him *and* the world. All my life, I have been trying to reunite with my family… I don't want to live in a saved world where I cannot."

Noct pursed his lips slightly. She could tell she was trying his patience. But Vi took his continued silence as an indication that she still held the upper hand on the matter.

"I've been told there is a shift around the Isle of Frost—much like the one here. I'm hoping there are tears in that shift, too—tears I plan to exploit." Vi tried to counter his argument before he could make it. "But I'd rather not risk that chance. I'd rather know that once I sail for the Isle of Frost, I will be able to get to my father. If you don't allow Arwin to accompany me for her own reasons, let her come to train me and ensure I can get past the Isle's shift. Please, I—"

She stopped shy of begging, but only just.

The king closed his eyes and sighed. When he opened them, he looked out on the courtyard with a sorrowful expression. Vi knew she was asking him to risk his family for her to save hers. She knew it wasn't a fair trade. Just as she knew exploiting the world's end was an underhanded tactic.

But Arwin also had her own reasons for going. She could see it on the woman's face. Even if Arwin's presence would help Vi, she got the impression it would help Arwin, too. She just wasn't sure exactly how.

"Did you not tell me we are to help the Champion?" Arwin asked, stepping forward. "Isn't that why you gave her the scythe and your hospitality?"

"I do not wish to give her my daughter as well."

Arwin knelt by her father. "You will not lose me, father. But I must put an end to the abominable shift that protects the bane of the seas—the shift that should've never been established and is a theft of our magic. I must put an end to the one who betrayed us."

King Noct looked only at his daughter, slowly lifting his hand. He cupped her cheek thoughtfully, lovingly. Vi's chest ached, thinking back to the few times she'd been with her own father and he'd looked at her with his heart in his eyes.

"If you take this burden on yourself, if you leave our lands… You know I must make it a royal decree. You will get no exceptions as my daughter."

"I understand."

"Then, my royal guard…" King Noct's whispering voice quivered slightly. "I command you to leave the protection of the Twilight Kingdom to atone for your past transgressions. I command you to venture beyond the embrace of the Twilight

Forest. You are to go, and on your way, you will teach the Champion so that she may save our world. You are to destroy the shift which should've never been—and you are to ensure it shall never be formed again by killing the one who created it. Otherwise, you will not be welcomed back into this court."

Vi's heart pounded so hard in her chest that it rattled her lungs. Breathing suddenly felt harder than normal. Cast out? Succeed, or live in exile? What circumstances were these? When she'd envisioned Arwin coming, she hadn't envisioned anything like this.

Vi was playing a game, though she knew precious little of the rules.

"Do you understand?" King Noct asked solemnly.

"I understand, my king. And as your royal guard, I live by your words."

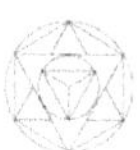

The next morning, Vi woke early. She dressed with more than enough time to get lost in her thoughts before there was a knock on the door.

"Come in."

Vi turned, surprised to see Sarphos rather than Arwin.

"I hear you're leaving," he said as he entered the room.

"So it seems." Vi leaned against the wall by the window, staring out at the bloody-ringed moon that never left the sky. "Can't say I'm surprised the King's hospitality has run short given that I'm responsible for his daughter's exile."

"King Noct holds no ill will toward you." Sarphos set a satchel down at the foot of her bed.

"I wouldn't blame him if he did," Vi said gently, giving him permission to be honest.

"Arwin made her choice."

I did a pretty good job of convincing him to go along with it,

Vi thought to herself. She'd replayed the conversation again and again for half the night. Wondering if she'd done the right thing. But Arwin had been eager to go along first. So Vi tried to set the worry out of her mind.

"I prepared something for the road." Sarphos motioned to the satchel. "There's some crackers in there that can fill an empty stomach like a meal, a specially woven blanket that will keep you warm even on the coldest nights without being bulky, salves, of course, and—"

"Why have you been so nice to me?" Vi interrupted. "You hardly know me."

"Do I have to know someone to be kind to them?"

"Too much kindness… too much trust… It will get you hurt, or killed," Vi muttered bitterly.

"The opposite is also true—but it'll be a much lonelier death."

"What would you know about it?" she murmured.

"A lot more than you give me credit for." He sighed and stood. "I don't understand everything about you or your world. But I don't have to, to see that you're hurting." Vi opened her mouth about to protest, tell him to stop any kind of diagnosis he'd been performing on her. "Trust me when I say you're not the only one who's been hurt by people they loved."

Vi pressed her lips shut as Sarphos started for the door.

"Look after her, please."

"Arwin is far stronger than I, she can look after herself."

"But her emotions get the better of her and cause trouble." He stopped, and the long pause that followed was what brought Vi's attention back to the healer one last time. "I've already lost a brother, Vi," Sarphos whispered. "I don't want to lose a sister, too."

With that, the man was off and Vi finished readying for her journey alone.

She inspected the contents of the pack. In addition to all Sarphos had promised, there were a few extra changes of clothes, wrapped around vials. It didn't matter what he said, Sarphos was a fool for giving away his kindness as he did… She certainly didn't deserve it.

Vi put the journal she'd been working in atop everything else in the satchel, slung it over her shoulder, and strapped the scythe to her back over the opposite shoulder. The strap from the satchel and the scythe formed an X over her chest. But thanks to the undergarments Arwin had gifted her, neither dug in uncomfortably.

Also thanks to Arwin, Vi no longer had to carry the scythe by hand. The woman had taken heed of King Noct's suggestion and stopped in last night with a special strap identical to those she used to carry her pole arms.

"It looks good on you," Arwin appraised as Vi met her on the arcade walkway.

"Thanks." Vi gripped the strap.

"Though, unhooking the strap can make for a slow draw. You may not want to have the weapon wrapped as well, in case you need to get to it."

They started back toward the entrance.

"If I don't have it wrapped, it'll draw too much attention." Vi patted the fabric covering the blade. She suspected her magic would be the first thing she fought with the moment she was out of the Twilight Forest. Vi was still more confident with a sword in her hand than a scythe.

They walked through the entryway and out of the palace, starting along the same road Vi had now traversed many times. Other than the occasional person who gave a nod or wave to Arwin, there was no fanfare.

"Not much of a going-away party," Vi said under her breath, tightening the bandanna around her forehead.

"They're used to my coming and going," Arwin replied. Vi hadn't intended for the woman to hear. "I'm usually patrolling the edges of our kingdom, checking the barriers daily. They don't know that this time I'll be gone a little longer than normal."

"Don't you want to say goodbye to anyone?" Vi couldn't help

but ask. Something about their departure reminded Vi of leaving Norin. A princess quietly departing her Empire… even if Arwin wasn't *technically* a princess.

"I said goodbye to my family earlier."

"Friends?"

"I don't have many of those."

"I'm shocked." The dry remark slipped through Vi's lips before she could stop it. Arwin looked over her shoulder in what could've been a glare, had it not been so obviously laced with pride.

"When did you get a smart mouth?"

"More like when did I get bold enough to share it with you."

"Don't get too bold," Arwin cautioned. Despite the warning, a grin was sneaking its way onto her lips. "Take my hand, I'll need the physical contact to get you through the shift. Don't let go."

Vi took her hand and refrained from pointing out that this would be the third time she'd passed through the shift. If Sarphos kept their secret up until the end, so would Vi. Even if one very big, Taavin-shaped secret was about to come to light.

Heart racing, Vi closed her eyes and sucked in a deep breath, allowing Arwin to guide her through. It seemed like a single step now—the transition between kingdom and forest becoming easier each time. Like waking from a dream, Vi blinked into the bright morning light.

She instantly raised a hand, shielding her eyes. She and Sarphos had only ever sneaked out at night. The light of the Twilight Kingdom was perpetually dim, the majority of illumination coming from unnatural sources.

"Your eyes will take a little longer to adjust… It's been a while since they've seen the sun. But don't worry, you'll be back to normal in no time."

Vi had an increasing amount to worry about, none of which had to do with her eyes. Squinting, Vi trying to discern her bearings. But there was nothing familiar. Trees, as far as the eye could see, and not the slightest bit of sound from the stream.

"Where are we?" Vi tried to ask calmly.

"Right near the western edge of the Twilight Forest." Arwin pointed. "We're about half a day away from Toris. It's a small fishing and trading town notorious for being a pirate stopover. We should be able to pick up a vessel there to get us to the Isle of Frost." Vi didn't miss the slight grimace at the mention of Adela's stronghold.

"Can we return to where Sarphos showed you the tear?" Vi's markings on the trees should still be there. With them, she could find her way back to Taavin.

"Why?"

"There's something I stashed in a cave near there. I want to retrieve it," Vi explained delicately.

"Oh, fine." Arwin rolled her eyes. "Come on then."

Scooping up Vi's hand once more and gripping it tightly, Arwin tugged her through the trees. Vi barely had time to close her eyes and hold her breath. Her lungs were on fire in a moment and her ears popped from the shifting pressure. But as quickly as it came, the uncomfortable sensation of the shift vanished and Vi opened her eyes once more to what had become a more familiar stretch of forest. She could hear the stream in the distance, and see the markings on the trees.

"Right, this way." Vi started forward, gripping the straps of her satchel. It was going to be a miracle if they didn't all end up dead. "Listen, Arwin… I want you to know how grateful I am for you coming."

"I have my own agenda."

"Yes, well… I still appreciate it." Vi continued. "And I hope that, on this journey, we can trust each other."

Arwin snorted. "I suppose I can trust you not to get yourself killed. Barely."

The cave came into view and Vi pointed at it. "That's where my things are. Wait here?"

"Get what you need and let's be on our way." Arwin folded her arms, resting against a tree, impatient.

Vi moved hastily, not wanting to sour the woman's mood even further. Uttering every prayer and good luck wish she knew, Vi crossed to the cave, set the scythe aside, and squeezed through the opening.

"Vi." Taavin's voice cut through her thoughts.

"Taavin." Vi looked over to him in the dim glow of Sarphos's stone. They stared at each other for what felt like an hour—long enough that Arwin should've come investigating. After their last parting, Vi was even more painfully aware of all that was left unsaid.

"Are you alone?" Taavin's eyes shifted over her shoulder.

"No. And it's not Sarphos who's with me."

"What happened?" Taavin's tone sobered and Vi wondered for a brief second if he'd thought she betrayed him.

"I can't explain fully right now, there's no time, and this introduction will be uncomfortable enough as it is. I'd rather not do it in a confined space." Vi sighed and rested her palm on his chest. "You have to trust me, all right? Please know, no matter what, I will never seek to bring you harm. Trust me like I trust you."

"What're you talking about?" His heart was beating faster underneath her fingers.

"You said it yourself—the morphi are not friendly to Fallor or Adela. Turns out, they have some unfinished business with the pirate queen and one of the royal guards wants to come and settle the score."

"*What?*" Taavin's voice dropped to a panicked whisper. He spoke so fast that Vi didn't have the chance to tell him Arwin stood far enough away that there was no way she could hear. "We can't bring a morphi along, especially a morphi royal. First, you saw how Sarphos reacted to me. Second, if they leave their kingdom, they risk exile. Third, they risk being hunted by any Faithful we run into."

"I know the risks. Moreover, *she* knows the risks." Vi dropped her hand, fighting the urge to glare at him and failing. "And so do you. You told me yourself of your hand in creating the decrees that would lead to the Faithful hunting her."

"And I told you not to judge me for the things I did in captivity."

Vi bit the inside of her lower lip and focused on the present. "We don't have a choice in this. Adela's Isle of Frost is shrouded by the morphi shift and I'm not about to leave getting to my father up to chance and hope that one of Raspian's tears allows us through. Getting to the Twilight Kingdom nearly killed me. That's not a viable strategy for us."

Taavin pressed his lips together into a thin line. Vi knew when she'd won. There was no better counter-argument. She'd run through every possibility already; having a morphi on their side was their best chance.

With that, she left the cave, trusting him to follow. But she didn't look back. Instead, she focused on quickly slinging the scythe over her shoulder once more and walking toward Arwin, trying to position herself right between the two.

Vi knew the moment Taavin emerged based on the change in Arwin's expression. It was a darkly fascinating thing to behold. She went from bored and grumpy, to horrified, to the picture of loathing in about an instant.

Spear in hand, Arwin let out a crazed cry and began sprinting toward Taavin.

CROUCHING SOME AND DIGGING in her heels, Vi braced herself as the woman approached, shifting to the side slightly and narrowly missing the point of her spear. She grabbed Arwin's shoulders with both hands, knowing full well she couldn't hold Arwin anywhere for any amount of time if she didn't want to be held.

"I need you to listen to me."

"Vi, you have no idea who that is." Arwin twisted from her grasp. Bringing an arm around, she pushed Vi behind her as if Vi was in danger.

"I know who that is." Vi gripped Arwin's forearm and bicep, clinging to the woman, futilely trying to stop her from moving.

"What have you done to her?" she growled at Taavin. Vi watched the man's eyes dart between her and Arwin, no doubt debating if or when he should step in. "What hold do you have over her?"

"He hasn't done anything to me, Arwin, listen!" Vi yanked

at her arm. It was as unflinching as one of the giant vines in the forests of Soricium. "He's…" Her eyes drifted to Taavin for a long second. So much was left outstanding and unsaid between them. But now wasn't the time. And sorting through that mess would be a lot harder if he was dead. "He's my friend."

"Your friend?" Arwin wrenched her arm free and stepped back, facing Vi without letting Taavin fully out of her sight. "Your *friend* is the Voice?"

"I can explain." Vi held up her hands.

"You lied to me," Arwin seethed, raising her spear. "You lying traitor. Curse you, your father, and your family."

"I didn't lie." Vi worked to keep herself calm even as Arwin spit venom.

"You said you weren't Faithful!"

"I'm not."

"No? You're just aligned with the worst of them all." Arwin swung her spear in Taavin's direction, though her eyes remained glued on Vi. When she spoke, it was with a bitter detachment that hurt more than any word. "I knew you were seeking to infiltrate and betray us from the first moment I laid eyes on you and I was right."

Vi allowed her blood to run cold. She knew the pain on Arwin's face all too well. It was the look of someone you trusted showing their hand and coming up with cards you never dreamed they'd be holding.

"If I had wanted to harm the Twilight Kingdom, I could've," Vi said calmly. "If I had wanted to lead a legion of Faithful though the tears in the shift, I could've." Vi actually doubted that. It had been the watch that had protected her through the tear. But Arwin didn't need to know that. "If Taavin had wanted to move against your people, he would've."

"The Faithful are devious. They don't function based on logic or reason. They act on hate alone."

"You don't have to like us," Vi spoke through Arwin's justified rage. "None of us are pretending to be friends. Our only link is that we're all working toward the same thing."

"I will never be aligned with a Faithful, and especially not the Voice."

"You already are. I need him to teach me how to bring down Raspian, but I need you to get to my father. And you need both of us to settle your old score if you ever want to return home." They didn't have to like each other. They had to work together. That would be good enough for Vi and it should be good enough for Arwin. If they all knew where they stood from this moment forward, there would be no more betrayal, because there wouldn't be any real trust between them. They would trust in their shared goals, and nothing more.

"I don't need you," Arwin seethed. She swung her weapon and pointed the blade right at the soft spot of Vi's throat. "My father may have told me not to come back until I settled my outstanding score, but I think he'd make an exception for bringing him the body of the Voice and his accomplice."

"Harm her and you'll never see the Twilight Kingdom again," Taavin cautioned dangerously. "Harm her and I will ensure every sword and sorcerer at my disposal will rally against you."

"You will not leave here alive."

"Do not underestimate me." Taavin raised his hands. Vi could feel the power gathering under his palms, ready to be brought to life with a word. Power Sarphos had nursed back into him at Vi's command.

One wrong word, and the whole situation would explode into violence and death.

"Listen, both of you, just listen!" Vi pleaded, trying not to move too much. She would've suspected talking would be much harder with a spear through her throat. "We all want the same thing! This doesn't have to be personal."

"You made it personal," Arwin growled. "And I will never want the same thing as a Faithful."

"You do though," Taavin interjected before Vi could. "And I could give it to you."

"What're you talking about?" Arwin's eyes narrowed at him, but she had yet to attack, which Vi took as a victory.

"What do you want more than anything else?" Taavin asked. "You want to see Ulvarth dead, no? You want an end to the Faithful as conquerors? I can deliver that opportunity to you."

Vi watched Arwin shift her white-knuckled grip on the weapon. She was holding the spear so hard that it squeaked as her calloused hands rubbed against the polished wood. The woman seemed suspended in place by her own tension.

"How?" Arwin demanded finally.

"I will give you access to Ulvarth. I know where he lives and works. I know the people who attend him. And I know the back doors that connect them all."

"You lie. No such back doors exist into the Archives of Yargen. The place is a fortress."

Vi had never thought of a library as a fortress. Her image of the Archives, and just where Taavin had spent the majority of his life, were shifting faster than a morphi.

"The Archives of Yargen are old. They've been added to by countless Faithful over the years, each one more neurotic than the last. Each trying to find a new way to protect themselves, escape if needed, or slit the throats of their enemies as they lay sleeping."

"Exactly—slit the throats of their enemies as they sleep. The Faithful are underhanded, so why should I believe you?"

"Because I am proof that such passages exist. It's through them that I finally staged my escape."

"Why would you have to escape?" Arwin seemed genuinely confused. "Why not just command your way out?"

"Because he's been their prisoner for years, and hates the Faithful just as much as you do." Vi dared to speak.

"Silence, you," Arwin growled.

"I want nothing more than to see Ulvarth dead and the Faithful returned to a quiet order built around Yargen—not blood-lust or power." Taavin stole Arwin's attention again with the declaration.

She laughed, bitter and icy. "You're a dog that would bite your master?"

"Let's say my master didn't spare me the rod," Taavin countered with a dangerous edge to his voice. "You don't get to beat this dog and expect loyalty."

"Betrayers, the whole lot of you," Arwin whispered. But she was also clearly weighing her options. Vi did the same, hoping they came to an identical conclusion.

Arwin could try to kill her and Taavin here and now—maybe she'd be successful, but she'd likely die in the process.

Or she could help them settle not only the score with Adela for the sake of her family, but slay Ulvarth as well, for the sake of her people. If she could muster enough faith in Taavin's deal, she had far more to gain. In fact, Arwin would get everything she'd ever wanted. Except there was a loose end in Taavin's proposal—

"And what about you?" Arwin asked, gaze intent on Taavin. "I could slay Ulvarth and you could find another just as ruthless to carry out your decrees."

"They are not my decrees."

"You are lying to save your skin!"

"He's not!" Vi interjected.

"I said silence!" Arwin pressed the spear farther forward. Its razor-sharp edge biting into Vi's throat was far more persuasive than words.

"Hurt her and die."

Arwin's eyes swung back to Taavin and the expression on her face almost had Vi wondering if she'd heard something Vi had not. A devious, deadly smile crept across her lips. "What does she matter to you?"

"Everything." There was no hesitation. No holding back. "She is everything." Arwin's grip faltered slightly; the spear sagged as surprise settled in on her.

What are we?

Vi finally had her answer. She was suddenly too hot and too

cold at the same time, keenly aware of the pain at her throat yet numb and tingling all over.

Everything.

She loved him. And he loved her… despite both of them knowing better. Despite neither being brave enough to say it in such plain terms. Those facts made no difference in the end. They had fallen in love despite themselves. They just had yet to be brave enough to say it aloud.

Taavin continued on as if the very world wasn't shifting beneath Vi's feet. Perhaps he was oblivious to it. More likely, his ground had shifted long ago. So had hers. She was only fully realizing it.

"Help us, help *her* get her father, do whatever you need to do to Adela, and then I will deliver you Ulvarth. And should his head not satisfy your need for justice—if I do not keep my word and do right by you and your people—then at that time, you may have me."

No! Everything in Vi screamed at once. She didn't care if it was justified, or righteous, for Arwin to seek Taavin's life. She didn't care if it was Taavin's right to make this deal. She didn't want to see him harmed. That was the sole thought in her mind.

Yet thanks to the blade at her throat keeping every breath shallow, nothing escaped her lips.

"How do I know you'll keep your word?"

"You'll have to trust me."

Arwin snorted. "Trusting a Faithful? That never worked out well for anyone. Just look at the spot I'm in now." Her eyes swung back to Vi. "*Her*."

"*What?*" Taavin asked and Vi let out something of a whisper to the same effect.

"If I so much as think for a moment that you will go back on your word—if I even *suspect* it—I'll kill her on the spot."

"That's too high a bar. You will be suspicious of my breathing."

"Then you should make an effort to breathe less," Arwin

snapped at him. "It'd do wonders for my mood, at least."

Vi searched the woman's face for any sign of warmth or familiarity, but there was none. This was the same woman who had accused her of being Faithful in the throne room. No, this was worse. This was a woman who had proof of the careful tapestry Vi had been weaving around her.

Vi didn't have the right to hope for anything from Arwin. *This was business*, her mind insisted. It always had been. Friendship was a luxury she could no longer afford.

"Do we have a deal?" Arwin asked neither of them in particular.

"I said—"

"You have a deal," Vi interrupted before Taavin could say something well-intended but foolish. "Help me get my father. Taavin will give you Ulvarth. And if at any point, you think we mean to harm you or the morphi, or that we will go back on our words… You have my life."

THE NEXT HOUR WAS uncomfortable, to say the least.

Vi looked to Taavin. Taavin glared at Arwin. Arwin watched her. None of them said anything. It was silence the entire walk through the forest. An uncomfortable, deafening silence of Vi's own making.

By the end of the day, Vi nearly wanted to scream just so she'd hear something in the too-still woods.

"We should make camp here." Arwin came to a stop just when the forest's edge was in sight. Through the trees, Vi could see a clear dividing line—not unlike where the jungles of Shaldan ended at the Waste. She wondered if this, too, was a scar left on the earth by the ravages of man's squabbles. "Get one more night of sleep somewhere that the only enemies we have to worry about are each other."

"We're not your enemy," Vi said tiredly.

"I'll be the judge of that."

"Suit yourself." Vi held up her hands as Arwin took a few

steps backward.

"Where are you going?" Taavin asked cautiously.

"I'm going to find dinner for myself, and perch somewhere you two don't know of so you can't slit my throat while I sleep." Arwin pulled her mass of golden hair back with a line of cord. "But don't think I won't be watching you."

"How do we know you won't go back to the Twilight Kingdom and return with an army?"

"I guess you'll just have to… how did you put it? *Trust me*," she said with a mocking smile.

The air around Arwin pulsed. Magic rippled in several equidistant rings, distorting the forest around her as though it were the surface of water. Arwin took a small step, then jumped into the air, slipping between the rings. Vi saw the outline of a bird taking her shape, identical to the dark fowl she'd seen when she'd first emerged from the cave nearly two weeks ago.

Before Arwin's feet could touch the ground again, she was gone, and there was just the flap of dark wings as the animal soared away. Vi and Taavin watched her leave, until it was impossible to see her outline from the deepening darkness between the trees.

"We should consider leaving," he murmured. "She could go back and—"

"She won't go back." Vi sighed softly, removing her scythe and leaning it against a tree. "She's exiled if she doesn't finish her mission."

"If the king can make those rules, he can break them," Taavin cautioned.

"I know. But the king who breaks his own rules is a ruler soon to lose his crown."

"Spoken like a true princess."

"Perhaps because I am one." Vi removed her satchel next, setting it down heavily. "Besides, we've made her a good offer. She stands to gain a lot more than lose."

"What's been happening this past week?" Taavin asked

cautiously, looking from the weapon she'd been carrying to the satchel Vi was rummaging through. "I've had precious little by way of information."

"I know, and I'm sorry." Vi sat, beginning to sort through the items in her satchel and looking for the blanket Sarphos mentioned. Of course, it was at the very bottom.

Vi took a deep breath and tried to fill in the gaps in Taavin's information with broad strokes. He remained silent as he positioned himself at her side to listen. The sun was low in the sky when she finally finished.

"So that's it, then?" Taavin nodded at the scythe. "This weapon the king claimed was from the Dark Isle and bestowed on you?"

"I believe him." Vi rested on her elbow and reached for the weapon, surprised once more at how light it was. Laying it across her lap, she slowly undid the upper strap and then unwrapped the cloth tucked around the blade.

Taavin let out a soft gasp. He slowly reached out a hand, then withdrew before he could touch it. There was a reverent expression on his face, as though he gazed on a holy object.

"I take it you believe his claims now, too?"

"Vi… This… It shouldn't exist," he breathed, eyes drifting up to her. "What do you know of its history?"

Vi ran her fingers over the shining crystal of the weapon. It was as if the whole thing—blade and shaft—had been crafted from a single, flawless stone. But there were no marks of the crafter, no sign of any tool on its surface. It was flawless in every way. She closed her eyes, feeling the magic pulsing from it, familiar and yet slightly unnerving at the same time.

The longer she was in contact with it, the more dangerous it felt.

"I've been thinking about that," Vi started thoughtfully. "Trying to piece it all together… I know Raspian's return aligns with the destruction of the Crystal Caverns—so I know the caverns were where he was sealed away. One of my final lessons from my tutors was how my mother had a role in starting the war that led to that destruction, beginning with a crystal axe she found in Soricium. And I know that, in the lore on the Dark Isle, there were four of these weapons—an axe, a scythe, a crown, and a sword."

"Yes, you have the main points…" His hand finally rested on the scythe. Magic swirled up from the crystals, wrapping around his forearm in hazy blue light—as if reaching out to him, before it sank into his skin. His eyes seemed to shine an even brighter green in the fading light.

"What am I missing?"

"Yargen's sacrifice." Taavin looked to her. "When Yargen defeated Raspian in the last great war, she broke off a piece of Meru, sending it into the sea and sealing away Raspian there for what was to be eternity. She then split herself—her power—to ensure he remained in place. A third was bestowed on the Champion as a staff of frozen fire. Another third encapsulated Raspian in the same frozen fire to prevent his return. And the final third remained here on Meru as living flame, to guide her world."

"Frozen fire…" Vi repeated. Before her lips could close, her jaw went slack. *Frozen fire*. "No, not fire," she uttered. What would frozen fire look like, if not magic captured in shining stone, faintly glowing with a power greater than any man had ever known? Stone that would turn to coal—obsidian—when the power diminished. "Crystal."

"Just so," Taavin said solemnly.

"But all the crystals are dark and dormant since the caverns were destroyed… why does this persist?" Vi stared at the weapon in her hands that still glowed with a life of its own over a thousand years since it was first created.

"As I said, the Crystal Caverns sealing away Raspian were one part of her power. The other part was given to the Champion in the form of a staff to guard the tomb and ensure none sought it."

"Then, this is not from the tomb… but from the staff?"

Taavin gave a noise of affirmation. "That's my belief. The

Champion was to use the power of Yargen bestowed on him to guard the tomb and ensure none came to seek it out. For over two hundred years, the Champion kept his lonely watch. But as with most things in time, details become hazy… the severity of a threat is forgotten.

"Eventually, people came to the Dark Isle, and the Champion did not send them away."

"Why?" Vi couldn't imagine why the Champion would turn back on his duty. But she also couldn't imagine spending centuries alone. The notion that such could be her own fate, that it wasn't beyond the realm of possibility, crawled under her skin like invisible bugs.

"Why does any man turn from duty? Love, loneliness, family… I can only speculate," Taavin murmured softly. Vi wondered if he was speaking about himself and the duty he'd left by fleeing Risen for her. "But he wasn't foolish. The people he let on the Dark Isle were mostly human—all born without magic."

"Without magic? I thought everyone has magic outside of the Dark Isle?"

"The vast majority do… but once in a hundred, a child is born without. And this world is not kind to those without magic."

"So they left to seek out a new world, kinder to them," Vi finished, imagining ships of dozens setting out for a barren land—an empty continent without anyone to judge them.

She'd always been told that people in the Solaris Empire feared sorcerers for their magic because it was rare, strange, and dangerous. Perhaps the real reason they hated sorcerers so fiercely extended back past anyone's memory. Extended toward the first peoples of the early kingdoms. People who held a deep resentment for magic—any magic—because it forced them from their homelands.

"And the Champion let them settle, either out of loneliness, or because he believed that these peoples without our magicks could be of no threat to the tomb."

"But… Solaris did eventually develop magic." Vi thought of

the elemental powers of her home. "You called the magic of my land fractured…" Then, it dawned on her. "The Champion used the power of Yargen within him to split the staff into an axe, a scythe, a crown, and a sword—the Crystal Weapons of lore."

"From the fractured magic of Yargen, new magic seeped into your world." Taavin gave a solemn nod. "And that new magic, the lure of power, drew them to Raspian's tomb long after the Champion had relinquished his mortal form by giving up Yargen's power. It was her magic that was extending his life beyond the hold of time, and when he no longer possessed it, he left our world."

"We turned Yargen's magic against itself. We were the ones to destroy it," Vi said in horror.

Everything made sense. Such loathsome, horrible, wretched sense. The fear of magic ingrained in people from the start, bolstered by the Champion's warnings, and cemented by time. Conventional wisdom maintained that the crystals in the Caverns tainted people, perhaps as a result of a power mortal hands weren't intended to hold. Or perhaps Raspian's power was slowly escaping through them, and that was the source of the deadly crystal taint.

"But this means there's hope." Vi clutched the scythe tightly. "This is hope. In the ruins of old Shaldan, I saw a figure of a man and a woman fighting etched on the wall. I didn't understand it then… but it was Raspian and Yargen. The likeness must have been made by those who remembered their story. Yargen wielded a *staff* against him. If this comes from that staff, then maybe we can fight him with it. Maybe we have a chance."

"I can only hope." Taavin looked from the scythe to the watch around her neck, then to her face. "I know that Yargen's power seems to seek you out. And that the other living piece of Yargen is in Risen, with the archives. If there's any information that will help us crack this—" his fingers landed on the watch "—and figure out a way to fight Raspian… it's in Risen."

"We'll go there." Vi closed her hand around his. The man's

skin was warm under her fingertips.

"As soon as we rescue your father." Taavin's fingers worked their way around hers, winding tightly together. A dull, sweet ache filled her chest. Even with the world on the line, he knew she would go to her family first. He knew her focus would be her father until Vi knew he was safe. And he was not doing anything to pry her from that task when he so rightfully could.

"Thank you," she whispered.

"For what?"

"Beginning to tell me everything."

"There's so much I've yet to say," he murmured, his other hand reaching up to lightly tuck a strand of hair behind her ear. "I'm just afraid to say it."

"Me too." Yet, in saying that much, she knew what was unspoken for both of them. She didn't need anything more for now.

"Just as I'm afraid I have already cursed you by it." Taavin brought her hand to his lips, kissing her knuckles. "I never wanted any of this to happen to you." Remorse flooded his words. Vi gave a small, bitter laugh.

"*Never?* Not even when I was just the woman who supposedly tortured you in your dreams?"

Taavin began to protest, but stopped when he saw the makings of a grin on her lips. "Hush, that didn't count."

His thumb brushed over her lower lip, his eyes dipping half-closed as he watched the motion with delicious intent. Vi's focus was shifting as well. The tiniest of touches flooded her with such bittersweet delight.

"If that doesn't count, then you couldn't have cursed me," Vi said gently. "Because the red lines of my fate were drawn by the goddess long before you met me."

He looked at her as if seeking permission. She tried to convey it to him as she held his hand tighter, as she leaned forward—awkwardly across the scythe still in her lap.

"Perhaps, we're both equally cursed," he murmured darkly,

close enough to her face now that she could feel his breath on her mouth.

"Perhaps."

They were from two different worlds. When it all was over—assuming the world didn't end—she would still be the crown princess. He was still the Voice. They couldn't be anything else to one another.

What does she matter to you?

Everything.

Their lips brushed, feather-light. His mouth quivered slightly, and a groan escaped him. Taavin's fingers curled around her jaw and he pulled her closer.

The scythe was forgotten, sliding off her knees as Vi shifted her weight forward. He leaned back and she followed him. She couldn't breathe if she didn't know her lungs were in time with his. She couldn't move if his hands weren't on her. Taavin laid back on the leafy ground, Vi atop him. He was light and life and everything she'd ever wanted without knowing it.

She was clumsy and inexperienced. But what she lacked in confidence she made up for in enthusiasm. She allowed every shift, kiss, and caress to fill her, fuel her.

If they were destined for heartbreak, she would steal as many nights as she could along the way.

It took two days, but on the afternoon of the second, Toris at last came into view.

The town was set aside a small inlet. Cliffs stood tall toward the sea, but they gradually sloped down as they wrapped around the sloping hills to the valley where Toris proper sat. A winding dirt path connected the town with a larger stoned road that ran from the Twilight Forest out into the great plains beyond—plains mottled with dark brown patches that looked alarmingly like decay.

"Grim little place, isn't it?" Arwin muttered. She was still barely on speaking terms with them.

"I suppose," Vi agreed purely for the sake of not starting an argument. She didn't see anything that grim. It looked like any other town.

"It's been a sheer delight to patrol these past few days," Arwin continued. She'd spent most of her time ahead, rather than with them. The scouting served a purpose they hoped to capitalize on, but Vi also suspected it had given Arwin an excuse to get away from them. "But the pirates haven't moved since I first flew in; they're on the ship in the morning, wreak havoc in town, drinks at the brewery, back at night."

"You're sure they haven't seen or sensed you?" Taavin asked.

"I'm certain I would know if they had. One of them would've been after me in an instant if he'd known."

"Who?" Vi asked.

"Another morphi. He's been flying the edges of the Twilight Forest relentlessly."

"Fallor?"

Arwin rounded on Vi the moment she said his name. "You know him?"

"He's been after me." Vi watched Arwin closely. There were emotions Vi couldn't quite put her finger on in Arwin's reaction. Fallor was obviously an exiled morphi who had betrayed his people, but there was more than that in Arwin's expression. This felt personal. "Do you know him?"

"He's an exile of the Twilight Kingdom." Arwin backed away from Vi, looking to the cliffs.

"I know that. But what I mean is, was he anyone… significant in the Twilight Kingdom before he was exiled?" Vi clarified. "Anyone important?"

"Not to the masses."

"But to you." Taavin keyed into the unspoken implication.

"Back off, Voice," Arwin snarled. "Whoever he was to me is

none of your business."

Vi's lips parted as her jaw relaxed. She put all of Arwin's past actions, statements, reactions together in a second.

"He's Sarphos's brother." The family likeness was undeniable, now that she saw it. "He's the one you were engaged to."

Who else would make a woman like Arwin leave her home and her post as guard to her father? Who else would have committed such a deep betrayal? Vi knew firsthand how hard it was to crack through Arwin's callous exterior. If she let someone in, and that person betrayed her, they would be forever dead to her.

Vi could relate.

Arwin's grip on her staff tightened. Her eyes were glued on Toris.

"What of it?" she muttered.

"We don't need personal feelings getting in the—"

"I will not have *you* lecture me, Voice." Arwin glared between him and Vi, a look that said she had seen them waking side by side more than once. "This is personal. All of it is."

So much for being just business, Vi thought grimly.

"Yes, Fallor was my betrothed. Yes, I was young and didn't see him for what he was. I made the mistake of trusting him. Those are the faults I've had to live with for years since."

"He was the one to set up the shift around the Isle of Frost, wasn't he?" Vi asked.

"Yes. He wanted to learn the royal shift—the way we pulled the Twilight Kingdom out of reality. He'd always been fascinated by the notion… but something changed. Mere curiosity became a relentless pursuit. I didn't know then, that Adela had already got to him. And fool that I was, I didn't want to lose him, so I gave in."

Vi stared at Arwin's detached and determined eyes. The woman had her jaw clamped so tightly, the muscles in her cheek twitched.

"When the time comes, I have to be the one to do it." She was talking about murdering a man she'd loved enough to marry at one point. "Neither of you will take this from me. I have to be the one to kill him."

"Are you sure?" Taavin asked, far too gently for a heart as ragged as Arwin's. "You and he were—"

"He's yours," Vi interrupted. Arwin looked directly at her now with all the same murderous intensity. "Adela took something—someone—from me, too. A woman who was a sister to me until I learned of her true nature. She was taken in by Adela, just as Fallor was. I had the satisfaction of revenge in her death. You will have your satisfaction today."

Arwin gave a small nod, the beginnings of what looked like a new foundation of shared understanding in her eyes. If Vi had read it correctly, it was coming from the last place she would expect. Without a word more, Arwin leapt from the crest of the hill on which they were standing. The shift rippled around her, and she was gone in a blink, a bird soaring off down to the town, ready to implement their plans.

18

"JAYME?" TAAVIN ASKED as they started down the sloping field toward the main road into Toris.

"I don't want to talk about it." Vi looked over the crops and land as they passed between fenced pasture and open field alike. An uncomfortable quiet had overtaken the hill. The houses were still; not a single farmhand was out tilling soil.

"I haven't asked about her because I assumed she'd decided to stay behind, but you said—"

Vi spun, rounding on him. "I said I don't want to talk about it. She was a traitor, nothing more." Her voice dropped softer as she tried to quell the rage. Vi wrapped her hand around his. "I don't want her name coming from your mouth. I don't want to associate anything of you with betrayal." She'd already toed that dangerous line once on finding out the true nature of the Faithful.

"Are you all right though?" Taavin held her fast as Vi tried to pull away. "Jayme was—"

"Jayme was no one. She was a traitor. She betrayed my family.

It's because of her Adela has my father. It's because of her Adela had me. I gave her a traitor's death and I don't want to speak about her ever again."

"Very well." Taavin released her and Vi quickly started on again.

It felt like she was running. But she didn't quite know from what. Just the mere thought of Jayme filled her with brutal darkness—not unlike the darkness that seemed to be settling on the land.

They quickly discovered the reason why no one was working the fields—the houses were abandoned. What crops there were had rotted where they stood. Tilled soil had turned to hard, cracked mud, small deserts breaking up what Vi assumed was once fertile farmland. An ox rotted where it fell, eye-sockets oozing white.

"Raspian's power grows," Taavin said, giving voice to their shared thought.

"How much longer do you think the world has?" Vi wondered aloud, gripping the strap attached to the scythe.

"Not long enough."

When they arrived in the town, there was no main gate to enter Toris. The buildings crept up from the earth. Most of the construction was waddle and daub, an ashy clay the same color as the raw earth of the central town square. By all appearances, it was not a wealthy place—but a few buildings boasted shingled roofs or intricately decorated glass in their windows. Where would money like that come from in a place like this? *Nowhere good*, Vi thought wryly.

"Good luck," Taavin whispered. "I'll keep you in sight. Stick to the plan."

"I will, and good luck to you too," she breathed back, before they promptly headed in opposite directions. Taavin wandered off to the side and Vi continued along the town square until it evolved into a market that extended right down to the docks.

Here, Vi could appreciate the majesty of Norin.

There were only two main docks and neither could tie up anything larger than a medium-sized vessel. The larger ones were anchored in the sheltered bay formed by the cliff sides, or further still, out at sea. Only dinghies were tied up at the docks.

It seemed incredibly… small. She didn't know what she'd been expecting, but after the greatest port in the world, followed by a magical city of twilight, Toris seemed lackluster. Though Vi supposed there were average or below-average towns everywhere, no matter how fantastical certain elements of the world were.

"Don't just stop in the road, girl." A man pushing a wheelbarrow laden with feed veered around her. "Daydreamin' kids."

Vi quickly stepped to the side and mumbled an apology. She positioned herself by the side of a building where she could see the whole market. She scanned the seabirds on the docks and the silhouettes against the late afternoon sky, looking for Arwin or Fallor, but Vi saw neither. Not that Vi could tell Arwin apart from a normal bird. The oil-slick plumage of the nightwisp was common in this region of Meru.

She settled into Step One of the plan: observe and be noticed.

After an hour of normalcy, Vi debated if she should move elsewhere in the town. She'd taken two laps around the market trying to make herself visible, and was just about to wander the docks when the sound of shouting filled the air.

Vi glanced over her shoulder and into the small store she'd been passing. Two men argued within, nearly coming to blows. The larger of the two scooped the smaller by the collar, pushing him out.

"Get out and stay out, you bloody cheat." The store clerk? Building owner? Gambling pit master?

"Just because you lose doesn't make someone a cheat." The man stumbled, but recovered before he ended up face-first in the mud. The larger man was already heading back inside with a shake of his head. "The nerve of some people," the shorter man muttered. His eyes drifted to Vi. A smile slowly spread across his lips. "All you want to do is play a game of cards and they cast you out, am I right?"

She hummed noncommittally, looking back to the market.

"Say, you wouldn't be interested in a game of cards, would you?" The man walked over, despite her showing no interest in him. That was a positive sign.

"I'm not really one for cards." She looked him up and down, trying to remember every detail Arwin had recited after her scouting. Could she be confident this was one of Fallor's men?

"Come now, that can't be true. I'll buy you a drink and we can play a game of cards—low stakes, I promise. We all enjoy a good game of cards now and then."

"Buy me a drink from there?" Vi pointed to the brewery.

"Only place in town." He gave a hearty laugh. As he tilted his head back, the collar of his shirt shifted, revealing the edge of a tattoo—three lines disappearing under fabric. A trident, she was sure.

Vi made a show of debating the proposition. But her mind was already made up. She had accomplished Step Two of the plan: find one of Adela's men.

"Perhaps you're right." She tried to make her agreement sound reluctant. "It's been a while since I let loose."

"Excellent, this way!" He linked his elbow with hers and pulled her off across the market.

Vi skipped a step to get in pace with him. She tried to take a quick glance around the market. There were shopkeepers talking with farmers about the harvest, rumors being swapped by two old men sitting at the docks… but no indication of Taavin or Arwin.

They'd better be playing their parts and in their positions.

Because Vi was about to initiate Step Three: offering herself up on a platter to Adela.

Vi would make herself an easy target and lure the pirates into a false sense of security. Then, when they were busy apprehending her, Taavin and Arwin would strike. With the pirates taken care of, they would steal their vessel.

Simple enough, and it was going off without a hitch so far.

Vi followed her escort into a dimly lit tavern. There were a few patrons scattered throughout, each scarier-looking than the last. Two burly men were seated at the far end of the bar. Another table was filled with a loud group well into their cups. Two others played darts at the back wall.

If Arwin and Taavin were to be believed about this town, most if not all were pirates—though not all Adela's men. Toris was a quaint fishing town on the surface, hub for the trade and sale of pirated goods underneath.

"What'll you have?" The man sat at one of the bar stools.

Vi did the same, feeling her legs slide into the divots made by countless patrons' thighs. "Whatever you're having is fine."

She needed to keep her wits about her and didn't plan on drinking much. Vi took one more scan of the bar while he ordered—Taavin and Arwin were nowhere to be seen.

"Two ciders, then." He motioned to the bartender. "The name's Charlie, by the way." Charlie raised his hand to his forehead, right between his brow, and lowered it. "And you are?"

"Marnie," Vi lied deftly, not knowing where the name had come from so easily.

"And where do you hail from, Marnie? You certainly have a strange accent."

"Monlan." Her days studying maps in the Twilight Kingdom had paid off. Monlan was a land-locked city, one she doubted pirates got to often. But for good measure, Vi added, "But my father was from Hokoh, so I grew up with a weird mix of accents." She knew very little about these cities other than the fact they were on opposite ends of the continent and surely produced different accents.

Vi was saved from having to elaborate further by the bartender placing down two heavy clay flagons.

"Two silver."

Charlie produced two silver coins from his pocket, laying them on the bar. On the front of the coin was a simple carving of three circles, a line intersecting them—a symbol Vi actually recognized. Her eyes widened slightly, trying to take it all in before the bartender collected it. She'd seen that symbol carved into the old trees of Soricium.

At least, she thought she had… Because the coin was gone with the bartender in a blink.

"To new friends." Charlie lifted his mug, holding it between them.

"To new friends." Vi lifted her mug as well, tapping it lightly against his. She brought it to her lips, taking a long sip. It drank somewhat like an ale, small bubbles tickling her tongue. But this was sweeter and had a bright, fruity quality—almost like an apple juice. Placing it back on the bar, Vi stared in wonder and said, with no acting required, "It's… really good."

Charlie gave a hearty chuckle. "Toris has a good brewmaster. He does creative things with palm fruits. Horse and Cask is one of my favorite bars to stop in when I'm sailing my route."

"What's your route?" Vi asked, hoping the query sounded casual.

"Oh, I go all over," he answered coyly. "I've been from Risen to Toris and beyond."

"So you're a trader, then?"

"Of a sort." *Pirate*. Definitely a pirate. "Do you have an interest in sailing?"

"I do, actually." Vi smiled sweetly.

"You must… Growing up in a land-locked city, I imagine a girl like you would find the high seas thrilling." He gave a nod to the scythe Vi had strapped to her back. "Though it looks like you may have been coming here to find work in a field. Too bad they're all going barren."

"I only told my father I was going to find work on a farm," Vi said lightly and took a long sip of her drink. "I wouldn't have traveled all the way from Monlan if I just wanted to farm."

"Then what do you want?" He leaned in slightly.

"Adventure," Vi said conspiratorially, leaning in as well.

"You're right, I do find the idea of traversing the ocean thrilling. But not half as thrilling as the men on those vessels." She said it so effortlessly, so smoothly, that Vi even shocked herself. She was a far cry from the girl stumbling over her words at the Noru races.

His pupils dilated slightly—just as she'd seen Taavin's do right before she was about to kiss him. Vi glanced down at his mouth, licking her lips for good measure. And then leaned away with a playful grin.

"I like the sound of that." He gave her a smirk and was back to shuffling his deck. "So I know we discussed a game of cards, but let's make it interesting, shall we?"

"What do you have in mind?"

"We could gamble for coin?" The way he said it told Vi he had no expectations of that actually happening. So she played right into those expectations.

"I'm afraid I don't have much. It'd make for a boring game." Vi made a show of thinking hard. "Say, if you're a trader… your vessel must be nearby."

"Anchored off the other side of the cliffs," the fool announced proudly, further confirming all of Vi's suspicions.

"Then how about this: if I win, you take me with you to wherever it is you're going next?"

"And if I win?" The man asked with such obvious expectation. Vi hadn't thought of that and she quickly rummaged her mind—but came up with nothing. Luckily, he had an idea for her. "How about you still come with me… but you're not my guest. You're my deck wench."

"All right," Vi agreed quickly. It didn't matter what she bet. This was all going to end with him having a sword in his gut. "I'm feeling lucky."

"Let's hope you are, Marnie."

Charlie shuffled and dealt. Vi's eyes were focused on his motions, trying to catch the sleight-of-hand she knew was there. She was so intent on him that she didn't even notice the man who had entered from around the back door behind the bar.

A hand covered the cards and Vi followed the forearm up to a shoulder, to the man who had a smirk smeared across his ruddy beard. Fallor leaned against the bar as though he owned the place; even the bartender gave him a wide berth.

"You don't need to flip those," he said. Vi narrowed her eyes slightly, not wanting to show for a moment that her hands were trembling. "I can already tell you, your luck has run out." Then louder, to the other patrons, "The rest of you—out."

As though issued a command from a lord, the rest of the bar came to its feet. There was some grumbling from particularly red-faced patrons in the back corner, but no one objected. Even the bartender calmly set down the glass he'd been polishing and left through the back door Fallor had entered from.

Fallor wasn't supposed to be there. Vi's heart was racing. He had been in his bird form almost exclusively according to Arwin, patrolling the edges of the Twilight Forest. They were supposed to have a chance to take out his lackeys before he even knew they were there. Or, at worst, catch him mid-fight.

They'd planned, and Fallor had been one step ahead.

"Now, last I saw you, you were traveling with the Voice himself. Where is he hiding?" A pulse of magic rushed over her, disorienting and powerful. Vi vaguely recognized it from the field that night—it was the same magic that had disrupted Taavin's Lightspinning.

"I'll never tell you." If Taavin was still operating to plan, he was positioned somewhere in the square, hood up, as inconspicuous as possible, watching the entrance of the bar.

"No matter." Fallor turned his eyes to her. "He's not here now. Good. I wanted to speak with you alone."

"And what makes you think I want to listen to you?" Fire crackled around her balled fists, singeing the bar. "I'm much stronger than when you last met me. I could—"

"Spare me." Fallor waved a hand through the air, as though he could wave away her words like a bad smell. "If you so much as make one move against me, your father dies."

"What?" Vi whispered. The spark stilled, iced over with horror.

"Adela is the *pirate queen*—do you think she rules by being everywhere at once?" Vi stayed silent, allowing him to continue in whatever way he wanted. "No, she delegates, as any good ruler would. As I'm sure you would understand."

"Get to your point," Vi ground out through clenched teeth.

"I know you're not threatening me, are you?" Fallor looked to Charlie. Charlie leaned against the bar, fumbling with a large hoop earring in his ear. "Because, you see, Charlie here has an imprinted token of Adela's."

Vi's hand went to her watch at the mention of an imprinted token. She knew what that was. It was what had started it all—it was the same as her watch. Though Vi had never seen one made, she knew they could be used to communicate over any distance.

"He's not the only one." Fallor's grin grew wider, verging on the point of mad arrogance. "Each one of my crew has a token. If Charlie so much as thinks you'll use one bit of magic, he'll activate it. If he, or I, don't return in due time, the rest of my crew will activate theirs."

Each one of his words was like a hook to her flesh—digging in, pulling, peeling, exposing her. They had so quickly put together a plan… none of them had thought for one moment Fallor would have a better one to counter with.

"So, not one more word. Not one bit of fuss for my colleague here," Fallor commanded as Charlie slowly collected his cards. "You're going to come calmly onto my vessel, or your father dies. Do you understand?"

Vi bit the insides of her cheeks. She wanted to scream *juth* at him until her voice was hoarse. She wanted to burn the whole brewery down to ash, them inside. She wanted to sever head from spine with the blade of her scythe.

Maybe Fallor was lying. Maybe she could kill Charlie fast enough that he couldn't get to Adela. But could she kill Fallor before he flew away? Could she, Taavin and Arwin take him down in the middle of Toris—a town where the majority of the population would stand for Fallor? And even if they could, how long until the pirates aboard Fallor's ship would raise an alarm?

These were risks Vi couldn't take—not with her father's life on the line.

All she could do was nod.

"Good." Fallor pushed away from the bar, starting for the back door. "Now, remember Vi, your father's life depends on what you do next."

More than you know. Because while Fallor had out-planned them, he had also overplayed his hand. Vi knew what she was dealing with. And most importantly, Fallor had just confirmed *her father was alive*. He was too valuable a bargaining chip for Adela to let him die without gaining something for it.

All Vi had to do now was get out of this.

19

"COME ON, PET." Charlie grabbed her wrist and tugged. He was stronger than he looked, *much* stronger, and if Vi didn't go along she risked having her shoulder popped from its socket.

The moment they were out of the bar he turned, starting for the port. Vi's eyes scanned the crowd, searching for Taavin or Arwin, but she found neither. The sun was already setting, casting the world in a bloody glow.

"Let's get to the boat before dark. They say pirates are in this town… we wouldn't want anything happening to you, now would we?" Charlie gave a laugh at his own joke, carrying on for everyone to hear, knowing full well that even if someone knew what was happening, no one would dare stop one of Adela's men. "The path is narrow. Don't try anything funny or you may fall off."

Charlie pushed her ahead along the narrow way that wound along the cliff-side just above the docks. Vi glanced back over her shoulder. Where were Taavin and Arwin? By now, they were supposed to be following her in some form or fashion, ready to strike against Fallor when the moment presented itself. But if they did so in a way his crew on the ship could see… her father would be dead. Unless Adela was playing games about that, too.

Vi's hands balled into fists, her nails leaving crescent moons in her palms. She hated this game of cat and mouse. She scanned the skies until she found a large bird soaring on the updrafts off the cliffs. She couldn't make out its color, but Vi would bet it was ruddy. Fallor was flying high enough to stay in sight of the boat on the other side of the cliffs.

They had barely crested the top of the cliffs. Vi knew from Arwin's reports that there was a switchback on the other side of the ridge, leading down to a narrow beach. There, a boat was anchored not too far off—a rowboat used to transport men to and from the beach. Vi scanned the plateau; she couldn't see the vessel, which meant they couldn't see her—she hoped.

Vi intentionally tripped herself.

She caught the toe of one boot on the heel of the other. Her hand raked against the rough wall for support, but she prevented her fingers from catching. Vi allowed herself to fall hard, knee splitting underneath her clothes.

"Get up." The man took a wide step around her, hand on his earring. "Get up or—"

"I tripped." Vi looked up at him, pushing herself onto her elbows. "I tripped, that's all. I'm coming, I promise." She leaned back onto her heels, rubbing her palms on her pants, trying to stall for every second she could. "Shite… I scraped my knee." Vi made a show of inspecting the bloody spot on her clothes.

"I don't give a rat's arse about your knee. Get up or it's your dear old father who's getting his blood spilled."

Vi put her palms on the ground, tucking her head and trying to sneak a look over her shoulder. Fallor was flying lower—no doubt coming to inspect the disruption. Vi took a slow breath.

"I said—"

Magic crackled through the air. Vi could almost hear on the wind the blessedly beautiful words of *loft dorh* leaving Taavin's lips. There was a spark of light, and the eagle seized mid-air.

Vi turned back to Charlie. Fallor may have tried to throw a wrench in their plans, but those plans could still be salvaged. They just had to move very quickly and stay out of sight.

"Get up or—" The pirate never had a chance to finish his sentence.

"*Juth calt*," Vi snarled, going right for the heart.

Charlie seized, wide-eyed. He crumpled on the spot, just as Jayme had, blood dripping from his lips. She had vowed to Fallor that she would see Adela's brood suffer. But Vi found herself beyond caring. There wasn't time to exercise the dark art of vengeance.

The world was ending and all that truly mattered were results.

The screech of a bird drew her attention. A nightwisp—half the size of the eagle—shot through the sky like a black arrow. Vi watched as it twisted mid-air, wicked sharp talons leading the charge. Before the eagle could fall from the sky, the nightwisp had dug its claws into it, using momentum to pin the eagle against the cliff wall.

Vi turned away from Charlie's body, keeping herself crouched and praying the men on the boat hadn't seen their comrade fall. Down the path was Taavin, shifting his stance and readying more words.

"Taavin," Vi called as loud as she dared—hoping the wind and crash of waves masked whatever of her voice would carry. Taavin looked up to her. "They have imprinted tokens to talk to Adela. If the ship sees a struggle, they'll have my father murdered!"

His eyes widened, no doubt putting together all Vi had in an instant: they had to move fast and with certainty.

With a pulse of magic, Arwin replaced the bird, landing on the path and sliding back slightly. The dazed eagle shook its head, slowly regaining its footing. When its eyes focused, they were trained on the spear Arwin was pointing at its neck.

"*Loft dorh hoolo.*" Vi thrust her hand at Fallor right as he was about to take flight. Her glyph surrounded him, stalling him in place.

Even with *hoolo*, she could feel him wriggling and writhing against her magic. He struggled to break free of her tethers and Vi realized she didn't know how long she could hold him. Sweat beaded on her brow.

"You're not leaving." Arwin ruthlessly stabbed her spear through the bird's wing. "Free him of your magic."

Vi did as Arwin bid. This was her kill, her moment of revenge. They didn't have much time, but they had time enough for this.

Fallor rippled in and out of existence. When he reappeared, his clothes were torn, blood pouring from deep slashes in his chest that Arwin's talons had made. His arm was pinned to the path, blood pooling around Arwin's spear.

"Arwie, let's not—"

"Don't," she snarled. Vi would've snarled too if a man like Fallor had tried to give her a nickname like *Arwie*. "If you have any scrap of honor, any trace of the man I loved, you will stay in place and let me gut you from naval to nose."

"Because you love me, don't gut me," he pleaded hastily, holding up a hand. "I-I never wanted to hurt you."

Arwin slowly tilted her head to the side as Fallor spoke. Vi couldn't see her expression, but she could see Taavin's reaction to it. And that was enough for Vi to know it was every bit as venomous as her tone.

"You had a poor way of showing it."

"Let me fix it. I can fix this," Fallor continued hastily. "Who would you rather leave here with—me, or the Voice and a foreigner? Adela will pay anything for them. She'll be indebted to the Twilight Kingdom. She's a worthy ally to have on your side against the Faithful. With her ships, you could even stand up against the Swords' armada. Start with the seas, then attack Risen."

Arwin went very still.

"Arwin…" Taavin started cautiously. There must have been something on her face, if only for a moment, that made him uncertain. But his expression changed in the next instant, as the woman herself no doubt swung on a pendulum of emotions.

Vi watched as Arwin ripped the spear from Fallor's arm and, in one deft motion, gouged his throat with the blade. The man fell back, took one last gasping, gurgling breath, and died. Vi didn't feel one drop of pity or remorse. But right now, it didn't matter what she felt.

It mattered what Arwin did.

"Don't think this means I like either of you now," Arwin said softly. "It's not that I chose you."

"You had a job to do." Vi finished the thought.

Arwin slowly turned and gave a nod. That was enough for Vi to count on her for what needed to come next.

"The two left on the ship. If they suspect something is amiss, they'll contact Adela and she'll kill my father." Vi looked to Taavin. "You'll wear Charlie's clothes and we'll ride out on the rowboat. Arwin, you fly in from behind. We strike them both at once, but only when we're certain we can take them out cleanly. If one survives for even a second, it could be enough time to relay a message."

A jump off the cliff, followed by a pulse of magic, and a bird rising on the updraft was all the affirmation Vi was going to get from Arwin. But she didn't need more. Time was of the essence now.

Still, she found herself staring at Fallor for one last, long moment. He was dead. She imprinted his bloody corpse on her memory. He was dead, and he couldn't come for her again.

Vi turned away, crawled toward Charlie's body, and began to tug at his clothes. "Taavin, help me, he's heavy."

The man appeared across from her, wordlessly helping lift the dead weight to yank off Charlie's long tunic.

"How did you kill him?" Taavin asked warily.

"*Juth calt*—I shattered his heart."

"You what?" he whispered.

"I shattered his heart, maybe his lungs, too."

"I've never heard of *calt* used that way," Taavin said warily.

"Well, now you have." Vi held out the shirt. While she waited for Taavin to take it, she ripped off Charlie's earring with her other hand and pocketed it. "I've had a long road to get here, and I've had to improvise along the way. Now, wear this—the sun is getting low and I don't want to test their patience."

Taavin yanked off his shirt. It was the first time she'd seen him in such a state of undress. The scar on his face extended down past his collarbone. There were other scars, too. Smaller, fainter, curving and intersecting… almost as if someone had taken a knife and lazily drawn lines across his body time and again until their bloody art left a permanent mark.

No doubt from Ulvarth, she thought darkly

He finished tugging the tunic overhead, bringing her back to the present.

"Good thing pirates are embroiled in shady business." Vi lifted the hood of the tunic. "Of course they'd have sewn a hood to everything."

"Vi, you saw—"

"Later." Vi gave his hand a squeeze, knowing where his mind was. She didn't have to know the stories behind those markings to know that it was likely something very few had seen, and that he'd want to keep them hidden. "When we're on our new boat."

Taavin gave a small nod as he stood. Vi did as well, taking a step in front of him. She kept her head down, starting on the switchbacks with Taavin close behind.

"Remember, I'm your prisoner. Push on my back a little, make it a good show."

Taavin did, but the shove was so weak Vi had to intentionally put a stumble into her step. She fought the smallest of smiles. Even acting, he didn't want to harm or demean her.

Sure enough, there was a rowboat moored on the beach. Just off the shore was a single vessel—narrow and fast looking with one main sail and a secondary. Perfectly hidden from view of the town.

Two silhouettes were drawn against the setting sun, standing at the railing. Vi held up a hand, blinking into the sunlight as they trudged through the sand toward the small skiff. She didn't see Arwin anywhere.

"Do you see her?" Taavin asked, pushing on the rowboat. He strained against the sand—clearly not a trained deckhand. Vi hoped Fallor's other crew would assume Charlie drunk.

"No," Vi murmured. She wanted to help him, but she doubted Charlie would've asked for help, so she just stood there, waiting and watching the other two pirates aboard the boat.

"What if she left?"

"She wouldn't. She still has to disable the shift on the Isle of Frost." Vi hoped to the Mother above that remained true.

The skiff was in the water and Vi boarded first, Taavin behind her. He took up the oars, pulling them hard through the water and fighting against the waves crashing along the beach. Vi looked at the surf splashing up against the sides, remembering the last time she had been in a rowboat like this.

Then, she had been a prisoner. Now, she held the upper hand.

"When we get close enough that you can be sure to hit your mark… use *juth calt*," Vi said under her breath. Taavin looked up at her, panting. "I'll take the woman, you take the man."

"I don't think I can…" Taavin nearly stopped rowing, continuing in an instant. "I've never been trained to use it in that way. What if I explode their whole body?"

"Then there's less for someone to find when the corpse washes ashore." Vi stared at him. In that moment, it was painfully clear that he was sitting where she had been months ago. He had never killed—at least not with his own hands—and had never considered doing so. Vi swallowed hard, looking over her shoulder. "Just freeze one, I'll take care of the rest."

"Charlie," the woman cupped her hands to her lips and yelled. "Have you seen an ice moon?"

It was clearly some kind of code—a code neither of them knew the answer to. "Get a little closer," Vi whispered, glancing over her shoulder. Taavin kept rowing.

"Charlie," the man bellowed, "have you—" At that moment, he was cut short by a sudden jolt of magic. Vi heard him make a gurgling groan before he landed heavy on the deck with a dull thud.

"*Narro h*—" the woman began.

"*Loft dorh*," Taavin said, eyes focused on the woman.

Vi turned in the rowboat, careful not to knock it over or rock it so much that Taavin lost his focus. Arwin was on deck pulling her spear from the dying man. Before she could thrust it through the woman, Vi uttered, "*Juth calt*."

With that, Taavin's magic was broken, and the woman fell limply to the deck. Arwin stood at the railing, looking down at them, regarding them both warily. Vi locked eyes with her, as if in warning.

As if to say, *Yes, beyond the Twilight Forest we are as deadly as you feared.*

20

"THROW DOWN THE lines," Vi called up to Arwin as they positioned the rowboat under two arm-like pulleys at the stern. "I'll tie them off to the boat and you can hoist."

Arwin walked over to the low deck rail, looking down at them. She wore a stony expression that guarded her innermost thoughts. Instinct would have Vi just as guarded, but she kept her face calm, relaxed. She didn't want to risk escalating tensions in an already-tense situation.

Without a word, Arwin threw the ropes down and Vi caught them, quickly fastening them off to either end of the dinghy. "Stay here," she murmured to Taavin, pulling off her scythe and setting it in the boat.

Grabbing one of the ropes, Vi hoisted herself upward with a small jump that set the dinghy to rocking. Kicking out her feet, Vi landed them on the side of the larger vessel. One hand over the other, one foot then the next, Vi walked up the side of the ship with the help of the rope.

"What was that for?" Arwin asked.

"Now you don't have to pull alone." Vi rubbed her palms on her thighs, working out the aches in her fingers.

"That was unnecessary. I could've done it on my own."

"Or you could accept help and make it easier." Vi moved to one of the pulleys, making sure everything was looped through correctly. Unsurprisingly, the riggings seemed to be in top shape, ready to go at a moment's notice.

"All right, let's get our dead weight aboard."

They pulled together until the small boat was up at deck level, tied off the ropes to secure the dinghy in place, then Vi reached out a hand for Taavin. He wasn't too proud to take it, allowing her to help him over the railing and onto the deck. Vi reached in after him, retrieving her scythe and slinging it back over her shoulders. She was finding the longer she carried it, the less she liked being without it.

"You're fairly confident on a boat," he observed.

"This is the third I've been on." Vi shrugged. She had a strong suspicion that neither Arwin nor Taavin had been on a ship. Maybe Taavin. But if he had been, it wasn't in any kind of sailing capacity.

Vi knelt down, taking the earrings from both of the pirate's ears. They were identical to Charlie's, further confirming her suspicion that this was the token.

"Are those some kind of trophy?" Arwin asked.

"No, they're communication tokens to Adela," Vi pocketed them. "They could be useful… or perhaps not. Either way, I'd rather keep them than lose them to the sharks. Now, a little help please?"

Taavin and Arwin both helped Vi push the bodies to the railing, twisting them until they slipped through the wide gaps and off the sides of the boat. Vi fetched a bucket attached to a long rope, drawing up seawater and splashing it across the deck twice to remove some of the man's blood. There was still a long red streak on the main deck, but it was clean enough. Spending too long cleaning a pirate ship felt like an exercise in futility.

"All right." Vi wiped her hand across her brow, taking stock of the setting sun. It was little more than a sliver on the horizon now. Was it just her imagination, or was it setting earlier than normal? "We should set sail before anyone can find the bodies. I can imagine there's at least a few in Toris who will be sympathetic to Fallor and Adela's men."

"Or who will at least want Adela's gratitude and bounty for turning over the people who killed them." Taavin leaned against the railing, a few steps away from the red smears.

"Taavin and I will give the ship a quick once-over and see the status of things. Arwin, will you fly back and gather up our supplies?" When the woman didn't immediately respond, Vi turned to face her. She looked back at the coastline with a conflicted expression. "Ar—"

"I heard you." The woman leapt into the air, soaring upward and back toward the cliffs where she'd stashed their bags.

"What's her problem?" Taavin muttered.

"She got what she wanted, and doesn't know how to feel about it," Vi answered easily, beginning a quick inspection of their new vessel.

The ship was fairly simple, one mainmast and a foremast. The rigging she'd already used on the davits was some of the most complicated of all the ropes. There was a tiny cabin that was half in the hull and half beneath a shallow quarterdeck. A break in the smooth lines of the deck toward the bow betrayed a storage area Vi inspected immediately, confirming rations within.

"You think she regrets killing Fallor?" Taavin followed behind her.

"Regrets? No." Vi shook her head. Thinking of Arwin right now felt like looking into a mirror that reflected what was inside, rather than out. Vi could recognize emotions and feelings—all the ones she didn't want to see. "But I don't think it's so black and white. Fallor betrayed her, yes. But she also loved him, once.

Those feelings were real to her before the discovery that they hadn't mattered to him."

"This isn't Jayme," Taavin whispered gently. Vi slowly lowered the storage hatch and turned, looking up at him from her crouched position. "Arwin has known who Fallor was for a long time."

"Some emotions are as sharp as knives that don't dull or rust with time." Vi stood, looking out over the water and seeing the dark bird gliding on the ocean breezes. "Even if you're right, after dreaming of his death for so long… how would it feel to actually get it? To have it be so easy?"

"I don't know."

"Me neither."

Jayme's death had been swift and sudden, and perhaps easier. Vi didn't have to live with the knowledge that the woman who had wronged her was still out there breathing. The chapter was closed, and while she still carried the wounds of it, she could try to move forward.

Arwin had been in stasis for years. Vi could only imagine how she must be feeling now.

The woman in question landed lightly on the deck, a pack over her back and Vi's bag strapped across her chest. She tossed them haphazardly into the cabin, reporting, "No problems with them."

"Arwin."

"What is it, princess?" Arwin sighed, leaning her staff against the entrance to the cabin. There was no door, merely a curtain stretched across the opening to keep out the night's chill and salt spray. She looked at Vi warily and, for a long moment, they merely held each other's gaze.

Vi didn't know what she'd intended to say. Had she wanted to tell Arwin that she understood in some way? Did she want to say it was okay to feel whatever it was she was feeling?

"Thank you for your help." In the end, Vi couldn't pry. Just as she didn't want anyone to pry about Jayme, she wouldn't inflict that on Arwin.

Rather than retorting back with something about having no other choice, or begrudging them both, Arwin gave a grunt in acknowledgement. That was the best Vi could hope for, and she let the matter drop.

"Taavin, how much do you know about rigging?" It was past time for them to be on their way.

"I grew up in the Archives of Yargen and spent most of my time making use of the fact. I may not have had a chance to apply knowledge very often, but I certainly collected it."

"Good, let's give you a chance to practice, then. You and Arwin will help get the sails ready while I plan a headway." Vi started for her satchel in the cabin, retrieving her journal and a compass. She didn't even make it back out before they were bickering.

"I wouldn't untie that."

"You said to untie this."

"No, untie *this* one." Taavin tapped on a rope knotted to a peg. "Not that one."

"Well you should be more clear."

"I'm being perfectly clear."

Vi ignored them, starting up to the quarterdeck. Consulting her maps and the compass, she quickly decided on the best headway. "Lower the sails. Taavin, as we sail out, please hide the ship."

"Why?" Arwin asked.

"I don't want anyone from Toris seeing us leave." She didn't want to give Adela any warning that they were coming. Though, despite her best efforts, Vi fully expected the woman to know. She was far too cunning not to. Vi was beginning to doubt that anything happened on the seas without Adela somehow knowing.

The wind hit the sails and Arwin finished tying them off as Taavin intoned, "*Durroe watt radia.*"

Light swirled out from him in glyphs that slowly wrapped up the whole vessel. They spun slowly over the deck, cutting through the walls of the vessel harmlessly. Magic settled on every surface with a dull shine.

Vi adjusted the tiller, checking her compass as the ship began to turn.

Arwin made a noise of disgust. "Even your magic feels slimy."

"Slimy?" Taavin asked. Vi was genuinely curious as well. Could Arwin detect a tangible quality to Taavin's magic, or was this just another opportunity for her to make a jab at the Faithful?

"It slithers, feels like wet seaweed over bare skin."

"Your magic feels different for us, too," Vi spoke before Taavin could, stealing Arwin's attention.

"It does?"

"I wouldn't say slimy though… uneasy, perhaps."

"Yet another reason why the morphi are hated without cause."

"Doesn't that go both ways?" Vi looked down at the woman on the main deck. "I mean… if you describe Lightspinning as slimy… doesn't that also sow the seeds of dislike?"

"Don't talk like you know things, Dark Isle dweller," Arwin grumbled.

Vi chuckled softly and turned her eyes back to the horizon. There was the same empty feeling she'd known all too well lingering between the spaces of Arwin's words—the feeling of not belonging. She hadn't belonged anywhere in her Empire, now she didn't belong with those of Meru. Arwin was right: she didn't understand because she wasn't a part of this world.

But would she ever have the chance to be a part of anywhere?

"Ignore her," Taavin said, placing a hand on Vi's shoulder. She didn't realize he'd even walked over, a testament to how lost in thought she'd been. "Do you have a headway?"

Vi nodded.

"How long until we arrive?"

"Depending on the wind… Perhaps two days? Three at most?"

"I'll know when we near the shift that surrounds the isle," Arwin declared with a determined stare over the bow of the boat. "I'll feel it."

"That's helpful, then." Vi looked back to shore. The land had become a narrow strip of black in the darkening night. The vessel was, indeed, a fast one.

"If we have a couple days, let's sleep in turns and get decent rest so we're ready," Arwin suggested, starting up the quarterdeck. "I'll take the first." Coupled with her thoughtful expression, the offer sounded almost like an apology for her earlier remarks.

"All right." Vi released the wheel and passed the compass to Arwin. "Head due southeast. We won't start cutting south until we get to the Diamond Sands isles."

"Simple enough." Arwin said. "You two get some rest."

Taavin paused, his gaze lingering on Arwin. Vi couldn't tell if the woman was choosing to ignore his hesitation, or just hadn't noticed. Not wanting to risk either, she tugged lightly on Taavin's sleeve.

"Come on, she's right. We should catch some shut eye."

He followed her down into the cramped cabin, crouching through the curtained opening. Vi pushed aside the heavy tarp, hooking it on a peg.

"Leave it," Vi requested as Taavin went to swing the tarp back down into place. "I'd rather it be open."

"Are you sure? The moon is full tonight—it may be quite bright."

"I'll sleep better if I don't feel like I'm trapped." Vi settled her scythe on the floor between the two hanging cots on either side of the narrow cabin.

"Trapped… like on Adela's vessel?"

She paused for a breath, then sat heavily. Vi rubbed her eyes. At every turn of her journey, no matter how much rest she managed to get at the end of the one previous, she somehow managed to feel even more exhausted.

"Yes," Vi said finally. "The idea of being tossed around in the hull of a ship again, confined, is one of the last things I think I could tolerate right now." In truth, there were a lot of things her patience was running thin on. This was just at the top of the list based on circumstance.

"Then we'll keep it open." Taavin took the bed across from her, laying down as she did.

Vi stared out the opening, the night sky barely visible over the rocking bow. Above her, Arwin stood, alone with her thoughts—and the knowledge of what she'd finally done to the person who'd harmed her.

Without warning, her chest was burning—brighter and hotter with every breath. She tried to slow her breathing, to stave off whatever was rising within her. But it was hopeless.

"Taavin," Vi croaked. "Are you still awake?"

"Of course," he whispered back. "What is it?"

"I…" Words escaped her. In the darkness, the burning of her chest flushed her cheeks and pricked at her eyes. All she wanted was comfort. Just the slightest bit of comfort. Why was that so hard to ask for? The longer the world forced her to be strong, the harder it was to accept weakness of any kind.

"Vi?"

"Can I sleep with you?" she forced out, finally.

Taavin shifted to face her, eyes shining in the darkness. Vi's shone as well, but for a different reason. He pressed his back against the wall and lifted an arm.

Slowly, heart racing, Vi moved from her bed to his.

The cots were far too small for two people. Vi felt like half of her was hanging awkwardly over the side of the bed, which meant Taavin undoubtedly had no room for his considerable height. Even if she'd wanted to be modest, there was no room to be.

Vi's eyes fluttered closed. No, she didn't care about modesty. He was warm. His arm snaked around her waist, hips twisting, legs intertwining… Taavin's whole body fit flush against her, as though it were made to be there. His comfort was enough to soothe the burning of her chest and racing of her mind.

"I find myself thinking, more and more, that I am cursed." Her fingers laced with his.

"You are not cursed, you are chosen." Taavin held her tighter.

"Are they really so different?" Being *chosen* had led her down a path she had never wanted to walk—a path laid well before her birth. "If I try, I can tie everything together. My mother's illness, my father's plight… It all leads back to the Crystal Caverns, Raspian's return. It's all connected. Were they being punished for me?"

"I can't claim to know the will of Yargen. None of us can."

Vi closed her eyes, shutting out the world. "What if it's all my fault? What if they suffered because they had to be the parents of the Champion?"

"Or what if everything was merely chance? Or what if their actions were what made you, out of everyone, the Champion?" His voice was low and soft, whispering across the shell of her ear. "I don't know what the truth is. I don't know if it lies here." His hand freed itself to rest on the watch around her neck. "I don't know if it's in the scythe. I don't know if there's a greater meaning to any of it."

"That's hopeful," Vi said sarcastically.

"I won't lie to you." The words sent chills down her spine. "I can't promise your mother will live, or your father will be saved. I can't assure that you will find your way back to your family and homeland, and selfishly… selfishly I…"

"You what?" she probed when he hadn't continued the thought after several breaths.

"Perhaps, selfishly, I don't want to see you go."

A sad smile crossed her lips.

Romulin had accused her of deserting her post. But everything Vi had done had been for her Empire and for the greater good of the world itself. If anything could inspire her to act selfishly, it would be Taavin. Perhaps, after all she'd been through, she wanted to be selfish, too.

"But…" Taavin continued, finally. Sorrow filled his voice, matching the sorrow that was beginning to fill her chest, extinguishing the burning fears that had risen there earlier. "I can guarantee one thing."

“What’s that?”

“Should you want it… allow my arms to be your home. Here is home. Because, as I told you once, here is where you are safe.”

The last holdouts of her stress and tension vanished. Vi sank further into his embrace, and his arm tightened around her waist, pulling her to him. There wasn’t a part of her that wasn’t flush against him, and Vi savored every bit of warmth he had, wrapping it around her like a blanket.

Despite feeling the most relaxed she’d been in some time, Vi disrupted the comfortable position they’d found to turn to face him. He didn’t seem surprised; a small smile played on his mouth, and his eyelids were heavy but not with slumber. Her arms were tucked between them, fingertips on both of his cheeks. Vi looked from his lips to his eyes.

This was not the man she’d kissed in Solaris. She was not the woman who had seized a moment in a tent for fleeting joy. She saw him for who he was—tortured and hopeful. A man who had done wretched and wonderful things alike. And she was no different.

Imperfection fit them both well. Maybe life had carved enough parts out of each of them that they needed each other to feel whole.

She leaned forward, and Taavin moved to meet her. His breath was hot on her cheeks, lips soft under hers. He kissed her tenderly, almost timidly. Vi pressed forward and Taavin’s arms tightened around her, drawing her close. A hand knotted in her hair. A sigh escaped from her lips between slow, languid, sensual motions that ignited something completely new.

Something worth holding onto as long as time allowed.

21

THE SCYTHE SAT STRETCHED across Vi's lap. Beside her, Taavin manned the helm as she ran her fingers along the smooth crystal. Magic swirled underneath her fingertips, trapped beneath its glassy surface. She'd spent the day running drills on deck with Arwin again and still felt no more confident using the weapon for battle.

"You'll master its use," Taavin said encouragingly from her side, as though he read her mind. "And I'll be scouring every book on the crystal weapons the moment we return to the Archives of Yargen for anything that could help you." Taavin pushed his sleeves back and massaged both his wrists, the golden bracelet shining in the light of Vi's flame, before grabbing the wheel again.

Suddenly, Arwin emerged from the cabin like a wild animal. She bolted on deck, hair a golden bird's nest, stance alert, head jerking about before her attention landed on them. "It's close."

"Is it?" Vi reached for her journal, opening it up to the maps she'd been referencing. They'd been sailing for about two days, so it wasn't impossible. Her maps were beginning to get as murky as the dark waters spreading beneath the hull of their boat the further they got from the Twilight Kingdom.

"I know the shift better than anything." Arwin turned slowly, looking to the left of the bow. "I can feel its magic in the air."

"How far do you think it is exactly?" Vi flipped her pages, looking at the sketched grid lines and trying to estimate where on their course they were.

"I'll know soon enough. I'm going to fly ahead and see if I can find it. I'll scout out a good point to enter through the shift." Arwin began to run for the bow. "For now, just stay on course. I'll find you!"

Before Vi or Taavin had a chance to reply, Arwin had leapt from the vessel, shifting into her form as a nightwisp and taking to the skies. Vi followed her with her eyes as long as she could. But she quickly lost sight of the woman in the darkness of the early morning. She didn't have a working clock at this moment, but the days seemed to be getting shorter, the nights longer.

Arwin returned a short time later, landing on two feet after a pulse of magic and starting right for the helm. "I'll take it from here to get us through the shift." Taavin stepped aside and allowed her to take the wheel. "There's a cliffside I think we can dock by without anyone seeing, near some caves that'll take us right into their stronghold."

"Will they know when we've crossed through the shift?" Taavin asked Arwin.

"I don't think so. They didn't seem aware when I crossed through in my nightwisp form." An intense look of focus was painted on her brow.

Vi stared forward at the open sea, her heart already racing. All of her maps—now safely tucked in her pack below deck—told her that somewhere in this vast ocean of nothingness was an island. But as far as she could see on the dark horizon, there was nothing but water below and a sea of stars above. The horizon remained unbroken.

There was a growing electricity in the air. The sensation of a terrible storm on the horizon pulled Vi's hairs on end from head to toe. She glanced over to Taavin, who wore as intense a look as Arwin's. Did he feel it too? Was she the only one who felt the edges of something transformative about to occur?

"Brace yourselves" was the only warning Arwin gave.

The ship rocked with a violent pulse of magic. Rigging groaned, the sail slumped in the still air. The world around them shifted: stars brightened, light kissed the edge of the horizon before darkening once more to the near-blackness of the hours before dawn. Vi kept her eyes open and held her breath.

Like a veil lifted, the Isle of Frost shimmered into existence before them.

It looked like a great storm on the horizon, a frigid mass of ice and snow fogging the air around a giant, craggy rock. Vi squinted, trying to see through the haze, but it was nearly impossible. The sea itself had begun to freeze all around the coast, the waves calmed by the unnatural atmosphere of the shift.

Somewhere, in all that, was her father.

Another pulse shook her. But Vi kept her feet under her, using only a hand on the deck rail next to her for support. She kept her eyes forward, waiting for the pop in her ears that signaled the shift passing.

"We're through. Take back the helm," Arwin said. She jumped down from the quarterdeck, heading to the bow much as she had before. "Full sails. There's not much in the way of wind here. Follow me." The woman leapt over the water and took to the skies as a bird.

"I have the helm." Vi rushed to Arwin's prior position.

"I'll man the sails."

They rounded the island, the only marker of their vessel the white foamy trail that faded into blackness behind them. A blustery gale picked up as they plunged into the perpetual frost swirling the coast. It crept under her clothes, clawing at every inch of exposed skin. Vi knew this cold. She'd felt it before on Adela's vessel.

She pushed the spark forward and felt its warmth bloom under her skin. Heat radiated off of her, melting snow to rain before it could settle on her. By the time they reached the ice that ran the perimeter of the coast line, her hair was slick against her face and neck.

"Shouldn't they have more patrols?" Vi asked in a low voice. She'd seen the first specks of light in the distance at the far end of the isle. "It seems too empty, too quiet."

"I imagine they feel fairly confident in their barriers… and the fact that no one in their right mind would walk into Adela's stronghold."

"Good to know we're all mad." Despite the weight of the situation, a grin struggled to form on her cheeks. "Here I thought I was alone in that."

"You're not alone. Not in any way." The thin line of his mouth almost made a smile.

Arwin continued to glide ahead, banking and turning on the swirling currents that surrounded the island. Vi worked to keep up, following her as closely as possible. But as the ice became thicker—its frozen tendrils reaching out into the surf—she began to fear for the vessel's integrity.

Luckily, Arwin seemed to think much the same. She did a wide loop before returning to their small ship.

"I think we should tie off here," Arwin announced. "The cliffs will keep their eyes off us, and there are no outposts I could find on this side of the isle. Those caves will be our way in." She pointed to a dark spot tucked into the side of a cliff.

Arwin and Taavin made quick work of striking the sails as Vi debated if she should take the scythe with her or not. Ultimately, she decided against it. She wasn't skilled enough yet to use it, and carrying it onto the island only risked it falling into Adela's hands.

After disembarking, Arwin guided them forward toward the yawning darkness of the cave. "I only scouted far enough to make sure this was an unguarded route. Once we cross onto the hillside beyond, we're all on our own."

Slowly, twilight filtered in, penetrating the blackness. It was carried on the icy wind and snow that piled at the mouth of the cave. The three emerged into a snow bank up to their knees, looking down over a small slope that ended with what could only be described as a pirate city.

Much like Beauty's Bend, the Isle of Frost was crescent-shaped, surrounding a lagoon packed to the brim with ships of all shapes and sizes. The coast of the lagoon was riddled with waterways. They snaked through ice-covered buildings, functioning as main thoroughfares for the pirate city below.

"How many pirates do you think there are?"

"Too many," Taavin said grimly.

"Enough to make our odds worse than grim."

Vi found herself agreeing with Arwin's assessment. This was certain suicide. They were walking into the hornet's nest. "Shall we, then?"

"Today seems as good a day to die as any other." Arwin gripped her spear tightly. "I'm going to dismantle the shift and then I'm back to the boat. Good luck finding your father."

"Wait, aren't you—"

"Going to help you?" Arwin interrupted. "I've helped you both more than enough to get here and I've my own business to settle. Hopefully, I'll see you both, plus a fourth, before things get bad enough that I have to set sail. It'd be a pain sailing that thing alone, so don't die."

Before Vi could get in another word, the shift pulsed around her and Arwin took to the skies.

Vi and Taavin trudged through the snow, sliding on packed ice and tripping on hidden roots and rocks. Vi glanced behind them, trying to cement the path of their return journey in her mind. The falling snow and blustering wind were already filling the tracks they'd made.

They stepped onto the narrow walkway that lined a canal.

People were busy going about their business as they would in any city. She heard music drifting over the wind and snow from taverns; laughter rang out in harmony to a shouting match. Vi saw a man slam his hand down on a card table in a gaming parlor as they passed.

It felt chillingly normal.

She looked for someone who looked like they knew what they were doing. Vi scanned the men and women on the streets, and in the boats traveling the canals. She searched the signs and doorways for any indicators, no matter how subtle.

If Adela was smart—which Vi had no doubt she was—she wouldn't let everyone know where she was keeping a prized prisoner. Even if the whole isle knew Adela had the Emperor Solaris, she would keep his exact location a secret. Which meant Vi needed someone—

She stopped dead in her tracks, a flash of red in the twilight catching her eye.

"What?" Taavin asked.

"I saw an elfin'ra."

"*What?*" he echoed, but this time the word said a whole lot more.

"Come on." Vi started for the building she saw the man slip into.

"I don't think we should be going toward the people trying to maim or murder us in order to bring about the end of the world."

"This whole island is trying to maim or murder us," Vi whispered hastily back.

"Yes, but the whole island can't bring about an evil god with our blood," Taavin muttered.

They slipped into a narrow walkway between two buildings that ended in a cliff-side. At their backs were the cliffs they'd entered from—and if the bluffs before them were anything like those, then these too had countless passages winding within them, no doubt attached in some way to the building.

"What're you looking for?" Taavin breathed, his back pressed against the wall as Vi leaned forward slightly to peer into a window.

"Anything." It wasn't a good answer, but her mind was moving too quickly. She barely had time to form her thoughts, let alone explain them to him. The elfin'ra she'd seen was inside, standing at the side of a table surrounded by four others—one more elfin'ra, a morphi, and what appeared to be two humans.

Vi brought a finger to her lips, motioning to Taavin for silence. Leaning against the wall on the other side of the window, Vi pressed her ear to the frosted wood of the building. She covered her other ear with a hand, closing her eyes and focusing on the muffled words, only catching every few.

"… patrols are…"

"So far there's no sign…"

"They'll… up soon…"

"Adela will want… keep them alive…"

"… prisoner?"

"Guard change will happen… far he's being quiet and…"

"… keep a close eye."

Vi struggled to piece together the missing blanks. She listened until her pounding heart drowned out the soft words. Was she hearing correctly? Or was her mind playing tricks on her and feeding her what she wanted to hear?

They had little else to go on. Her suspicion that Adela would keep the elfin'ra close was supported by the conversation. Surely they were talking about her and Taavin showing no sign of coming to rescue her father.

There was a shuffling of chairs and Vi leaned forward slightly. Whatever little council she'd been overhearing disbanded. The two elfin'ra headed back, the others started for the door. Vi motioned for Taavin and they stepped back further into the shadows of the alley as half the group left the building, none the wiser that the very people they were on the lookout for were right under their noses.

Vi kept her ear against the wall, hearing the creaking of wood, the closing of doors, the dull metallic thud of locks being engaged and disengaged. She ran toward the back of the building, getting ahead of the elfin'ra moving through it. Leaning forward, Vi peered through the frost clouding the window of a dark room.

She squinted, making out shapes moving within it. A flash of red. Vi pulled back, pressing herself flat against the wall. Taavin mirrored her motions, trusting her without word or explanation.

"... thought I saw something." One of the voices from earlier drew near.

Vi wriggled her fingers, keeping her magic at the ready. The spark was eager, curling like lightning right at the edge of each of her movements.

Another voice said something Vi couldn't make out.

She glanced at the window, trying to make herself as flat and small as possible. The heat radiating off her beaded the frost into water at the bottom edge. *Please don't let them notice*, she silently prayed.

"It's nothing." Footsteps thudded away, carrying the voice with it.

Vi closed her eyes, breathing, counting to twenty. The room was completely still for the second half of her count. She dared to lean forward, peeking through the lower corner of the window.

The room was empty.

Vi stood, stepping around Taavin, pressing her ear back to the building. There were no more sounds of doors. No more footsteps.

"We're going in." Vi started for the main street with wide, hasty steps. She had no idea when, or if, the previous three people would return. Or if another group would soon arrive.

No one stopped them as they rounded the front. Vi's hand fell on the metal handle, pushing on it. But it didn't move.

A scream wriggled up in her throat, but it escaped as a few hushed words.

"*Juth calt.*" The metal around the lock splintered, cracking. Vi pushed her way in before anyone on the street could look in their direction. Rushing over to the table, Vi propped up a chair against the door underneath the handle. It wouldn't stop someone for very long, but it would at least keep the now-broken door closed at a glance, and make noise if anyone tried to follow behind them.

"Was that wise?" Taavin asked, as though she could somehow change her actions now. Vi shot him a dumb look that seemed to communicate the fact. "The morphi have a way to sense when Lightspinning has been used in their lands. What if Fallor has set up the same here?"

Vi hadn't considered that. "Even if he did, it's likely as Arwin said: he's the only one who would've been able to sense it. And even if there are morphi here who can sense it—they have Lightspinners on their crew, remember?"

Taavin nodded, looking over his shoulder warily.

"*Juth calt,*" she said again to the next door that barred their progress, glancing over her shoulder at Taavin and making sure he followed her into a narrow hallway. Vi continued to press straight back through the building and toward the cliff wall.

A short humming sensation pulsed through the air. The air pressure changed and Vi's ears popped. She rubbed them; Taavin did the same. They exchanged a look as a bell tolled, its frantic, high-pitched ringing echoed over the whole city.

"Any chance that isn't for us?" he asked grimly.

"Us or Arwin, and it doesn't matter which." Vi pushed forward, no longer holding back with her magic. "*Juth calt!*" It exploded from her, knocking down the final, heavily locked door at the end of the hall that led to the back room she'd seen from the alleyway.

"A dead end?" Taavin turned, looking back the way they came. So far, no one was in pursuit. But Vi suspected it wouldn't be long until someone was. If the pirates knew she would be coming for her father, then they knew right where she'd be headed.

"No, there's a passage here." She knocked along the back wall softly. Her hastening heartbeat led to trembling hands. But she tried to keep her rapping as quiet as possible. The pirates may know they were here given Arwin's presumed progress on the shift, but they hopefully didn't know where they were just yet. "Help me look."

Taavin lifted a hand. Vi felt the swell of magic like a rolling tide around her ankles. "*Uncose*."

The unfamiliar word rattled her bones. Magic ignited around his fingers, exploding forward from the glyph—most of it bouncing off the walls in an array of sparks. However some sank in like water slipping through a grate.

"How…"

"*Uncose* means to expose truth," he explained, starting for the wall where the magic had vanished. "It's a word Yargen recently gave me."

"Convenient, when you were looking for a way out of the Archives of Yargen." Taavin pushed in a knot of wood and the whole panel slipped open—jagged at the edges to completely hide the passage behind. He motioned for her to take the lead and Vi did so without hesitation. "Can I use that word?"

"Unfortunately not… It's a word given to me by the Goddess herself. I doubt I could teach you if I tried."

"If we survive this, I may want you to try." Her voice dropped low as they started into the narrow passage. It was rough-hewn and natural in appearance—much like the caves they'd entered through—but this one was far better maintained and… she heard voices.

"… hear the bells?"

Vi recognized the voice from one of the two elfin'ra from earlier. She slowed as amber light danced off the outlines of stones, pressing her back against the wall. Taavin did the same on the wall opposite.

A second voice. "Do you know what it means?"

Vi pressed her eyes closed, taking shuddering breaths. She had to keep her head about her. She couldn't give in to hope—not yet. Not when there was so much risk still and so much at stake.

"It means your darling daughter is here." The first voice again. Vi inched forward. Her magic was building to an inferno inside her, ready to be unleashed on the whole room. It was a rage she didn't know she'd been carrying. A rage she knew could melt the whole island into the sea.

"She thinks she can save you." The second voice again.

Let there be only two.

She and Taavin inched forward to the mouth of what looked like a cavern. From Vi's field of vision she could see a row of cells. Two were occupied with the husks of other unfortunate souls Adela had deemed too valuable or too lowly to give the comfort of death—people she already knew she couldn't risk trying to save.

She was here for one thing only.

"She's like a lamb, coming to slaughter."

How many? Vi mouthed to Taavin silently. He held up two fingers, confirming her earlier suspicions. They could manage two.

A deep chuckle interrupted her thoughts. Its rasp echoed through the caverns and was attached to a voice richer than even Romulin's. Even weary and worn, Vi knew the sound. She'd know it anywhere in this wide world.

"I think it's you who will be slaughtered." Vi felt as much as heard her father's declaration.

"Do you think you can scare us?"

"No, and I think that will be your downfall. You should never underestimate a Solaris… least of all my daughter."

Magic swelled on pride. It flowed out of her as sparks of fire and light, dancing on waves of power and heat that scattered off her skin. Vi pushed from the wall, swinging her hand in the same motion. Power for the glyph was already collecting under her fingers before they turned. Vi took a breath.

"*Juth mariy!*" One of them hissed. The glyph shattered and Vi used it like a starting gun on a line.

They'd been paying attention to the wrong hand and the wrong glyph.

"*Mysst larrk,*" Vi breathed between wide steps. Her right hand was held behind her, grasping the sword that bloomed from the light under her palm. She swung it wide, putting all her force behind it, both hands clasped around the grip.

It sank with a satisfying crunch into the elfin'ra's side. Vi shredded bone and sinew, dark pride rising within her. It felt good to wield a sword again.

You should never underestimate a Solaris... least of all my daughter.

She'd prove her father's words right as he watched in shock and awe.

22

THE SCREAM THE ELFIN'RA let out was sweeter than any music she'd ever heard.

"*Mysst xieh*!" Taavin's voice called out from behind her. A shield appeared at Vi's side. Magic ricocheting off of it. "*Loft dorh*." The elfin'ra at her left was frozen still.

Vi had only taken her attention off the man before her for a moment, but it was long enough for him to grip the blade of her sword with a hand, blood streaming from between his fingers as he ripped it from his side and her fingers. She moved to take a step back, but wasn't fast enough. His hand clasped her face.

His dark blood smeared across her skin, red lightning crackling between the blood and his fingers as he pulled away.

"*Narro vah'deh*." He rasped at her.

She knew what *narro* meant—acts of the mind. But *vah'deh* was a new and foreign phrase. It rumbled across her uncomfortably in a dissonance that made Vi's teeth clench to the point of pain. There was something distinctly *wrong* about it.

Something that made her toes curl and her head hurt instantly.

His eyes flashed a brilliant red, brighter than anything she'd ever seen. So bright, her mind went blank. The world was awash in that crimson shade. Shadows carved shapes from a bleeding reality before her, but Vi could no longer make sense of what she saw.

This is wrong, something in her screamed—a voice she knew once. It was her voice. But she couldn't figure out how it had become so distant. She couldn't fathom anything. Her mind wouldn't move. Every time a thought formed it was gone, falling through her fingers like the magic that poured from them.

Another scream and Vi awoke back to the room, not as she'd left it.

The elfin'ra who had been holding her was ablaze, thrashing to try to put out the flames. The other elfin'ra had lunged for Taavin and the two tumbled on the floor. Her head was splitting in two, pain seeping out from her ears. But Vi forced her thoughts to work enough to conjure the symbol and sounds she needed.

"*Juth calt.*" This time, the other elfin'ra couldn't stop her. The one assaulting Taavin crumpled as Jayme had on the beach, blood dripping from his mouth. Vi turned in place, repeating the process before the remaining man could put out the flames. "*Juth calt.*" As soon as the glyph was gone, Vi gripped her head, wincing in pain. "Mother above," she hissed.

"Vi—" Taavin pushed himself from the ground, rushing to her. "Let me—*halleth maph*—better?"

"More or less," Vi mumbled. He had stinted the pain, but a dull throbbing in the back of her skull promised it'd be back with a vengeance soon enough. She needed to find out what that elfin'ra had done to her. But first…

She turned to face the jail cell, and the man within.

Her father was a shade of his former self. He looked more like the man on the beach than the man in her memories—but somehow, even worse. His clothes hung limp on his emaciated frame, torn and tattered. Dark circles lined his sunken eyes and cheeks. Icy shackles Vi recognized coated his wrists.

But his eyes were alight, shining in the darkness. They were eyes Vi knew well from looking into the mirror.

"Do you know who I am?" she whispered, even though Taavin had only just said her name. She was overcome by the inexplicable fear that he might somehow deny her. So much had happened. She was so far and away from the girl he'd last met years ago when he'd managed to escape the pressures of ruling to visit her in the North.

A smile spread across his cracked lips. "I would know who you are anywhere. Not even a haircut can hide you from me, my daughter."

"I've come for you." She took a slow step forward. Her voice echoed in the cavern. Or maybe it just echoed in her ears. Vi couldn't be certain. "I've sailed across the world for you. I've come to bring you home, father." Vi looked to the heavy padlock on his cell, not even bothering to search for a key. "*Juth calt*." It fell with a heavy *clang* and Vi swung the door open.

"I should scold you for this—coming to such a dangerous place." Even as her father spoke, there was a prideful smile on his mouth. He stared up at her as though in a daze, as though Vi had become the Mother herself.

"Let's save the scolding for when we make it out alive." Vi knelt down, looking at Adela's icy shackles. "Taavin?"

"It's strange magic." He stepped forward, looking over her shoulder.

"It stints my power." Aldrik cursed under his breath—colorful language Vi had never heard from her father before.

"I know, I wore them once." Vi glanced up at her father, then to Taavin. "It took a bunch of fire to get them off me."

"Then I'd try fire," Taavin suggested. "If Adela really is from the Dark Isle, her initial training may be closer to that of a Waterrunner than anyone on Meru—like your training with fire. But you may want to hurry."

"Are you ready?" Vi looked to her father. Fire shouldn't hurt a

Firebearer… but her magic seemed so different from his that there was a twinge of worry she may actually harm him.

"Yes."

Vi placed her hands on the shackles.

The ice was so cold it burned her skin. Even the initial flames Vi pushed forward were snuffed in a puff of steam. She narrowed her eyes, pushing through the barrier. More flames, more power.

"Taavin, *starys*," Vi ground out through clenched teeth. Her magic was hardly making a dent on its own.

Without hesitation, he uttered, "*Juth starys.*"

A glyph appeared around her hands and her father's. It swirled slowly in orbit above the shackles. Fire blazed inward from its outer rings in a breathtaking display of power. Vi was a wildfire compared to the measured elegance that was Taavin.

Fire around her. Fire within her. Fire within her father.

Call it forth, she silently pleaded. Sweat dotted her brow. Adela's power would be stunning if it weren't so stubborn.

All at once, the ice shattered, dissipating into steam before it could even hit the ground as water. Taavin's glyph vanished, but Vi's and Aldrik's hands were still engulfed in flame. Her father shifted his grip, taking her hands in his. Flames danced up their forearms, illuminating the grimy jail cell in bright yellows.

They slowly stood, the fire remaining on her father even after their hands dropped.

"Are you ready?" Vi asked him.

"To get out of here? More than ever."

She nodded at her father and turned, starting for the exit. Taavin fell into step beside her, his long strides almost putting him out in front. Aldrik took a step and stumbled. The sound of his body hitting the open bars of the jail cell rang in Vi's ears.

"Father!" She hurried back over to him. "What is it?"

"He's weak." Taavin assessed the obvious.

"I can't say they were the most mindful about how much, or what, they fed me," he said grimly. Aldrik's eyes, full of sorrowful dread, swung to her. "I'm sorry, daughter… after you came all this way…"

Don't consign yourself to die! She wanted to scream at him. Not after all she'd gone through. Not when the pieces of her family were finally all within reach. He was like a firefly: brilliant, blazing, and fading all too soon.

"You will not apologize to me," she said firmly. "You will move." Vi looked back to Taavin, a plan quickly forming in her head. "Taavin, I need you."

"Anything," he said hastily. Perhaps a little too hastily, judging from the sideways look her father gave her.

"Put my Father's arm around your shoulders. Support him. Get him to the boat."

"Vi—" She wasn't sure which one of them said her name first in that disapproving tone. But Vi wasn't about to let either finish.

"One hand, manage *halleth*—heal anything you can on him before moving, then sustain *maph* on the same hand to stint his pain so he can push through." Vi knew pain was only a small factor. Exhaustion and malnutrition were the bigger ones. But she could only do so much. "With your other hand, *durroe watt*. Only focus on those two. Conceal yourselves and get out of the city. Don't do *sallvas*."

"Why not *sallvas*?" Taavin asked slowly, horror already creeping into his voice. He knew what she was planning. He knew it from his sad eyes to the slight tremor in his words.

"I'll be making enough of a commotion that it won't be needed."

"You can't do this." He took a step toward her. Vi held out her hand, slowly walking past him with a straight arm barring him from coming too close, as though he was some wild animal.

"I can, and I will. Because you both need to get out of here alive and you and I both know you're no fighter."

"Vi, these pirates are deadly and well trained," her father cautioned.

"So am I." He'd seen what she'd done to the elfin'ra, hadn't he? "Wait a moment, begin healing, then move. I'll only need a minute to bring about destruction."

A sinister grin found its way onto her lips and Vi turned before either of them could notice. They didn't need to see her like this. She barely wanted to see herself like this, and some part of her curled up in the far back of Vi's consciousness, remaining oblivious to the horrors she was about to unleash.

She'd entered the isle unsure. She'd been taken over by sympathies for the people here. But Taavin was right: these people were murderers. It took seeing the brutality of the elfin'ra and the state of her father to remind her of that.

Vi's hands balled into fists at her sides.

She wouldn't forget it again.

Banging echoed to her through the cave, dull and distant. Vi pushed her feet harder against the ground, picking up speed. With a wave of her hand and an utterance, the opening to the cave was blown wide open with an explosion of splinters. The chair she'd propped against the front door rattled with another loud bang.

Vi imagined the men on the other side, slowly rearing back. Perhaps they had a battering ram. Perhaps they were just putting their shoulder into it.

She hoped for the latter as she shouted, "*Juth calt!*"

The whole front of the building exploded outward. Vi leapt through it, over the bodies that had been sent tumbling by the shockwave of her magic. Her feet hit the wooden walkway bordering the city's canals.

Vi pinwheeled her arms, preventing herself from tumbling in. She took a step and a small leap onto a nearby bridge and started running. She had no headway and no purpose other than to burn it all.

She was a blaze of fire through the dark night. Her flames licked through the permafrost of the buildings and ignited tinder as they had on the *Stormfrost*. But unlike the *Stormfrost*, Vi was at her best—she'd recovered, she'd been trained, and she'd learned how to channel the darkness within her.

A man lunged from an alleyway with a curved sword. Vi took a step back. Magic flew from her lips and hands—a shield to block, a blade of her own to plunge into the soft spot of his throat. She was moving forward again before the body even hit the ground.

Where was Adela? Adela must be here. She'd been expecting them—preparing for them. Where would she hide?

Sliding to a stop across snow and ice alike, Vi sent out a wave of fire, giving herself a moment's reprieve. She pulled one of the earrings she'd taken from Fallor's crew from her pocket and said, "*Narro hath.*"

The glyph appeared above the earring and the sensation of a communication channel being opened pulsed through her.

"Come and face me," Vi demanded and dropped the earring, letting go of the magic.

Her challenge issued, Vi continued through the city, zig-zagging as arrows were fired from rooftops and stoking more flames. She started heading away from the port, setting buildings and boats aflame left and right, then dashed across the bridges that spanned one of the canals and looped back. Pirates came at her from all directions, but none could manage her flames. They were all too disorganized, too startled, or too under-trained.

Without warning, a crack of ice snapped across the ground and a large spear jolted upward in an attempt to impale her.

Vi spun away at the last second, flame at the ready, turning to face the pirate queen.

Neither of them said anything. For a brief moment, they were the only two people in the world. But pirates filed in around Adela, emerging like rats from every alley and doorway.

"You finally show yourself," Vi called over. She smothered the flames around her fingers and readied her next attack. If the woman was smart—and Vi knew she was—half of the men surrounding her were Lightspinners ready to cancel her magic. All it would take was one good *juth calt*.

"Give it up, girl."

Vi would grant Adela this—even in the moment she should feel most panicked, most worried about defeat as her pirate city burned around her, she remained calm and composed. The command was said as though Vi was nothing more than a child who had wandered too far from home and needed to be scolded.

"I may have lost your father, but I will not lose you."

"Let me go, and I may let you live," Vi threatened.

"How long have we been doing this?"

What?

"We're alike… aren't we? It's how you got this far. It's how you destroyed my ice around the crown decades ago. You have their blood, too, don't you? Was it your mother or your father who was elfin? Who are your real parents?"

Vi took a small step backward, feigning shock; really, it was an excuse to look around and get her bearings. Let Adela yammer on about parentage in an effort to distract her—meanwhile, Vi sighted the cave she and Taavin had entered from. The snow leading to it was disturbed, but Vi couldn't be certain if it was their footsteps from earlier, or if those were fresh tracks from Taavin and her Father.

"Let's end this, finally. Just you and I, girl." Adela held out her icy hand. The fingers elongated, combining into a single column, and crashed into the ground. It was as if the pirate queen was merging with the isle itself. "The elfin'ra can kiss their Dark God's arse. This will be the night when one of us dies."

Vi was torn.

She knew she should run for it. She should make her way to the cave tunnels by all means necessary. This didn't matter.

Her vengeance didn't matter.

"*Mysst larrk,*" Vi uttered darkly, her eyes on Adela. The satisfying weight of a sword filled her hand. She sprinted into battle, bringing the sword across her body. Adela shifted slightly, magic pulsing with the movement.

"*Juth mariy.*" Vi made a flick of her wrist with her right hand, stopping the shift in power. She danced over cracking ice, her feet remembering every step Sehra's warriors had trained into her, every movement Jayme refined, each new step Arwin had drilled into her. Vi moved with the strength of each of them and with something none of them could give her—a power that had been bolstered by their teaching but was entirely her own.

Adela narrowed her eyes. There was another shift in the magic, but this time it seemed to split into several parts—none of which Vi could focus her sole attention on. The canal on the next street over came alive, a tidal wave of ice shards roaring over Vi.

She didn't have time for a word, so she swept her hand overhead, incinerating the deadly hail before it could reach her. Her left foot slipped out. Vi spun on her right, bringing the sword to Adela's shoulder.

The woman ripped her hand from its column of ice, fingers reforming at her magical command. The limb stopped her blade before it could strike true. Ice chipped off, but Adela was otherwise unharmed.

Vi leaned forward, closing what little gap remained between them. She had no reason to think this would work… and yet…

"*Narro vah'deh*," Vi echoed the words of the elfin'ra from earlier, whispering them as a lover would to Adela. She remembered every syllable with perfect, deadly clarity.

There was something about this twisted magic that she didn't need to understand the way she did Lightspinning glyphs. It was an abomination—an adaptation of Yargen's words gone wrong. It tapped into the most ruthless, brutal nature that hid in the corners of her humanity.

This magic thrived on hate—not logic or skill.

Adela's face glazed over. Her hands went limp. Vi saw the world both through her eyes and the eyes of the pirate queen simultaneously. Everything was doubled and vastly too large as Vi occupied the mind of her adversary.

It was a spell to control the mind of another, Vi realized quickly. This explained the world as she'd seen it earlier, when she had been under the same command. It also explained the screaming voice in the back of her mind that sounded identical to Adela, demanding freedom.

Vi pushed herself and the magic. *Die, die, die*, a voice in the back of her mind screamed. With Adela under her control, she could make the woman do anything. *Die, die, die!* The voice grew louder, and all too late Vi realized that it had not been the voice of Adela, but the same voice she'd heard at the first tear—Raspian.

There was a thunderous crack in her chest.

The whole world exploded with bright yellow, red, and blue light. Tendrils of red lightning shot out from Vi, exploding against the buildings around her and Adela. Vi was thrown backward, hit a wall hard, and slumped on the ground.

Everything the magic touched seemed to wriggle and thrash, like the tears in the Twilight Forest. Raspian's magic was breaking down the buildings, turning them to dust before her eyes. Turning the minds of the men it struck to madness.

Vi blinked, trying to bring her mind back into focus. Adela was hunched over on the ground, turning over the contents of her stomach. One of her men, still in possession of his right mind, levied a crossbow directly at Vi.

Move. She had to move. Vi pushed against the ground, struggling to regain her feet, to somehow dodge the incoming shot. Her whole body was a shuddering mess.

The man's finger squeezed the trigger and in the same moment one of the other pirates crashed into him. The bolt dug into the wood at the side of Vi's head, but she hardly flinched. She watched in horror as the now white-eyed pirate mounted the man who had once been his ally and began to tear him apart with hands and teeth, like a wild animal.

She'd be sick if she looked on any longer.

Move, she commanded herself again. Everything hurt. Red magic crackled over her skin, splitting it, only to have it heal with the blue and yellow tendrils of flame that coated her.

Somehow, Vi found her feet.

"G-Get her!" Adela struggled with words, pointing in her

direction. But there wasn't anyone able to heed her command.

Vi looked over her shoulder and, for a brief second, debated going back to finish the job. This was her chance to kill the pirate queen…

Ultimately, she didn't take it.

Getting to her father would be sweeter than any revenge, and the longer she lingered here, the less likely it became that she'd make it back to him. She'd already made the mistake of lingering once.

Vi tried to move faster. Her head was splitting and body aching. Flames still licked over her body, dancing with red lightning. Every time she blinked, there was a red and violent edge to her sight.

A little longer. She was so close now. The darkness of the cave coated her and Vi paused, several steps inside. The mere idea of her magic was like torture, and yet…

"*Juth calt*." Vi pointed up at the entrance to the cave. The earth groaned and split, rumbling as the supports for its frozen mouth caved in. Vi didn't wait to watch the first rocks collapse with the power of her glyph. Instead, she turned and sprinted through the tunnels on the last bit of adrenaline she had.

Flames birthed with her every footstep, cutting through the darkness and smoldering against the wet, frozen rock. She heard crashes behind her. The island itself was trying to bury her now, chasing her through its frigid bowels. It wanted to punish her for the magic she'd unleashed on it.

Magic she still didn't fully understand and should've never touched.

Vi emerged on the other side just as the cave-in caught up behind her. There'd be no pirates getting through there and Arwin would figure out that she needed to fly around… If Arwin survived at all. Vi swallowed hard.

"Vi!" Taavin's voice cut through her thoughts.

Her attention jolted to the ship still tied to the thick ice surrounding the island.

"Vi!" Her father echoed, hands cupped around his mouth. "We're here!"

They'd made it.

She began sprinting once more. She slipped, falling hard, landing with a cry, but pushed herself upward, ignoring the red that smeared the blue ice from where her shirt ripped at her elbow.

Get to the boat. Get away. Get to the boat. Get away.

The mantra was on repeat in her mind. Vi leapt to the rope that dangled down the side of the vessel. With the last of her strength, she pulled herself upward. A strong hand closed around her belt, hauling her over the deck railing.

"*Juth calt,*" Vi said with a glance at the rope tying down the vessel. It snapped in two. Between heaving breaths, she panted out a soft, "Go."

"Arwin?" Taavin asked, though he was already stepping away and heading for the ropes connected to the sales.

"She'll make it back," Vi murmured, blinking up at the sky above her. She'd never seen a sky so violent. Red lightning crackled overhead like the tentacles of a writhing beast, ready to escape. Dull light, the color of dried blood, seeped over the horizon, staining the sea, staining the sky.

Her father may be saved, but there was still much for her to do. Yet for now… Vi twisted, looking at the man who sat at her side.

Her father was saved.

"Father…" Vi lifted a hand. It felt heavier than lead.

"Daughter." Aldrik's fingers clasped hers. Neither had a strong grip. Adela had stolen both of their strength. "You did well."

Vi pressed her eyes closed, only just now feeling the wetness on her cheeks. Things were only beginning. He didn't understand what still awaited them.

"You did well," her father repeated softly.

Even though she knew all that lay before them, three words had never sounded so beautiful.

"MAY I?" TAAVIN asked, kneeling down on the other side of Vi. He held out his hands, his intent to heal her obvious. Vi gave a small nod.

But no magic flowed, and no words were said. Taavin looked on in horror.

"What is it?" Vi rasped.

"What happened?" Taavin whispered, reaching for her watch. As his hand drew near it, a spark of red lightning streaked from watch to finger and he pulled away quickly.

"What—" Vi struggled to prop herself up, looking down at her chest. The watch had cracked, half the cover had vanished—a molten line still smoldering in the metal. The glass that had protected the face was shattered and the face itself had been charred completely black. "I… I don't know." She looked up to Taavin, frantic. "What does it mean?"

"I have less of an idea than you. What happened out there?"

Vi was about to answer when the cry of a bird overhead

stopped her.

Hovering on gusts and gales sweeping over the sea was a bird with a crooked wing. It coasted low before a bloodied Arwin tumbled onto the deck with a pulse of magic. Her eyes were dazed and unfocused, blinking slowly.

"They did *not* want me to break down the shift," she groaned, nursing her arm. Vi noticed her weapon was nowhere to be seen. "Yet, somehow, you look worse than me."

"Thanks." Vi fought to sit.

Taavin looked between her and Arwin. His eyes fell to the watch and that seemed to make up his mind. He quickly walked over to Arwin and hovered near the woman, looking down at her. "Want me to heal you?"

"Don't touch me, Voice," Arwin droned. The bite was gone from her words. Their hatred for each other had lost its venom, becoming more residual habit than impassioned feeling.

"Let him heal you," Vi called. "We need the hands to set sail."

There was a long stretch of silence and, finally, "Fine. Though if you tell anyone I let Lightspinning touch me, I will kill you."

"I thought you were going to kill me anyway," Taavin mumbled.

"I thought I was killing Ulvarth, and you were still to be decided."

Vi slumped, resting her forehead in her palm. The whole world spun, and it had nothing to do with the rocking of the boat. She had to get herself in order. They needed to get away from the Isle of Frost. Yet she stayed frozen, her hand clutching the now broken watch.

"Daughter." Her father's hand rested heavily on her shoulder, jolting Vi from her thoughts. "Is there anything I can do for you?"

She stared up in momentary awe. *He was really here.* It had been years since they'd last seen each other. Now, they were together for the foreseeable future—no meetings, no Imperial business, nothing to tear them apart. Nothing save the end of the world, that is.

"Actually, yes." Vi forced her mind to move again and not just gawk at him. "In the cabin there's a satchel. Bring it to me?"

Aldrik stood slowly, and walked even more slowly to the cabin's entrance. Vi watched him carefully. Even though she had been far more beaten up during the escape, he looked worse for wear. The gray streaks by his ears had never seemed wider.

Still, he moved with the grace of an Emperor. Every motion was fluid and purposeful. Even at his worst, he was still better than most at their best.

"Is this it?" he asked, returning with the bag.

"Yes." Vi placed it on the deck, rummaging through it for the vials Sarphos had given her. She quickly read through their various labels and found the two she was looking for, downing them in a large swig. "Thank you."

Vi wiped her mouth with the back of her hand. Sarphos's abilities never failed to impress her. It felt as though the potion never even reached her stomach, seeping into her blood and restoring strength to her muscles near instantly.

"Here—" Vi held up two more vials to her father. That only left them with one more—for disease, specifically, which didn't seem applicable at the moment—but if there was ever a time to use them, it was now. She also took out one of Sarphos's ration crackers. It looked like a biscuit but really did fill the stomach as though you'd eaten a meal. "Take these."

Her father didn't question, uncorking and drinking from the vials as Vi stood. Taavin and Arwin were on their feet as well.

"We should get moving." Time was strange for her at present. She couldn't tell how long she'd been on the deck, waiting for the world to settle back into place. Yet it felt like far too long. "I think Adela has enough on her hands but—"

"We don't want to be around when chaos turns to rage," Arwin finished.

"Taavin, you take the helm, Arwin and I will get the sails ready." Vi looked to her father, a small smile spreading on her lips at the mere sight of him. He was alive, and with her. It was every dream come true. She'd actually done it. "Father, you just sit tight and rest."

"I can help."

"We have this," Vi insisted. "The three of us sailed here, we know the ropes."

Her father relented, still slowly nibbling Sarphos's biscuit as he sat on the steps that led up to the quarterdeck. Taavin walked around him, and Vi didn't miss them sharing a small look that spoke volumes she couldn't hear. For now, she ignored it. They had a few days trapped on a ship together; there'd be enough time to deal with everything.

Arwin began readying the sails. They got the ship moving without so much as a word among them. Vi looked out over the Isle of Frost as they turned away; smoke plumed into the early dawn from the still-burning pirate town. Not one ship had limped out from the lagoon.

"I saw it," Arwin said softly, startling Vi from her thoughts.

"Saw what?"

"When I broke the shift around the Isle of Frost… I saw the spider-web red fractures in the veil between this world and the next."

Vi turned her gaze over the horizon, leaving the isle behind her. So what she'd seen in the sky hadn't been a hallucination of magic and pain. Taavin's words—some of the first he said to her when she arrived on Meru—echoed back to her: *We're running short on time. The end of the world is near, and we must be ready to meet it.*

"The world really is ending, isn't it?" Arwin whispered.

"It's heading in that direction."

"Can you truly stop it?"

"I'm going to try." Vi looked over at her companion, the woman's eyes locking with hers.

"We'll have to keep training you with that scythe, then." Arwin gave her a light pat on the shoulder, the touch brief but shockingly reaffirming. "So rest up today, princess. We're back at it tomorrow." All Vi could do was nod, startled by the woman's sudden change in attitude. "Speaking of… How many days are we going to be stuck on this thing this time?"

"That's an excellent question." Vi returned to her bag, grabbing the journal.

"I was about to ask for a headway—more than 'away from Adela'." Taavin joined the conversation.

"That headway sounds good enough to me for now," Arwin declared. "I'll take the helm. You should give her a look-over and make sure her wounds have healed…" Arwin glanced between Vi and Aldrik. "And I suspect you may want some time with your father."

"Thank you." Time with her father was a luxury Vi could barely comprehend. She almost didn't know what to do with it now.

"So where are we heading?" Arwin looked over Vi's shoulder at the map.

"Risen," Vi announced. She looked up at Arwin. "There, you can kill Ulvarth."

"You sound almost eager about that," Arwin mumbled with the tiniest grin on her mouth. Vi ignored it, looking to Taavin.

"And we can find out the truth about this." She held the watch, broken metal jutting against her hand uncomfortably. "And find a way to stop Raspian."

"Risen it is." Arwin took the journal from her, bending over to scoop the compass from the satchel. "North, then northwest after we pass the southern tip of Meru's crescent?"

"You have the right idea," Vi affirmed.

"Then I think I can manage for a while."

Taavin was already descending the stairs as Arwin went up. Vi looked over her shoulder again at the Isle of Frost. There were still no signs of ships in pursuit, and the land was growing smaller and smaller with each passing minute.

"Looking for the *Stormfrost*?" Taavin asked from her side.

"Yes. Though I don't think they'll give chase…" She thought back to the magic she'd unleashed—the pirates going crazed, red lightning mixing with blue and yellow fire. As her thoughts wandered, Taavin's hand drifted over her and he murmured spells. The haziness in her head began to clear and the last of the aches vanished. But before Vi could thank him, Taavin's fingers rested against the watch. This time, no magic lashed out at him.

"What happened?" he asked again.

"I used the words the elfin'ra had used on me to control Adela." She could still feel the echo of power rumbling within her like a dark storm.

"You used those words?" He looked up at her, his expression darkening. "Are you insane?"

"Maybe. It was that or die," Vi said firmly. She didn't want to be made to feel guilty for doing what it took to survive.

"Those words are Raspian's work… As Yargen's words evoke her magic, those evoke his." Taavin tapped the watch. "You invited his power into you willingly."

Vi clenched her jaw as she looked out over the ocean. She could continue insisting it had been to survive… but was it? Or had she wanted to find the most brutal way to end Adela's life? Where did her justice end and her darkness begin?

"No wonder it reacted poorly with the watch," he said grimly. "Yargen's magic was likely trying to protect you."

"Protect me from what?"

"Vi, *think.*" Taavin gripped her upper arm to the point of pain. "Raspian seeks a living host to let him walk among this land once more, and fully usher in an Era of Darkness. To do that he needs one of us, or the ashes of the flame. If you *invited his magic into you…*" Vi felt her shoulders tense, and it had nothing to do with the pain of Taavin's grip. It felt like a crank was winding the muscles in her neck, making her head hurt all over again. "One way or another, as his power continues to grow, he'll find a way into this world. Let's not make it easy for him."

"I won't," Vi whispered. "I won't use those words ever again."

"Good." Taavin relented, quickly releasing her as if he hadn't realized he'd been holding onto her. His fingers trailed down her arm, wrapping around hers tightly for a long moment. "I don't know what I'd do if something happened to you."

Vi gave him a small smile. Their lives—their love, however unspoken it was—seemed so insignificant in the face of the needs of the whole world. No wonder neither of them could bring themselves to say it aloud.

"Now, I'm going to get some rest…" Taavin looked over her shoulder. Vi thought he was looking to the cabin, until she turned, realizing he'd locked eyes with her father. "You finally have your father. You should spend some time with him."

Vi squeezed his hand once before letting go.

Taavin crossed to the cabin and disappeared behind the curtain. Arwin was at the helm, focused and silent. Her father slowly stood and walked over to her. Vi's throat was thick with emotion, and tears prickled her eyes but didn't fall. Aldrik's eyes seemed just as glassy.

But the deeply ingrained stoicism of royalty won for them both.

They had shared words. They had been reunited. This moment felt different. This moment felt like the first time they were actually seeing each other, free from panic, fear, and worry.

Vi took a deep breath.

"It's been a while. I've much to tell you.

"IT STARTED WITH a watch…" Vi began as they sat at the bow of the boat. The seas were blessedly smooth, the salt spray from the hull cutting through the ocean misting her legs as she hung them over the side between the railings. "This watch—or what's left of it, to be specific."

"I recognize it."

"You do?"

Her father hummed softly. "Even charred and broken, I'd know it anywhere. After all, it was this watch that gave your mother her magic back."

"Magic… back?" Vi repeated.

"Have we never told you that story?"

"I suppose not." Vi had heard of rare cases where sorcerers lost their power through a process called *eradication*—diminishing magic to the point that it created a block in the channel. But she'd never heard of her mother going through it.

"When the Mad King rose up, he gravely injured your mother

and, in the process, robbed her of her magic. There was a brief time when her command of the wind was gone." Aldrik's eyes drifted closed and he sighed, for a moment living in a time well before Vi's birth. "We didn't think she would ever regain her power. But it seemed she had made an unintentional vessel—that watch. It housed enough of her magic to reopen her channel."

"Fritz said that Mother was reunited with her power when the world was darkest, thanks to this. But I didn't know…" Vi turned the watch over and over in her hands. *Magic has an odd way of finding us when we need it most.* He couldn't have known when he'd sent the watch how right he'd been. "It gave mother a connection to her power; it gave me a connection with mine," she whispered, mostly to herself.

"Your magic, Vi…" Her father left the sentence hanging, clearly expecting her to fill in the blank.

"It's not like yours, after all." She looked back over the deck, toward the cabin. Her mind was an ocean of memory and Vi was sinking into its depths. "It's like his."

"His?" Her father turned, following her attention. "*Ah…* Taavin, you called him?"

"He's a Lightspinner. Like me." Her voice nearly quivered at the end. "I-I'm not a Firebearer."

Aldrik was quiet, looking back out over the sea for a breath. Eventually he turned to her, tilted his head, and asked, "So?"

"My magic isn't like yours, like grandmother's, like anyone in the Ci'Dan line or anyone on the Dark Isle for that matter."

"Just as Sehra predicted."

Her parents had known, thanks to the traveler, that she would have unique magic. At first, Vi had hated the traveler and what she'd done to her life. But now, sitting next to her father—a father she had rescued thanks to that magic—Vi found her rage had quelled. Had it not been for the traveler, Aldrik would be dead.

"Speaking of family, does your mother know where you are?"

"I'm not sure." Vi glanced at him, feeling as if she was about to be scolded. "I told Romulin. He may have mentioned something by now."

Aldrik shook his head, letting out a chuckle. Had her father always looked so old? Sounded so tired? It seemed he'd aged ten years in the five it had been since she'd last seen him.

"My foolish daughter… You could've been killed, you know." His face fell from the controlled mask of the Emperor into the raw emotion of a father.

"You could've been killed if I hadn't come to rescue you," Vi countered stubbornly.

"This streak of recklessness, you get it from your mother." Despite his words, her father had a proud smile, as if he were silently taking credit for the fact.

She blurted out rough laughter. "Mother would say differently I think."

"Exactly. She's reckless *and* stubborn." His eyes were glassy and tired. But still, no tears fell. This time it had nothing to do with the trappings of royalty, and everything to do with the fact that they were soaking in the relief of being finally, *finally* reunited.

"I know about her," Vi confessed. "I know why you left."

"You do?"

"Yes. And I want you to know that I'll save her, just like I saved you." Vi stared out at the sky. The bloody dawn had turned into a pastel blue with spots of white in the distance. Not a cloud of red lightning in sight.

But Vi could still feel Raspian out there. She could feel him in her blood now—in the weight of the broken watch around her neck. Taavin was right: Raspian's power was growing day by day, perhaps in part because of her. She had been the one to first sail through the storm of red lightning, to inspect the tears in the Twilight Forest, to throw herself into one of those tears, and then to use his words…

It was possible her actions were giving him footholds in the world. Vi's jaw tightened. It didn't matter; she'd be the one to undo him.

"Vi," her father said painfully soft, "Sometimes, you can't save everyone."

Vi jerked her head toward him.

Aldrik Solaris had always been an imposing figure. Dark hair, taller than most. He wasn't particularly broad, but he could command a room with little more than his presence and a look. Vi loved her father dearly, but he could be frightening to a young girl, especially when she'd done wrong. She had always seen him as an insurmountable force of nature.

But right now he looked like a tired old man.

"I will save our family," she vowed. "First our family, then the world." She'd saved him from the clutches of Adela; the rest suddenly seemed manageable.

"How did you even know to save me?" Her father shifted, bringing up a knee and resting his forearm on it. The skin of his shin was exposed through a long rip in his clothes. Everything he wore was in tatters—a shadow of former Imperial glory.

"I had a vision of the future, specifically of you on the Isle of Frost."

"So you can see the future?" Vi made a noise of affirmation. "You share that much with your grandmother—my mother—then."

"I thought so but… It's a different sort of sight." Vi tucked her head, running a hand through her hair with a sigh.

His father tapped her chin. "Do you not peer along the lines set out by the goddess?"

"I think so but—"

"Do you look into flames?"

"Well, yes, but that may just be because I—"

"Daughter, you are of her blood, as you are of mine, as you are of your mother's. You don't need proof in magic or tokens. You don't need the world to validate it. It's here." He tapped her breastbone under her collarbone and above her heart. "It's in the woman who's sailed across the world and risked her life to reunite that family."

Vi hung her head now. She would not allow the world to see the few stray tears fall. Her father's arms wrapped tightly around her for a long moment, his chin on the top of her head. As if he understood, as if he knew that for one long minute she needed to hide from the world and give in to the overwhelming emotions before she drowned in them.

She straightened, finally, rubbing her face when her tears would no longer betray her.

"But this talk of saving the world," her father finally continued. "You've risked enough, Vi. Come home."

"Father… I can't," she protested weakly. It was a tempting prospect, even before he elaborated.

"You can. You are the crown princess of the Solaris Empire. Your home is on the Main Continent."

Vi sniffed as a bitter smile crossed her lips. Her father still called it the Main Continent, and she had long since begun to refer to it as the Dark Isle. Vi could argue it was because that was how those on Meru knew it. But it was more than that.

She had called it the Dark Isle more because that was how she saw it. Her worldview had changed, and Vi didn't know what it would take for it to change back… if it ever would.

"You've done your share, return home," he repeated.

"What about mother?"

"You've been on the Crescent Continent longer than I. Do they have a cure?" Vi shook her head. "Then them summoning me to discuss a cure was a lie." Vi glanced at her father, filing that information away. Who had summoned him? Ulvarth, or the queen? Had Taavin known? Her heart protested against that last question. "Let's go home."

"But mother…"

"Your mother is strong. The strongest woman I have ever met." Nothing short of wonder, admiration, and love filled his voice. Vi watched as her father gazed out to sea, his brow softening. Only to nearly choke on his next words. "But I have been away from her long enough, and if ill is to befall her, I should be by her side, as she would seek to be by mine."

"But *I can save her*," Vi reiterated, stressing each word.

"How? Daughter, I believe you can move mountains. But I need your help filling in the blanks of how you believe so adamantly that you can accomplish something the most skilled clerics and sorcerers on the Main or Crescent Continents have not."

"Have you ever heard of the Champion of Yargen?"

"I can't say I have."

Vi chewed on her lower lip a moment, trying to figure out her next words. She knew of the rise of the Mad King and the fall of the Crystal Caverns. It would be an understandably trying topic for her father. How could she broach it all without sounding as though she blamed him? She didn't, of course. No one knew what the Crystal Caverns really were and it was not his fault they had been opened.

"Long ago, Yargen—we know her as the Mother, and Raspian—we know him as the Father, were at war."

"At war?"

"Yes, well, the Crones of the Sun got their stories a little twisted at some point in history. They're not lovers; they're sworn enemies. Anyway, when the war was over, Yargen won and sealed Raspian away. That seal was broken, and he's back now. He's behind the White Death."

"If you stop him, or seal him away again, the White Death goes away too?" Vi gave a nod. That was the same logic she had used—the same thought she'd hung all her hopes on these past months. "But how can you accomplish such a task?"

"Well…" Vi picked at the hem of her tattered, sun-bleached shirt. "Because I am Yargen's new Champion."

"You?"

"Yes, and because—hold on."

Vi scrambled to her feet. She had to prove to him she wasn't talking madness. Heart pounding against her chest, Vi sprinted over to the cabin, quietly leaned in so as not to disturb Taavin's slumber, and grabbed the scythe. She returned, sitting back down and setting it between them. Her father regarded the bundle warily and Vi took a deep breath.

"I think—know—I can defeat him because I am Yargen's Champion. Taavin is her Voice; he can hear her words and knows how to get to the flame of Yargen in Risen. That's the other piece of Yargen's power." Vi knew she was talking too fast, but couldn't slow down. She was working up to this moment and her words were in a race with her heart. "And because I have this."

Vi undid the straps wrapped around the scythe, pulling back the fabric covering it. Even in the bright, early morning light, it sparkled and shone with a magic that filled her with delight and hope.

At least it did until her father scrambled backward, looking on in horror.

"Throw it overboard," he demanded.

"Father—"

"That, Vi, is not the solution. *That* is the problem."

25

"I KNOW WHAT THIS is," Vi insisted.

"You clearly do not." Aldrik reached forward, hesitated with his hand hovering above the pole of the scythe, then made up his mind. He grasped it, but not before Vi gripped it with both her hands on either side of his. She held on firmly as he tried to wrench it away and make good on his demand to throw it overboard. "If you knew what this was, you would not be holding it in the first place. Now let it go, Vi."

She knew that tone. It was the same tone that would have had her shaking as a child. But she wasn't a child any longer.

"No. You need to listen to me, Father."

"Vi—"

"Listen, please," Vi pleaded. But she knew that alone wouldn't be what got through to him. Vi knew she had to prove she wasn't the reckless child he thought she was. "I know this is a crystal weapon and I know their history. I know Mother found a crystal weapon that led to the rise of the Mad King and the destruction of the crystal caverns."

"Do you know it was that same crystal weapon that stole her powers?" Aldrik's voice lowered, becoming sterner by the moment.

"What?" Vi breathed.

"Do you know it was a crystal weapon that also began the War of the Crystal Caverns *before* the Mad King?"

She didn't. Her father was pointing out dangerous gaps in her knowledge left and right. "No," Vi said calmly, leveling her eyes with her father's. "I don't know those things, though I would like to. What I do know is that the Crystal Caverns are gone. All the other Crystal Weapons—fragments of Yargen's power—are gone with it. And this may be the last thing we have to stand against an evil god trying to destroy this world as we know it."

They engaged in a staring contest. Vi didn't back down. Her father sighed heavily, releasing the scythe and staggering away as though it had wounded him.

"Neither of us should be touching it…" he murmured, running a hand through his dark, limp hair. "You may have gotten recklessness and stubbornness from your mother, but damn if I didn't pass along that fire in your belly."

Vi felt somewhat proud. Continuing her efforts to calm the situation, she acquiesced to his request, slowly laying down the scythe.

"I think I'm able to touch it without issue since I have Yargen's magic—I've felt normal handling it for some time now. But you're likely right in that you should limit your contact." Vi didn't know if the scythe could taint him in the way the crystals of the Crystal Caverns were said to have tainted men who had come in contact with them. The scythe had been removed from the Dark Isle so early, perhaps it had escaped the slow weakening of the barriers holding back Raspian and the affects of his powers on the crystal.

It was a plausible theory. But to test it, Vi would have to risk the crystals twisting her father into a monster. So she wasn't about to find out if she was right or not.

Aldrik settled back into his earlier seat. Vi glanced at Arwin over her shoulder, but whatever thoughts the woman had about the outburst, she was keeping them to herself. Luckily, Taavin hadn't seen Aldrik nearly throwing their one crystal weapon overboard. She didn't want him to have a negative impression of her father.

"Vi, nothing good comes of a Solaris touching a crystal weapon."

"Father, I—"

"It was a crystal weapon that sparked a whole new thirst for conquest in my father."

"How?"

"Our family has a dark history tied to these. One we cannot seem to escape." Her father stared at the scythe as though it had hypnotized him. "Your great grandfather held one in his vaults—a crown stolen by Adela that was later recovered by my brother."

"Uncle Baldair fought Adela?" Vi had heard stories of Baldair's prowess with the sword. Still, she couldn't imagine anyone without magic standing against Adela.

"No. I found out much later he discovered it in an old pirate hideaway one summer at Oparium." Aldrik sighed heavily. Talk of his late brother always cast a cloud over him. Usually, Vi would change the subject. But this was the first time she couldn't afford to spare her father from these thoughts; she needed the truth. "But it was brought back, and my father eventually learned of that crown. He thought he could use it to someday conquer the Crescent Continent..."

"Grandfather was born with a taste for conquest," Vi tried to say as delicately as possible.

"It was a crystal weapon that led to my mother's death."

"*What?*" Vi had to open and close her mouth several times before she finally found words. "She died in childbirth."

"So the official story goes. But it was really because she was the last head of the Knights of Jadar."

"The extremist group?"

"They weren't always so." She'd been taught as much. But it was still odd to hear. "My mother as the head of the knights was said to have been in possession of their sacred relic—the Sword of Jadar, which was—"

"A crystal weapon," Vi finished with a whisper. "And then mother found the axe." Sword, axe, crown, scythe. They were all accounted for. And all of them had passed through her family's hands.

"Fiera was ultimately killed by men who sought to unleash the powers of the caverns. She died protecting that sword."

"Was the sword destroyed in the rise and fall of the Mad King as well?" Vi asked delicately. Her hushed tones had little to do with Arwin. Her father's eyes seemed more sunken and haunted with every word, despite his voice remaining level. These were old wounds, yet they still oozed.

"No, it was destroyed when I used it to kill a man. And with that act, I began the War of the Crystal Caverns."

"You…" Vi placed a hand on the deck, leaning, trying to catch her father's eyes. But he avoided her gaze at every turn. "Father, you—"

"It's the truth, Vi," he spoke firmly, leaving no room for doubt. "I was taken to the caverns. I was misled. But that is no excuse. It was my hand and my actions that led to the death and suffering of our people—that helped pave the way for your mother to be used as a tool and nearly die in search of that same power. Now you—" Aldrik reached upward, grabbing her shoulders, shaking her gently "—you wield one as well. And I will not see you suffer the same fate. These weapons attract lies as easily as foolish, power-hungry men."

Tears shone in his haunted eyes. Vi's lips parted, but no sound escaped. She was held in place by her father and by the weight of his truths.

"Father, this is different," she finally insisted, her voice weaker than she would've liked.

"Is it? Or is this just another turn of a vortex that every Solaris will drown in?"

Vi didn't have an answer. She wanted to. She desperately wanted to. But nothing came. And, as if sensing the crack in her determined exterior, her father continued.

"Leave this behind and come back to the Main Continent with me. Return to your family."

"I…"

"Vi, please. I have longed for our family to be together as much as you have. Leave the world to the hands of fate." His father's arms tightened around her, pulling her to him. "Leave it all behind, and come home with me."

Vi closed her eyes, returning her father's embrace. No matter how old she became, part of her would always be the girl soothed by her parents' arms.

"Vi…"

She whispered, "I'll talk to Taavin about starting a course for Norin."

Her father tightened his grasp, holding her to the point of pain—though Vi couldn't tell if the ache came from his hold, or from within.

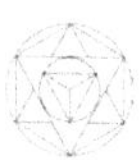

She was behind the helm, adjusting course slightly. The wood was weathered and worn, ashen from the beating sun. Vi felt the same heat on her cheeks, deepening the natural tan of her skin.

On her left was Meru and the end of the world she was expected to meet. On her right, across the Shattered Isles, was the Dark Isle and her waiting family. At her feet was the scythe that was part of a far more bloody history than she fully understood.

And she was trapped between them all.

Movement below deck wrenched her back to reality from her tangle of thoughts. A familiar mess of dark hair emerged from the cabin, the late afternoon sun picking up purple notes as the sky turned to red. The days were undeniably shorter now. Vi would bet they only had six or seven hours of daylight now—a change too dramatic to have anything to do with the summer months stretching toward winter.

"My father?" she asked as Taavin approached.

"Asleep. It seems to be restful," Taavin said softly.

"Arwin?" Vi had expected Taavin to emerge the moment Arwin entered the cabin after Vi had offered to take the second shift. But he hadn't, and Vi had been too grateful for the silence to investigate.

"Asleep on the floor." Vi gave him a look and Taavin let out a low chuckle. "I was just as shocked."

"I expected her to kick you from your cot."

"Me too." Taavin looked out over the bow of the boat, where Vi's eyes remained transfixed. "How long until Risen?"

"If we go straight there… perhaps two days?" Vi answered delicately.

"Why wouldn't we go straight there?" Taavin shifted mostly in front of her, making it impossible for her to avoid his piercing stare.

"I was thinking of making a quick stop in Norin."

"No."

"It would only add two—three days."

"Vi—"

"We can drop off my father." She decided not to bring up the fact that her father had begged her not to go onward with her plans to seek out her destiny involving the scythe.

"We risk being caught." Taavin frowned. "Moreover, what makes you think your father will let you go once he has you back on the Dark Isle?"

"I'm his daughter, not his prisoner."

"You're right, a prisoner would be better because he'd care much less about a prisoner."

Vi rolled her eyes and looked away, doing anything to avoid his gaze. "I don't want to bring him to Risen," she finally whispered.

"Why?"

"Because it was someone in Risen who contacted him—claiming they had a cure for the White Death." The surprise on Taavin's face reassured her that he hadn't known. It didn't rule out Ulvarth; in fact, Vi's bet would still be on the Lord of the Faithful. But she took solace in the knowledge that Taavin had no hand in this particular machination of Ulvarth's. "Why do they want him?"

"I don't know." Taavin shook his head. "I had no idea he was summoned."

"Then I'm inclined to believe it's not a good reason." Vi stressed. "I always told you that you'd have my undivided attention to figure out the watch—the scythe—as soon as my father is safe."

"But your father will always be at risk." Taavin grabbed the helm, standing right in front of her. "How long will you make the world wait in the name of your personal problems?"

"As long as it has to, because a world without my family is not a world I want to live in."

"None of us may have a world if you keep dallying."

"I am *not* dallying." Vi glared up at him and fought to keep her voice hushed.

"Every delay brings us closer to the end. Raspian's power is growing exponentially by the day. You've seen it. You must surely feel it, perhaps better than I. You can't deny it. And yet you stall."

They were in a deadlock, each holding a peg on the helm's wheel. Vi gripped and released the wood several times. It felt as though they were now at the moment when he would turn the wheel west, and she would spin it east.

There was a weighted, heavy sensation. Every nerve-ending firing. The spark was alive under her skin, flushing, radiating heat.

This moment had weight to it.

It was the same sensation she felt before they had entered the Isle of Frost. Perhaps their every decision now carried so much weight that nearly each choice affected the outcome of the world. Maybe this was how an Apex of Fate was formed.

The thought sparked an idea.

"Let's let the future decide." Vi was acting on a hunch.

"What?"

"I'll look into the future. I have the scythe. The watch has been broken, some of Yargen's power unleashed. Perhaps I will see a vision; perhaps I can command them now." Vi released the wheel, giving it to him. Taavin regarded her warily.

"And if you don't?"

"Then we'll keep arguing after." Vi sat, holding the scythe in one hand. "It can't hurt to try."

Before Taavin could say anything else, she summoned a flame in the palm of her other hand. The bright, yellow fire burned on and around her palm, snaking through her fingers. She held it at eye level, staring, waiting expectantly.

"Vi, I don't think…"

"It will work," she insisted. "I will make it work." Her grip on the scythe tightened. A shot of energy went straight through her—from the hand holding the scythe to the hand holding the flame. It tinged the flame with blue, barely visible at the edges.

"What the—" Taavin's voice was lost as Vi was pulled into a vision.

The world blurred and overexposed before slowly fading back into place. Things were hazier than normal. Nothing seemed sharp. Vi squinted, trying to make out the shapes being painted into a dark reality.

There was an arc of blue in the darkness, and a flash of red. The blade of the scythe came into focus first, floating mid-air, quivering with her strain as she tried to push it through a tangle of red lightning.

The blue-green magic that swirled within the blade illuminated her bruised and bloodied face. She had a split lip and swollen eye, and blood streamed down her temple to her cheek from trauma hidden by her matted hair.

Out of the darkness, a figure emerged opposite her future self. The lightning was his forearm, his face the haunted, skeletal visage of death itself. His hair writhed like snakes, silvery like moonlight. His mouth was a perpetually open maw of razor-sharp teeth.

The man's gaze shifted away from Vi's future self and toward *her*—as though he could look straight at her.

Raspian saw her.

Vi took an involuntary step back, though she didn't know how she would escape even if she wanted to.

In the vision, lightning cracked through the scythe. It shattered into a thousand pieces, magic propelling outward in a shock wave. Raspian grabbed for the throat of her future self and his nightmarish mouth ripped soft flesh from bone.

The Vi facing off against the dark god collapsed, grabbing her throat and gasping. She gasped as well, her consciousness blurring between reality and the Vi she witnessed die. Then, the air that filled her lungs was salty. Her throat was in one piece. And Taavin's face appeared over her.

"What did you see?" he asked solemnly, kneeling down by her, ignoring the helm.

"I… I don't know." Vi rolled onto her elbow, just in case she was going to be sick.

"Vi—"

"I don't know. I think it didn't work right because I forced it. Or because I let Raspian's power in me. Or because—"

"What did you see?" he demanded harshly, both his hands closing around her cheeks and jerking her face toward his. They were inches apart, his green-eyed gaze devouring her soul far more effectively than Raspian ever could.

"The scythe won't work," Vi whispers. "In the end… he wins."

Taavin's grip on her face relaxed. His eyes slowly widened as all tension left his face, his lips parting. He sat back heavily and breathed a soft, "No."

"I fight him, and he wins."

"No."

"I saw it."

"You saw wrong," Taavin snapped.

"And if I didn't?"

"Then we are headed to Risen, and we will find the information we need there to change this future. There's still time, there has to be time…"

Taavin stood, grabbed the helm and turned east, but set his gaze westward toward the fading sun. That was the problem with her vision: she didn't know what choice led to the outcome she saw. Was the scene she just witnessed the result if they chose to go to Risen, as Taavin wanted? Or if they headed to Norin, as she intended?

She rubbed her throat thoughtfully.

"For now, we stay on course. We'll decide if we are off to Risen or Norin later. I'll speak with my Father—" though Vi doubted she'd ever find the right words to explain that "—and make the best choice for us all."

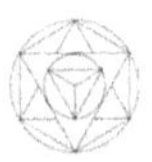

Vi eventually relented to the need for sleep, leaving Taavin at the helm. He hadn't argued with her for hours, so she decided their plan was settled. Arwin was just stirring as Vi entered the cabin, but her father slept on.

As soon as she was horizontal, a deep and thankfully dreamless sleep overtook her as well.

When she woke, it was still dark.

Moonlight winked through the cracks in the curtain that closed off the cabin from the main deck. She blinked away the sleep from her eyes. Her head felt heavy and aching, but it was nothing compared to her body.

It felt as though a noru sat on her chest.

There was creaking and the sound of ropes straining… and *voices*. Her eyes widened and Vi shot upright, heart racing. More hushed voices than Vi could count lingered on her ears. She pushed off from the cot slowly, reaching over to her father. He was rousing as well with a soft groan.

"Father," she whispered. "Father, do you hear—"

Vi never finished her thought.

"The bastard betrayed us!" Arwin's scream cut through the night. "Vi—"

Vi bolted upright, grabbing for the scythe. But Arwin had been right—she couldn't get it unwrapped fast enough. The curtain to the tiny cabin was pulled open with such aggression that it ripped clean off its pegs. Vi stared in confusion, her mind struggling to process the face that looked at her. He had a beak-like nose and short cropped back hair pulled tightly against his head.

He wore golden armor, embellished with mother of pearl, and a heavy sword strapped to his hip. The man's bright blue eyes—almost steel-like in their iciness—peered down at her, shining in the moonlight. A terrible grin spread across his face.

"Aldrik Solaris, Emperor of the Solaris Empire," he said to her father, and then turned to her. "Vi Solaris, Crown Princess of the Solaris Empire… I hereby place you under arrest by the order of her Holiness, the Goddess Yargen."

It hit her all at once.

Vi was staring at the face of Ulvarth, Lord of the Swords of Light.

VI KNEW WHAT SHE saw. But it didn't make any sense.

"You must be Lord Ulvarth," she said, as if saying the words aloud could remedy the disconnect between the realms of what should be possible and impossible. How in the Mother's name was Ulvarth staring her down?

"If you know who I am, this should go smoothly." His voice was a light and airy tenor. The man was clearly so full of his own hot air that she was shocked he didn't drift away. "I'm willing to grant you both the decency your stations deserve, assuming you grant me the decency of mine and do not resist capture."

"If you know who we are, you should not be arresting us." Her father tried to stand. But he was hunched in the small cabin. "Your queen sent for me. We are to discuss how the magicks of Meru could possibly be used to—"

"*I* was the one to send for you," Ulvarth interrupted. Vi only wished she could be surprised. "And I answer to no queen. I answer to the Goddess."

Vi balled her hands into fists. The scythe, still wrapped, was locked in her grip. If she swung it hard enough, she could cut straight through the cloth around it. But could a crystal blade cut through metal plate armor?

"What are our charges?" her father asked.

"You," Ulvarth spoke directly to Aldrik, "are charged with destroying the Goddess's confinement of Lord Raspian, and unleashing him—and the death and destruction he brings—back into the world."

"Raspian doesn't yet have a mortal form. He's not truly returned," Vi tried to counter. Even though she well knew that without a mortal form he'd still managed to kill countless people, thanks to the White Death.

Ulvarth turned to her and continued as though she'd said nothing. "And you are charged with kidnapping the Voice."

"*What?*" Every word Taavin had ever said about Ulvarth and his wicked nature was turning out to be true—not that Vi had doubted him. "I did no such thing."

"That will be for the High Counsel of Light to decide. Now, if you please." He stepped aside with a swing of his arm, as though he was ushering them into a party and not onto the dark deck of a stolen pirate ship.

Vi shared a look with her father, but neither of them seemed to have any better ideas about what to do. So they both emerged from the cabin and onto the deck. Several other knights in heavy plate armor stood in a semi-circle. Vi fantasized briefly about pushing them each over the railing and watching them sink far below the waves, no matter how hard they struggled against the weight of their plate.

"Where's Taavin?" Vi spun in place, looking Ulvarth in the eye. She was oddly satisfied by the fact that, even in his greaves, he was no taller than her.

With an emotionless expression and movement faster than she would expect of someone wearing such burdensome armor, Ulvarth slapped her across the face with the back of his hand. Vi was sent stumbling. She tasted blood in her mouth and knew from the instant throbbing it would leave a colorful bruise.

"That is *the Voice* to you, Dark Isle dweller."

"How dare you," her father snarled, fire crackling up his arm.

"Father, don't." Vi clasped her hand over his, extinguishing the flames and straightening. A smirk spread on Ulvarth's lips.

"Listen to the girl and keep your head about you… or we may just take it early."

"Where is the Voice?" Vi demanded, drawing up to her full height once more. He could not beat her into silence.

"We've already taken him aboard *Light's Victory* so you could not beguile him further." Ulvarth pointed over her shoulder and Vi dared to turn.

Not far from their own vessel was a large ship. Vi could hear voices drifting over the water and the creaking of its hull against the waves. Those must have been the noises she'd heard when she'd woken.

The whole situation finally began to come into focus.

"How?" Vi whispered. Certainly, they had been consumed with Adela and rescuing her father.

Vi hadn't so much as spared a thought for the fact that she wasn't the only one being hunted. For every step of theirs, Ulvarth had taken one just behind, following their tracks. She could imagine him casing the towns around the Twilight Forest—setting checkpoints on the main road. She could see him getting word from Toris that the pirates had been made fools of by a girl with a strange accent, accompanied by a morphi and an unknown Lightspinner.

It wasn't hard to piece together their intended route. Mother, the Swords of Light had likely known Adela had captured her father. He'd been coming to Meru under their order, after all. Adela may have even tried to sell him back to them.

Her hands clenched into fists at her side. She'd been so focused on herself and her own missions that she'd forgotten to account for the other pieces in play. And now everyone she loved was going to pay for it.

"Your hold over the Voice would not last forever." Ulvarth smiled, teeth shining in the darkness. "He was bound to call out to us."

A pulse of magic drew Vi's gaze upward. Arwin was perched on the stern railing. "There's no way they found us in a dark sea. He betrayed you, Vi! Don't trust him."

"What?" Something wasn't adding up.

"Archers!" Ulvarth shouted across the waves. Arrows peppered the back of the boat and water behind, but it was too late; Arwin had already taken flight again, disappearing into the dark night. "Keep your eyes on the morphi!"

Vi didn't know how they could—she had already lost track of the nightwisp. But a second pulse of magic above the large warship gave away Arwin's location aboard a mast's crossbeam.

"Taavin," Arwin shouted at the top of her lungs, so loudly that her voice was perfectly clear even over the crash of waves and creaking of boats. "I will not forget your promise to me. You will pay in full, and then some. I will have blood!"

The archers had readied another volley. But by the time they shot, she was off again. Vi watched as the nightwisp flew across the dark water, blending in with the sky and sea.

"Morphi scum," Ulvarth muttered. "My work is never done." Vi glared up at him and Ulvarth must have sensed it, because he locked eyes with her once more, an amused expression sliding across his face. "Do you have something to say, dark-dweller?"

Vi opened her mouth to speak, but before she could, Ulvarth continued.

"Consider your next words carefully. Come peacefully, use no magicks, and I shall not be forced to gag and shackle you." Ulvarth took a step forward, trying to loom over them. But he seemed so very small in Vi's eyes. To her, he was little more than a boy wearing too-big armor. "Come peacefully and you will receive an imprisonment befitting your station. Fight me, and you shall know the full spectrum of pain I inflict on all those who stand against Yargen."

He said it like he was doing them some great favor. Vi wanted to punch him square in his teeth. No magic required.

"We surrender peacefully," her father said for both of them.

As much as Vi wanted to object, she didn't. She'd reached much the same conclusion as her father—there was no point in fighting this now. They were out maneuvered and outnumbered and their best bet was to keep as much ground as they could beneath them as they tried to plan their next advance.

Plus, her jaw ached at the mere thought of another gag.

"Take them to *Light's Victory*," Ulvarth commanded his soldiers. "And torch this dinghy."

Vi looked back to the cabin. Her meager supplies. The journal with all her notes and maps. Once more she was ushered away from what little she'd managed to scrape together and claim as her own.

The knights directed them to the side of the vessel; Vi took a step forward. Ulvarth snatched the scythe from her grasp.

"Give that back," Vi demanded, knowing it was both foolish and futile. But seeing the man holding the weapon was enough to curdle her stomach. Ulvarth opened his mouth and it was her turn to interrupt. "You don't know what you're holding."

"You dare question me?"

"I will not fight you, but that is mine to carry."

Ulvarth leaned forward, passing into her personal space with a sneer. "Get in the rowboat before I change my mind."

Vi stood her ground, hands balling into fists.

"Daughter, come," her father said sternly. But she still didn't move.

"Listen to your father, girl."

With one last glare, and one last look at the scythe, Vi moved forward. She was oddly reminded of the *Dawnskipper* and her last moments aboard that vessel. Life on the high seas was exhausting, and seemed always to end badly.

She and her father slowly climbed down into one of the two rowboats. They sat side by side, right at the front, as the rest of the boat filled with Ulvarth and his knights. The remaining men and women piled into the other dinghy and were off rowing in an instant.

"A farmer's scythe, of all things to carry…" Ulvarth glanced at her from the corners of his eyes. "What a useless weapon."

Vi bit the inside of her lip, keeping silent. Perhaps if she let him believe that's all it was, he wouldn't investigate further and peel back the fabric.

"Unless your determination surrounding it is something more?" She remained silent. Ulvarth chuckled. "You'll talk eventually. They all do. Now, burn the boat," he commanded his soldiers.

Three soldiers set their stolen vessel ablaze with circles of light. Vi stared at it, watching as what had once been Fallor's ship burned into the sea. She wondered if she should feel something toward it, but she must've retreated once more into that dark place within her that Jayme had created. Arwin's words echoed in her mind: *He betrayed you.*

It seemed like no time had passed at all before she was back on deck, but this time aboard a far more massive craft than even the *Stormfrost*. *Light's Victory* was no doubt a flagship of the Sword's armada. Its sides were riddled with cannons and a long ramming spear dominated its tall front.

"Take them below," Ulvarth commanded to the knights still surrounding them, walking in the opposite direction.

Vi and her father obliged as they were led below the main deck. A long hallway with many doors stretched the length of the vessel before dropping off in another stairwell. Judging from the outside, the gun deck was beneath them now, which meant there had to be yet another subdeck for the crew to sleep.

"In here." One of the knights opened a reinforced door heavy with various locks. "You will have a guard posted day and night. If we so much as get a whiff of magic, Lord Ulvarth's patience and extreme generosity will run dry very quickly."

"More generosity than they deserve," one of the other knights muttered.

Vi and her father held their tongues as they walked into the small cabin. It wasn't what she'd been expecting in the slightest. It was sparse, but comfortable enough. Certainly a very different type of confinement than what Adela had given either of them. The linens on the two cots looked clean, the bedding plush and fresh. Water sloshed in a jug on the shelf, threatening to spill with every sway of the ship. She was already trying to figure out Ulvarth's goals in giving them this much comfort. What game was he playing?

The door closed behind them, and the sound of locks engaging brought her back from her thoughts.

"So much for a rescue," Vi murmured.

"Far better than my last imprisonment." Her father sighed heavily. He'd just been liberated and here he was, back again under lock and key. He sat on one of the cots.

"Mine too." She went over to the small porthole—barred—and looked out over the sea. The last pieces of Fallor's ship smoldered in the water.

"Yours?"

"Adela had me for a while, but I managed to escape."

"You escaped her?" Aldrik said, wonder softening his voice.

"I nearly died doing it." Vi looked back to the door. "I think if I tried to escape this imprisonment, I would die." She had no doubt she could make a good run of it. But there were too many trained soldiers here. They'd get her, sooner or later.

"We're not going to try to escape. It makes the most sense for us to get to Risen and sort this there. Perhaps their queen will be able to assist."

"I doubt it." Vi put her back to the wall, sliding to the floor. "Ulvarth said it himself—he doesn't answer to the queen."

"But—"

"The Swords of Light are part of a religious order on Meru—the Faithful—and they're trying to consolidate power. They're using fear of the end of the world to do it."

"Little good consolidating power does if you have no one to rule because the world ends." Her father made a good point, one that brought a tired smile to her lips.

"The only hope we have is Taavin. As the Voice of Yargen, he *technically* supersedes Ulvarth."

"Technically?" Aldrik must've heard the strain in her voice.

"Ulvarth will do what he wants, regardless of what Taavin says. And if Taavin doesn't say what he wants to hear, Ulvarth makes his life a misery," Vi said bitterly, not wanting to go into more depth than that.

"This Ulvarth sounds like a tyrant in the making," her father said solemnly. He'd know; he'd seen tyrants. Some claimed his own father had been one.

The words left a heavy silence in their wake. Vi took a deep breath, tilting her head back and staring at the ceiling. Her eyes drifted closed.

"I'm sorry. "I really was going to take you back to Norin if you'd wanted to go."

The floorboards creaked as her father stood, walking over to her. He slowly sat next to her on the floor and covered her hand with his. "Only me?" he asked.

Vi cracked her eyes open, tilting her head to look at him. She couldn't manage words. She couldn't hurt him with the truth, but she didn't want to lie to him either. She settled on a small nod.

"If there's even a chance I can save this world, I have to take it." The memory of Raspian was seared in her mind, the dark god tearing into her flesh. "No matter what happens."

Her father was deathly still. When he finally spoke, it was a repeat of words he'd said before. "This recklessness—you get from your mother."

"So you've said."

"Have I told you that you also inherited her profound

compassion?"

Vi gave a small smile.

"There are so many things I would've done differently, were it not for her. Before your mother, I was a man who would have watched the world burn. She was the one to show me how my actions impacted others, and how to care." He let out a heavy sigh. "But that compassion has a cost, Vi. Trying to save just our Empire nearly took everything from her… Are you certain you understand what you would have to pay to save the whole world?"

"I do." The words felt like a lie. But she couldn't back down now and she couldn't hesitate. She'd made up her mind.

Her father pressed his eyes closed, not hiding a wince. He slowly shook his head. When he opened his eyes again, he couldn't seem to bring his gaze to rest on her.

"Why do you think it has to be you?"

"Because every step of my life feels like it was planned—everything led me here. You said it yourself: Solaris has a history with the weapons. You and mother have a history with the Crystal Caverns."

"Then you are paying for the crimes of your forebears."

"No, not just that." Vi squeezed his hand and leaned forward. "I was born with magic I wasn't supposed to have, in a land that knows nothing of it. I was given a watch that, somehow, connected me with the one man in this world who could help me understand myself—who had visions of my destiny before we ever met."

"Taavin." Aldrik turned to her. The way he said Taavin's name gave her pause. "The young woman… the bird woman…"

"Arwin, yes," her voice had fallen to a whisper.

"She said he betrayed you."

"I…" Every fear raced to be the first to overwhelm her. The memory of Jayme. Learning the truth about Taavin. Seeing nothing but betrayal in Fallor and Arwin's worlds. "He would never hurt me," Vi insisted. Taavin had said so; she had to trust him.

"Do you love him?"

"I… I do," she whispered. She hadn't even managed to tell Taavin yet. But it felt surprisingly good to say it aloud. "But it's also very complicated."

The makings of a tired smile spread on her father's lips. "Now you sound much like your mother, or how I imagine she sounded, when she talked about me."

"I didn't expect to. And I certainly wasn't looking for it to happen. The only love I've ever been certain of—ever looked for—has been yours, mother's, and Romulin's. I've never thought about anything else. I've never considered it because—"

"You never thought you had a choice." He stole her thoughts and gave them form. Vi must have given him a shocked look, but she couldn't be sure—her face had gone numb. Her father chuckled and continued anyway. "You forget, Vi, I was a crown prince before I was an Emperor. I, too, fell in love with someone I wasn't supposed to."

"How did you navigate it?"

"It was nearly impossible… and I messed up, greatly." Aldrik's gaze swung to the door. "As I fear he may have," he added very softly. Then, continuing louder, "But that love was the best thing I ever surrendered to. It gave me your mother, and it gave me you and your brother." His palm rested on the crown of her head, stroking her hair twice like he would when she was a child.

"I don't know if I can manage it all," Vi confessed. "I'm scared of being hurt and of hurting him."

"You may not have that choice. Love often decides for us. Do you trust him?"

"I do."

"Then you have to have faith in him, his decisions for himself, and in what you just said—that he will not hurt you."

Vi let out a heavy sigh, tipping her head back against the wall. Her chest ached and all she wanted to do was see Taavin. She wanted to curl in his arms again and merely exist quietly, hidden from the world, hidden from the pain of trying to sort through every complex and uninvited emotion she felt.

"How did you two meet?" her father asked lightly. Vi could tell the tone was forced, but the question was sincere.

"It's a long story."

"I think we have time."

Vi took a deep breath, and as she let it out, the whole story poured from her.

It was a mess of emotion and facts, tangled together in a way she was certain barely made sense outside of her own head. The horrific visions of the world's end fell heavy from her lips, the scenes of the dying men and women in the clinic tumbling alongside them. She spoke of Jayme, recognizing her own shock on her father's face, her own anger at the betrayal in his eyes.

Vi finally spoke of Taavin. And, just like that, he transformed from her precious secret to a known person she held dear.

She detailed her trials on Meru, in the Twilight Kingdom, and finally on the Isle of Frost. Her father asked few questions, not because she was such a coherent storyteller but because he realized the telling was as much about catharsis as information-sharing. For the first time, she felt like all her burdens weren't completely on her shoulders.

Vi's voice was hoarse and ragged when she finished. Every detail had been explored and every truth confessed. Her father was the only person in the world other than her who knew everything.

When she finally laid down that night to sleep, Vi rested easier than she had in weeks.

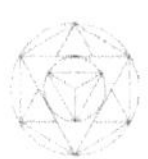

Over the next three days, there was no word from Taavin or Ulvarth, which left Vi and her father to their own devices. The first day, Aldrik repaid the favor of her story with stories of his own. He elaborated further on the crystal weapons. He spun tales about his brother. And he told her stories about visiting the North when Vi was too little to remember.

On the second day they dared to ask for a deck of cards when food was delivered, both surprised when one was granted to them with dinner that night. So they played cards and discussed tactics, speculating what would happen when they finally got to Risen. The next day they discussed magical theories—not daring to practice—and played even more games.

Vi had never had so much time with her father all to herself and felt downright guilty for enjoying it. Their circumstances were terrible. But getting imprisoned with the Emperor seemed an effective way to secure his time and attention—attention Vi had never fully admitted she was starved for.

On the morning of the fourth day, they were woken by the same knight who had been bringing them food and leading them to the latrine. As usual, he strode in as though he were a god himself.

"Up with you both. We shall be anchoring off Risen shortly."

Risen. This was the city Taavin had grown up in, and the capital of Meru. Curiosity swelled in her with every step up the stairs and back to the main deck.

Sure enough, in the distance was a vast city. It was settled among rising hills that sloped to the docks and down to a wide river that cut the city in two. On one side a large castle dominated the tallest hill. On the other, a circular building smaller in overall size than the castle stretched taller into the sky.

Without needing to be told, Vi knew that the two were the residence of the Queen of Meru and the Archives of Yargen. She knew it in their opulence, and in the way their very construction seemed to square off against each other.

A city of stone stretched out before them. Buildings were packed against each other so tightly that Vi had no idea how roadways fit between them. Every one was three or four stories tall and had a tile roof with metal gutters—not unlike the buildings in that long-ago first vision of her father.

She glanced at him from the corners of her eyes. His attention was still on the cityscape, and he was none the wiser. Taavin had said that her visions of the future were malleable. Had she changed the one with Adela? Or had the pirate queen taken him onto the beach before they'd arrived? Would he still end up in that square before the queen to bear witness to the plagued man in the cage?

Had she changed the designs of fate at all? Or had she merely played into the path that led to the world's end? Vi grabbed the watch at her throat, nervous energy sparking across her skin, leaving goosebumps despite the warm air.

"It's magnificent." Ulvarth seemed to materialize from nowhere, leaving Vi to wonder what hole the snake had slithered from. "I imagine you're in awe of it, coming from a land so… uncivilized."

"It's clear you've never been to Solaris, if you think us uncivilized," her father retorted.

"I don't recall giving you permission to speak," Ulvarth said lightly, as if talking about the weather. "Do I need to have you fitted for a gag?"

Vi bit her cheeks, barely resisting the urge to rise to her father's defense.

"Which reminds me… when we arrive, we shall proceed to the Archives of Yargen."

At the mere mention of the Archives, she swung her gaze across the deck. *Where in the Mother's name was Taavin?* What had been confusion turned to frustration, and now to worry. All this while, Ulvarth had been threatening to gag and chain them… What if he actually had done so to Taavin?

Surely he knew that Taavin had escaped of his own accord. His blaming her was to save face for losing the Voice. She couldn't fathom the wrath Ulvarth harbored for Taavin.

While they docked, Vi looked for Taavin, continuing to worry over him.

Despite all Taavin had said, she realized she had vastly

underestimated Ulvarth's cruelty. And she should've spent her time aboard worrying more over herself rather than playing card games.

27

THE SHIP ANCHORED JUST off the docks of Risen and they took tendering vessels to get ashore.

Vi sat with her father, silent once more. They were both keenly aware of the fact that any movement or noise could, and likely would, be used against them in some way. Ulvarth's efforts to lull them into a sense of security had come to an end. Vi turned into the salt spray splashing up against the side of the boat, allowing it to mist her face. She'd taken the time to rake her fingers through her hair and braid it. Her father had helped, knowing some of the more intricate plaits her mother usually wore. He had used a splash of water to slick his own hair back in the style he'd always worn.

They were a far cry from their regal personas, but it made Vi feel more put together and more like a princess. It made her feel less like some horrible sea goblin rising up from the muck to stumble through a gilded city.

The boat came alongside a dock that had a small army waiting.

Ulvarth's Swords were a group larger than Vi had previously given them credit for. She counted at least fifty, and that was excluding all the men and women who had been aboard *Light's Victory*. She wondered how much of the whole militia of Meru was composed of the holy order—how many men and women were positioned in and out of Risen who reported to Ulvarth instead of the queen.

"My Lord." A man sank to his knees. He wore a bright purple sash around his shoulders pinned with a medal that Vi had never seen before. Ulvarth held out his bejeweled fingers and the man reverently scooped them in his hands, kissing his knuckles for an uncomfortably long time. "We have made all the necessary preparations."

Vi spared a glance for her father. Aldrik seemed calm and composed, but an uneasy panic was rising in her. But she knew everything Taavin had said about Ulvarth, who was not the calm, collected, respectful individual they'd been dealing with to date.

He was a monster.

"Good," Ulvarth almost purred. Without so much of a glance back toward them, he started down the dock, a wave of knights dropping to their knees as he passed—as if he were a god. "Get them in irons for the parade."

"Irons?" Vi blurted. Ulvarth paused. She didn't know if she was glad or not he'd heard. But she had his attention now. "My lord," she ground out the honorific, hating herself for every syllable. "We have complied with you without struggle. You said there would be no irons or gags."

Slowly, Ulvarth crossed back to her. The assembled soldiers seemed to hold their collective breath. What set her heart to racing was their curious anticipation—as though they were about to witness a show.

"You did, didn't you?" he said softly. "And I do thank you for making it very easy for me to get you here." Vi narrowed her eyes as a satisfied smile crept across his lips. Ulvarth leaned forward, whispering in her ear. Vi barely resisted the urge to shove him away. "Now continue to be a good pet and I'll let you keep your skin. I have hides of far more fearsome creatures than you hanging on my walls."

He straightened away, leaving the strong smell of peppermint clouding the air in his wake. Ulvarth turned and Vi took a half step forward, fantasizing about shoving a blade right between the vertebrae of his neck. But the only blades drawn were pointed at her.

Four knights had closed in on her in a moment. Their weapons rested right under her chin. Ulvarth looked back with an amused smile.

"Muzzle that dog. She may bite the hand that's feeding her."

"Do not—" her father stepped forward as knights with irons approached. Vi grabbed his forearm, stopping him.

"I've endured worse, Father," she said loudly. "I've endured worse and thrived while the people who forced me to endure it suffered."

If Ulvarth heard, he gave no indication.

Outnumbered and out-manned, the knights were met with no resistance when it came to shackling them. A gag was pressed between Vi's teeth. *At least this one isn't cold*, she thought darkly. Two gags were too many, Vi decided; she was developing a preference.

As the knights pushed them down the dock, another vessel came up to a pier one slip over from theirs. A litter was situated on it—so heavy with gold that Vi was shocked it didn't sink the boat. Twelve men strained to hoist it, carrying it off the boat and onto the docks so that the man within was never forced to have his feet touch the ground.

Taavin.

Drawn by an invisible tether, Vi stepped toward him. Arms restrained her. She struggled against them. Incoherent noises slipped around the gag in her mouth.

Taavin didn't so much as look her way.

He was dressed in golden plate, a long cape draped behind

him. A legion of knights maneuvered to surround him. Pennons flew at the front and back of his detail. Taavin kept his eyes forward, face passive. Were it not for the breeze ruffling his hair, Vi would've thought he was sculpted from clay, not flesh and blood.

"Move!" A knight shoved her hard and Vi stumbled, barely keeping her feet beneath her. "If you stop, or try to run, or fight, we will cleave you straight in two."

Vi glanced over her shoulder at the man. He had golden hair and light brown eyes. He'd be plain, if not for the malice that permeated his very aura. She looked to her father, who stared back helplessly. He'd told her he'd endured much in his ascension to the throne, but Vi was left wondering if this could top it all.

Taavin was back in Ulvarth's hands. She and her father were captive. Her mother and brother were still back on the Dark Isle, left very much in the dark as to their predicament.

What had she accomplished? What had every step of struggle and effort until now been for?

Horns blared, echoing a short, lively tune off the tall buildings. The knights arranged themselves into a single line, falling into place. At the front of the procession was Ulvarth on a white steed—easily the largest warstrider Vi had ever seen. Behind him was a stretch of soldiers, then Taavin—the Voice that gave Ulvarth the power to lead, the foundation of his unjust rule. Then another long stretch of knights, a gap, and Vi and Aldrik.

Behind them was another gap before more knights, who kept their distance as though they were tainted.

"Lord Ulvarth has returned. Rejoice!" A voice boomed from the front, magnified by some kind of magical or mechanical device. Vi couldn't see which. "Lord Ulvarth has returned. Rejoice! The Goddess has smiled this day! Yargen's children celebrate, for his mighty campaign has been successful! Thanks to Ulvarth, the Voice has returned to Risen!"

The proclamations echoed off every wall as they entered the city proper. The knights must have been keeping the populous at bay. Because suddenly they were inundated with people. Citizens stood in line, pushing against each other to get a better look at the parade.

"Lord Ulvarth has returned. Rejoice!" the crier at the front of the line continued. Vi would've guessed Ulvarth, not Taavin, was Yargen's Voice, the way he was carrying on. "He has brought evil to justice. He has liberated the Voice from evil. He has recovered the Voice from the hands of those who would do him harm."

It was then Vi realized they were talking about *her*. She saw the people surrounding her for the first time, their skeptical and angry faces glowering from the shadows of their marbled buildings.

"Those who have brought the plague? Justice! Those who turned our fields barren? Justice! Those who unleashed the Dark God Raspian? Justice!"

Vi looked over to her father. His jaw was set so tightly that Vi wondered how his teeth didn't crack. His hands were balled in his shackles and fire crackled around them. But he kept his rage checked—for both of their sakes.

"She who took our Voice? Justice!" Cheers increased, the crowd chanting along, all crying for "justice."

Vi kept her eyes forward, no longer looking at the people and their lavish clothes or buildings. She could hear their jeers without needing to see their angry eyes. She would let their vitriol slide off of her, just as her father was. She would follow his example.

Something wet and rotten-smelling crashed into her temple. Vi stumbled, more from surprise than pain. She felt the slime from whatever it was—*food, rotten food? Let it be rotten food*—dribbling down the side of her face.

"Lord Ulvarth has returned. Rejoice!" the crier began anew, methodically repeating himself to the crowd.

It seemed all of Risen lined this wide road. All of Risen had come prepared with their best insults to levy and trash to throw. Vi and her father were pelted. The slimy, sticking, stinking things hurt less than the bottles and rocks—those Vi actively attempted to dodge. But the former coated her in yet another layer of grime.

Something particularly large smacked into her shoulder. This time she did stumble and falter. A knight grabbed her roughly, righting her.

"Keep going or lose your head," he snarled.

Vi found her feet once more, looking to her father. His dark eyes were filled with all the sorrow of the world. Sheer agony covered his face, agony that compounded the longer he looked at her. But when he spoke, his words were strong and even.

"Keep that head high," he dared to utter. "Even if you wear a crown of filth, you are still a princess of Solaris."

They can't take that away from you. The words were left unsaid, but Vi heard them with her heart more than her ears. She felt them—saw them, in every one of her father's movements.

Vi straightened, holding her head high, and continued their slow march to the Archives of Yargen.

At long last, they crested the top of the final set of stairs, reaching a large square. The heavy irons had cut into her wrists, blood dripping down her fingertips. But Vi continued to hold her head high. The small act of defiance was all she could manage now.

The Archives of Yargen towered over her in a single spire. At its base, triangular buildings stretched out like points on a sun, connected by glass-topped, floating archways and walkways. Every building was nearly five stories tall—taller than anything else surrounding it. But even they were only half the height of the main column.

Vi craned her neck awkwardly, jaw aching. Smoke billowed from a ring of windows near the top of the spire. *The Flame of Yargen.* Which meant Taavin's home—his prison—was just above that.

"Take him to the dungeons." Ulvarth's voice drifted back to her. The public had been pushed away from this square, leaving just Ulvarth and his small army.

Taavin was gone as well, but Vi hadn't seen where they'd

taken him.

"And bring the girl to me."

The words took a second to register. It wasn't until her father was being forcibly ripped from her side that Vi understood. She turned for her father. Vi screamed against her gag—more incoherent sounds.

In truth, she didn't know if she had words at all. Her mind was pure rage, and the daze of such a new and overwhelming place, peppered with the sheer confusion of exactly how all this had happened.

Two strong arms closed around her, pulling her backward, hoisting her off the ground. Vi kicked her feet and thrashed. She was done being the polite princess. The masses were gone; there was no longer the need to represent the Dark Isle with regal pride, and Ulvarth's Swords already thought her a monster. She would prove them right to defend her father.

Aldrik looked back to her, worry in his eyes. He still said nothing. *How could he say nothing?* She was the one wearing the gag, but he was the silent one. It was a level of self-control Vi had yet to gain.

"You have fight in you, don't you?" Ulvarth stepped into her field of vision, blocking her view of her father. Vi twisted and struggled against the arms holding her, trying to catch sight of him again. But he'd been lost in the sea of golden armor, purple sashes, and cruel eyes.

She'd lost him again.

She'd lost her father.

Vi glared at Ulvarth. She'd show him how much fight she had in her. Fire crackled around her knuckles, popping underneath the iron biting into her flesh at her wrists. It didn't take much for the iron to heat to a red glow under her white-hot flames.

Ulvarth covered the flames with his hand. She didn't know if he had somehow smothered her fire—or if it was the sheer surprise of the motion that extinguished her spark. He leaned in, the thick scent of peppermint making her dizzy.

"Now, now, you've done so well. No need to fight."

Vi would spit in his face if she could.

"Especially not since I'm willing to make a deal with you."

Her body went still. Warning bells tolled violently in her mind. His mere proximity had her whole body aflame with caution.

"You'd like that, wouldn't you? A deal to save yours and your father's skins?" Ulvarth waited long enough that it became clear he was waiting on her. His mouth twitched into a brief grimace, but he kept his composure. "*Well?*"

Vi nodded begrudgingly, and the sinister smile returned.

"Good, I thought so." Ulvarth leaned away. "Take her to my throne," he commanded the knights holding her before starting off ahead.

Vi was all but dragged behind him, ushered into the shadow of the Archives of Yargen, through the lofty stone archway, framed by two open doors.

And into the Light of Yargen for the first time.

28

THE ARCHIVES OF YARGEN were barely comprehensible. They should be an impossibility. Surely a place like this couldn't exist.

Vi forgot her body for several blissful minutes as she was half-carried, half-dragged through the ground floor of the Archives. She was too distracted by the shelves on shelves on shelves of books. Surely, every piece of knowledge that ever existed was compiled and packed into the overflowing bookcases that lined the spire all the way to the top.

Rings of walkways—connected by stairways and ladders—spread out at varying intervals all the way to the top. At the summit, a brazier hung over the center of the room, larger and more opulent than any Vi had ever seen. Several archways extended from the bookcases to support it, with chains hanging from points on the ceiling to further secure its suspension above the center of the tall, hollow room.

She squinted at the flame. It was so bright that it lit the whole of the Archives like daylight, even though there were no other light sources positioned among the bookcases.

Underneath her feet was a tiled floor of mother-of-pearl mosaic grouted with gold. At the center, directly under the flame, was a large golden sun. At the sun's center was an intricate engraving of a glyph Vi recognized from the coin Charlie the pirate had used to pay at the tavern. It was the same glyph she'd seen carved in the trees in Soricium—three interconnected circles, stacked vertically with a line through their center.

"Keep moving." One of the knights shoved her and Vi stumbled forward.

They led her across the room, directly under the flame. From where Vi stood, it seemed massive—and she was at least ten stories beneath it. Vi couldn't fathom its size up close. Even from here, she could see sculpted women fanning outward and linking arms to hold the main basin with their frozen, reverent faces.

Above the flame was a stone ceiling—likely the floor of Taavin's room. His prison.

She had no further opportunity to study the Archives as the knights led her through a side door tucked between bookcases. They wound up a narrow stair sandwiched behind the bookshelves, illuminated by glowing stones—not unlike those in the Twilight Kingdom—and emerged in a hallway through one of the soaring arches she'd seen connecting the main archives to the pointed buildings fanning around it like sun rays. Through another carved and gilded door they went, into what Ulvarth had aptly described as a throne room.

He sat on a chair of gold, plush with purple velvet. A sun rose up from the back of his chair, its points giving the illusion of a crown on his raven hair. A sash was draped over his shoulder and he wielded the crystal scythe in his right hand. Just the sight of him holding the glittering weapon made her feel ill.

"Kneel." The brown-eyed knight who'd been manhandling her kicked the back of her knees. Vi fell hard, biting against her gag to keep back a shout of pain. "You're in the presence of High Lord

Ulvarth, Lord of the Swords of Light, Destined Savior of Meru and Champion of Yargen."

Ulvarth's hateful eyes glimmered as he looked down on her. Vi had no doubt that while he didn't respect her land or people, he still delighted in seeing a princess brought to her knees before him. And a man that delighted in debasing others was a man who could never be trusted.

"If I remove your gag, do you promise not to try to use magic against me?"

Vi thought about it for a long moment and eventually nodded. He'd said something about offering her a deal, and she wanted to hear him out. Taavin was still at play in all of this. *He wouldn't betray her*, Vi's heart insisted for a countless time.

"Remove her gag, leave the shackles, and get out," Ulvarth commanded his knights.

"My Lord—"

"I did not ask for your opinion," Ulvarth said smoothly, almost lightly, as though he was making a passing suggestion and not levying a very obvious threat.

The knight removed her gag and left, closing the door behind them. Vi listened for their footsteps—they promptly stopped just beyond the door. Maybe she could kill Ulvarth, but she wouldn't make it out alive.

"Are you thinking of killing me?" he asked with a surprisingly smug grin.

"It's tempting." Vi rose to her feet.

"You won't make it out alive."

"So I gathered. It's still tempting." Vi gave him a mad grin. Perhaps she was mad for talking to him the way she was. But Vi had seen the death that was coming for her, and knew she wouldn't die here.

"Do you wonder why you're not dead yet?"

She doubted he'd believe her if she said she knew it was because she was currently fated to die fighting Raspian with the scythe he had his filthy hands all over. "I have the distinct feeling you're about to tell me."

Ulvarth lifted the scythe before slamming it down on the dais. The low thud was a cue and, on command, Taavin emerged from behind the throne. He wore the same finery she'd seen him in on the litter—gold and white. They were the Solaris Imperial colors as well, and for half of a second her treacherous mind wondered what he would look like as a Solaris Emperor, ruling at her side.

But now was certainly not the time or place to indulge such fantasies.

Especially not when her and her father's survival was up for debate.

"Our Voice has told me something most interesting," Ulvarth started. Vi didn't miss the hint of annoyance already in his voice. "He has told me that you are Yargen's new Champion, destined to defend the light against the coming darkness."

"And yet your men honor you with the title." Vi arched her dark eyebrows. Ulvarth's eyes narrowed slightly.

"You." Ulvarth's eye twitched. "The divine chose *you*. A small girl from the Dark Isle. The daughter of the man and woman who wounded Yargen so—who went against her will and acted in favor of the dark god."

Vi pressed her lips together and kept her mouth shut. He hadn't asked her a question and she didn't feel like indulging his chatter. She glanced over to Taavin, but he had yet to make eye contact with her. Wherever he was mentally, it was a world away.

"What can you possibly do?" Ulvarth grumbled. Vi didn't have a good answer, but once more, he wasn't looking for one. Ulvarth adjusted his seat, narrowly avoiding a position that would make his sulking even more obvious. "It's no matter… you're here now."

"You said you had a deal for me." Vi had no interest in his pity party over not being chosen as Yargen's Champion. She suspected if he really knew the trimmings the job came with, he'd be happier without it. He was just another man who wanted power and none of the responsibility attached. Vi had dealt with men like him her whole life—she called them Senators.

"I do. You see, Vi Solaris, I am not a man without mercy. I would be willing to send you and your father back to your forgotten rock on one of the Sword's fastest vessels."

"What would you want in return for such a kindness?"

"The Voice has assured me that, with your help as Champion, we will be able to rekindle the Flame of Yargen and return it to its former glory."

Former glory? Rekindle? Taavin had said as much… But the flame she passed under looked incredibly glorious from where Vi stood.

"If the Faithful have any hope to make it through the dark age Lord Raspian will usher in, we shall need her barrier, at the least. Yet the flame is so weak, it can barely protect this temple—let alone all of Risen."

Vi gave a small nod. She heard his words but didn't fully understand them. Yet she had the distinct feeling Ulvarth was the sort of man who didn't appreciate questions.

"Should you rekindle the flame for me, and commit to eternal silence on the role your family played in weakening it in the first place, I shall let you and your father return to your isle and do… whatever it is you do on that desolate rock."

"And my role as Champion?" Vi glanced at Taavin. He was still avoiding looking at her. This had to be some kind of plan he'd put together… right?

"I think you mean *my* role as Champion." Ulvarth gripped the scythe tighter, as though that alone distinguished him as the Champion.

"I see…" Vi said. He saw the crystal weapon as a trophy. Even if he knew it could be used to stand against Raspian, Vi doubted he would. All he wanted was the flame rekindled and a barrier around Risen—the rest of the world be damned. Taavin had kept information from Ulvarth and that meant she had to trust him and play along. "In the meantime, while I rekindle the flame and keep my silence, you'll keep my father safe?"

"No harm shall come to him while he awaits trial for his crimes."

"My father committed no crimes against you or your lands. This is the first time he's ever stepped foot on them." Vi shifted her wrists, trying to adjust the pressure of the shackles. Her blood slowly dripped on the floor from where the iron had cut into her flesh on the long walk.

"Your father allowed Raspian to return to this world."

Vi expected him to seem more upset about such a truth, but he delivered the line with the same concern one might reserve for reporting the weather. That was proof enough that he was lying. Ulvarth knew it wasn't entirely because of her father that Raspian had returned. This was all just a game.

Think like him.

Something was wrong with the flame of Yargen, and Ulvarth couldn't fix it—not without her help. The man likely hated the notion of "lowering himself" to asking someone from the Dark Isle for help. If she succeeded, and he sent her away… he planned to take the credit.

"No harm comes to my father while he awaits your trial," Vi reiterated, confident she now understood the full terms of the deal. "You keep him safe, comfortable, and in quarters befitting his station."

"You think you can order me, now?"

"I'm not ordering, I'm bargaining. Didn't you say you had an offer? Well the offer has turned into a negotiation." Vi rolled her shoulders back, standing straighter and ignoring the weight of the shackles trying to pull her down. "You keep my father and me safe and comfortable. When I have finished rekindling the flame, you allow us to go home without any other hindrances. You make no move against the Dark Isle or my family ever again. And then I will say nothing of my role here. I will let no one know that it was really I who helped rekindle the flame."

Ulvarth's expression soured like a too-ripe fruit. Vi smirked. He hadn't expected her to figure his game and she hoped he hadn't figured out hers.

Rekindling the flame had always been part of her mission. But so was figuring out the secrets of the watch and the scythe. Her arrival in Risen hadn't gone according to plan, but she was where she needed to be—the Archives of Yargen.

Fate had yet to abandon her.

"Do we have a deal?" Vi tilted her head. "I do everything you need and you can take credit for all my work."

"You think I need you that desperately?" he sneered.

"I do, because you are only pretending to be Yargen's chosen Champion. You need me," Vi stated with all the royal arrogance she'd avoided her whole life. "Do we have an understanding?"

Ulvarth was silent for several long breaths. Vi wondered if his heaving chest was a method to attempt to calm himself down. If it was, it didn't seem to be working. But then again, he didn't scream at her when he opened his mouth again, despite the bright flush in his cheeks.

"I think we have an understanding," he said finally.

"One more thing."

"You are a greedy woman."

"Blame my royal upbringing." She was in rags, covered in filth. He was on a gilded throne. Yet in that moment, Vi felt like the more powerful person in the room. "I need free access to the Archives of Yargen, and to that scythe."

"You think I'm just going to let you wander with a weapon?"

"It's required to rekindle the flame." She had no idea what was required. But she wanted as long of a leash as possible. She wanted to get her hands on those books for more reasons than she had fingers and toes. And she wanted full access to the last crystal weapon.

"Very well. I will let you have access to the Archives. But take one step outside and you will not make it a second step."

"And the scythe?"

Ulvarth considered for a long moment, slowly turning to the

statue called Taavin. "The Voice shall keep it, and perform any necessary research. He shall report to me on his findings and, as needed, you shall have supervised access to him and the crystal weapon."

Vi tried to keep disappointment off her face. The more she fought, the more he'd know he had something worth holding over her head. It'd give up the strength of her position. So instead, Vi kept her face passive, emotions hidden.

"Then yes, my lord. We do have an understanding."

"You have one month to rekindle the flame. One month before my patience and kindness expire."

Vi didn't know what she was doing, so she didn't know if that was long enough. Taavin had no reaction and gave no indication one way or another. He hardly looked like he was breathing.

"Now get out," Ulvarth snarled.

She gave a bow, just for effect, and turned for the door. The scythe thudded dully on the dais beneath her as Ulvarth struck it twice, signaling for the knights on the other side of the doors to escort her away.

"Remove her from my sight and find a place for her in the Lark's dormitories. Let them be forced to deal with her," Ulvarth commanded. "And for the love of Yargen, clean her before she stinks up the entire place."

29

THERE WERE THREE ASPECTS of the Faithful, Vi quickly learned. The first were the laymen—Faithful who studied Lightspinning and followed the teachings of Yargen but did little else. They were civilians. Followers, but not active participants in the structure of the Faithful. The laymen were scattered across Meru.

Next were the Swords. Vi had had enough of them for a lifetime. And, judging by how they shoved her into the care of a beady-eyed, sagely man, the feeling was mutual.

The final aspect were the Larks of Light. These were men and women who had pledged themselves to Yargen. But where the Swords where the militaristic strong-arm of the Faithful, the Larks were the teachers, theorists, theologians, scholars, and preachers.

They were quiet, calm, and kind.

Three things Vi hadn't experienced in a long time.

"This way, young one." The elderly man's demeanor reminded her instantly of King Noct. "Let's take you to a bathing chamber."

"What's your name?" Vi asked. She rubbed her wrists, gently inspecting the clotted blood and torn flesh left behind from the irons.

"They call me Kindred Allan." He spoke without turning. Likely because every movement seemed stiff and painful for him. "And your name, young one?"

"Vi Solaris."

"Not the same Vi Solaris as the Crown Princess of the Solaris Empire?"

"You know of it?" Vi asked cautiously.

"It is the Lark's job to know of it," he said thoughtfully. "We record all Yargen's light touches, and even the places where it cannot, to keep record of all her designs and the ways mortalkind seeks to change them."

It was a pleasant surprise not to have someone immediately telling her how terrible her home was. Allan seemed emotionally detached, but genuinely interested. Vi counted it a victory.

Allan lead her down a spiral stair in a different building from the one Ulvarth had occupied. It was the northernmost point of the triangular buildings surrounding and connected to the Archives. Every flight of stairs opened to either a long hall or a warm room. There were crackling fires, and men and women working quietly at desks or talking, while sinking further into plush cushions wrapped in warm-hued fabrics.

"This way, your highness."

"Just Vi is fine."

"Is it not your custom to always use some kind of honorific or title in Solaris for royalty and nobility?"

"Usually, yes… But we're not in Solaris. And it's not common for those who are close to royalty." Besides, Vi had enough of being the crown princess for one day. She'd invoked her royal persona for Ulvarth and her walk through the city. Now, she felt too tired to deal with it.

"Are we close?" he asked.

"That depends on your actions, I suppose."

"Spoken like a true princess." He gave her a weathered smile as he opened a door, allowing steam to billow out. The room was tiled from floor to ceiling. A faucet continually poured hot water into a large copper tub, the overflow draining underneath the vessel. There was a small wooden stool with a soap bar and a few other scouring agents in jars.

Another shelf at her left had a variety of brushes, combs, razors, and other barbering tools. Over which was a mirror. *A mirror*. Vi hadn't seen herself in a mirror since the small one in the bathroom of the Twilight Kingdom.

She stalled before it, slowly bringing a hand to her cheek.

"I shall leave you to soak. Please enjoy at your leisure. While you are soaking, do pull the screen before the door. I shall send one of our female Larks to come with clothing for you and she will drape it over for your convenience and modesty."

"Thank you," Vi murmured, too distracted by her reflection to say more than that.

The woman she saw didn't reflect the woman Vi thought she knew. Her fingers trailed over cheekbones that were sharper than she recalled. As sharp as her father's—she could recognize now that she had seen him again so recently. The harsh sun of the seas had further darkened her skin, as Vi suspected from her arms, but her hair was still as black as midnight and as fine as spider's silk.

She slowly undid the braids she and her father had coiffed for their arrival to Risen. Vi turned her head this way and that, looking at how it fell just beyond her shoulders. There wasn't the slightest bit of wild body to it, not even with the kink of braids—nothing like her mother's and brother's.

She was, indeed, her father's daughter.

Stripping, Vi balled and burned her clothes. Once more, she incinerated everything of her last incarnation in life. What version of Vi would walk the Archives of Yargen when she emerged from the tub?

Pulling the screen mostly shut, Vi sank into the water, spilling it over all sides. It completely engulfed her and for a few moments she let the warmth soak off the filth that covered her. With the constantly running tap, the water was perpetually hot and the grime flowed over and away as she began to scrub.

Vi had just started rubbing her legs raw when the door opened.

"Princess?"

"Just Vi is fine," Vi called over the screen.

"Vi, then… My name is Serina. Allan told me to attend you. I have clothes here; shall I drape them over the screen?"

"That sounds lovely." Vi rested her elbows on the edge of the tub, looking at the clothes that appeared by two dainty hands. A towel was draped last at their side.

"I'll wait just outside for you to finish to show you to your room… But do take your time. It sounds as though you've had quite a journey."

"Thank you," Vi said softly. For one moment, she thought about asking the girl to stay. Vi had questions about this place, about the Larks, and about the flame. But she ultimately decided to save them for Taavin.

She had no interest in making friends here. This was like the Twilight Kingdom—like Arwin. It was business. Vi retreated further into the tub, thinking of the morphi woman. She had definitely not grown any attachments to her, Vi insisted to herself. She only wondered how she was doing out of pure curiosity.

The door clicked closed and Vi finished, dried, and dressed. The robes were basic—not unlike those she'd seen the crones wear on the Dark Isle. They were a deep, sunset-red hue, cinched tight at the waist with a wide, golden sash. One benefit of clothes so basic—they were designed to swim on their wearer, and Vi didn't have to worry about how her hips were going to squeeze into anything.

Vi opened the door to find the woman waiting just as she'd said. She had silvery hair, though she didn't look much older than Vi, and bright hazel, nearly yellow eyes. There was something distinctly cat-like about her movements and Vi couldn't fight the notion that if the woman ever became a morphi, her shifted form would be some kind of lynx or leopard.

"The rooms are two floors up." She pointed upward as she walked to the stairs. "They're not much, but we've managed to rearrange ourselves so that you will have a room of your own."

"You didn't need to do that."

"We thought it appropriate," she said with a note of finality that suggested there were more layers to *why* they thought it appropriate than Vi understood.

They walked up the stairs, passing one landing that led into a workroom, and then up once more to a long hall nearly identical to the last. Her door was the first on the left. It was just as Serina had said—simple. A bed, a small desk, a washbasin, an empty bookcase.

"Should you need anything, you can ask any of the Larks." Serina paused, stalling before she headed back to the stairs. Her eyes dragged over Vi from top to bottom. She opened her mouth, promptly closed it, and turned.

"Ask." Vi let a slightly regal tone seep into the word, turning it into more of a command. "I know what it looks like when someone has a question."

With a guilty grin on her cherubic cheeks, Serina turned. "They say you kidnapped the Voice."

"So I've heard."

"Yet they tell me you are to be made comfortable while you are here…"

"And?" Vi kept her face passive.

"Those two things seem contradictory."

"They do, don't they?" Her attempts at stoicism failed, and a small grin made it onto her face.

"So are you our enemy, or our friend?"

"What do you believe?"

"I don't know. I don't have all the facts." Serina spoke as though that should be obvious. "That's why I ask… to collect them."

Vi smiled tiredly. Something about the girl reminded her very much of her mother. She couldn't put her finger on what, but it was there. Which was odd, given that she looked so young. The comparison already filled her with a dull ache.

"I'm not allowed to say much," Vi answered honestly. She would honor her deal with Ulvarth only as far as it benefited her. But Serina seemed sharp enough to figure out the undercurrents on her own—she was already seeking to piece together the facts. And while Vi wasn't looking for a friend, she could use an ally. "But I will say this: Taavin is the last person I would ever harm."

Serina seemed startled Vi had used his name so confidently. Eventually saying, "You seem honest enough about that."

"Good."

The woman continued to hover. Her eyes drifted down to Vi's hands. It was then that Vi noticed she was dripping blood onto the floor. The clots of her wounds, left behind by the shackles, must've been washed away in the bath.

"Would you like me to heal that for you?"

"I think not," Vi said, after a long moment's debate.

"It'd be no trouble."

"I know it wouldn't be as I, too, know *halleth*." She wasn't very good at it, but she knew it. Now the Larks also knew that she possessed Lightspinning. "I don't think I want to heal these with magic. I think I'd like the scars from Ulvarth's *hospitality*. It seems a fitting reminder of my time here."

Serina regarded her warily, as if seeing her for the first time. It was the same look Arwin had given Vi when they had stolen Fallor's boat, after Vi had killed a pirate with two words. Now, like then, Vi reached the same conclusion: *Let her be wary.*

Finally, Serina bowed her head, turned, and started for the stairs, not quite hiding her relief at the prospect of making her escape. Which only made Vi more surprised when her door opened again a short time later. Serina popped in just long enough to leave a small roll of bandages on the foot of her bed before leaving again without another word.

Vi debated her next move as she wrapped her wrists in the bandages. The mere mention of Taavin was all the direction she needed. She closed the door and headed back up the spiral stair the way she came, across the lofty bridge high above Risen, and back into the main tower of the archives.

She started up the first ladder she came to, arced around the wide landing that granted access to this stretch of shelves, then up a second stair. Up and up she climbed, higher and higher. It was nearly impossible to keep her attention on her destination among the ocean of books.

Close to the top of all the walkways, Vi was nearly level with the sculpted women holding up the brazier she'd seen from the first moment she'd entered. The light was blindingly bright and the fire that raged behind their arms was white-hot. How could anyone say this flame needed rekindling? If someone were to spark it further, they risked burning down the whole building.

Oddly, no heat reached her cheeks. She didn't feel the slightest bit of warmth from the blaze. Even as someone who first learned to interact with fire as a Firebearer, she still suspected she should feel *something*.

Vi squinted at it, holding her breath. She was waiting for something… but she didn't quite know what. A sign from the Goddess, perhaps? Taavin heard Yargen's voice in the flame; surely as her champion, Vi should hear something, too?

"Magnificent, isn't it?" Vi turned, startled. She grabbed the railing for stability, suddenly off-balance and aware of the dizzying height. Ulvarth had ascended the stairs opposite her, the imposing man slowly walking around the brazier. Vi regarded him warily, still gripping the railing. "I asked you a question."

"I thought it rhetorical, given it's obviously magnificent."

"I didn't bring you here to admire it." His voice went low and dangerous.

"Didn't you though? I am to find a way to reignite the flame, am I not?"

He smirked. "You don't already know how?"

"I couldn't go into it, really… It's something that can only be understood fully by the Champion and the Voice." Vi borrowed the morphi's explanation of their magic. He didn't seem to notice, but for her it felt like a double-edged blade to shove between his ribs. Vi had the satisfaction of one-upping him, and the knowledge that she'd borrowed an explanation from people he unjustly hated.

"I hope you're right, for your sake." Ulvarth gave her a sinister smile. "After all, your father starts his trials at the queen's earliest convenience."

"Let's hope it's a fair trial."

"Oh, I'm sure it will be." Ulvarth finally came to a stop only a few steps away. "You think me a monster." Vi kept her mouth shut and let that be answer enough. "But this is one thing I don't have to be monstrous about. Your father dug his own grave, by digging the world's."

She searched his unflinching gaze. Ulvarth may be a monster. He may be ruthless and calculating and obsessed with his own power. But there was confidence in those blue eyes. Not just arrogance, *confidence*. At least in this instance, he genuinely believed himself right and just.

"So maybe I am a monster. But you're the spawn of a monster. So you're really no different."

"Call me a monster and I'll show you my fangs." Vi sneered widely for emphasis. Ulvarth chuckled.

"A shame you were born a human to such poor parentage. We may have gotten along in another life, you and I."

Vi was certain she'd hate him in any and every lifetime. She hated him from his pointed ears to his mirror-polished boots.

Ulvarth sauntered away as though he owned the whole world. The megalomaniac likely thought he did. Vi tracked him with a piercing stare as he ascended the staircase to the next ring of walkways, then up one more ladder to the highest walkway. She began moving, as quickly and silently as possible, following behind him.

Up the first set of stairs, Vi wound back, looking for a sign of

Ulvarth. He had disappeared. She quickly climbed the ladder, not even caring if Ulvarth saw her or accused her of following him. But when she finally ascended… he was nowhere to be seen.

Vi walked all the way around the wide rung of the archives, her fingers trailing along the books. There was nowhere for him to hide. And no door for him to walk through. The only exits were the stairway she'd ascended and the rectangular windows at the top of the bookshelves—allowing the flame's thick smoke an escape. But Vi didn't think Ulvarth had gone through one of those.

Tapping her knuckles against the railing, Vi looked at the pillars that supported the roof above the flame. From all Taavin had said, she suspected this ceiling was also his floor. The pillars between the openings were wide enough to be hollow and fit a man though.

Taavin had said there were many secret passages in the Archives and he'd used *uncose* to find those passages. Vi didn't have the same skill. But she would make up for it with her knowledge of blueprints, architecture, maps, and planning.

30

VI SCOURED THE BOOKS for an hour. She walked through the archives—up staircases and down ladders—until her legs and arms were tired. But she didn't stop until she located the tall shelves containing the information she sought.

"*The Building of Risen*," Vi mumbled, selecting the book from the shelf. She set it down on a stack she had already collected, then pulled two more. The Larks had said they recorded all knowledge, so surely, somewhere in this vast labyrinth, there was something on the construction of the archives.

She continued flipping, searching, ignoring the growling in her stomach and Larks moving in and out of the Archives. Vi scanned pages on pages of blueprints until she began to find ones that matched the structure she recognized around her. To a layman, the sketched cross-sections would be difficult to line up. But for Vi, the whole building was slowly rebuilt in her mind's eye.

Her focused stayed on the uppermost portions of the buildings, no matter how fascinating the rest of its construction was. The triangular buildings that stretched out from the central spire were a web of bridges and passageways. The foundation of the building was a feat of engineering—brilliant minds had outdone themselves here. There was more than enough substance for her to be engrossed for months.

Vi's attention drifted upward to the flame. She didn't have months; she had days, weeks at best. Tracing the lines in the book with her index finger, Vi could clearly see the layout of the uppermost portions of the archives—much simpler than the rest. Away from the outer buildings and their connecting bridges, it was only the hollow column of the inner archives, and whatever the architects had hidden in the walls.

Sure enough, just as Taavin had said, within the walls behind the bookcases were passages that swirled and crossed over each other.

"Where's an entrance?" Vi murmured. She suspected one of the bookshelves was false—it wouldn't be the first such trick door she'd seen. But she couldn't find any indication of a hidden doorway in the blueprints.

Not wanting to give up on the theory, Vi went up to the landing and paced one, two, three times, running her hands along the bookshelves.

They didn't yield their secrets.

She retreated back to her perch and her books. There was a way to Taavin from up there, but it may not be the only way. As Vi searched for alternate routes, she kept an eye out for Ulvarth—though there was no sign of him. He had been gone for a long time—long enough that suspicion frayed the edges of Vi's concentration. The only good thing about his absence was that she could search in peace.

Closing each of the books, Vi tried to place them exactly as she'd found them on the shelves, giving no indication what she'd been looking for. She returned the way she'd came.

Vi stopped at the entrance to the walkway that soared atop a giant archway to the Lark's halls. There was no one in sight—

hadn't been for hours. Still, she waited for Ulvarth, waited for someone to show up. She waited long enough that the sun began to dip, changing the light that streamed through the glass ceiling of the walkway from gold to a deep amber.

"Very well then." Vi lifted a hand, Taavin's voice echoing in her mind. "*Uncose*."

Nothing. No magic sparked. No glyph came to life underneath her fingertips. It was just as Taavin suspected, though Vi didn't regret trying. With the merest flash of disappointment, she proceeded with the manual route.

Rapping her fingers along the side of the bookcase that met with the stone of the outer wall of the Archives, Vi listened closely. Her first couple taps sounded dull, with little reverberations. The fifth rang hollow.

Vi looked up the wide panel of wood. At about chest height, there was a thin line in its surface—one she'd overlooked at first—and another a short distance away. Vi pushed in a few different places before the panel popped loose and swung open. She hoisted herself into the narrow tunnel, closing the door behind her with a fraying leather strap on the inside.

It had been some time since anyone had come this way, if the cobwebs and bug carcasses were any indication.

Vi trudged on, determined, until the tunnel opened up into a proper secret passage. Working to rebuild the Archives in her mind as she walked, Vi wound upward once more from the inside. She kept a low flame over her shoulder, just enough to see by, though she extinguished it the moment she heard voices.

"You will tell me its secrets, and hers," Ulvarth rasped, as though struggling to keep his voice quiet. Vi crouched low in the darkness, closing her eyes and trying to imagine how high up she was.

Second walkway from the top? Maybe?

"Don't think I will let you see her unsupervised," he snarled. Taavin, for his part, remained worryingly silent. "You will not make a fool of me again. You are mine."

A door slammed so hard that Vi could almost feel the stones of the archives rattling. There was the sound of metal sliding against metal, followed by heavy footsteps. She held her breath, creeping on hands and knees upward—just a little farther.

A glow stone cast eerie light on the inner wall. She stopped, flattening herself on the ground. Ulvarth stomped across the narrow hall, oblivious to her presence. Vi couldn't see what he was doing, but she could hear him fumbling with something, footsteps on the other side of her, and… silence.

Vi kept a hand over her mouth, trying not to breathe. Her fingers trembled. Not from fear, but from loathing she didn't know if she had ever felt so strongly before. She pushed herself off the ground and continued upward to a four-way intersection. Directly ahead, the passage sloped down into the darkness. At her left was a ladder and at her right, a short ramp up to a flat wooden surface.

That was when it hit her.

Each of the landings in the Archives was in the shape of a right triangle, jutting out into the hollow center. The walkway was flat and formed a right angle with the wall, but the hypotenuse sloped down and away. Initially, Vi had thought it merely an aesthetic choice. Now, she realized otherwise.

The passage to Taavin wasn't in the bookcases. It was in the floor. Casters invisible to the naked eye slid a trap door underneath the bookcases she'd been looping around, looking for one such secret passage when it had been right under her nose the whole time.

Cursing herself, Vi turned away from the ramp and toward the final option at the intersection—a ladder upward.

The passage narrowed slightly as she climbed, and Vi imagined herself in one of the columns above the bookcases—fire from the Flame of Yargen billowing out on either side. Farther on, a faint ambient light glowed.

Stepping off the ladder and onto a small landing, Vi found the source of the light—or at least, the heavy door around which wisps of light managed to escape past the heavy latch and lock tightly on the outside. Sandalwood incense curled through the door jamb.

Vi swallowed, working to get rid of the lump trying to form in her throat.

"Taavin," she whispered. Nothing. The panic from Ulvarth's departure returned in full force. "Taavin?" A little louder.

"Who…" his voice was muffled. But she heard footsteps nearing the door.

"Taavin?"

"Vi, is that you?"

"Yes."

"How did you—"

"Given everything that's happened, I think me figuring out how to get to you should be the least surprising thing," Vi teased lightly. "There's a lock on the door. How do I get in?"

"The lock is new. I think only Ulvarth keeps the key. He says he'll only let me out at specific times to collect whatever research I need." Her blood instantly boiled at the words. She had grown up in a beautiful prison as well… but never one with locks on the doors.

"If I break the lock, he'll know." It was still tempting to do it, just to mess with him. But Vi suspected Taavin would be blamed—and punished. She ran her fingers over the rung the heavy padlock was slipped through. Such a delicate-looking piece of iron for a door that was bolted so tightly. "But I have an idea."

"There's no way to fix the lock with Lightspinning," Taavin cautioned hastily, needlessly.

"I know. I'm not breaking the lock, and Ulvarth doesn't need to know."

Vi pushed the spark into her fingertips, rubbing the rung again and again. The iron heated slowly. She wanted it hot enough to be malleable, but not so hot it dripped off the door. She'd have to fix it before she left, after all.

Her left hand held the lock in place as her right worked. Vi dug her nail into the soft metal, pulling back and separating it. She widened it just enough that the padlock could slide out. Vi set it on the floor carefully, giving the metal time to cool before she undid the latch and opened the door to the face of a very shocked Taavin.

"That's the problem with metal locks." Vi gave a small smile. "They're not really the best at keeping Firebearers out."

He stuck his head through the open door. His eyes fell to the still locked padlock on the ground. Vi tapped the rung attached to the door that she modified.

"You heated the rung." He went to rest his hand on the now separated metal. Vi stopped him with a touch.

"It may still be hot."

"Fire truly doesn't burn you."

"No, and thank the Goddess for that holdover from my Firebearer training." Vi looked to her hand, opening and closing her palm for a moment before shifting her attention to him. His eyes were worried and sunken, face pale. He looked more harrowed being around Ulvarth for a few days then he had on the run or while dying in a cave. "May I come in?"

"What?" Taavin's attention was jolted from the door. "Oh, yes, of course."

He stepped to the side and Vi entered, though Taavin's eyes remained on the door and the dark ladder that stretched away from his quarters. Vi caught the longing look from the corners of her eyes. It was the look of a man presented with the notion of false freedom. They both knew if Taavin left, Ulvarth would find him—and the consequences would fall on both their heads. Besides, all the answers they needed were here, anyway.

He'd described his room once to her and Vi had worked to imagine it in her mind's eye. She'd been right about a few things, wrong about others.

The whole room was in the shape of an octagon—that much she'd managed to get right. The walls were, indeed, painted in soft grays and whites, but mostly white. The gray was a delicate embellishment in tiny patterns of birds, swords, and suns across the room. It was such a subtle contrast that in certain light, it disappeared completely.

A single shelf on the wall to the left of the door held a handful of texts. The bookend on one side was a bunch of inkwells. On the other, screws and scraps of metal rested, little cogs shining in the low light. He'd mentioned his hobby of watchmaking and Vi had entirely forgotten. They'd been forced to leave behind so much of their peacetime lives since starting this journey. Vi thought back to the hobbies she'd had, the things she'd enjoyed—things she may never be able to do again.

Other than the shelf, there was a single chair and ottoman, facing a lonely window on the wall opposite the door, one other window to the right.

"This is where you live," Vi murmured. It was obvious, but she had to say it aloud. It didn't seem real. It couldn't be.

"My whole life."

Everything was immaculately clean but worn with age. She tried to imagine a young Taavin, running laps around the chair to dispel the energy that graces all children—even children chosen by Yargen. She imagined a young man standing at the windows, looking out at the world beyond and wondering if he should scream for help. She imagined the man he was now, cultivated in his captivity, seeking solace in the tomes beneath him.

Turning back to face him, Vi found he was suddenly blurry. She blinked rapidly, trying to draw him into focus once more. She could imagine the man before her now sitting in his lonely chair, waiting for the "daydreams" that tortured him to pass.

"Don't look at me with those sad eyes," he said softly, crossing over to her. Taavin collected both of her hands in his, bringing them to his mouth and kissing her knuckles.

"I can see you," she whispered, her voice steady. "I can see you here… alone."

"I was never truly alone." His voice was low and warm on her skin. "I had you."

Vi laughed bitterly. "My face was torture."

"Until seeing you became my light."

Her fingers curled tighter around his and Vi guided him toward her. Moments like this, moments of quiet, were so rare that they were more precious than any token or object she'd ever held.

She reached upward, fingertips smoothing along his jaw. Tilting her head, Vi guided his mouth to hers. Taavin's eyes dipped closed slowly, as if he wanted to see her there until the last possible second.

A soft sigh escaped her at the blissful moment of warmth and rest. Their kisses had yet to solve anything for her, but they made the days so much easier to bear.

As gently and slowly as his lips had met hers, Taavin pulled away. Vi looked at him through heavy lids.

"Would you like me to heal these?" Taavin ran his fingertips over the bandages around her wrists.

"They're fine," Vi said, shaking her head. What she'd said to Serina about the wounds still stood.

Taavin didn't insist further. He must've seen the blood dripping from the shackles in Ulvarth's throne room. So perhaps he had some idea of why she was allowing those marks to remain on her flesh.

"I want to show you something." Keeping her hand in his, Taavin stepped away, guiding her toward the set of doors next to where Vi had entered from. He pulled them open to reveal a small, dark room.

There was nothing inside. No gilded statues. No signs or sigils.

On a single pedestal in the center of the room stood a plain marble candlestick holder with a flame flickering at the top. There was no wick for oil or candle wax. The flame burned impossibly, hovering just above the candlestick.

"This is it, isn't it? The real flame."

"Yes, this is the legendary Flame of Yargen," Taavin affirmed.

"Or what's left of it."

Vi took a step forward, her eyes never leaving the small flame or the dull ash collected around its base. "What about the brazier in the Archives?"

"The flame used to burn that brightly, barely controlled. Now, it's nothing more than an illusion maintained by a few High Larks sworn to secrecy."

That explained the lack of heat, and Ulvarth's delight—she hadn't immediately identified the false flame.

"Why has it dimmed?"

"I suspect because of the destruction of the other parts of Yargen's power. The Crystal Caverns, the crystal weapons… they're all connected."

"We're all connected."

"What did you say?" Taavin took a small step forward into the room.

"We're all connected." She clutched her watch, thinking back to her father's words. Members of the Solaris family had been wrapped up with the crystals for generations, likely going further back than she understood. "Fate is a road that is made, laid by the generations before us."

"Vi—"

"And us," she turned to face him, clutching her watch. It felt hot under her palm in a way not even burning through iron had felt. "We're connected too, drawn together by her power. It lives in you, and in me, as it did in the crystal weapons and the caverns, and does still in the scythe."

Vi's hands went to the nape of her neck, slowly unfastening the watch. It was the first time it had left her neck in months, and she felt naked without it, bare before the Goddess. Taavin did nothing to stop her as Vi slowly turned toward the flame, compelled by an invisible force.

"I did what you asked. I've brought this to you." Beseeching the Goddess had just as much chance of working as her trying *uncose*. But she hadn't come all this way not to try. "Tell us, what do we do now?"

She slowly lifted the watch, and as soon as it drew level with the flame, the world was overcome with white.

Wind rushed around her, soundless. Even though it should whip her hair and tug at the robes she wore, Vi remained perfectly still. Untouched.

The world was completely dark, only the immediate radius visible to her. Underneath her feet was a barren landscape of pale gray ash, piled thick. Whatever fire had raged here had burned so hot that not even the stumps of trees or foundations of buildings had survived.

Cloying heat sank into her, trying to smother her, despite her detachment from the dead world before her.

She began to walk.

It was impossible to tell her direction, or what she was walking toward. But it was equally impossible for her to stomach the idea of standing still. If she stood still, *it* would get to her, something within Vi nagged. But she had no idea what *it* was.

Vi came to a stop.

A shard of obsidian jutted out from the ash—a dormant crystal. There was another not too far away, and another closer to the second. Vi followed the trail to a scattering of obsidian fragments. Her gaze landed on a hand, clutched around a large shard, even in death.

The woman was mostly covered by the thick ash, but one all-white eye still stared lifelessly at the world. Even with a sunken face, collapsed with rot, even mostly covered in ash, Vi recognized her own corpse.

Her pulse returned to her first as the vision faded. It beat like a war drum in her ears. No… it wasn't. It was a word.

Thrumsana. Thrumsana. Thrumsana, the soft voice repeated. It was strong, yet pleading—whispering, yet loud.

When Vi opened her eyes once more to the real world, light surrounded her, like flames condensed into glyphs she couldn't recognize. They spun against symbols wrought in a faint blue magic she recognized as Taavin's.

"Taavin," Vi groaned. The man lay across from her, his body twitching slightly. "Taavin." Vi pushed herself up, the magic fading. "Taavin," she shook him slowly. Her whole body felt leaden, her mind exhausted. Her magic spent. Yet she still found energy enough to worry over him. "Please, Taavin."

The minor convulsions stopped, and with them Vi's panic abated, though it didn't fully retreat until his eyes blinked open.

"Taavin, I think I… I…"

"I heard the Goddess," they both said at once.

31

"YOU... YOU HEARD Yargen?" Taavin pushed himself up slowly. He seemed to be in as much pain as her.

"I think so. She said a word, one word, over and over, she said—"

He pressed a finger against her lips. "Don't say it out loud... not until it sits in your mind and unravels. Think of her words like an egg: you must incubate it before it hatches understanding."

"But—"

"What if it is a word to summon Raspian so that you may face him? Or level a city?"

Vi ran a hand through her hair, shaking her head. He was right, she didn't know what it was for and until she did, caution was the best path forward. "I came to Risen for answers... but I only have more questions."

"But we are getting answers." Taavin leaned forward, bending his knees and locking them against the inside of his elbows. "There are layers and layers of magic here—magic the likes of which I've only ever seen in one place before."

"Here?" Vi motioned around them.

"Here." He reached out, tapping the watch that had fallen to the floor between them. "I was right to make sure we came back to Risen. We need the watch and that scythe to reignite the flame. It's just as the traveler foretold."

Vi ignored the mention of the infamous traveler. "You were right to make sure we came back to Risen," she repeated. "Taavin… what did you do?"

He looked at her with those worried eyes. Vi slowly shook her head. She'd asked the question and now, suddenly, would do anything to not hear the answer.

He betrayed you, Arwin had said.

He betrayed you, and Vi hadn't believed it.

"No," she whispered. Vi placed a hand between them, leaning forward. "Taavin, what did you do?" He turned away. "Answer me," she pleaded softly. "Taavin, please tell me I'm jumping to conclusions."

Still, silence.

"Tell me you didn't contact the Swords." Adela had used communication tokens. Why wouldn't the Swords, or Ulvarth himself? Why would she assume Taavin hadn't been carrying one with him the whole time? Her eyes fell to his bare wrist; the bracelet she'd seen him wear through their whole journey was gone. "Tell me—"

"You wanted to go to Norin… and there was no time…" He had the decency to sound ashamed.

Vi pulled away. Her whole body had gone from acutely pained to completely numb. The word Yargen had told her vanished from her ears, replaced by ringing.

"You… You carried a token to contact Ulvarth on your wrist." Taavin wouldn't even look at her as she spoke. "Tell me, yes or no?"

He gave a small nod. Vi shifted onto her knees.

"You were contacting him the whole time, telling him where we were. You didn't escape. He let you leave. He let you leave to get me. This was all one big game crafted by both of you." Vi's voice rose, cracking like her heart.

"No. I only contacted Ulvarth at the end. I tried not to the entire time—not even when I was near death in that cave. I only contacted him then because I knew he would be tracking us and there was no way we would make it to Norin. He'd stop us first. And this way I could try to salvage—" Taavin grabbed her hand.

"Don't touch me," she seethed. He slowly released his grasp. "Don't you dare touch me."

"Vi—"

She stared at him and slowly shook her head. It didn't matter what he said or claimed. Whatever they were—whatever they'd shared—was breaking right before her eyes.

"Listen, please," he pleaded. "The days are becoming shorter, the nights longer. Raspian's power only grows. The end of the world is near and *we are not ready*. We couldn't afford a delay—if we even made it to Norin."

Vi stood, turning her back to him. Still he spoke. She heard his boots sliding against the wooden floor as he stood as well, relentless.

"I knew if we came back, we would figure out the way to end this—the way to save us all. Your father, your mother. Then you would be reunited with your family not in the final hours, but for a lifetime together.

"I wanted to give you everything you desired, but this was the only way."

Vi stared out at his small room—the lonely chair, the window to the world. The pity she'd felt was crumbling. It started a landslide that slipped underneath the dark waves she'd carried since her time aboard the *Stormfrost*.

"You don't know it was the only way."

"I knew delays wouldn't help."

"You couldn't know." She slowly turned, lacing and unlacing

her fingers to try to keep the spark from springing forth and burning him alive. "Because you do not see the future. That is *my* destiny."

"And you have." He stared, unflinching in the face of her seething rage. "You have seen the future and it is one of failure. We must remove ourselves from this line of fate that leads only to our end."

"Well, you have brought me here." Her voice was quiet and quivering as Vi fought the urge to shout. "And the world is still headed toward its end."

"What?" he breathed.

"I saw it here, now. The scythe still breaks. I still die. Raspian still wins."

Taavin stared at her, dumbstruck. Vi watched him crumble under her unrelenting gaze. She looked down on him like the traitor he was, and he couldn't stand under the weight of her judgment. Vi took a small step forward and he stepped back so hastily that he gripped the wall to prevent himself from tripping over his own feet.

"The only thing you changed is that now I will have to watch my father die at Ulvarth's hand before I die fighting Raspian."

"We can still figure it out," he said weakly, less confident than she'd ever heard him. "We can still—"

"We? That's the other thing you changed, Taavin." Her voice cracked. Damn it all. It cracked. "There is no 'we,' not anymore."

"Vi…" His tone was pleading, begging. So much said in the single syllable. Yet her heart ignored it.

She was the fire of her forefathers. She was the bitter ice that had hardened her. She was the frozen flames of the Goddess herself embodied in crystal: hard, unmoving, unfeeling.

"Count your blessings," Vi whispered. "The last time someone betrayed me and my family, I killed her. But I guess I really did love you, Taavin. Because here you stand, and here you'll stay."

Vi started for the door. He didn't move to stop her. She briefly considered leaving the lock broken and letting Ulvarth's wrath befall Taavin—but if she sought revenge, now or ever, it would be by her own hand. Just as it had been with Jayme. Just as Arwin had shown her with Fallor.

So Vi returned the lock, sealing Taavin away once more, and vanished into the darkness of the secret passages of the Archives. She walked down the way she'd came, heart thundering in her chest, eyes blurry with anger.

She made it all the way back to the secret entrance, crouching to crawl through the passage. But Vi couldn't bring herself to move another step. She sat down heavily, leaning against the wall, knees at her chest in the narrow space.

In the darkness, the crown princess felt herself burning alive, from her heart outward. But she didn't cry. She didn't call for help.

She let the fires within burn.

Until there was nothing left but ash.

She was alone now.

Without Taavin, there was no one on Meru she could depend on beyond her father. But he was locked away somewhere Vi couldn't find and likely couldn't get to even if she could find it. So rather than wasting the effort, she focused on research. She focused on the one thing Taavin had been right about: the only path forward involved finding a way to prevent the world's end. And sulking wouldn't accomplish that.

Vi sat perched on a high rung of the Archives. From her vantage point, she observed the Larks coming and going. Much like their namesake, they flitted in and out, carefully selecting tomes to bring back into their chambers to study. She wondered how many recorded new histories, how many studied the old in order to provide counsel, and how many merely maintained the massive library.

After watching them for an hour, she stood and began

nonchalantly following behind one man, then the next, lingering at the shelves long after they'd left. Vi watched as books were taken and returned. *What had them so busy?*

"*The Kingdom of Solaris*," she murmured, reading the title of the most recently replaced book. Vi plucked it from the shelf and opened to the first page, where a large family tree spilled over onto the next four pages.

It was strange to see her father's name there among the rest and, in a fresh ink, her own. The book was on the lineage of the Solaris kings, and later, its emperors. The conqueror who had brought the continent to heel was none other than her grandfather, Tiberus.

Vi replaced the book and moved on to the next.

The War of Light. Lord Noct had mentioned the last great war in relation to Yargen and the Dark Isle. Vi flipped to the first chapter, scanning the text:

In the fifteenth century following the end of the last Dark Era, Lord Raspian escaped his previous imprisonment in the heavenly body, the prison of night's light.

The book was factual and dry, but the subject matter was so vibrant, so fantastical, that Vi read it more like a story book than a historical text.

A horn startled Vi from her reading. Her head jolted upward, looking on instinct to the open windows above the fake flame where the sound echoed from. It was a sweet melody that rang throughout Risen, bells accompanying the trill of the horns. She could've sworn she heard drums in the mix.

The sound drew nearer and Vi closed the book to listen. The music increased in fervor. It was bright and full of life—the sort of thing she'd associate with a celebration of some kind. All at once, it stopped.

The large doors to the Archives opened with a mighty groan and Vi sprinted around to get a better look, dashing down a set of stairs. She positioned herself opposite the doors peering at the group waiting to enter.

A company of knights were revealed to be on the other side of the door. But these were not Ulvarth's Swords of Light. They wore silver armor and had bright red plumage extending from their caps. Without any further invitation, they marched in slowly.

Behind the first line of knights was a row of men and women, dressed in heavy layers of embroidered finery. The only similarity among them were the silver pins they wore on their left breasts—each in a different shape. Behind this row of people came a single woman.

Vi couldn't actually see her face. In fact, the woman wore so many layers of fabric that she couldn't tell it was a woman at all from the shape of the body. But Vi knew it was a woman, because atop the long veil that covered her from head to toe was an ornate, silver crown.

Lumeria, the Queen of Meru, had come to the Archives.

She leaned over the railing slightly, watching as the queen passed underneath. They went through a door opposite the entry, toward one of the pointed buildings Vi had yet to explore. Two more groups of knights took up the final rows, and Vi waited until they'd passed under her to step back and sit against the bookshelves.

Ulvarth had said her father's trial would begin at the queen's convenience. If the queen was here, that meant his trial was beginning. Vi ran a hand through her hair; the sensation of it, free of braids, was odd, but she didn't have the energy to coif it.

She should keep reading, keep searching for ways out of the mess they were all in.

But she couldn't.

She was so lost in thought that she didn't hear the footsteps of someone approaching. Two unfamiliar booted feet appeared next to her and Vi followed them up to a silver-armored woman. She had bright blue eyes, ringed in purple. Eyes that stared at her for so long, Vi began to feel uncomfortable.

"Vi Solaris?" the knight asked, after that seemed like forever.

"Yes?"

"Your presence has been requested."

"By who?" Vi slowly tilted her head away from the bookcases, though she already suspected she knew.

"The queen." The knight took a step away. "If you'll please follow me."

Book in hand—because Vi wasn't about to risk a Lark taking it off the shelf again—Vi trailed behind the knight to ground floor. They walked through the same door the queen and her retinue had disappeared into, and across a tunneled walkway. The windows were laden with fragments of heavily tinted glass that distorted the world beyond.

From time to time, the knight glanced over her shoulder. Vi caught her odd looks. It wasn't suspicion, and Vi didn't get the sense the woman viewed her as a threat.

"Is something the matter?" she finally asked as the hallway split in two, absentmindedly scratching at the bandages around her wrists.

The knight paused, allowing Vi to catch up. They stood side by side before a staircase leading upward. "You look just like someone I once knew." Her voice was filled with a longing that made Vi inexplicably sad. "A good friend that I lost."

"I'm sorry," Vi murmured. The knight shook her head, refusing Vi's sympathies.

"Perhaps we will meet again someday, in a different place and time." It was an optimistic world view—one Vi couldn't share after seeing the end of the world. "I'm Deneya." She raised a hand to the center of her forehead, pushing aside the dark brown, almost black fringe there to touch her skin before lowering it.

Vi did her best to replicate the greeting. "A pleasure to meet you."

Deneya led her up the stairway and to a small landing. Another knight in identical armor was positioned by a door. He gave Deneya salute and opened the door.

"Please, come in." A voice summoned them.

The long room was dominated by large windows that ran the length of both walls. Vi was distracted by the inner wall that overlooked a courtyard. She knew she should be bowing before the woman at the far end of the room, sitting poised in her endless folds of fabric on the edge of a plush chair. But for a moment, all of her regal training was forgotten.

"I know this place," she whispered, horrified.

The last time she'd seen it, she'd been nothing more than a specter. She'd seen the carved gutters and tiled rooftops. She'd seen the covered stage where the queen would sit and before which her father would kneel. But that time, the square had been full. And now it was unnervingly empty.

She'd seen this moment long ago in a cave in the North.

"Do you?" The queen's voice sounded nothing like Vi would expect. For all the flowing silks and chiffons she wore, the woman's voice was low and sharp, every word enunciated in the thick accent Vi had come to associate with all of Meru.

"I saw it in a vision once," Vi explained. Secrecy wouldn't serve her now. Vi pulled herself from the window, crossing to the small sitting area where the queen waited. She dropped to one knee. "Forgive me for forgetting myself before you, your highness."

"I thought the Solaris family saw themselves as rulers of the world entire. Is it common for you to kneel before other nobility?"

"I've found 'the world' a bit generous to describe our borders." Vi lifted her gaze with a small smile. "And you are not even the first ruler I have knelt before since coming to Meru." The one downside to all the fabrics covering the queen was that Vi could not read the woman's facial expressions. She was left to judge her reactions from voice alone, and the length of pause she took to collect her thoughts.

"Please sit." Lumeria slowly raised a jeweled hand. Vi would move slowly if she was forced to wear that much silver on her fingers.

Vi stood, sitting on the stool across from the queen's chair. She very much felt like a child at her mother's knee.

"I have summoned you because I would like a word with you before your father's trial begins."

"How may I be of service?" Vi asked cautiously.

"Merely speak with me. I ask nothing more of you." Vi gave a tentative nod. She knew just speaking could be dangerous enough, especially when her father was about to stand trial before this woman. "Do you know what is happening with your father? Have they told you?"

"I believe the Faithful think he had some role in harming our world," Vi answered delicately. She didn't know how much Lumeria knew about the impending doom that awaited them all—or if keeping it a secret from the queen would be beneficial in some way. Proceeding with caution seemed the only choice.

"They believe he set free Raspian from the god's tomb on the Dark Isle." Lumeria paused for a brief moment. "This doesn't surprise you? I didn't think the War of Light was compulsory education on the Dark Isle."

"It's not. But I have had ample time to research and learn over the past year." Vi looked to the window. Everything seemed too bright, too harsh. "My father is not guilty—not to the letter of the accusations. The man who truly destroyed the Crystal Caverns and tried to harness their power was the Mad King Victor, and he is dead."

"Do you think Ulvarth will care?" She could almost imagine Lumeria's eyebrows rising underneath her veil.

"Hardly. He cares for little beyond himself. I think his sham of a holy crusade to undermine your power and work to put the real control of Meru in his own hands through brutal tactics is enough proof of that." It would be plain speaking between them, then. *How refreshing.*

"Tell me why he has yet to put you on trial."

"Because I am the Champion reborn," Vi answered honestly, deciding her best chance was to ingratiate herself to the queen.

She had just lost one powerful ally on Meru; she could use another. "So I can help rekindle the flame."

"I have always known Ulvarth to be greedy, but not stupid," Lumeria murmured. Then, louder, "Can you rekindle it? Can you bring Yargen back to us and collect her scattered power from your lands?"

"Scattered power from my lands?" Vi repeated. She suspected she understood—she had heard about Yargen's fractured power—but sought clarity nonetheless.

"To seal Raspian away, Yargen split herself—one part into the staff she gave the last Champion, one part to the seal Raspian's tomb, and one part to the flame."

"As you know, the tomb is gone," Vi said.

"The staff, then. There are records it was split and—"

"Transformed into a crown, an axe, a sword, and a scythe," Vi finished. "Yes… But all that remains is the scythe."

Lumeria was silent for a long time. She folded her hands in her lap and Vi heard a soft sigh. Underneath the fabrics of her veil, the queen hunched slightly.

"Then it may already be too late."

"I have the scythe in my possession," Vi said quickly. "Well, Ulvarth has it. But it is here."

"I will pray for that to be enough," Lumeria said wistfully. "But a fragment of a fragment of the Goddess's power does not seem like it would be sufficient to stand against a god."

And Vi had the visions to prove it wasn't.

"Deneya, you may escort the princess back to the Archives now. Thank you for speaking with me, Vi Solaris."

Vi stood at the dismissal. Deneya guided her back through the door and down the stairs. They crossed the walkway in silence, the knight pausing at the entrance to the archives, hovering like the clearly unspoken words.

"Vi," she said delicately. "You have a path more difficult than any can comprehend. The only one who can truly understand it is the Voice."

She bit back protest that Taavin was clearly the last person in the world who understood her. If he did, he would've never put her and her father at risk.

"But should you ever need me, no matter the time or place, seek me out. My sword is yours."

"Thank you," Vi said, trying to hide her discomfort. She didn't trust the woman's eagerness. Perhaps Lumeria had put her up to the task.

Or perhaps she was another trying to get close to her for their own gain.

"Good luck, Champion."

Deneya gave a small bow, returning back the way she came.

Vi watched her leave before wandering back into the Archives. She returned the book she'd started reading on the last War of Light to its place on the shelf. Her mind was too full to try to process the knowledge within.

A fraction of a fraction of the goddess's power wouldn't be enough to stand up against Raspian.

It made sense and gave credence to her visions of Raspian shattering the scythe and striking her down. But all the other crystal weapons had been destroyed. Her father had told her that much.

Vi clutched the watch around her neck and for the first time wondered if, perhaps, the future of their world couldn't be saved.

If there was only one path forward—into the eternal darkness of death.

32

THE LIGHT STREAMING THROUGH the window of her room dimmed to night as Vi paced. It seemed like now the days were more darkness than anything else. The moon dominated the sky almost perpetually and daylight was only a couple hours.

Finally her feet came to a stop and Vi let out a groan of frustration. She knew what she needed to do. But it was the last thing she wanted to do.

Ulvarth would be at the trial, which meant he was tied up for at least a few hours. This was the perfect time for her and Taavin to work, though he was the last person she wanted to see.

She was up the stairs of the archives despite heavy feet, through the trap door she'd discovered during her last excursion, up the ladder, and worrying away the ring holding the lock on his door without so much as knocking. Vi allowed the padlock to clang as she set it aside, the only warning before she opened the door.

Taavin stood at the opposite window in all his heartbreaking beauty. He didn't so much as look at who entered.

Vi hovered in the doorway, trapped in the snare of wanting to scream at him and, at the same time, flee. Freeing herself from the hold of fear, she crossed the small room to the man. His eyes—distant, *different*—drifted to her. They felt like the eyes of a stranger.

Things had been damaged between them and they both knew it. Vi held his gaze for a long moment.

"Listen." She knew she had to be the one to get the first word in. "I am not here for you. We still have a duty."

There was the little matter of the end of the world, and Vi would let him assume that was all she referred to. In truth, her treacherous heart still bled from the wounds he'd inflicted that her past experiences had only made worse. She still felt for him. She wanted to be ambivalent, but her emotions had yet to catch up to her mind's stoicism.

A small part of her still loved him. And that terrified Vi more than anything.

"That's putting it mildly," Taavin said dully, leaning against the wall behind him.

"I met with Queen Lumeria." Vi stepped away, pacing. She noticed the scythe leaning against the doorway to the flame. Good, they wouldn't have to go hunting for it.

"Did you?" He looked back to the window, as if the sight of her was too painful.

"I think I know what we need to do." Her voice was little more than a whisper, though Vi didn't know why. "I think the watch holds Yargen's power. We need to use it and the flame to give more power to the scythe. When Yargen fractured her power, giving the staff to the Champion, he later fractured it further. It is only a part of her power, and it's too weak to stand against Raspian on its own."

Vi turned away from the scythe to find him staring at her. "It's not a terrible theory."

"I'm glad it makes the high mark of 'not terrible,'" Vi

muttered dryly. "It's far better reasoning than the logic you used before betraying me," she mumbled under her breath.

"Vi, I—"

"Don't." She glared at him, equally angry now at herself for her own pettiness. "I won't bring it up again and you shouldn't either. We have to focus now… we can deal with all that later." Of course, there might not be a later, which suited her well enough. She worked to get them back on track, trying to keep her venom in check. "I think the word the Goddess gave me was for the watch."

"You *think*, or you know?" Taavin took a step forward.

"I know," she lied. She didn't have time enough to sit on this particular egg, waiting patiently for it to hatch. All she knew for sure was that merely thinking of using the word filled her with confidence. She was right; she had to be. Vi lifted the scythe and opened the door to the flame. "Come and hold this with me."

"Why me?"

"Because you're the Voice. You also have a part of her magic in you, don't you?" Taavin gave a small nod. "Surely that's important. We're trying to collect as much of the Goddess's power as possible."

Taavin crossed over, grabbing the scythe around her hands. Vi kept him at arm's length, but he still felt too close. She wasn't strong enough around him yet—her mental defenses hadn't been sufficiently fortified. Because her heart still wanted to love him—her mouth still ached to kiss him.

"Are you sure about this?" he asked softly, nervously.

"Yes," she insisted. But his worried look got the better of her. "Why?"

"I have this weird feeling… as though I'm in two places at once."

"What?" Vi remembered the same sensation the first time she'd seen the scythe in the Twilight Kingdom. "I've felt something like that around the scythe before."

"Right. Perhaps it's normal then." He looked up at her, the soft blue glow of the crystal illuminating his face. "Whenever you're ready."

Vi took a deep breath, then a second, a third. Her nerves rose alongside the pounding of her heart with each stabilizing breath. She let her mind go blank, staring into the swirling magic of the scythe, allowing herself to feel the heat of the flame of Yargen.

"*Thrumsana.*"

Glyphs appeared from the watch on her chest. Layers on layers of them—just as Taavin had said. They swirled around them, filling the room with symbols Vi didn't understand.

The voices she'd heard at the tears—whispers, cries, screams, songs, and shouts—filled her ears once more. The cacophony was softer than she remembered, sharper, but overwhelming to her senses as it seemed to flow through her.

Taavin let out a scream.

He fell, and Vi dropped the scythe alongside him in shock. He writhed on the ground, clutching his head. Vi stared on, helpless, as veins bulged at his neck and temples.

"Make it stop," he begged. "Make it stop!" he screamed loud enough that Vi was certain someone had to have heard.

"Taavin, Taavin!" His thrashes were too violent, not even allowing her to get near. "*Th-Thrumasana!*" Vi tried again, trying to imagine the glyphs going away.

They did not.

The magic began to shine brighter. The noise filled her ears. Taavin's mouth was locked in a soundless scream and Vi watched in horror as his whole body tensed and arched off the floor. The glyphs condensed on him like ropes, sinking into his flesh. He shuddered with each one that collapsed in on him.

Taavin gasped for air; tears streamed down his face, his eyes wide and unseeing as the assault continued. Vi covered her mouth, collapsing to her knees beside him. He may have betrayed her… but she had not wished this on him, had she? Had *thrumsana* somehow done this? Had the word somehow known the dark corners of her heart?

"Taavin…" Vi said his name weakly, helpless as more glyphs poured from her watch into him. She did everything she could to bring the magic within her once more, but the powers had a mind of their own and Vi was helpless.

He curled into the fetal position, crying out with each circle of light that crashed against him. His eyes were unfocused, his mouth hanging open, fingers contorted at odd angles with pain, his whole body quivering. All she had ever been to him was pain… and now she may well kill him.

Vi unhooked the watch from her neck and thrust it toward the flame. "Take it!" she cried. "Yargen, make it stop!"

The watch shattered. Light tinged with blue filled the room—but this was not a vision of the future overtaking her. It was Yargen's pure magic. And rather than seeking out the scythe as she had hoped it would, it all flowed into Taavin.

One final scream, and it was over.

He lay on the ground, limp and lifeless. Tendrils of magic swirled off of him, fading into the darkness. Soon there was nothing—no sound, no movement.

"T… Taavin?" Vi whispered, crawling on her hands and knees to him. Her eyes were still adjusting to the dim light of the flame. "Taavin." Vi rested a hand on his shoulder and he flinched.

At least he was alive.

"Taavin, I—"

"Get out," he rasped.

"But you—"

"Don't touch me," Taavin seethed. "Don't touch me ever again. Not in this lifetime or the next."

"I didn't mean for…" What hadn't she meant for? This to happen? Hadn't she loathed him for betraying her not hours before?

Nothing between her heart and mind made sense right now.

"I said out!" Taavin roared, sitting at once. The irises of his eyes were a green so bright and pale, it nearly matched the whites surrounding them.

Vi bounced to her feet and ran.

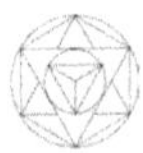

She sat alone in the darkness on the edge of her bed, clutching herself.

What had happened? What was that?

Questions swirled through her mind. Answers eluded her. Even after using the word, its meaning was no clearer to her. It felt as though a part was somehow missing. Perhaps that was why it had gone so awry. Perhaps a meaning was hidden in those seemingly endless glyphs.

Vi rested her elbows on her knees and sank her face into her hands. The watch was gone. One more token of Yargen had been destroyed and Vi doubted the flame seeming dimmer after was only in her imagination.

Slowly, she turned, looking out the window at the dark city. Maybe this would be the day the sun stopped rising altogether. The end of the world seemed more inevitable by the hour.

The door opened suddenly and Vi's eyes with it. She turned to face the man in the doorway slowly. Taavin stood, staring at her with a fire in his eyes she'd never seen before.

"We have to move," he said. "Now."

"Move? Where? Are you—"

"There's no time." Taavin's expression darkened. "The trial ended and your father will be put to death tomorrow."

It was her worst nightmare come to life. This was the reason she hadn't wanted to come here.

"If we hadn't—"

"Spare me." Taavin glowered at her. After the events earlier, it now seemed the rift between them spread both ways. "It doesn't matter I brought him here—none of this matters. I know now how to rekindle the flame and stand against Raspian."

"What do we have to do?" Vi asked softly. No matter the tension between them, it seemed they could still work toward this singular, common good. Perhaps when the world was saved, they could solve the rest—if things didn't become too broken between them along the way.

"Follow me."

Vi did, into the hallway and up the spiral stair that led to the walkway to the archives. As they crossed, Vi could hear noise and commotion growing. They were making preparations to kill her father. Vi didn't have to walk up to the railing and look down to confirm it. She felt the dark truth in the air itself.

"Through here." Taavin pushed on the same trap door Vi had used. "The Swords are patrolling the Archives. They expect you to try to escape."

Vi moved quickly and quietly, not arguing. She wriggled through the narrow tunnel and into the passage where she could stand. A small flame appeared over her shoulder, illuminating them both.

"What have you figured out?" Vi asked over her shoulder.

"I was right—the traveler was right. The watch was the key to everything."

"But—"

"Quiet," he interrupted with a whisper. "Don't talk here, it's not safe." They continued walking upward in silence, Vi's nerves setting her hands to quivering. The shakes only stopped when Taavin's firm grasp wrapped around her closed fist. "Wait here. Let me go ahead and make sure Ulvarth hasn't decided to pay me a visit."

Vi pressed herself against the wall to let him pass. They were practically stepping on each other's toes and his chest slid across hers. She wondered if his heart was beating just as hard as hers, or if she only imagined feeling it through the thin fabric of the Lark robes she wore.

He disappeared in the darkness and Vi remained leaning against the wall, rubbing the bridge of her nose. The one good thing about everything happening all at once was that she didn't have time to think or worry about any one thing. She needed to save her father, save the world, rekindle the flame… all while continuing to navigate the strained relationship between her and Taavin. She was so focused on surviving that she didn't have time to be afraid.

At least, until moments like this, when she was still and waiting.

Unfocusing her eyes, Vi looked to the flame dancing over her shoulder, the one that had been lighting her way. She scratched at her bandages; the wounds were constantly itchy now. Vi tried to keep her mind on the tangible so it didn't get too worked up over the possible horrors emerging from the shadows around her.

But it was Taavin who appeared next. Not a Sword. Not Ulvarth himself.

"Well? How does it look?"

"Safe, for now. Let's hurry."

Taavin started off into the darkness once more and Vi followed behind him. She paused, turning slowly. Their interaction was seared into her memory.

She'd seen it before, Vi realized with a sense of growing dread. It wasn't bright in her memory because it had just happened. It was seared in her memory because—

"Taavin!" she hissed, grabbing his arm. Her words burst forth as fast as her heartbeat. "I've seen this before. My first vision… Here…" Vi looked down at her clothes, the simple, drab robes—the cowl—the bandages over her wrists and hands. "We haven't changed anything." Her eyes darted back up to him.

"We haven't changed anything, *yet*." Taavin pulled his arm from her grasp and took a full step away, as if to see her clearly. His eyes burned brighter than the flame at Vi's side. They were wide enough to swallow her whole—the wide eyes of a fear Vi didn't know if she had the strength to acknowledge. "That's what we're going to do now, tonight… We're going to change this world."

Vi nodded her head like she understood and when he continued into the darkness, she followed. It was possible he was leading her to a trap, Vi realized. He could be setting her up for yet another betrayal.

She swallowed. She didn't want to trust him again. But if she couldn't trust him, she had to trust the fact that he had just as much of a reason to want to fix their future as she did. She had to trust in mutual goals, if not in the man himself.

Up the ladder, Vi found out how Taavin had escaped.

"You broke the door." She stared at the scattered splinters and the annihilated lock. "But Ulvarth—"

"After we rekindle the flame, Ulvarth won't matter." Taavin started in. He went to the shelf on his wall, lifting something from his watchmaking supplies. "Here, I made a new watch, you'll need to hold it."

Vi held out both her hands to accept the small token. When Taavin's fingers vanished, she stared at something nearly identical to the watch she'd carried across the world. The links were uncannily similar. The face was the same. The only difference was this one was shiny, new, so pristine that Vi could see her face reflected in it.

Whereas the one she'd been gifted, the one Vi had received from Fritz, showed its age in every scratch, dent, and smear of tarnish.

"What do we need to do?" Vi whispered. "Why do I need a new watch?"

Her mind was jumbled. She'd packed it so full of information and plans that it was now about to explode. This would be the final straw.

"Listen to me, there's little time to explain now, but I will soon. After you are settled, summon me as you once did. I can explain it all then."

"Tell me now?" she asked, wishing her voice was stronger.

Taavin lifted the watch from her numb fingers, fastening it around her neck as he spoke. "When the War of Light ended,

Yargen fractured her power to keep Raspian at bay."

"One third to the tomb, one third to her Champion in a spear, and one third here in Risen as a living flame," Vi recited. "And we have a piece of that staff in the scythe."

"But the scythe alone… it isn't enough." He stepped away, starting for the open doors. The flame cast him in silhouette. "The scythe with the power of the flame, your watch, my power—it's not enough. We need all the crystal weapons to stand against him. We need the full power of Yargen."

"The full power of Yargen is gone," Vi needlessly reminded him. "The caverns, destroyed. The other crystal weapons—"

"Destroyed," he finished for her, glancing over his shoulder, the light of the flame illuminating his profile. "I know it all. Thanks to your word, I now know every step this world has taken for hundreds of years, time and again."

"So then how do we rekindle the flame?" Vi asked, taking a small step toward him. "If that power is gone, if the crystal weapons were destroyed, along with the other third of Yargen's power held in the Crystal Caverns… What do we do to reignite the crystals so we can bring her power back to the flame? What do we do to bring her power back so she can fight off Raspian?"

"It's not a what, Vi. It's a *when*."

WHEN.

When.

Her mind sputtered and came to a halt on the word. Vi stood, swaying slightly. There was magic in the world. Powers great and small. Powers to heal and destroy.

But there was no power that granted one the hold over time itself.

To have that… one would have to be a… a… a goddess.

"Vi." Taavin summoned her from her haze. Vi looked up, startled. She hadn't realized he'd crossed over to her. Now, he towered above her with every inch of his height. "You cannot lose yourself now. I need you here with me mentally. If we dally too long, we're met with a great deal of hardship. Ulvarth comes and… Well, what happens then doesn't matter because we're not dallying."

Taavin rounded behind her, pushing her to motion. He pushed her toward the flame and Vi's body only obliged because it was that or collapse in place. Luckily, her physical form moved on instinct, even when her mind refused.

"I'm going to say some words," Taavin was saying. Vi barely heard him.

None of this was real. None of this was happening. It couldn't be. He was speaking insanity. And yet her other option if she didn't go along with it was walking back down into a hornet's nest of Ulvarth's men who would execute her father by dawn—if dawn even came. If they hadn't already executed him.

What if Taavin had been lying about that to get her to move? What if they'd killed him in that courtyard and Taavin knew if he told her she would be a grieving mess? Could she trust him to tell her the truth?

Right now, the answer was a resounding no, and Vi felt as though she would be sick.

Taavin stopped pushing her and rounded in front of her. His hand cupped her cheek, but Vi could barely feel it. The motion was too familiar, too caring, for the strange man in front of her now. Madman or traitor—she didn't know who he was.

"This is the only way forward. This is the only way to save your family. Repeat what I say, Vi. And I will be there to guide you in the new world, I promise. This is my destiny as much as it is yours." He turned, his back to her, and knelt.

Destiny. She hated the word.

Vi was living a nightmare that ended with the world's destruction. For the third time in three short days, she was overcome by a sensation of déjà vu. She'd had a vision of this very moment and she knew where it led. She knew what was about to happen.

"N-no." Shaking her head, Vi stumbled a few steps back. "No, Taavin, I—"

Taavin stood slowly, looking to her. He advanced and Vi took another wide step—too wide. She stumbled, falling, landing hard because she didn't even bother to catch herself.

"No, not this… don't make me do this."

"Don't you hate me now?" His face was shadowed by the flame behind him, his mess of hair falling into his shining eyes. "Aren't I the one who betrayed you?"

"Taavin, if I do this, you will die." The words were a whisper, little more than a breath. "I have seen this—I told you. I will not burn you alive."

"It's because of me your father will die. I betrayed you, Vi."

"Stop," she pleaded. He was speaking truth right to the darkest part of her—the part she so desperately wanted to ignore.

"You wanted to take him to Norin if he wished, and I stopped that from happening."

"Taavin—"

"You must do this!" His expression was a cross between pained and impatient. "This is the only way. This is the only path forward."

"I'm not a murderer!"

"Then hate me more for making you one." Taavin knelt before her. Even as she shouted at him, his voice didn't waver and his gaze was set. He really was going to let her kill him. "Hate me because I will never let myself love you again. Hate me because you truly are the cause of all my torment. You are my nightmares. It was always you."

Hate me, because I now hate you, his eyes said. That same burning feeling she'd embraced the other night was sparking again within the charred husk of her ribs. She wanted to sob and let out all the tears it felt like she'd been holding in for a lifetime. But if they fell now, they would merely evaporate on her cheeks.

"You must do this," he reiterated, his voice gone soft. Taavin reached for her arm, pulling her upright.

"What happens if it doesn't work?" Vi croaked, standing on shaking knees. "What happens if you're wrong and I just kill you?"

"Death comes for us all." He echoed the same sentiment as the first time she'd told him he was going to die. He looked her right in the eyes, so close his features went blurry. Perhaps, somehow, if everything he was saying was true, some part of him had known even then. “And if I am wrong, death will come for me before you when Raspian walks this earth once more… and you will have the satisfaction of killing someone else who wronged you.”

“You’re not making any sense!” She wanted to slap him. “Do you hear yourself? This isn’t logical and this magic, it doesn’t exist, and—”

“The watch was power—my power mingled with Yargen’s, and yours,” he spoke over her hastily. His hands gripped her shoulders, hard. “Layers and layers of magic, Vi… countless times. Countless attempts to stop this failed future from coming to pass. You have to return the power that’s in me to her, along with you, along with the scythe. Only that will give her enough power to send you back.”

“You truly are mad.”

“And you truly are the worst thing to have ever happened to me,” he seethed, so close their noses almost touched. Part of her wanted to kiss him, kiss the pain away. The other part of her was more tempted by the minute to give in and kill him. He was begging for it, after all. “Now, help me do this.”

Why was the line between love and hate so confusingly thin? She stared at his back, at the scythe positioned on the pedestal before the flame.

She wondered if she was about to trade some part of her soul—and if so, for what. It didn’t feel like much of her soul was left. Whatever was still there after all she’d endured, she may as well give to the Goddess.

Taavin knelt and Vi hovered behind him, swaying unsteadily.

Without so much as looking back at her—without even reaffirming what it was they were about to do one final time—Taavin begin to chant.

The words blurred together into a litany that would be his dirge. She could stop this now. She could clamp her hands over his lips and silence those infernal words that were already flowing through her.

But if she did that… then what? Taavin would likely perish anyway, as fodder to bring about a dark god. She would likely die fighting that same god. The world would end. Her family would be forever lost.

Perhaps Taavin was the one to have it right all along—*death comes for us all*—and Vi was the one to have her worries tied around the wrong priorities.

Vi took a slow step forward. She knew her role. She'd do it just like she had in the vision she was given back in Soricium.

Her hands settled slowly on Taavin's shoulders. Light was already peeling off of him, merging with the halo of brightness surrounding the flame. Barely-formed glyphs seemed to wrap, collapse, and form anew in complex patterns Vi couldn't follow.

His magic, shimmering and bright, pulled hers forth as well. Together, it looked almost like a white-hot fire, but with a cool pale blue at the edges. Vi gave into the flow like a ship to a current. She shut off her mind and let him pull her along.

If she thought too much about what was about to happen next, she may not be able to do it. Her will might fail her.

She spoke.

Vi didn't know the words she was saying, she didn't know the meanings, but she echoed him anyway. She allowed the magic to be pulled from her. It felt almost like an invisible hand plunged into her chest, pulling forth all she was with a violence that seemed appropriate for an unnatural act.

They were two mortals, playing at godhood.

Taavin's head tipped back and he let out a scream as his magic exploded in a burst of flame, mingling with the fire of Yargen. In the distance, voices. Ulvarth or the Swords were coming to investigate. They must have discovered her absence.

But it was too late.

The Voice was immolating under her hands, with the help of her magic. The fire before them blazed brightly, brighter than anything Vi had ever seen before—so bright, she was certain to be blind when it faded.

The whole world was consumed…

And Vi was falling into the void it left behind.

THERE WAS NOTHING BUT light, so bright she squinted and her head ached. Vi tried closing her eyes, but she couldn't even do that to block it out. The light was in her mind, in her flesh. It seared through her from the inside out.

She felt every layer of skin boiling. Red lightning finally broke through, flesh disappearing into the void above her as she continued to fall. She felt her tongue crisp and her hair singe. She felt the burn down to the clean white of her bones.

There was nothing left of her. At least, Vi couldn't *feel* anything. All sensation had vanished from head to toe. She was a spirit, her body gone.

Tick.

Tock.

No… perhaps, there was something. The watch Taavin had given her still ticked. Vi was aware of magic swirling from the timepiece as time and space whipped around her like wind. From the magic that had been stored there with their final act together, life began again, and Vi let out a scream more animal than woman as everything rushed back all at once.

A new heart—her new heart—beat in time to the watch. Veins sprouted from it, unfurling outward like bloody ribbons. Bone and sinew became her foundation, sprouting muscle and then layering on flesh. Her nails grew back in place, her hair flowed past her shoulders.

And her freshly made, still-falling body began to finally, *finally*, slow.

Tick. Tock.

The end of the world is near, and we must be ready to meet it. Taavin's voice echoed and Vi turned, trying to find the source of the sound. Her new heart began to race.

Tick. Tock. Tick. Tock. Tick. Tock.

Vi covered her ears, trying to blot out the noise. The faster her heart beat, the faster the incessant ticking. It would drive her mad before she even—

"Young one," a voice that sounded like every man, woman, and child in the world speaking all at once startled Vi from her thoughts. There was silence, then the voice again. "My Champion."

"Y… Y…" Vi could barely form a word. Her mouth was new, foreign, strange.

She turned in place, aware she was no longer falling. But all around her was nothing more than bright light, swirling yellows mixed with blues and whites. The same colors and intensity as the flames that had engulfed her.

"I am here."

"Where?" It felt like eternity stretched in all directions, all possibilities contained within.

Vi looked behind her, and when she turned forward again she was startled to see the shadow of a woman. A long veil covered her face, bolts of silk hiding her form. A crown of pure light sat on her head.

"Queen Lumeria?" Vi said, finding her voice once more.

"No. It is I… I who have seen this world from its start. I who sowed the seeds of life. I who gave you ground to grow in. I who gave you light to grow by."

Yargen. Vi would've dropped to her knee, but she was too stunned. She also wasn't completely certain she could move her knees. Her body was as fresh and primordial as the light around her, yet it mirrored the woman she'd always been.

The magic of the Goddess was within and around her. But mortal flesh still covered that power. She was neither divine nor mortal. A familiar sensation for the princess who had never belonged in any one place—who had never been any one thing.

"Yes," Yargen spoke as though she heard Vi's thoughts, because of course she heard Vi's thoughts. Vi stared at the face—veil—of a goddess. "I am in everything. I am everything. My essence, my being, cannot be comprehended by you or any mortal mind. So this is merely a form your consciousnesses has created, to make me something you can understand—a meager shell for all I am…" She slowly raised her hands, fabric floating unnaturally weightless through the air. "Because *this* is all I am.

"Or, should I say, all I was." Her hands lowered just as slowly. "I have given you a boon once more, my Champion. Your mind does not deceive you—in you is the last of my power from this world, collected from what fragments were left. The flame has been extinguished. With it, the world you knew is gone."

"Gone?" Vi repeated in quiet horror.

"The world you were born into, the people you knew, the way you knew them, are no more."

Gone. Everything was gone. Everything Vi had ever loved, would ever love, vanished at the whim of a goddess. Her mind ached and Vi didn't know if it was from the struggle of trying to comprehend what was happening, or from what she'd already endured. She would cry in the face of such a truth, but Vi wasn't sure she even remembered how.

"Do not despair," Yargen soothed. "They are not gone forever. Just as you are not gone forever. You now possess a new shape…

as shall they."

"What? But you said—"

"This is the only way to thwart Raspian. The only way we can prevent him from destroying my world of light. We must begin anew in the shell of the former world and preserve my power, this time, so that I may face him once more in our deadly, eternal dance."

"A new world," Vi whispered.

"Yes, but a familiar one. Everything as you knew it has been wiped away. But the lines of fate remain. The life that was cultivated can still thrive. Everything is as it was, but new once more."

"I… I don't understand." Vi shook her head. She wanted to. She desperately wanted to, because somewhere amid all the talk of the world ending was hope. Vi could hear it, and she lived for that hope, even if she didn't yet understand its foundations.

"You will, in time," Yargen assured her. "We begin anew. I return you to before the first moment where fate was changed. I place you back in a new world. You will be free of the bonds of time because my magic is in you. I have given you the power that lived in the watch your past self carried. I have bestowed the power of my Voice and the last vestiges of power from the flame on you as well.

"Together, we have scraped together my meager remnants to make this attempt at a world in which I am not weakened. When I rebuild this new world, you shall enter it as you are, knowing all you know. However, you shall be immune to time's flow, a traveler among mortals."

A new world. A traveler. If Vi understood correctly, the world was being remade with the crystal weapons still intact. But that meant…

"But what about *my* world? My father, my mother?"

"The only world that exists now, is the one we exist within. I am the fount of life and time. There is no other world."

Vi shook her head and fell to her knees. What was it for? *What was everything for?* She'd struggled and fought to spare the world from ending, only to see the world end anyway? Raspian wanted to destroy the world, so Vi fought against him… only to see it destroyed by a different god.

Yet, if Yargen spoke true, there was still a chance to save it.

The Goddess approached, stopping before her. Queen Lumeria's shifting silks floated through her vision as Vi stared up like a hopeless acolyte, beseeching forgiveness and mercy.

"Regain your birthright as Champion," Yargen intoned.

The spear that was bestowed. A voice that both was and wasn't her own replied from within her mind.

"Assume your mantle as Champion."

To defend the Crystal Caverns.

"See my power is never turned on itself again. See I am not weakened. See I am able to stand against the incomprehensible darkness that rages at the edge of your mortal world."

The air was sucked from Vi's lungs.

Light turned to darkness and she was falling again. Yargen vanished from before her and Vi was left alone. The wind sped around her. Her eyes dipped closed.

If she hit the ground at this speed, she'd die.

Perhaps that was the best end she could hope for.

But she couldn't die. For in her was the power of Yargen. Wasn't that what the goddess had said? And that power condemned her to remain adrift in the sands of time.

Vi gasped for air, opening her eyes wide. She lurched upward, the watch around her neck thumping dully against her chest. The world around her was bright—uncomfortably so—but not the same brightness she had just endured.

And certainly not the same brightness that peeled off her skin like some primordial, godly afterbirth.

Rubbing her hands over her arms and shivering in the heat, Vi looked around. She'd thought of herself in the sands of time… but now she was just in regular sand. Hay was scattered at her side, damp-smelling and foul. Whatever animal lived here would need something fresh, if the animal was still alive at all. The stables she was in were completely empty.

People drifted past on the other side of the gate. None of them noticed her or looked her way. Perhaps they couldn't see her at all.

Vi stared down at her trembling hands. She opened and closed her fingers slowly. They still worked. She could keenly feel her nails digging into her palms when she balled them, just as she could feel the thin layer of sand shifting over hard-packed earth beneath as Vi pushed herself off the ground.

Swaying, she took one step forward, then another. She knew where she was before she emerged from the stable. The people were easy enough to identify, the architecture of the city even easier.

The city stables of Norin stretched on either side of her as Vi emerged along the main road. She remembered passing through these markets and streets with Jayme. At least, she thought she remembered…

Perhaps this whole time she'd been in one endless fever dream. Perhaps none of it had been real. Perhaps she'd been marching home with her family, took a detour to Norin she couldn't recall at this moment, and suffered heat fainting. She'd only dreamt her father gone, her mother ill. She'd only dreamt of Taavin and Meru and—

"What do you think will be in the proclamation?" a wife asked her husband as they passed. Her voice was low, and as weak as her body looked.

Vi turned and stared. Luckily, the woman didn't notice, because Vi didn't think she could wipe the shock off her face if she tried. The wife hadn't been speaking common. She was speaking the old language of Mhashan—and Vi could understand it with perfect fluency.

"Hopefully an end to this war," the man murmured in reply.

War. Vi's whole body continued to tremble. She ran her hands over her arms, trying to comfort herself. But her palms smoothed over fabrics she hadn't ever owned in a style she didn't recognize.

Dragging one foot forward, then the next, Vi began to march with the rest of them. Ahead was a castle. Her gaze drifted over familiar spires, working to make sense of them. She'd read enough to know the architecture of the castle of Norin anywhere. But seeing it now was impossible.

She had just been in Risen. Her head ached as her head tipped back and her eyes lifted. She squinted at the sun, wondering if Yargen was watching her right now—watching her attempt to complete the task she'd been given.

Watching her attempt to make sense of what on the Goddess's earth had just happened.

A crowd collected in an open area at the end of a long bridge that connected the castle and city over a dry moat. Guards were gathered in a semi-circle, blocking entry to the bridge. None of the populous seemed interested in fighting them. The people were harrowed and gaunt. Every man, woman, and child had the haunted eyes of a soldier who had seen far too much.

Without warning, a woman stepped up onto a tall box that had no doubt been carried out expressly for this purpose. She was just high enough to see over the people. Vi stared, slack-jawed, at an oddly familiar face. It was not identical to hers. But it was so close that it was like looking into a mirror.

Even from Vi's distance, she could see the woman had angular black eyes, jutting cheekbones, and a sharp chin. Her skin, a deep tan darker than Vi's own, paired with straight black hair. Hair identical to Vi's.

Vi opened her mouth to speak, but couldn't form words. Not that she knew what she would have said, anyway.

"People of the West," the woman began, "this siege has gone on for nearly ten long years. But I am Fiera, Princess of Mhashan, youngest daughter to King Rocham, and head of the Knights of Jadar, and I have received a vision from the Mother above. The end is near, and we must be ready for it."

The story continues in...

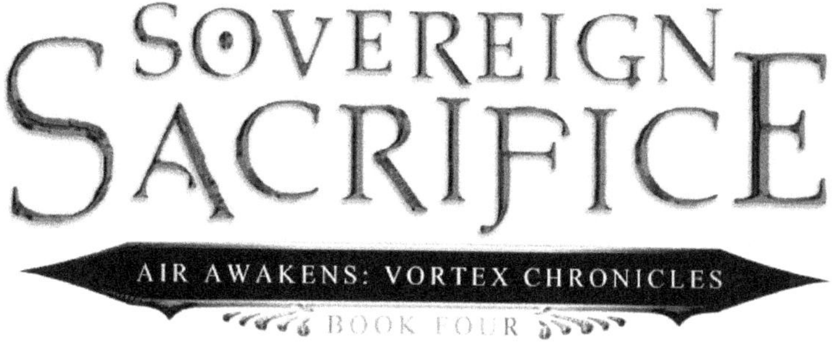

Learn more about SOVEREIGN SACRIFICE (Air Awakens: Vortex Chonicles, #4) and grab your copy at:
http://viewbook.at/SovereignSacrifice

Want to make sure you never miss a giveaway, cover reveal, or release day?

Sign up for Elise Kova's Mailing List:
http://elisekova.com/subscribe

ELISE KOVA has always had a profound love of fantastical worlds. Somehow, she managed to focus on the real world long enough to graduate with a Master's in Business Administration before crawling back under her favorite writing blanket to conceptualize her next magic system. She currently lives in St. Petersburg, Florida, and when she is not writing can be found playing video games, watching anime, or talking with readers on social media.

She invites readers to get first looks, giveaways, and more by subscribing to her newsletter at: http://elisekova.com/subscribe

Visit her on the web at:
http://elisekova.com/
https://twitter.com/EliseKova
https://www.facebook.com/AuthorEliseKova/
https://www.instagram.com/elise.kova/
See all of Elise's titles on her Amazon page:
http://author.to/EliseKova

Enjoy Vi's Story?
See where it all began by reading Vhalla's tale...

THE AIR AWAKENS SERIES

A library apprentice... A sorcerer princes... And an unbreakable magic bond. The rare elemental magic that lies in Vhalla Yarl will not only change the Empire's future, but the heart of its Crown Prince. Perfect for readers who want magic and romance!

Series complete!

"I read the full series in a just two days. The worlds was thrilling and the characters endearing... Recommend for fans of Sarah J. Maas and high fantasy"

- Kristen, 5 Star Amazon Review

Find out how Jax became known as The Crown's Dog in...

Three stories filled with mystery, romance, and adventure. Learn how the most illustrious fighting force of the Air Awakens world — the Golden Guard — came to be.

Series complete!

"These books were great! I wish I knew the back story of these characters before reading the other books. It added a lot of dimensions to the character interactions, and it leaves me wanting more!"

- Jessie, 5 Star Amazon Review

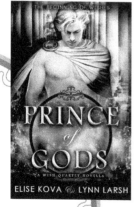